T0332834

STAR WARS: THE RISE AND FALL OF THE GALACTIC EMPIRE

STAR WARS: THE RISE AND FALL OF THE GALACTIC EMPIRE

By Dr. Chris Kempshall

DK | Penguin Random House

Senior Editor David Fentiman
Project Art Editor Stefan Georgiou
Senior Production Controller Laura Andrews
Production Editor Marc Staples
Managing Editor Rachel Lawrence
Design Manager Vicky Short
Managing Director Mark Searle

For Lucasfilm
Senior Editor Brett Rector
Creative Director Michael Siglain
Art Director Troy Alders
Story Group Leland Chee, Pablo Hidalgo, Kate Izquierdo,
Matt Martin, Emily Shkoukani
Creative Art Manager Phil Szostak
Asset Management Chris Argyropoulos, Elinor De La Torre,
Gabrielle Levenson, Sarah Williams
With special thanks to Steve Blank, Chasidy Lowe, and Jeff Yang

Cover artwork: Maurizio Campidelli
All images: © Lucasfilm
With thanks to John Friend for proofreading.

First published in Great Britain in 2024 by
Dorling Kindersley Limited
DK, One Embassy Gardens, 8 Viaduct Gardens,
London SW11 7BW

The authorised representative in the EEA is
Dorling Kindersley Verlag GmbH. Arnulfstr. 124,
80636 Munich, Germany

10 9 8 7 6 5 4 3
006–339032–Jul/2024

A CIP catalogue record of this book is available from the British Library.
ISBN: 978-0-2416-5504-7

Set in 10.6/16pt Minion Pro
Typeset by Jouve (UK), Milton Keynes
Printed and bound in Great Britain by Clays Ltd, Elcograf S.p.A.

www.dk.com

To those who kept the dream alive

Research Report EXG-107

Reporting Officer: Beaumont Kin

Location: Exegol

Academic Background: Previously a lecturer at the Historical Institute of Lerct. Specializing in the ancient history of the Sith

Rank: Captain (Intelligence Division)

Current Assignment: Exegol Excavation Lead

Transmission: Much has happened in the months since the Battle of Exegol. We have begun the long and difficult process of rebuilding the galaxy following the destruction wrought by the recent First Order–Resistance War. In the aftermath I have been tasked with leading the excavation of the Sith temple on Exegol. However, while this has taken a great deal of my focus and time, it has not been my only consideration. This study has been made freely available across the holonet in the hope that it finds an audience willing to read it and take on board the message within it.

Contents

Contents

Part Three: The Galactic Civil War

Part Four: Fall and Continuation

Introduction

History tells us that, given enough time, all empires will fall. But if we do not also come to understand how and why they rise, we will remain trapped in this cycle forever.

Since the end of the Galactic Civil War, for most of the last thirty years, it was thought that the history of the Galactic Empire was clear and easily understandable. That the New Republic had successfully taught the next generations about the horror inflicted upon the galaxy by Palpatine and his followers. It seemed to be an easy message to explain something that was now safely behind us. My colleagues and I congratulated ourselves on the ways we'd been able to take the realities of the Empire and convert them into lessons in schools and universities, which would then further ripple out across the galaxy. We were so sure that we had created the perfect way of preventing future conflicts and a return to Imperialism. We were fools. I was a fool. As much as we might have wished that the remnants of the Empire could have been left to rot beneath the sands of Jakku, it seems that we could not be free of it so easily. I recall the shock I felt when Resistance agents brought back from Batuu—among other things—word that there were traders in Black Spire Outpost selling busts of Emperor Palpatine and other trinkets of his fallen Empire. How could this be? What must have happened to make the image of the Emperor—a man responsible for the murder of billions—acceptable enough to sell and own, even long after his apparent death at Endor? How could we all have gone so astray?

Recent events have shown us that Imperial ideology was not, as once hoped, a thing of the past and its return pushed the entire galaxy over the edge of disaster. The First Order brought death and tyranny with them out of the Unknown Regions. Hosnian Prime was destroyed just as Alderaan once was. Billions died across the galaxy as the New Republic disintegrated in the face of an enemy that sought to subjugate all worlds. This alone was bad enough. Then came the transmission from Exegol heralding the return of Emperor Palpatine. The exact techniques he used to cheat death are currently unclear but Rey Skywalker has been certain that what she fought on Exegol was Palpatine, returned in some twisted form and set on reconquering the galaxy and ruling it forever. His subsequent defeat and the destruction of the First Order— and its true face as Palpatine's Final Order—was achieved only through the desperate actions of the Resistance and brave people from across the galaxy, who came to Exegol prepared to fight to the death. I was among them. I saw many of my friends make that sacrifice.

In the aftermath of the battle, those of us who survived celebrated our victory on Ajan Kloss. It was here, surrounded by jubilation, that I noticed the things that have troubled me ever since. I heard people talk in joyous terms about how "the Force had been with us" at Exegol. I watched them discuss how the final death of Palpatine had liberated the galaxy. I could feel the relief that was over them all. But I did not feel, or say, or agree with these things. To be a historian is, at times, to be cursed. Perpetually watching patterns or seeing similarities and worrying about whether whatever comes next will resemble the past behind us. On Ajan Kloss I began to wonder and worry if the celebrations we were involved in were very different from those on Endor more than thirty years before. They too had, seemingly, killed an Emperor, won a war, and sought to create a better life for the people of the galaxy. It is time to admit that both they, and those of us who followed in their footsteps, failed.

This failure had understandable roots. Having fought a long and desperate war against the Empire it was only natural for the leaders and soldiers of the Rebel Alliance to turn their eyes to the future that the New Republic would provide. The years after Endor and Jakku were marked initially by hope and optimism. But the line between hope and *blind hope* is a dangerous one to walk. In the post-war years people became so determined to look forward that they did not spend nearly enough time looking back at what they had left behind. They tied themselves so tightly to the belief that this should never happen again that they neglected to take the steps to ensure that it *could* not. They did not understand the Galactic Empire. They did not understand how it had functioned, how it had operated, and how it had ruled the galaxy. They did not comprehend why so many had served, seemingly voluntarily, within its ranks and perpetrated so many heinous crimes. They viewed the Empire as Emperor Palpatine and with him gone, so too was his Empire. But that Imperial ideology did not disappear overnight. How many ex-Imperials escaped to form the First Order? How many continued to undermine the New Republic from within? How many celebrated as Hosnian Prime burned? The Empire had endured. Though it may have reappeared with a new name and new uniforms, the roots of the First Order led all the way back to the Galactic Empire that we had resolutely failed to understand.

I do not believe we can risk that again. The idea that we achieved victory at Exegol because the Force was with us, overlooks just how close to complete destruction we all came. We were hugely fortunate to achieve victory and I do not wish to trust to that again. I am not a great Jedi like Rey. I am not a leader like Generals Poe Dameron and Finn. I do not have the insights and abilities of Commander Rose Tico. I do not know how to do the things that the leaders of the Resistance must now do—to lead us forward and to help us rebuild—because I am not like them. Before the war I was just a historian. I liked reading and researching. Then came the Hosnian Cataclysm and I realized that the galaxy needed soldiers. So, I fought, as best I could. But now—in the earliest stages of the peace we fought for—I believe that the galaxy needs a historian again. Someone who can help us understand the past, so we do not have to fight again in the future.

Before we can even begin to analyze the intricacies and events of the Empire, there are things that need to be further explained and understood. I have spent years researching and examining the nature of the mystical energy field generally referred to as "the Force." Similarly, I have spent much time uncovering mysteries of the Jedi and Sith orders that drew upon different aspects of the Force, but I am well aware that much of this knowledge is not widespread across the galaxy and can, at times, seem frankly beyond belief. While I have attempted to become an expert in this topic the actual usage and intricacies of the Force are far beyond my comprehension. In fact, one of the Empire's greatest successes has been to erase and suppress even the very memory of the Jedi—a group who once served the Galactic Republic for over a thousand years. The members of the Jedi Order were able to access what was referred to as the "light side" of the Force. It granted them almost magical powers including telekinesis, athletic ability, and meditative foresight. Within the Republic they served as diplomats, advisors and, very occasionally, warriors. That was, at least, until the Clone Wars. Because the Jedi were not alone in being able to draw upon the Force.

The Sith were essentially the opposite of the Jedi. They too could use the Force, but where the Jedi prized its ability to grant knowledge and inner peace, the Sith saw in the "dark side" the potential to provide power fed by their raw emotions of anger and hatred. For the Sith the Force could—as will be discussed in forthcoming chapters—provide a variety of unnatural powers. While I cannot access or utilize the Force myself, I have seen and read many things that make its existence undeniable. For untold millennia the Jedi and the Sith fought each other for control of the Force and the galaxy. Until the dying days of the Republic, it had been thought that the Sith were extinct. But this was not the case. They had survived in the shadows, biding their time. Perhaps the greatest practitioner of the dark side of the Force had risen to finally defeat the Jedi and seize the galaxy. His Sith name was Darth Sidious. The rest of the galaxy knew him as Sheev Palpatine—one-time supreme chancellor and, more notably, Emperor of the galaxy. Through the infrastructure of the Galactic Empire and his knowledge of the Force, Palpatine is likely to have been the most powerful individual who ever existed. But, as we will discuss, Palpatine's arcane or supernatural abilities should not give us a false sense of security. While he was able to utilize powers that most of the rest of the galaxy could not, his desire for power and control were not summoned from the Force. They existed within him in the same way they could conceivably exist in anyone. Palpatine was not a demon. He was a man. It is that aspect I find most terrifying of all.

The first part of this study will deal with the rise and consolidation of Palpatine's regime. It will examine what we know of Palpatine himself and factor in recent events in helping to understand what his objectives were for the Galactic Empire, and the role he played at the center of it. Though Palpatine no doubt benefited from the various strange and supernatural powers—some of which will be discussed further in forthcoming chapters—granted to him by his study of the arcane aspects of the dark side of the Force, he was still just one person. He was not the totality of the Empire, nor did he administer it on a day-to-day basis. So, this part will also explore some of the institutions that administered the Empire such as the Commission for the Preservation of the New Order (COMPNOR). It will explain how its economy functioned, its industrial outputs and controls, and its approach to education. It will show how the Clone Wars were part of a wider plan to destroy the Republic and bring about the Empire's ascendancy. It will also show that, despite Palpatine now ruling, the Imperial Senate remained, at least until the destruction of Alderaan, as a key part of Imperial infrastructure for years. Though a much-maligned body, it was clearly still seen as a necessity by Imperial officials while they secured power.

The second part will explore exactly how the Empire sought to achieve dominance over much of the galaxy. It will analyze the Imperial military and the ways in which it expanded the Empire's borders through a system of conquests and annexations. It will also identify leading figures within the Empire's military. Figures like Grand Moff Tarkin, Darth Vader, and Grand Admiral Thrawn are all infamous, but how much about them do we actually know? Do we fully understand how they served within the Imperial hierarchy? It is time to analyze those operating below Palpatine who ruled large swathes of the galaxy. We also need to understand what the Empire did with that level of control. The prejudice. The bigotry. The restrictive laws. The brutal punishments. The massacres. The genocides. The Empire was held together by violence and horror. We cannot look away from these truths.

In the face of such a tyrannical government, rebellion was not just an inevitability but a moral imperative. The third part will therefore deal with the Galactic Civil War. We were blessed in the years after Endor that enough of the leading figures of the Rebel Alliance had survived to help record their own thoughts and recollections on the war. They outlined the different strategies and decisions undertaken by the rebels and how, together, they had achieved victory. But what of the Empire? How much time has been spent looking at Imperial strategy during the war? The Death Star was supposed to be the end of resistance in the galaxy. Its destruction left a huge vacuum of personnel and planning at the center of the Imperial military. Who and what filled that vacuum? Why did the Empire wage war in the way that it did? How did it understand the rebel threat? All of these questions must be answered in order to fully comprehend the lessons of the Galactic Civil War and the reasons why the Rebel Alliance eventually triumphed.

The fall of the Galactic Empire is the focus of the fourth and final part. While the Battle of Endor may have, seemingly temporarily, spelt the end of Palpatine, the war itself continued for another year. In many ways it was one of the worst years of the whole war. Operation: Cinder saw the Empire's remaining forces raze entire worlds as some form of punishment for the Emperor's death. In the absence of the Emperor various Imperial factions began to appear as the military and government split apart. The Battle of Jakku marked the end of official hostilities, but clearly this was not an end to the Empire. The New Republic instigated systems of truth and reconciliation to try and heal a war-weary galaxy. Some of these programs worked. Others did not. Complacency and appeasement became policy. Remnants of the Empire continued to endure in the galaxy while, in the Unknown Regions, the First Order gained strength. The recent disastrous war was the result.

When it comes to chronicling the events of the Empire's lifespan there has long been a divide and debate among historians regarding dating conventions. Some have favored a calendar which takes the birth of the Empire as a starting point. Others have preferred to base their "before" and "after" periods around the Battle of Endor and the—apparently first—death of Palpatine. I understand both of these approaches but have not utilized either. As my research progressed it became increasingly clear that the history and activities of the Empire could be split into two different sections. Those before the emergence of the Death Star and its destruction at Yavin and those afterward. While the Empire was never truly "at peace," the onset of the Galactic Civil War greatly accelerated many aspects of its rule and the ways in which it would interact with—and often murder—its own citizens. Therefore, I have come to favor a dating system that highlights the years before the Battle of Yavin (BBY) and those that came after (ABY). I have no doubts that this will produce the sort of stringent debate from both my colleagues and other readers which often accompanies such decisions.

As alluded to above, this is not the first study or examination of the Galactic Empire, but it may now be the most relevant. Through the course of my research it has become apparent that many of the previous assumptions and understandings that were widely held and accepted about the Empire may have been built on flawed information. It is possible that much of what was once believed about how the Empire operated and the ways in which the regime undertook the Galactic Civil War were wrong. Furthermore, the very reasons for its eventual fall and collapse do not appear to have been adequately researched and analyzed at all. We know why the Rebel Alliance believed they won the war. Do we know why the Empire lost it? Because the Galactic Empire was so misunderstood, it is necessary to begin the process again. That is the point of this study. To deconstruct the entirety of the Galactic Empire beyond just notions of Palpatine himself. To see how it actually worked, the ideas and ideologies that drove it, the ways it waged war, and the motivations behind its most awful crimes.

This research has not been a simple undertaking. The Empire was a gargantuan state that ruled for years. Even before the most recent conflict, investigating the history of the Empire was not easy. There is no single repository for material relating to that fallen state, instead it is spread across the galaxy on many planets and in many databases which, when linked together, have become something more commonly known as the "Imperial Archives". There exist similar such collections for the Rebel Alliance, and both the Republic destroyed by Palpatine and the New one that replaced the Empire. In fact, the recent destruction of the New Republic has granted access to some material, such as the interrogation records of Imperial officers at the end of the Galactic Civil War, that was previously classified. Trying to access all this material would have been challenging in normal circumstances. From my current position on Exegol it was impossible. However, I am absolutely indebted to the archivists, librarians, scholars, and record-keepers of the galaxy who have maintained the surviving records available to us of the Galactic Empire, and who granted me remote access to them in order to undertake my research. They recognized, as I do, the importance of this study and I will endeavor to highlight their important work throughout it.

While some archives of the time have endured, many have also been lost. The Empire burned or buried many records. Other collections have been lost in the recent fighting. However, the excavation of Exegol and the capture of various First Order ships have presented us with new sources of material. The ability to cross-reference existing records with this new information has allowed me to uncover important new insights and understandings about the way the Galactic Empire governed, ruled, and waged war. In time many more records may also be uncovered. If so, it is possible that this study may become obsolete and replaced by more up to date research. That is always the risk of historical writing but, in this case, I welcome that development. Further research will help us avoid the fate that concerns me so much. It is entirely possible that in a week, a month, or a year I may find information that contradicts my findings here. But that is not a reason to delay. People so often misunderstand the purpose of historians. They think that we are just here to recount past events. To provide details without analysis. Facts without insight. Data without argument. This is wrong. The role of a historian— my role as a historian—is to try to tell you not just *how* but *why* these things happened. To try to make you understand the importance of these past events and what they mean for us today and tomorrow. This study is not just a work of history but of necessity. The galaxy needs to understand exactly what the Galactic Empire was and how it brought us to our latest brush with disaster. I can think of no more important undertaking than this one and no more required moment.

What is interesting to me is that I am not the only one to recognize the importance of this moment and the need to reexamine galactic history in light of recent events. A number of my colleagues—including some of the most illustrious figures in the field of galactic conflict studies—appear to be collaborating on a new overarching work of military history that aims to explore the series of wars that have been waged across the galaxy under the direction of Palpatine. I wish them good luck in their endeavor. Furthermore, the noted journalist and biographer Kitrin Braves is currently undertaking a detailed and exhaustive biography of the Skywalker dynasty. The recent deaths of Luke Skywalker and General Leia Organa were—while crucial in helping the Resistance survive and triumph—a tremendous loss to all of us who grew up idolizing them. It is long past time that we learned more about this family that appears to have given so much to our galaxy. Kitrin has been kind enough to share some information with me regarding the entire Skywalker lineage which—as will become clear—has been of great use in my research. I can think of nobody better than her to undertake this task.

This study will not always make for easy reading. As has already been mentioned, and will become clear in time, the depths of the Empire's crimes were truly horrifying. They were also not always equally felt. Many planets and species suffered far more than those in the Core Worlds. Similarly, while some humans—such as the Alderaanians—lost everything to the Empire, the inherent prejudices of that regime often focused in on those who were not human. The Empire, and those who orchestrated it, often spoke with a mix of disdain and disgust about "aliens" across the galaxy. There is no hiding the fact that, as a human, I have no experience of living with this type of prejudice, which still, sadly, endures. There are, however, things that can—and should—be done to mitigate this. While it may be necessary to sometimes quote the words of the Galactic Empire regarding the targets of its violence, there is no need to replicate their mindsets and use of language outside of this. The term "non-human" is problematic in its own ways but in the absence of a better one it is infinitely more acceptable than the pejorative "alien" that the Empire was so fond of using. Furthermore, where possible, I have attempted to highlight the experiences, writings, and voices of those who actually suffered under the Empire's prejudices and genocides. We should not follow the Empire's lead when it comes to silencing the victims of its many crimes. These are not perfect solutions and I accept the knowledge that they may fall short of what is both expected and required by those across the galaxy who lost both loved ones and worlds to Imperial aggression. They have a right to criticize failings of my own making, and I apologize to them for any of my own shortcomings. I can imagine that there will be those within the field of history and elsewhere who will find a declaration of my own potential blind spots to be unnecessary, but to them I say simply, this is an integral part of being a historian. As I recognize and analyze the relevant sources for this study I must too recognize and analyze myself.

The survivors of the Battle of Crait have become fond of saying, in moments of sorrow and loss, that "no one's ever really gone." It seems to bring them solace and I respect that. But I do not feel it. I have immersed myself in the existing records and writings and sources that relate to the Galactic Empire. And all I feel is the absence of lives that it brought. The multitudes who suffered and died. The further into this dark history I have gone the more horrified and haunted I have become. That is why this study now exists and why it is so important that you read it. Others in the Resistance will now lead and shape the galaxy. I cannot do that. I can only try and explain where we have come from. Why we have ended up here. But I need you to come with me. I cannot do this alone.

Part One

RISE AND CONSOLIDATION

Chapter 1

Emperor Palpatine

To begin to unravel the intricacies and details of the Galactic Empire it is impossible to begin anywhere but with the Emperor himself. It is difficult to think of any single figure who has had more of an impact on the entire galaxy than Sheev Palpatine but, despite this, so much of what we know about him is open to question, interpretation, or doubt. His recent apparent resurrection and return on Exegol immediately forces us to reconsider much of what is known about Palpatine and the powers supposedly granted to him by the dark side of the Force. As we continue the excavation of Exegol and the interrogation of captured First Order officers we may yet uncover more details of Palpatine's return. But beyond this, even re-examining what has been collectively "known" about him, there are many questions and concerns that need to be confronted. Palpatine existed in many guises and identities and trying to decipher which of them was really "him" is a challenge. Was he Sheev Palpatine the senator for Naboo and later supreme chancellor? Was he the Emperor—a man who tyrannically ruled the galaxy for a generation? Was he Darth Sidious the manipulative Sith Lord? Which of these aspects of his character was *truly* him?

Answering these questions is not easy. In the Galactic Republic, following the Naboo Crisis, Palpatine was one of the most prominent and publicly recognizable individuals in the galaxy. As the supreme chancellor he was beloved by the people and seemingly every movement he made outside of the Senate was broadcast by HoloNet News chan-nels.[1] As Emperor he became a far more secretive and secluded figure. Various Imperial agencies then either rewrote or removed huge num-bers of records that related to Palpatine's early life, to such an extent that there are now serious issues regarding the veracity of much that has previously been written or accepted about him. How do we go about understanding the background, the life, and the motivations of a man like Palpatine when there is so much contradictory information avail-able? I would suggest that, for understandable reasons, previous studies of Palpatine have often contained the same flaw. They have looked back at specific moments in his life—the decisions and actions that he took and the way he ruled the galaxy—and from there tried to draw conclu-sions about his personality and character. Ordinarily this approach makes a great deal of sense. But given the issues with the archival records relating to Palpatine, the concern remains that since much of the publicly available material from the years of the Galactic Empire is compromised, the surviving items exist for a reason—presumably to paint an acceptable image of the Emperor. I have no interest in creating a biography of a man with the materials he handpicked.

So, I am suggesting a different approach. One that has not been fully attempted before. Instead of looking at these past events and establishing Palpatine's character from them, we reverse the process. We take what is apparent about Palpatine's character and then consider how these impacted key moments in his rise to power. The difficulty of this is that many people have been distracted or blinded by Palpatine's abilities. The dark side apparently gave him powers that are beyond the reckoning of most of us, and will be discussed in greater detail shortly. The ability to see at least ele-ments of future events allowed him to lay out a grand plan of manipulation, subterfuge, and domination. As Emperor he appears to have, in some way,

[1] Imperial Archives, Section: Galactic Republic, File: Press Coverage of Supreme Chancellor Palpatine

cheated death, suggesting Palpatine may be the most powerful Force-user to have ever existed. But these are not character traits. The dark side did not create the ambition or desires within Palpatine, they just provided him with the tools to achieve them. Palpatine, for all his power, all his ability to pull the strings of government, his charisma as a senator, and his scheming as Emperor was not a flawless or insurmountable genius. If you strip away all these aspects and all his mystical powers, what you are left with is the real Palpatine. An arrogant, vicious, petty man. A man so utterly deter- mined to rule the galaxy in as oppressive a manner as possible and yet, simultaneously, so full of wounded pride that even the smallest acts of rebellion or rejection produced violent responses. A man who, for all his power, was so terrified of death that he effectively burned the galaxy to the ground to avoid it. With this in mind, we can now examine Palpatine's rise to power as a senator and supreme chancellor, his reign as Emperor, and his activities as Sith Lord through the lens of what we can already establish about his personality. Taking these aspects as the starting point we can begin to see things differently.

Rise to Power

Many of the details of Sheev Palpatine's early life are sketchy at best. Some records do remain and are useful for us, but either due to the gen- eral passage of time or, more probably, the actions of Imperial censors there are notable gaps. Despite this it is important to work with what is available and present educated theories regarding absences.

The Palpatine family was a reasonably notable—but not excessively so—wealthy house on the planet of Naboo. Records, backed up with sur- viving media reports from the time, suggest that Sheev Palpatine was born around 65 years before becoming Emperor.[2] Given the tendency of

[2] Naboo Planetary Archives, Section: Media and Press, File: Theed Birth Registration: #TC846317

the Naboo nobility at the time, he was likely the beneficiary of a private education at one of the various elite colleges on the planet. Surviving information from the Naboo Planetary Tourist Bureau highlight the fact that Dee'ja Peak had a notable theatre and was a major center for the arts at the time of Palpatine's youth.[3] Given that Palpatine nurtured a love of opera and ballet throughout his adult life, it is plausible that he spent some time around Dee'ja Peak during his formative years.

Little information now survives about the fate of Palpatine's family. By the time he was elected as a senator he did not appear to have any remaining relatives, but what happened to them is a mystery. It is entirely possible that they had simply passed on from old age but the complete absence of even an obituary for them in Naboo's records leads me to be suspicious as to their fate. It also presents perhaps the first example of Palpatine's underlying insecurities. What was he trying to hide regarding the eventual deaths of his family? If they were through natural causes then why hide them? Why continue to devote Imperial resources to maintaining this censorship? If he was already Emperor then what did it matter what people knew of his family? Unless perhaps they had rejected him on some level and his ultimate revenge was to remove all traces of them.

This is not the only notable gap in Palpatine's life before becoming a senator. In the years following his education Palpatine appears to have spent a great deal of time traveling the galaxy. It was a topic he would sometimes reference during political speeches.[4] The purpose of these travels is somewhat unclear. Ostensibly, Palpatine developed an interest in various forms of art and sculpture and became somewhat of a collector. Many of the pieces that would later decorate his political offices were supposedly collected in this period. But we also know that

[3] Naboo Planetary Archives, Section: Tourism, File: Dee'ja Peak
[4] Imperial Archives, Section: Galactic Republic, File: Supreme Chancellor Palpatine's Speeches #W108, #V211, #D492

Palpatine was a master of hiding his real intentions behind plain-sight activity. It is not clear at what point in his life Palpatine first became aware of the Sith. It is only through material recently uncovered on Exegol that we even have an indication that the individual who would become his master was named Darth Plagueis.[5] According to scrolls and writings that appear to have been dictated by Palpatine shortly before his most recent death, Plagueis had spent much of his life as a Sith Lord attempting to discover the secrets of eternal life. Such power appears to have greatly interested Palpatine himself.

But it seems fair to suggest that many of these lost years provided him ample cover to travel the galaxy either with Plagueis, or under his orders, while building his skills in the Force. Similarly, we can also wonder to what extent his collection of art provided Palpatine with cover to accrue ancient Sith artifacts. While serving as supreme chancellor, Palpatine was known to display in his office a carved bas-relief of a battle between Jedi and Sith forces which, given what we now know of his Force alignment, is an unsubtle display of allegiance that was seemingly completely missed by the Jedi of the time.[6]

When Palpatine became the senator for Naboo, around the age of 32 or 33, we must consider it likely he was already a Sith apprentice. However, certainly in the years before the Naboo Crisis, Palpatine exhibited what might have been one of the truly defining characteristics of this phase of his life: patience. Whether it was at the urging of his Sith master or just an innate part of his younger character is unclear, but Palpatine fostered an identity for himself over many years as an

[5] Exegol Excavation Project, Section: Sith Lords, Files: Darth Plagueis* *This information was recovered from the Arcane Library and appears to have been defaced. The discovery of this new material, which has brought to light the existence of Darth Plagueis, has helped to further construct the existing, but so far incomplete, hierarchy of the Sith Lords, which was a significant part of my ongoing research before I joined the Resistance.
[6] Imperial Archives, Section: Galactic Republic, File: Supreme Chancellor Palpatine's Chambers—Image #R187

amiable, pleasingly charismatic, and yet ultimately irrelevant political figure for a Mid Rim world. In the years to come, Palpatine would need to become a master at hiding in plain sight and his time as Naboo's senator allowed him to hone his craft. The Senate of the Republic was populated by more than its fair share of careerists and bureaucrats, corrupt figures, and mediocre minds. There were noble senators among them. Those who truly wanted to serve their constituents and the wider galaxy. Some of these played crucial roles in the founding of what would become the early political wing of the Rebel Alliance. But the unfolding rot of the Galactic Republic and the bureaucracy that kept the system in permanent cycles of stasis, best served the corrupt and the complacent.

In such company the best camouflage was not to appear as an honest man—who might be perceived as a danger—but rather as an unthreatening and unassuming one. Many looked at Palpatine and, seemingly seeing nothing in him, looked away again. This was an error that Palpatine seized upon. Because he was widely dismissed as an irrelevance, he fostered a position of counsellor and confidante for other senators in the Mid Rim. Many of whom—before taking a position on the political issues of the day, making speeches, or supporting bills—would seek out Palpatine for his calm, neutral, and unbiased opinion.[7] Opinions that it appears he readily gave and asked for nothing in return.

By the time of the Naboo Crisis—where the forces of the Trade Federation blockaded the planet of Naboo in protest at a proposed taxation bill—Palpatine had been a senator for twenty years.[8] He had spent more than two decades carefully building his public persona, all to then cash it in at this moment. Many, including officials in the Empire,

---

[7] A cross-reference of the following files makes for highly illuminating reading: Imperial Archives, Section: Galactic Republic, File: Senate Proceedings, and; Imperial Archives, Section: Galactic Republic, File: Meeting Records—Senator Palpatine.
[8] Naboo Planetary Archives, Section: Naboo Crisis, File: Trade Federation Blockade

have claimed that the Senate turned to Palpatine at this point out of recognition of his skills and sympathy with Naboo. This is probably, at best, only partially true. While it is hard to authoritatively declare each senator's agenda, given the way they rose to oust his predecessor Finis Valorum it is arguable that Palpatine was not so much elected but that the previous supreme chancellor was ejected. While Valorum came to be looked back upon fondly by some senators in the Empire there is little to be gained in overlooking the fact that he had long lost control over the actual running of the Republic and that the state had indeed become bloated and corrupt. Some of that rot was likely the work of Palpatine and his Sith master, but they did not create the issues of the Republic. They manipulated them to their own ends. There is a difference.

Regardless of the motivations of those who lifted him to the position of supreme chancellor, Palpatine took on the role largely safe in the knowledge that, should his plans come to pass, he would never leave it.

The Naboo Crisis should not be overly detached from the Clone Wars that eventually followed. The defeat of the Trade Federation—a major company that had foolishly been elevated to the same level of power as entire star systems—pushed it and other conglomerates into seeking alternative pathways to even greater power. Systems in the Outer Rim had long chafed under the control of Coruscant and a Republic that appeared happy to take their money but not recognize their concerns. The Separatist movement had bubbled under the surface within the Senate. Perhaps this too was a reason people were happy to drop Palpatine into the seat of supreme chancellor—it would be his problem to deal with. Palpatine's solution was Count Dooku—previously a Jedi Master and now, as has become apparent from the records on Exegol, a Sith Lord by the name of Darth Tyranus and Palpatine's apprentice.[9] Dooku would tip the galaxy into war and lead the

[9] Exegol Excavation Project, Section: Sith Lords, Files: Darth Tyranus*
*Information retrieved from the Arcane Library

Separatists, Palpatine would fight back as the Republic. The two men would play both sides of the same war. In desperation and fear of what this conflict would mean, senators willingly gave Palpatine ever increasing amounts of power and control without him ever having to request it. In this sense Palpatine did not take control of the Republic—it was presented to him.

While the Clone Wars will be covered in a subsequent chapter it is important to note that as supreme chancellor, even as he made changes to the constitution and begrudgingly—at least in public—accepted additional executive powers from the Senate, Palpatine's mask of civility was already beginning to slip. Various political figures from the time describe Palpatine as becoming testier and possessing an increasingly brittle temper during the Clone Wars. Members of the Delegation of the 2,000—before their subsequent arrests—told Mon Mothma and Bail Organa that Palpatine had come remarkably close to threatening them in a meeting when they attempted to present their petition.[10] At the time some of his detractors wondered if it was just the stresses of the war effort but, as we now know, there was no such stress. Palpatine already knew who was going to win. Instead, I would suggest that what they were seeing—as some like Mon Mothma suspected—was the real Palpatine shining through the façade. There was clearly only so long that even Palpatine could maintain the act and cloak his real nature.

For a man who we have already noted was clearly patient, that aspect of his character seems to have begun to run out in the final years of the Republic. One of the curiosities about Palpatine's position as supreme chancellor is that it also kept him safe from the Jedi's scrutiny until it was too late—the Jedi had believed that the Sith Lord they were searching for was someone who wanted to assume control of the galaxy, not

---

[10] Senator Leia Organa, personal writings: *Lessons from serving in Palpatine's Senate** *This story was recounted to Leia Organa by Senator Bail Organa, as a warning about Palpatine while she became further embroiled in the Rebel Alliance.

someone who already had. But Palpatine did not just want this power and control. He wanted it to be unquestioned and unchallenged. As supreme chancellor he seemed to find it increasingly difficult, or perhaps even tedious, to welcome those who would not automatically accept his wishes and commands. The unwillingness of others to bow to his rule had begun to grate upon him. It would evaporate as Emperor.

Galactic Emperor

For a plan as long-sighted as Palpatine's, timing was everything. The end of the Clone Wars was a messy, confused, and chaotic affair. There are parts of it we still do not adequately understand, but clearly Palpatine decided the time to act had come. His first step was to dispense with his existing apprentice, Count Dooku, and target the Jedi prodigy Anakin Skywalker as his replacement.[11] With Skywalker's assistance secured, Palpatine moved to eliminate the Jedi Order as the primary obstacle to his ambitions. We may never know what actually happened in Palpatine's office when representatives from the Jedi Council attempted to arrest him. The version recounted by Palpatine is obviously not remotely reliable.[12] What is clear, however, is that the man who emerged from that room appeared to most observers to be very different from the one who had previously entered it.

Palpatine was, in his own words, "scarred and deformed" by the Jedi. In immediate response he gave the command to the clone army, codenamed Order 66, to turn upon their Jedi commanders. The outcome was the extermination of almost the entirety of the Jedi Order.[13]

[11] Anakin Skywalker's role as the feared Imperial enforcer and Sith Lord, Darth Vader will be discussed in a forthcoming chapter, but for a more in-depth examination of his life as a Jedi then see Kitrin Braves' forthcoming work.
[12] Imperial Archives, Section: Formation of Empire, File: Emperor Palpatine's Speeches A00001
[13] We will examine the ending of the Clone Wars in greater detail in the next chapter.

This would be the first mass killing of Palpatine's rule. It would not be the last.

Palpatine's declaration of Empire was perhaps the most important and horrifying moment of recent history. Not just because of what it meant; the dissolution of the Republic and the rise of the Galactic Empire, but because of how it was received in the Senate and on many of the Core Worlds. Palpatine had been a beloved wartime leader. His life had been threatened repeatedly during the Clone Wars—he had only recently survived an abduction by General Grievous and an apparent assassination attempt by the Jedi. He was now a man who had won a war and, by his own statements, brought peace to the galaxy. Many in the Senate made the exact same assumption that had recently doomed the Jedi; Palpatine was already running the galaxy, how serious could a reorganization with him as Emperor really be? So, they cheered and broke into spontaneous applause. Princess Leia Organa would note years later that her adoptive father Senator Bail Organa had once, sadly, recounted a story to her where an unnamed senator—one whom he implied was a close friend—had noted that the jubilant acclaim was "how liberty died."[14]

Interestingly, having now apparently achieved everything that he had schemed so long for, it appears that the end result was not exactly what Palpatine was aiming for. As supreme chancellor he was one of the most public and recognizable figures in the galaxy. He was feted for the long hours he worked, the many committees that he met with, and the energy and vigor with which he threw himself into maintaining the Republic war effort.[15] Yet effectively overnight after declaring himself Emperor, he became a recluse. The public explanation was that he

[14] Senator Leia Organa, personal writings: *Lessons from serving in Palpatine's Senate*—This material was provided to me by C-3PO and appears to have been originally dictated to a droid named L0-LA59.
[15] *Coruscanti Society* #3269 featured an entire section on "Palpatine—Supreme Chancellor at War."

needed time to recover from the apparently horrific wounds he had suffered at the hands of would-be Jedi assassins. While there may be some truth in that, it is unlikely to be the real reason. I believe that another underlying assumption about Palpatine has obscured our understanding of him. For too long we have accepted at face value that his quest to be Emperor was one motivated by the desire for absolute control. And, again, there is a large element of truth to this, but it misses a crucial aspect: Palpatine wanted to rule the galaxy, but he had no interest in running it.

Even in the latter stages of being supreme chancellor, Palpatine had set in motion a process whereby power would be centralized under him, but the actual responsibility for the administration of the galaxy would be placed under the control of various regional governors and, under the Empire, Moffs. The most important of these was Grand Moff Wilhuff Tarkin—a man who we will be dealing with a great deal in this study. Political operations on Coruscant were effectively handed over to the likes of Mas Amedda, Pollux Hax, and Sate Pestage. How these different figures would run sectors and systems was, as will be discussed in a forthcoming chapter, largely up to them. As long as order and Imperial authority was maintained, Palpatine had no interest in the minutiae. However, that is not to say that Palpatine was entirely oblivious or uninterested in the state of his Empire.

In the Imperial Senate a common joke about Mon Mothma, as she would later recount, was that she was obsessed with trying to save the Empire from the Emperor.[16] Others within Palpatine's administration seemingly shared similar thoughts. In imagery that was, briefly, broadcast on the holonet in 2 BBY, Minister Pitina Mar-Mas Voor who led the Coalition for Progress—a propaganda ministry—declared that Palpatine himself was "ruining everything" when it came to trying to

---

[16] Chief of State Mon Mothma speech to the New Republic Senate: *The construction of power and governmental balances*

convince the galaxy of the benevolence of the Empire. She described the Emperor as "unlovable" and someone who "feels no need to promote the myth of prosperity because he has no interest in it coming true." Instead Palpatine's "only joy is watching his pet cyborg snap throats." Such treasonous statements immediately led to her execution by Darth Vader, but they do provide an insight into the transformation Palpatine had undergone now that he no longer felt any compunction to pretend to be a diligent and devoted civil servant.[17] However, despite this there still appears to be a significant part of Palpatine that wanted those who feared him to also—on some level—love him. Princess Leia has recounted how Mon Mothma had once explained to her that "the people of the galaxy *know* Palpatine is corrupt and cruel. They've known that for a generation," but despite this it didn't stop Palpatine from attempting to rewrite history to present a more acceptable version of himself.[18] Why did it matter so much to him?

Presumably Palpatine enjoyed the power of ruling the galaxy. Firsthand accounts from former Imperials, such as Mas Amedda—though these should be treated with some caution given the circumstances in which they were offered—suggest that he reveled in watching Darth Vader carry out his orders and executions, and took joy in the death and misery of others.[19] But he also took any attempted resistance to his rule or act of rebellion incredibly personally. Fourteen years into his rule, in 5 BBY, a small group of rebels staged a successful heist in the Aldhani system and escaped with a considerable chunk of Imperial payroll. The Emperor was, apparently, furious. Records of meeting minutes and communications transcripts from the Imperial

[17] Imperial Archives, Section: Treasonous Behaviour, File: Pitina Mar-Mas Voor. See also: Rebel Alliance Archives, Section: Propaganda Material, File: Pitina Mar-Mas Voor's Broadcast

[18] Senator Leia Organa speech to the New Republic Senate: *Reflections on the life and career of Mon Mothma*

[19] New Republic Archives, Section: Imperial Prisoners, File: Mas Amedda—Interrogation Notes #12-216

Security Bureau (ISB) show that Colonel Wullf Yularen met with Palpatine personally in the aftermath and took the lead in a series of sweeping and brutal galaxy-wide legal responses.[20] Shortly afterward an attack by the Neo-Separatist Anto Kreegyr was defeated on Spellhaus. There were no prisoners taken from Kreegyr's group in order to "wipe the taste of Aldhani from the Emperor's mouth."[21] How brittle and bruised was Palpatine's ego that such an event could cause this sort of response? It makes sense for the Empire to strike back in order to meet rebellion with further oppression, but Palpatine appeared to take such acts of resistance to heart. For an unlovable man a significant part of Palpatine appeared to want people to bow and suffer under him and to do so willingly and with gratitude.

If this was Palpatine's aim, then his reclusiveness did not help matters. In the Core Worlds Palpatine remained an ongoing figure even if he only ever made rare appearances in the Senate. But further out in the galaxy, beyond the Mid Rim and on the Outer Rim, the Emperor himself was almost an irrelevance. He barely even existed as a symbol, replaced instead by stormtroopers, TIE fighters, and Star Destroyers. As peculiar as it sounds there are serious questions over whether or not some people on these planets even knew what the Emperor looked like. While his Declaration of Empire was broadcast widely on the holonet and, as a result, showed Palpatine's new physical form after his battle with the Jedi, elements of his old appearance still proliferated. The propaganda poster "Leadership, Order, Power" that was displayed on multiple worlds such as Naboo and Vardos did not use the Emperor's current appearance but instead reverted to how he had looked as supreme chancellor.[22] Similar images were regularly displayed on the walkways of Coruscant and they too showed a much younger version of

[20] Imperial Archives, Section: Imperial Security Bureau, File: Aldhani Response Briefing
[21] Imperial Archives, Section: Imperial Security Bureau, File: Spellhaus Operation
[22] Imperial Archives, Section: Propaganda Material, File: "Leadership, Order, Power"

Palpatine, as did the Emperor's museum on Coruscant. The docent in charge of that institution would regularly take guests on tours through the exhibitions outlining Palpatine's rise "from humble beginnings" to becoming one of "the heroes we need."[23] There are also indications from within old Imperial records that, at times, Palpatine would use a filter on his hologram projections to appear as he once had rather than how he currently did.[24] Perhaps the reason for this was ego, but again it makes us wonder why Palpatine cared at all about what people thought of him when he was already Emperor. Maybe he realized the issues his current appearance caused, and feared his mutilated visage would be interpreted as a sign of weakness, but I'm not convinced. Given Palpatine's ongoing arrogance I think it is reasonable to suggest he wanted people to buy into the propaganda images for more personal reasons. Regardless though, for the most important figure in the galaxy to have no clear visual recognition on some worlds is staggering, though interestingly the previously mentioned busts of Palpatine currently available on Batuu depict his face after the injuries inflicted by the Jedi.

There also exist further questions regarding what exactly Palpatine did with his time, having essentially become a malleable figure rather than something present in people's lives. His appearances in the Senate were so rare as to become notable events in themselves. His public appearances were even scarcer than that. He maintained a private box at the Grand Imperial Opera House but it is unclear how often he visited. Other guests sometimes noted the appearance of the red-robed Royal Guards within the building but that is not definitive proof that Palpatine himself was in attendance.[25] It could just as easily have served his purposes to make people believe he moved around. Having become

---

[23] Senator Leia Organa, personal writings: *Lessons from serving in Palpatine's Senate*

[24] Imperial Archives, Section: Emperor Palpatine, File: Projection Filter B003

[25] Various editions of *Coruscanti Society* during the reign of the Empire make reference to the appearance of the Royal Guard at the Grand Imperial Opera House.

Emperor he had relocated himself to the old Jedi Temple, rebranding it as the Imperial Palace so that he could rule the galaxy from the home of his defeated foes. He also had a small retreat in the countryside of Naboo, but whatever he did there is not clear. The building was stripped of all equipment and material before it could be explored by the New Republic following the planet's liberation.

Having acquired all of this power, the Emperor did not seem inclined to directly wield it himself or to ever interact with outsiders again. If he had no interest in seeing the lies and promises of prosperity come to pass and he was not actively involved with the running of the Empire, what was he doing?

Sith Lord

It is possible that an additional assumption about Palpatine's long-running plan has blinded us to an extra-important element. The notion that Palpatine rose to power, then destroyed the Jedi Order and the Republic, simply in order to become Emperor and rule the galaxy, makes a great deal of sense but it also suffers from the supposition that this form of recognizable power was all that Palpatine wanted. But this power was not eternal. Palpatine could sit upon the throne for decades but eventually he would die and the Empire would pass to another. It is here that we must understand the potential underlying element to his Sith studies. Palpatine did not simply want to rule the galaxy, he wanted to rule it *forever*. He had no interest in having a reign that expired at the end of his life and he does not strike me as the sort of person who was interested in retirement or succession. Should we now perhaps be wondering if everything Palpatine did as senator, supreme chancellor, and Emperor was designed to provide him with the time, safety, security, and resources to pursue his actual goal: discovering the secrets of immortality? If we consider the enemies removed along the way and the ability to now spend the wealth of the galaxy in whatever ways he wanted, we must wonder if Palpatine saw the Empire as a means to an end—the swiftest and easiest way to ensure that his will was enforced upon the galaxy so absolutely that he would be free to uncover the solution to eternal life without challenge or distraction.

The knowledge that Palpatine was also a Sith Lord going by the name of Darth Sidious was probably one of the most closely guarded secrets in history. At some point in his time as supreme chancellor he must have revealed his identity to the likes of Mas Amedda and other bureaucrats and officials who would later go on to effectively run the Empire. We can only be sure that those who continued to serve accepted this information and kept the secret. Any who were repulsed by it likely did not live much longer, and it may be worth a more detailed examination of officials who worked with Palpatine over the years but then either faded into obscurity or unexpectedly passed away.

I am aware the extent to which discussions about the Force, the Jedi, and the Sith can come to sound increasingly implausible. Even before the recent war, I had spent years researching and uncovering the historical ruins and material left behind by generations of Sith. Among these remains I have encountered stories of powers and prophecies that stretch the very limit of credulity. But I have also seen things that I cannot rationally explain without accounting for the existence of the Force. During an archaeological dig on Yoturba I believe I saw the remnant of a long dead Sith Lord take control of one of my colleagues. I saw Luke Skywalker use the Force to levitate him clean off the ground. Both Luke Skywalker and Rey have given detailed accounts of their own encounters with Emperor Palpatine. Both mentioned how he could shoot lightning from his fingertips. How he could move things with his mind. How he claimed to be able to view the future. Many of these stories are supported by testimonials from ex-Imperials. And if these stories about Palpatine are true, if he could do these things, then the tales of the ancient Sith must also be reconsidered.

I spent years chasing around the galaxy searching for sites of Sith activity or temples, where some few scant clues could be dug from the ground to illuminate a fraction of the mystery. This was all before Exegol. Excavating the temple here may take an entire generation. Never before have we found so much material relating to the Sith in a single place. It appears, given our preliminary surveys, that Palpatine had spent years, either before or after his "death" at Endor, gathering up relics from worlds that had previously been thought to be myths like Moraband (or Korriban as it is referred to in Sith texts) and Dromund Kaas. This wealth of material could prove to be revelatory to our understanding of the Sith and of Palpatine's life as a Sith Lord. As a historian this is hugely exciting; we now stand on the verge of knowing more than we ever have on these topics. But we must also exercise caution. I have seen enough of Sith relics to know that they can be tremendously dangerous. Most forms of historical and archaeological research cannot be rushed, but that is particularly true in this case. There are plenty of Sith legends which speak of ancient relics or weapons that will not just take a victim's life but also their soul.

At present we know precious little about Palpatine's time learning under Darth Plagueis and barely any more about how he trained his own apprentices, but there is a clear hope that this will soon be expanded upon. It appears clear from the earliest results of our survey on Exegol that at various points Palpatine had at least three Sith students: Darth Maul, Count Dooku, and Darth Vader.[26] It is also clear that Palpatine had no qualms in dispensing with his students should circumstances dictate or better opportunities arise. According to these records Maul was taken from his people on Dathomir at a young age and spent years learning from Palpatine but, following his defeat on Naboo, he was— although presumed dead for some time—discarded. Maul had been a

[26] Exegol Excavation Project, Section: Sith Lords, Files: Darth Maul, Darth Tyranus, & Darth Vader* *All details retrieved from the Arcane Library

ferocious warrior but he did not have the charisma or leadership skills that would be necessary to lead the Separatists. Dooku was a much better fit for that role. However, Dooku would also be tossed aside once he had fulfilled his purpose in favor of Anakin Skywalker who was both younger and possessed significantly more power potential. What did Palpatine want to use that power for? Vader, as will be discussed, would often operate as the Emperor's roving enforcer. But this was after the severe injuries that left him encased in foreboding armor and dramatically weakened as a result. Palpatine may have nominally adhered to the Sith Rule of Two—a directive which ensured that there could only ever be a pair of Sith Lords in existence; a master and an apprentice—but I find it unlikely he wanted to train Skywalker so he could be overthrown.[27]

My previous research into the ancient lore of both the Jedi and the Sith often found references to a prophesied individual. The Jedi called them "the Chosen One" while fragments of Sith writings make mention of the coming of the "Sith'ari." Both of these legends share certain aspects and details regarding the coming of one who was born of the Force itself and who would wield tremendous power. The Jedi believed this individual would bring balance to the Force, the Sith that they would lead them to glory. Prophesies are difficult things to decipher and are often more a matter of faith than of destiny. But it appears, both from tales within the Jedi Order in the last days of the Republic and from scrolls retrieved from Exegol, that both sides believed the individual in question to be Anakin Skywalker.[28] Anakin was trained as a Jedi before falling to the dark side of the Force and adopting the identity of Darth Vader. If, as the stories suggest, Anakin Skywalker was

---

[27] *The Lerct Historical Institute Review*, Volume 3119. Article: *Historical Examples and Implications of the Sith Rule of Two*—by Beaumont Kin

[28] In particular, see: Rebel Alliance Archives, Section: Ahsoka Tano, File P23—Reflections on the Jedi Order; and also Exegol Excavation Project, Section: Sith Lords, Files: *Sith'ari* Prophecy* *This scroll appears to have been annotated by Palpatine.

conceived purely by the Force, it seems plausible that Palpatine believed Anakin may have held the solution to a way of unnaturally extending his own life.

While others ran the galaxy for him, Palpatine may well have spent his time and energies in communing with the dark side of the Force and undertaking a variety of Sith experiments. The facility that was constructed on Exegol and that appeared to bring him back from the dead was not constructed overnight. Palpatine must have been funneling incredible quantities of resources and trusted personnel into the operation. Such long-standing investment must have been coming from a place of fear that he may not crack the pathway to immortality in time. Palpatine had good cause to be afraid. No sooner had he declared himself Emperor, than the same day he was attacked by Grandmaster Yoda—the head of the recently destroyed Jedi Order—in the Senate building.[29] Though the two fought each other to a standstill, Palpatine must have realized how close to defeat he had come. This may also account for some of Palpatine's reclusiveness: a desire to never be that vulnerable again unless he was able to pick the battlefield.

Which produces another strange quirk of Palpatine's personality—he was remarkably willing to risk his own life at points if he deemed the potential rewards great enough or had "foreseen" that he would be successful. He allowed himself to be captured by General Grievous at the end of the Clone Wars, almost dying when the *Invisible Hand* crash-landed on Coruscant, and, while Emperor, he used himself as bait during a visit to Ryloth that brought a rebel group out of hiding. When each of these gambits worked, it helped shore up Palpatine's power. When one finally did not, it cost him everything. His plan to try and convert Luke Skywalker on the second Death Star while fighting ensued on Endor must rank as one of his most arrogant and foolhardy. The dark

[29] Imperial Archives, Section: Emperor Palpatine, File: Jedi Assassination Attempts—Yoda

side had given Palpatine significant power—both Luke Skywalker and Rey reflected upon their encounters with the Emperor and described him as terrifying. But, as noted at the beginning of this chapter, the dark side did not create Palpatine's ideas and persona, it just empowered him. Having already succeeded with Anakin Skywalker, Palpatine could not conceive of failing with Luke. Here again we see signs of the man who would take the rejection of the galaxy personally. Whether Palpatine believed he would be successful or simply could not countenance Luke's rejection is unknown, but he certainly did not anticipate Vader's.

Luke Skywalker noted that, clasped by Darth Vader and hurled into a reactor shaft, the Emperor screamed in horror and fear.[30] Betrayal by your own apprentice is the Sith way and yet, clearly, Palpatine had not considered it a possibility. This should have been the end, and a fitting one, for such a man. Sadly, we now know this was not the case. In time we will attempt to discover more about how Palpatine returned to Exegol, but we should not let his resurrection distract us from his reality. We should not let the raw power of the dark side blind us to the fact that Palpatine, beneath it all, remained the same scared man he always had been. For all the pain and misery he caused and reveled in, he spent his life chasing immortality only to fail because of his own shortcomings. Twice. The regime he created has cast a shadow over all of us for too long. This chapter will not be the only point in this study where we discuss and explore the actions of the Emperor, but it was a necessary starting point. However, to really understand the regime that Palpatine created we must look beyond him and come to understand the actions of those who drew authority and permission from Palpatine, but rarely—if ever—interacted with him. We must separate the Emperor from the Empire.

[30] Rebel Alliance Archives, Section: Luke Skywalker, File: Debriefing after the Battle of Endor—Emperor Palpatine

Chapter 2

The Clone Wars

Our galaxy has been split by three major conflicts within—at least for some species—living memory. Previously the Clone Wars and the Galactic Civil War had been considered two different events. However, given what we have since learned about Palpatine's involvement with both conflicts and the more recent First Order-Resistance War, perhaps it is better to think of them as key markers within a longer period of galactic warfare. It seems that many of the worst things that have happened to the galaxy across most of the last century can be attributed to Palpatine and the empire he wished to create.

Like many of the events of recent history, the Clone Wars have been taught and understood in very different ways since the conclusion of the conflict. The Empire went to great lengths to frame the war in a manner that fully justified Palpatine's decision to dispense with the Republic and usher in the new regime. The Empire was positioned not just as the natural outcome of the issues and problems inherent within the Republic but also as a necessary intervention from the one man capable of saving the galaxy. For years, a very carefully constructed version of the Clone Wars was delivered to the galaxy by the Empire with the aim of justifying the totalitarian government that now ruled. More recently, the New Republic found itself caught between a desire to learn lessons from the past and the urge to move forward and leave the darkness behind them. So, while the fall of the Republic remained an important moment for both lawmakers and teachers, both aiming to solidify the new government in different ways, the actual nature of the conflict itself became less relevant after the more recent civil war that had taken place.

However, understandings of the past change. The details that have been retrieved from within the archives of both the Empire and the records of the First Order can, when combined with the new material being uncovered on Exegol, help tell a different story about the Clone Wars.

It is not possible to fully understand the Empire, the Galactic Civil War, and all that Palpatine hoped to achieve without also knowing a great deal about the conflict that preceded it.

A Galaxy in Flames

It is never easy to deconstruct accepted facts about momentous events of the past. As time goes on, the rough edges of memory are worn away until what remains is an easy to accept and understand recollection. But the past is rarely easy and, certainly for historians, when we encounter versions of it that appear to be widely shared across the population the reaction is generally one of concern or suspicion. This is true of how the Clone Wars has come to be understood and, of greater importance, how alternative views of the conflict have been effectively suppressed to maintain the dominant one. It is time for us to begin the process of re-examining the war by beginning with accepting a simple truth: there is no single unified history or memory of the Clone Wars because it was written by the only side that actually won—the Empire—at the expense of the experiences of Republic and Separatist participants. While the purpose of this study is not to build a new and fully rounded under-standing of the Clone Wars, I hope it can serve as a starting place for such an endeavor in the future.

The basic facts of the Clone Wars are well-established but, given the length of time since the conflict's conclusion, still bear repeating.

It is largely accepted that the origins of the war can be found in the Trade Federation's blockade of Naboo that was, ostensibly, over taxation in the Outer Rim. Though that blockade would eventually fail, following the involvement of the Jedi Order, it helped lay the seeds of the coming conflict, the fall of the Republic, and the rise of the Empire. The Trade Federation had previously achieved a great deal of power within the Republic Senate but, following their failure at Naboo, their fortunes dramatically fell. While enduring a form of political exile they found like-minded allies among other super-conglomerate corporations and worlds across the Outer Rim. While these companies feigned neutrality within the Republic, in reality they made clear their potential allegiance to the emerging Separatist Alliance, planets who had long believed that the Republic scarcely functioned as a governing body and certainly was not serving their planetary or commercial interests. While it would be these worlds who would provide much of the political momentum for the forthcoming secession, their industrial backers prepared for war and—cynically—profit. What this movement lacked was a leader and soon enough one emerged in the form of Count Dooku. A former Jedi, Dooku had left the Order citing grave concerns with how the Jedi and the Republic were failing the galaxy. He provided the charisma and political leadership that the Separatist movement required. Following a series of attempted, but failed, negotiations between the two sides, warfare broke out at the planet Geonosis and spread across the galaxy. The conflict would rage for years, and see whole star systems ravaged, before finally ending in defeat for the Separatists.

While these details sketch out the broadest strokes of the Clone Wars, they do not fully explain the underlying tensions and machinations of the conflict and nor do they really explain why it ended in the manner it did and what it meant for the dawn of the Galactic Empire. Wars are complicated things. In order to understand the Clone Wars it is necessary to accept one fact that seems contradictory but is also incredibly simple:

despite seeming to be one and the same, the Republic and Palpatine were fighting very different wars with very different objectives. That is why Palpatine won and the Republic lost. The Trade Federation did not just pick Naboo at random to stage their initial blockade. They did so because they were urged to by a Sith Lord named Darth Sidious.[1] After that blockade failed, they and the rest of the Separatist movement were led down a path to war by the same individual. What they—and the Republic along with them—failed to realize was that Sidious and Palpatine were the same person. While the supreme chancellor led the Republic, his Sith Lord persona—with his apprentice Count Dooku—orchestrated the Separatists. And beneath it all Palpatine made his own plans to achieve his goals. None of them included the success of the Separatist movement or the long-term survival and stability of the Republic.

As a result, the various military campaigns and battles of the Clone Wars—while of definite interest to military historians in seeing how the commanders and soldiers of both sides waged the war—are effectively irrelevant to this study. Though there was very real danger to those involved in fighting the war, there was no real jeopardy involved for Palpatine himself, as he was going to win regardless. Instead, we should focus our attentions on the moves and decisions that were taken to herald the age of Empire that Palpatine had always intended. Within these plans and schemes we can see the actual lasting impact of the Clone Wars on both sides that were supposedly fighting it.

Preparing the Way

The underlying tensions and issues that had beset the Republic in the lead up to war must have been of great interest to Palpatine. They proved

---

[1] Imperial Archives, Section: Seized Trade Federation Records, File: Naboo Blockade* *This material was heavily censored and sealed during the era of the Empire and was only recovered in the years after the war.

that there was already significant demand for a change in the way the galaxy was governed. Beyond this, even if just in localized factions, there was also significant willingness to fight for that change. With both the Republic and the Separatists effectively viewing the war as a necessary one to preserve their very existence, Palpatine and Dooku would just have to ensure that neither side won it too quickly nor felt motivated to sue for peace. The war-weariness of the galactic population would be a crucial factor in its acceptance of the new regime, and Palpatine himself had to be welcomed, eventually, as a savior. Which is why it was so important that most of the political controls that he planned on keeping had to, publicly at least, appear forced upon him. Palpatine had to play the role of a reluctant figure grappling to end a conflict that was constantly spiraling out of control.[2]

For one of the primary purposes of this war was to brutalize the population of the galaxy. Palpatine knew that desire for change was not enough on its own. Peaceful movements might lead to an election or a change in the organization of the Republic, but neither of these things would upend the system, effectively leaving Palpatine in a position at the top. To achieve this the population, both of the Republic and the Confederacy of Independent Systems, had to be made to suffer the realities of a war raging around them. This war had to be more destructive, more chaotic, more disruptive, and more horrifying than they could have believed. It had to have effects and impacts that were keenly felt both in the Core and in the Outer Rim. Civilians had to die in huge numbers on besieged worlds. Property had to be destroyed. Economies had to collapse. Planets had to starve. The people of the Republic had to fully invest in Palpatine as a hope for peace, while the civilians on Separatist worlds had to question whether independence was worth the

[2] This can be seen in recordings of Palpatine's speech upon being granted emergency powers shortly before the Battle of Geonosis, available at: Imperial Archives, Section: Emperor Palpatine, File T271 and New Republic Archives, Section: Galactic Republic, File X S409.

horror.[3] Because when Palpatine was ready to bring about the end of the conflict, both populations had to be so desperate for that moment that they would gratefully embrace peace. They must be so grateful that they would not care about the price it came at or what was traded away to achieve it. And Palpatine intended to charge a very high price for the end of his war.

In many ways this was the true target of the Clone Wars. It was not clone troopers against droid armies, or loyalists against separatists. It was the use of weapons of war against the spirit and the morale of ordinary civilians. People needed to be led right up to the edge of disaster so that they would give anything to go back the way they had come, without noticing that the landscape had changed around them in the interim. In this sense it was important that the war should, at least on the surface, end with a Republic victory. Most of the population involved with the war had continued to operate under the Republic. Palpatine was already installed as leader of that faction. In the earliest years of stabilizing the Empire, at the period when it was most vulnerable, it was important that people accepted it as the natural evolution of the war's end. In short, many civilians did not object to the changes going on around them because the Empire arrived wearing—initially at least—similar clothes to the Republic that had existed before. This level of acceptance was invaluable in securing the Empire's control across the galaxy.

What was equally important was the presence of a beaten enemy. Palpatine and those he installed to run his new Empire knew that there would be resistance to the new order of things.[4] The Separatists had proven themselves useful as a willing participant in the recently concluded conflict but given they had rebelled against the Republic they

---

[3] New Republic Archives, Section: Luke Skywalker, File: *The Horrors and Spiritual Impact of War* *This appears to be a lengthy message provided to Luke Skywalker by Lor San Tekka, a companion of his whom I met on several occasions.

[4] Imperial Archives, Section: Occupation of former Separatist Systems, File: Plans for Preventative Measures

posed a liability to the Empire that replaced it. Planets with a history of armed resistance could not be left to their own devices for long. Key systems such as Raxus Secundus, the capital of the Separatists, and Serenno, Count Dooku's homeworld, were the targets of early and brutal Imperial occupation in order to stamp out any last surviving flames of insurrection. Palpatine needed the spirit that had driven the Separatists into open warfare to be crushed as quickly as possible. But having the specter of secession linger in the galaxy was also useful. The Empire was able to justify many of its early expansions and actions in the name of eliminating surviving holdouts from the Clone Wars, whether the targets actually had any relationship with the Separatists or not. The wider population was happy to accept such military endeavors in the name of safeguarding the seemingly hard-won peace.

There were other benefits for the Empire arising from activities and actions undertaken during the previous war. Early in the conflict the Republic had come to an arrangement with the Hutt Cartel regarding access to hyperlanes and trade routes into the Outer Rim. These were hugely useful to Republic fleets during the conflict as it granted them new pathways into contested territory that circumvented Separatist blockades. The true value of these new routes, however, was not to the Republic but to the Empire. Along the Outer Rim there were any number of worlds and systems who had remained untouched or inaccessible to the Republic and fiercely guarded their independent status. Now they were within reach of an Empire that cared little for— and respected less—the desires of star systems to maintain their own sovereignty. Following the conclusion of the Clone Wars, as will be discussed in a forthcoming chapter, the first waves of Imperial expansion focused on those worlds who had remained neutral in the previous conflict but now found themselves living alongside the borders of a belligerent neighbor.[5]

[5] See Chapter Seven

Former Separatist worlds that had been converted into industrial hubs in order to fight the war were also welcome prizes for the Empire. The droid factories of the Trade Federation, Baktoid Industries, and the Techno Union all now fell under Imperial control. The leadership of these companies was purged but the machinery and the industrial opportunities they provided were swiftly nationalized in service to the Empire in a process called Imperialization. Similarly, the huge stashes and collections of weaponry abandoned by the Separatists at the end of the war would swiftly be claimed by the Empire, who would later find inventive uses for it.

Beyond the material benefits of the war, and the damage it did to the wider galactic population, there was an extra important and overarching objective for Palpatine in the way he waged it. The events of the Great Jedi Purge have become confused and complicated over time. Imperial propaganda pushed very clear messages about the Jedi while at the same time making clear to the average citizen how important it was for them to forget about the Order and leave the topic very well alone. It should therefore not be surprising that the actual details of the events that saw the extermination of the Jedi and the conclusion of the Clone Wars remain largely uncertain. Hopefully we can start to illuminate some of the events from here.

Destruction and Legacies

The roots of the Jedi's downfall lay in the creation of the clone army itself. In the lead up to the beginning of the war the Republic Senate had been paralyzed with debates over the creation of a military force through which to defend itself against the emerging threat of the Separatists. Seemingly from nowhere such an armed force was discovered in the form of a clone army created under contract by the Kaminoans. The exact series of events behind the creation of this army remains unclear and records relating to it are scarce. The popularly accepted version at the time was that a rogue Jedi by the name of Sifo-Dyas had independently contacted the Kaminoans, 10 years before the war, to place the order for the clone troops.[6] Given what we now know, and what shall be shortly discussed, it seems highly unlikely that Sifo-Dyas did this without at least some form of involvement or manipulation by Palpatine or his agents. The arrival of the clones at the exact moment they were required is far too convenient for there not to have been a long-running plan behind their creation.

As part of the training and creation of these clone soldiers, each one was inserted with a piece of organic technology generally referred to as an inhibitor chip. These chips were ostensibly designed to ensure that the clones would only follow legitimate orders but, within their programming, also lay various contingency plans for the clones to react to, should various disasters befall the Republic war effort. Only the supreme chancellor could issue these select orders and, as we know, Palpatine was assumed to be working in the Republic's best interests and therefore would not do anything to damage the state.[7] A very dangerous and misplaced assumption. Because within these set directives was one titled "Order 66." It was to be issued should the Jedi turn against the Republic and need to be eliminated.[8]

Ever since the clone army had arrived to "rescue" the Jedi on Geonosis at the outbreak of the war, much of the Republic's propaganda efforts had been designed to elevate and venerate the actions of these

[6] Information regarding some of this background was provided to the Rebel Alliance by the former Jedi Ahsoka Tano while serving in her role of "Fulcrum," a rebel coordinating agent. Rebel Alliance Archives, Section: Ahsoka Tano, File H23—Reflections on the Clone Army
[7] For a full list of these various codes and their corresponding orders, see: Imperial Archives, Section: Galactic Republic Military Operations, File PG004—Executive Order Codes for the Grand Army of the Republic
[8] Details of the inhibitor chips and their functions for the clone army have survived in selected Imperial archives. Additional information is drawn from testimonies by the clone captain known as "Rex" within Rebel Alliance records. Rebel Alliance Archives, Section: Clone Army, File XD461—Rex

soldiers. Images such as "Support the Boys in White" and "Buy Republic War Bonds" placed the image of the clone trooper right at the forefront of the public's mind. A monument enshrining the identifying numbers of clone soldiers who had died on Geonosis was unveiled on Coruscant to commemorate their sacrifice to the Republic. The Jedi were, despite serving as generals and commanders in the war, relegated to the sidelines. During the war the Republic instituted a program of Population Observation, where ordinary civilians would be regularly surveyed for their opinions on a range of aspects regarding the war effort.[9] A recurring trend as the war dragged on and became more destructive was the extent to which the Jedi were viewed as either a part of the problem or culpable for the conflict.

As the war continued and suffering spread throughout the Republic many, especially on Coruscant, came to look at the Jedi Temple and its occupants with resentment. If the Jedi were so powerful, how had they failed to win the war? If they were so wise, how had they not foreseen the coming dangers? If they were so important to the Republic, why were so many new clones required? With no obvious forthcoming answers to these questions, anger and distrust continued to blossom. Palpatine must have been delighted. His planned eradication of the Jedi would only be truly successful if the population either already hated them or did not care about their fate. The Separatists had spent much of the war creating their own propaganda warning about the "Jedi Menace," so that side of things was already taken care of. Palpatine just had to ensure that the population of the Republic was prepared to do without the Jedi Order.

Following the failed attack on Coruscant by the Separatist fleet that cost Count Dooku his life, Palpatine—who almost certainly orchestrated the whole thing, including his own staged abduction—appears to

---

[9] Some of the records for this are still available at: Imperial Archives, Section: Galactic Republic—Population Observation File: Directives and Responses.

have decided that the end of the war was now approaching. The Jedi Order had, supposedly, been hunting for the Sith Lord Darth Sidious who was orchestrating the war from behind the scenes. It seems logical that, given the attempt to arrest Palpatine in his offices, the Jedi had discovered his true identity. The failure to arrest him triggered the final stages of the war. From his offices Palpatine must have transmitted a short statement to the clone army: "Execute Order 66." On countless worlds, clone soldiers who had spent years living and fighting alongside the Jedi instantly turned on them. On Coruscant itself a battalion of clones led by Anakin Skywalker—newly dubbed as Darth Vader— stormed the Jedi Temple and executed the occupants. From masters to younglings, none were spared. By the time the clones stopped firing, the Jedi had effectively been exterminated. The extinction of the Jedi removed a serious obstacle to Palpatine's plans. He must have known that if an organized Jedi Order remained that they would continuously oppose him. Their deaths became a necessity for his Empire to live.[10]

It would not take long for the symbols of the Clone Wars and the Republic to be actively dismantled by the Empire. Imperial forces soon destroyed Tipoca City—the center for the Republic's cloning facilities— on Kamino. Imperial involvement in this act was only later exposed by a senator, with the blame being ascribed to a rogue vice admiral named Edmon Rampart, though it is hard to believe he had truly gone rogue and was not acting under the orders of senior officials. Regardless of his motivations, Rampart's actions helped bring about dramatic changes in the Empire's military. The end of the war had also brought about an effective end to the long-term viability of the clone army. As will be discussed in a forthcoming chapter, various figures within the Imperial military, including Grand Moff Tarkin, came to view the clones as an expensive and unnecessary undertaking for the Empire. Growing and

[10] See Chapter Ten for more details on the ongoing Imperial efforts to eliminate the Jedi.

training them took time and resources that could potentially be put to better use elsewhere. Furthermore, there were lingering concerns regarding the true loyalties of the clones. While many continued to serve in the armed forces of the Empire much as they had with the Republic, there were others who appeared changed by their time spent with the Jedi. The Empire had no interest in maintaining an army that may have been corrupted by exposure to the Order. They would shortly be phased out in favor of the new Stormtrooper Program.

One curiosity that did continue into the Empire was the emergence of amateur historical reenactments of key Clone Wars battles, complete with costumed "clone troopers" and de-militarized droids. There were groups across the Core Worlds who indulged in the practice and, strangely given their reputation for pacifism, a particularly strong presence for it existed on Alderaan. Why the Empire tolerated such overt harking back to the Republic and its obsolete symbols is perhaps on the surface unclear. There were some Imperial officials who believed that the Clone Wars reenactment movement "provided young persons with the military skills and training that would be invaluable for service in the Empire."[11] Though whether this viewpoint was widely held is uncertain. It is noticeable that this was one of the few ways in which imagery and uniforms from the Republic were permitted within civilian life. Again, this might seem unusual, but when you remember that the Republic that gave way to the new regime had already been through a period of militarization, it becomes a much more understandable evolution. The Republic that existed in the latter stages of the Clone Wars was not the example of peace and prosperity that had once existed. It was not a great leap to go from the Republic venerating the military during the Clone Wars to the Empire using it as cover to expand its armed forces while celebrating them at the same time. The annual

---

[11] Colonel Toln Yurak, Imperial Army, in an interview with the periodical publication *Clone Wars Quarterly*

Empire Day parades, which were a feature on many worlds, celebrated the end of the Clone Wars as well as the dawn of the Imperial state. The major difference between how the Republic and the Empire viewed the Clone Wars was the removal of all references to the Jedi, often in favor of a greater acknowledgement of Palpatine. That many of the participants of the reenacted scenes were from the upper classes of the Core Worlds may also provide an explanation as to why it was permitted. The Empire would often allow the wealthy to create their own diversions and entertainment as long as they were not using their resources for things that actively undermined the Empire.

There was, however, one significant holdover from the transition between Republic and Empire that continued to hold a deal of power and significance. While the Empire wished to sweep away many of the trappings and systems of the failed Republic, the aftermath of a war—even one that had served its purpose—was difficult. For the Empire to have a long-term future it needed to solidify its hold over the galaxy, shore up its power, and survive the tumultuous aftermath of the conflict. To achieve this, the Empire maintained the existence of the most obvious relic of the Republic: the Senate. In order to understand how the Empire intended to organize and rule the galaxy, we must also understand the ways in which it accepted or circumvented limits on its political power.

Chapter 3

The Imperial Senate

The continued existence of the Senate, as one of the enduring elements of the now-fallen Republic that carried over into the Galactic Empire, has previously provoked a good deal of confusion among those studying the Imperial state. This is understandable. If we accept that Palpatine intended to reign over the galaxy as a dictator, retaining a publicly elected body that had some powers to thwart his plans seems counter-productive. However, this confusion often overlooks the fact that the Empire's control was not instantaneous—it was an (at times) incremental progression away from the Republic following the Clone Wars. While Palpatine may have wanted to dispense with the Senate entirely, the fact that it took years to be able to do so is instructive as to how secure he and his primary advisors felt in the Empire's stability. As will become apparent as this study progresses, Palpatine—and Grand Moff Tarkin alongside him— had a very definite endpoint in mind for the Senate.

Furthermore, as will also become apparent as we progress, the upper echelons of the Empire were often creative in solving significant obstacles in their path. There is certainly evidence to suggest that the Senate was not simply a powerless body, but an institution that did have the power to directly impact Imperial plans and activities. While its eventual dissolution was the inevitable end stage of Palpatine's plans, this would take time. Before this point could be reached, the Empire would have to find ways of dealing with this political body. Though they could attempt to circumvent its reach and oversight, this was not always possible. The solution to this issue was as inventive as it was cynical. Rather than continually try and dance around the Senate, the Empire took a different approach—one it would repeat at various levels for other administrative and military personnel and organizations. That is, the Empire wove the Senate into the decision-making processes for some of its most unsavory crimes. Rather than allow the politicians to stand apart from the grim reality of Imperial rule, the Empire sought—as this chapter will outline—to make sure they were also culpable.

Maintaining the Balance

There has been a tendency, as already mentioned in this study, to idealize the Senate of the Republic. To view it at the time of its fall through the lens of its highest moments. Histories of the—admittedly long gone—era now collectively referred to as the High Republic have noted how the state aimed to be a unifying force and that slogans such as "We are all the Republic" and "For Light and Life" motivated both the ordinary citizenry and the Jedi to move the galaxy forward. A few of these studies have overlooked some of the growing problems within the High Republic. Though idealism can form a powerful bond, the motives and directives of individual senators were a source of potential erosion. Similarly, that government's response to aggression from a pirate group known as the Nihil was—initially at least—less than impressive and significant civilian casualties were sustained before the situation was brought under control. However, what *can* be taken from this period of history is that the galaxy, and its various institutions, could still be rallied together against an emerging menace. There remained a desire to try and improve both the Republic and the galaxy, and the system of government allowed for those efforts to be undertaken. However, the final hundred or so years of the Republic were a far cry from the ideals that had gone before. The Senate that existed during the last years of the Republic had fallen a very long way from those lofty heights.

The sad irony of the Republic's fall is that it came at a time when some of the most capable and idealistic politicians for a generation were present and attempting to prevent the unfolding collapse. The likes of Mon Mothma are, of course, legendary for their leadership of the Rebel Alliance and then the New Republic. There is a reason why her life and career are considered key parts of school education. Similarly, before his death during the destruction of Alderaan, Senator Bail Organa had been a key figure in opposing Palpatine. During the Clone Wars, he joined with like-minded senators—including Padmé Amidala from Naboo—in trying to derail some of the more egregious attempts to place additional power into Palpatine's hands. Following the declaration of the Empire, Organa then secretly worked with Mon Mothma and other allies to help found the Rebel Alliance.

However, set alongside these figures were a variety of loyalist groups and factions that supported Palpatine's rule during the last years of the Republic for a mixture of personal and political reasons. When Palpatine's new Empire was greeted with seemingly unanimous consent in the Senate chamber, not all of those who cheered and applauded did so out of corruption or political expediency. There were those who had supported Palpatine during the war and voted him additional powers and controls because they believed he could be trusted with them. This is an important lesson for the galaxy moving forward: there will always be those who are prepared to accelerate the death of democracy if they believe power is being given to someone worthy.[1] However, there was also a potential danger for Palpatine within this situation. It was easy enough to rely on the support of those senators

---

[1] This was, as Chapter Twenty-Three will show, an area of concern for Mon Mothma when attempting to define the role of the New Republic's chancellor.

who had been bought or bribed or coerced into supporting him. They weren't going anywhere—particularly now that the Empire was unopposed. But support from those who chose to believe in him could be more precarious. Should those same senators be presented with evidence of atrocities, or grow aghast at decisions undertaken too quickly, they might start to turn on the Emperor.

This required a careful balancing act by the likes of Palpatine, Mas Amedda, and other political figures within the nascent Empire. Because underlying everything was the realization that regardless of what they may wish to achieve in the long term, following the end of the Clone Wars, the Empire needed the Senate. It could not hope to rule the galaxy without them. The war had done grave damage to wider galactic infrastructure and the shift to Empire did not immediately translate into fully centralized power. Therefore, if the Empire was going to function—and at some future point dispense with the Senate entirely—it was necessary to make use of them as an organizational and administrative body for as long as required.

As a result, very little of the actual process and responsibilities of the Senate initially changed as the Republic gave way to the Empire. The Republic had already allowed member worlds to effectively define their own electoral procedures and the limits of their senators' terms of office. While galactic standard time was used across both the Republic and the Empire, trying to legislate for a senatorial standard across thousands of worlds with differing orbital cycles and species lifespans was an impossible task. So, each member system generally produced a representative through whichever means and methods best worked for them. Given that this system ensured that Mon Mothma continued to represent Chandrila and Bail Organa did the same for Alderaan, it might seem perplexing that the Empire did not actively involve themselves in the electoral process to ensure that more favorable candidates were successful. Both Mothma and Organa were subjected to varying degrees of unofficial surveillance while they were on Coruscant, though the surviving Imperial Security Bureau files on Mon Mothma proved how difficult it was to pin any truly seditious or criminal activities on her, save for repeated mention of non-political infractions committed by her husband.[2] It would certainly have made life easier for the Empire in the long run if both Mothma and Organa had been removed before the rebellion spread too far.

But perhaps this also misunderstands the Imperial plans for the Senate. There were undoubtedly any number of senators serving within it that were nuisances in some way or another. But the benefit of having them all operate on Coruscant was that it made it easier to keep track of them, rather than trying to maintain surveillance on all their homeworlds. If any of them did become a serious issue, there were various means through which they could be arrested on corruption charges, or something similarly convoluted that would tarnish their name back home while also removing them as an obstacle. Additionally, as we now know, the Empire did not view the Senate as a long-term proposition. Senators would continue to serve for as long as Palpatine deemed it necessary and not a moment longer. But while they were there, they could provide a significant service to the Empire. Not through serving their various constituents and maintaining the smooth running of the state. That was largely expected and—in the sectors the Empire was intending to expand into or take direct control of—largely irrelevant to the current moment. Instead, what the senators could do, especially those viewed as potentially problematic, was be forced into scenarios where they would have to dirty their hands with Imperial crimes and misadventures. In this way, they would deflect any blame away from the Emperor and onto themselves.

[2] Imperial Archives, Section: Imperial Security Bureau, Section: Mon Mothma, Files: UG043-219—Perrin Fertha

Wielding Power

There is sometimes a tendency to overlook the political experience Palpatine gained through his years of work in the Republic Senate. His understanding of the ebbs and flows of political fortunes and how best to achieve the results he wanted was invaluable in now managing the Imperial Senate. Leia Organa once spoke about how Mon Mothma had explained the ways Palpatine would lay traps for senators that would force them into doing his bidding by accident.[3] Leia Organa herself was the victim of several of these attempts while she was serving in the Apprentice Legislature and learning the ways of Imperial politics. The Apprentice Legislature was, in principle, a program designed to allow the politicians and administrators of the future the chance to learn the methods and bureaucracy of governing the galaxy while they were younger. In reality though, many worlds ceased to send representatives to participate, and the Empire had come to view the system as an easy way to drag young volunteers into various forms of culpability before they'd even been elected into office.

A prime example, according to Leia Organa's own records, was the decision by her cohort of the Apprentice Legislature to select the planet Arreyel, instead of three other options, to be the home of a planned Imperial academy of aeronautical engineering and design. The decision was made because of how the academy could benefit Arreyel's economy and populace. However, following Imperial scans of the planet, a significant radiation source was discovered and the world was seized by Imperial authorities. As punishment for having never declared the radiation source, the inhabitants were given a matter of weeks to evacuate with no compensation. Leia Organa, almost certainly correctly, reflected that the entire process had been a ruse designed to allow those scans to take place and discover the radiation source that the Empire already

---

[3] Senator Leia Organa speech to the New Republic Senate: *Reflections on the life and career of Mon Mothma*

suspected was there. Out of a desire to do good, Leia Organa and her compatriots had been tricked into furthering the Empire's aims.[4]

Leia Organa, along with the likes of Mon Mothma and Bail Organa, learned that there were very few ways in which any form of sustained ethical choices could be made while operating under Palpatine's rule. If decisions were put before committees or raised as bills and amendments on the Senate floor, they were often liable for alteration or manipulation by Imperial political advisors or governors to create the outcome they desired, while also smearing the reputations of those senators who had been the driving forces. So complicated was the process of navigating the various pitfalls of Imperial politics that Senator Daho Sejan once wrote to a compatriot that "the Senate increasingly resembles a rigged casino. Given that Palpatine always wins the political games, it seems pointless to play unless you can also secure your own prizes at the same time."[5] Sejan was later executed for some unspecified form of treason, so it appears that he did not end up playing the game well enough.

Records of the decisions taken by the Senate—records that the Empire itself made sure were well-preserved and dispersed to the relevant worlds—are replete with examples of senators signing off on decisions that then had widespread negative effects. Campaigns to help the starving population of Wobani resulted in the planet being converted into a prisoner and labor camp, thereby providing "accommodation and food" for those trapped there.[6] A bill requesting additional employment opportunities on Corellia led to the shipyards becoming an associated offshoot of Kuat Drive Yards to help construct new Star Destroyers. The result for the inhabitants of the planet was heavy pollution in the upper atmosphere.[7] For everyone else it was the growing shadow of Star

---

[4] Senator Leia Organa, personal writings: *Lessons from serving in Palpatine's Senate*
[5] Imperial Archives, Section: Senator Daho Sejan, File: ZE14—seized records
[6] Imperial Senate Proceedings, File: VK139.5
[7] Imperial Senate Proceedings, File: DL221.8

Destroyers in orbit above their worlds. Shortly after the Empire was founded, Senator Riyo Chuchi of Pantora was a strong dissenter against the planned Imperial Defense Recruitment Bill that would seek to phase out the clone army and replace them with civilian soldiers recruited, or conscripted, from the wider population. The bill had already been defeated once before but had been returned to the Senate again. Senator Chuchi garnered opposition to the bill from existing clone soldiers and then exposed the destruction of Tipoca City and its cloning facilities on the orders of Vice Admiral Rampart—who was the bill's main supporter—on the floor of the Senate. Rampart was immediately arrested as a response. Chuchi and her allies may have briefly thought that they had won the debate, but the sudden arrival of Emperor Palpatine changed all of this. He expressed his concerns that Rampart's clone soldiers had obeyed the order to attack Kamino without hesitation and that such blind loyalty represented a threat to the Empire—something that a conscript stormtrooper army would not. In response the Senate enthusiastically supported the bill and Chuchi discovered that she had been outmaneuvered all along.[8]

Because of the ongoing fear that any action would be twisted to either support the Empire or result in senators being held responsible as culpable participants in ongoing Imperial activity, many of them found themselves effectively paralyzed by indecision. When faced with several, even seemingly contradictory options, fear that all of them somehow served Palpatine prevented lawmakers from acting decisively or, indeed, at all. This did nothing to remove the reputation of the Senate as a body that achieved nothing but talking, with only Imperial governors seemingly able to act without the obstacles of politics. Amid this indecision various unscrupulous politicians took the decision to simply accrue their own personal wealth and power at the expense of their home systems, given that little could be done to assist them anyway.

[8] Imperial Senate Proceedings, File Y D19.6

Orn Free Taa had been the senator for Ryloth since the Republic and had been a staunch loyalist of Palpatine during the Clone Wars. During the reign of the Empire he continued his role in the Imperial Senate and was willing at various points to impede and threaten the Free Ryloth movement on his home planet, viewing its leader Cham Syndulla as a political rival who threatened his own position and wealth.[9] Domus Renking served, for a time, as the senator for Lothal but seemingly spent most of his time gathering additional wealth through a variety of corrupt deals with regional industry and trying to block the fortunes of political rivals like Governor Arihnda Pryce. His avarice and political machinations eventually came to an end when Governor Pryce was able to have him implicated in a bribery scandal.[10]

There were also other ways for Imperial senators to prove their loyalty to the Empire while also being complicit in some of its most cynical crimes. In the years before the Battle of Yavin, Gall Trayvis, the Imperial senator for Osk-Trill, resigned from his position and began to garner a reputation as a wanted dissident through a series of covert broadcasts criticizing the Empire. Seemingly in an attempt to build up an organized rebellion, he made contact with various groups across the galaxy who were resisting the Empire. However, following an encounter with the rebel cell on Lothal it was discovered that his persona was nothing more than a façade organized in conjunction with the Imperial Security Bureau (ISB).[11] Trayvis had retained his loyalty to the Empire and had been working to identify rebel groups across the galaxy so they could be rounded up by Imperial forces. Following the conclusion of the Galactic Civil War, Trayvis was put on trial by the New Republic where evidence was presented that he had

[9] Rebel Alliance Archives, Section: Hera Syndulla, File: Free Ryloth Movement
[10] Post-Imperial Lothal Archives, Section: Governor Arihnda Pryce, File: Personal records 59
[11] Rebel Alliance Archives, Section: Resistance Cells, File: Spectre—Lothal

been complicit in the imprisonment and deaths of hundreds of beings from across the galaxy.[12]

Because of Palpatine's scheming and the tendency of some senators to choose corruption over actual service, it would be easy to assume that the Senate had very little actual power or ability to intervene in galactic affairs. But that is not entirely true. Before my first mission against the First Order, I had a prolonged conversation with General Leia Organa. I told her that I was not really a soldier and merely an academic. I told her that I was afraid. She smiled and told me that when she was captured on the *Tantive IV* with the Death Star plans, she had also been afraid. But, despite the fact she was a prisoner, she had stood before Darth Vader and told him that she was on a diplomatic mission and that the Imperial Senate would not accept his attack on her vessel. She meant this story to reassure me about bravery in the face of fear, but I also took something else from it. If you are going to threaten Darth Vader with something, it must be something he might be afraid of. If the Senate truly had no power, why did Leia use this line of defense? One of the last recorded actions of the Imperial Senate was to receive the notification of a distress signal from the *Tantive IV* and the additional details that all aboard had been killed.[13] This is clearly not what happened so, again, if the Senate posed no threat to the Empire, why lie to it? The Senate had also only recently been informed that Jedha City had been destroyed in a mining accident rather than by the Death Star.[14] This was also a lie and, if the Senate was an irrelevance, seemingly an unnecessary one.

We may have to reconcile ourselves to accepting the seemingly contradictory nature of the Imperial Senate as something that Palpatine was largely able to manipulate but also an institution that could cause him significant problems. The Emperor did not maintain the political

[12] New Republic Archives, Section: Post-war Tribunals, File: Gall Trayvis
[13] Imperial Senate Proceedings, File HY8364.7
[14] Imperial Senate Proceedings, File UE8364.2

body out of a sense of desire but rather one of necessity. Until he could fully rule the galaxy as he chose, he had to walk the line between dictator and accountable political figure. While many of the controls and plans of the Senate could be circumvented, the senators could still cause problems if they overtly supported the burgeoning Rebel Alliance. Mon Mothma's speech denouncing Palpatine and his role in the massacre on Ghorman was enough to send her fleeing into exile, but the Imperials would not have chased her so hard if they were not concerned about what her words might provoke. Similarly, the Imperial Senate was able to enforce limitations and restrictions on the Imperial military at various points. This included things like the mandatory completion of Imperial Naval Regulation 132.CAT.ch(22) documents to justify any ship opening fire on an escape pod. The form was adopted by the Imperial Navy in response to Senate investigations into possible war crimes. The Senate was a multifaceted entity, and it is necessary to fully understand these different aspects of its operation in order to understand why the Emperor thought it necessary to first sustain it and then remove it.

Dissolution

As previously established, during the early years of the Empire, the Imperial Senate was viewed by the likes of Palpatine and Mas Amedda as a necessary inconvenience which they aimed to manipulate and circumvent where possible. Palpatine maintained a veto over laws passed in the Senate but, in the interests of maintaining the careful balance with the legislature, would allow some policies into law even if they provided an obstacle to his current plans. The senators who opposed Palpatine seemed to believe that, given enough time, they could prevent too much damage being inflicted upon the galaxy. As noble as this viewpoint was, at least some of them did not recognize the precarity of their situation. Palpatine viewed the Senate as a temporary nuisance, not a permanent or long-term one. The moment he no longer needed it, the body would cease to exist.

The roots of the Senate's eventual obsolescence lay in the restructuring of the galaxy through appointed regional governors and Moffs who would regulate and administrate different sectors and star systems. The Senate initially opposed these measures when they were first floated in the Republic toward the end of the Clone Wars, but Palpatine and Grand Moff Tarkin were able to achieve the same result over an extended period, as they gradually diverted much of the day-to-day administration of the Imperial state out of the hands of elected politicians and into those of loyal officers. With this administration now solidified under Imperial control, the Senate lost much of its actual power and relevance, and with the burgeoning Rebel Alliance gaining support among some senators, the political benefits of maintaining the body also began to erode. While this transfer of political power was underway, Palpatine and Tarkin had been secretly orchestrating the final stage of the plan to solidify Imperial control across the galaxy. At the moment of its completion, Palpatine made his move.

It can surely be no coincidence that within days of the Death Star being declared fully operational following its test firing at Jedha—and having been witnessed in action by the rebel fleet at Scarif—that Palpatine dissolved the Senate. The entirety of the Death Star project had—as will be discussed in greater detail in a forthcoming chapter—been kept secret and hidden from the eyes of the Senate. Funding and requisitions of equipment to enable the weapon's construction were diverted through various different systems and sectors, and were spread across so many different Imperial accounts as to make it extremely difficult for even the most dedicated senator to discern what was happening. With the weapon completed there was no need for any further secrecy. Palpatine's solution to the political body was ready. Where the Senate had served to represent the voices of the population—even in a hobbled state—the Death Star existed to silence them either through fear or through destruction.

Following the announcement of the dissolution of the Imperial Senate, it has long been supposed that many of its representatives were subject to immediate arrest warrants and incarceration. There is certainly evidence of some cases of this taking place. Senator Nadea Tural had served as a representative for Thrad and had, over time, come to be seen as a vociferous rebel sympathizer. She and several other rebel supporters were arrested and imprisoned in the Arrth-Eno Prison Complex where they were subsequently executed. But the fate of Tural and her fellows was surprisingly rare. Some of the most ardent supporters of the Rebel Alliance were not even on Coruscant when the dissolution came, having already traveled to the Alliance headquarters on Yavin 4 to receive news of the Death Star's existence. The ordinary senators who had not sided with the Rebel Alliance were simply removed from office and then ignored. In the lead up to the dissolution of the Senate full sessions had actually become incredibly rare. This was partly because of the aforementioned transfer of real power from the politicians to Imperial governors. But many outland senators often dispatched proxies or did not bother with the journey to Coruscant at all. Empty senatorial pods were an increasingly common sight. By the time of the dissolution, some senators had not been to Coruscant in months and simply stayed home. The plain fact was that Palpatine and his administrators had barely cared about any of them individually when they had power, and he cared even less when they had none. The sudden destruction of Alderaan was enough to get the message across to these newly unemployed senators about what could happen to their worlds if they aimed to cause trouble. Many returned to their home systems, some eventually becoming contacts and agents for the rebels as the Galactic Civil War unfolded, while others sat back to watch with curiosity which side would triumph. Some even re-emerged in the New Republic Senate to lead their worlds again, the greatest irony being reserved for those who witnessed the Senate fall once more, this time in the flames of Hosnian Prime.

It remains unclear what system of government or form of representation we will now adopt across the galaxy to replace the destroyed New Republic and the defeated First Order. But there are clear lessons for us to learn from the Senates of both the previous Republic and the Empire it became. Devoted politicians and civil servants can do great work to benefit their own worlds and the wider galaxy. But the cynical and the corrupt can slip between the cracks of government and, if given the opportunity to embed themselves, become difficult to remove and dangerous to empower. How we avoid this cycle repeating, is perhaps the most difficult and important question of all.

Chapter 4

The New Order

While the Imperial Senate was, as has been discussed, nominally charged with orchestrating the political aspects of the Empire, the actual administration of the newly formed state was managed from elsewhere. As with the Senate, certain aspects of bureaucracy and legal construction were adopted from the now-disbanded Republic. This was partly because it was far easier and more convenient to adapt existing laws and infrastructure than create brand new ones immediately, but also to help avoid the transition being too dramatic for the galaxy's population, regardless of what the end goal of that transition might be.

The structure of the Empire, once the new regime was established, has always appeared to be a complicated collection of departments, organizations, and bureaus often working at a cross purpose.[1] Previous studies have wondered how the Empire ever actually managed to achieve or organize anything, given the apparent tangle of authorities. However, I feel this position to be a misunderstanding of the very particular intentions and designs behind the Imperial structure. There is something deeply ingenious about the way Imperial officials organized

---

[1] Indeed, most administrative recruits who entered the bureaucracy of the Empire were provided with a copy of Chief Administrator Svete Naemon's gargantuan work *A Thorough Guide to the Bureaucratic Operation and Diligent Administration of the Galactic Empire* which, from my own research, was not an easy read.

those who would actually carry out orders and maintain the administration of Palpatine's Empire.

The myriad of advisors and officials who operated in the level below Palpatine undertook a form of administrative triage to avoid bothering the Emperor with issues and decisions that were beneath his notice or would distract him from other matters. But, as we shall see in this chapter and in others, none of them had even remotely the power or authority to replace Palpatine at the top of the hierarchy. It was a system expressly designed for two purposes: to undertake the monumental task of administering the Empire, and to solidify the rigidity of Imperial structure. They called it The New Order.

Competition by Design

When understanding the ways in which the various aspects of the Empire came together to function, it is important for us to further accept something established in an earlier chapter—the Emperor was the only one who could have the full authority of ruling the Empire, while also having no interest in its day-to-day operation. Without understanding and accepting this aspect of the Empire it is not possible to fully recognize the nature of the Imperial hierarchy and state apparatus. Huge amounts of energy and time were spent in weeding out almost all aspects of Imperial bureaucracy, administration, and operation before they ever reached Palpatine's attention, therefore ensuring he would only ever have to interact with the specific projects and undertakings that interested him.

The result of this was a system of hierarchy that placed the various arms and aspects of Imperial governance into well-defined silos of influence and power. The purpose of these silos was to ensure that the various branches of the Imperial machine would require each other to perform their own duties while, simultaneously, not having clear routes of interaction between them that would enable the circumventing of the overall system. For example, the Imperial military relied upon funding to maintain operations and pay the wages of soldiers. However, this funding was administrated by the Imperial bureaucracy and diverted out via COMPNOR, which we shall come to in more detail shortly. Planetary governors may have wished to have additional controls over military forces deployed in their regions, but the chain of command went up through the Grand Moffs and dedicated Imperial advisors before it reached various military commands. Throughout this system the opportunity to take shortcuts through proceedings is denied because the various institutions and bodies have no official means of contacting each other directly, and unofficial attempts to do so would quickly draw the attention of the relevant authorities. While at times of crisis or during moments of serious military concern, this rigid framework prevented Imperial forces from reacting quickly to changes of circumstance, in every other way it worked exactly as intended. No parts of the Imperial state could circumvent the chain of command or, crucially, plot against the Emperor without it becoming immediately apparent. In this way any attempts at an organized coup were almost inevitably doomed to fail because of the warning signs that would be picked up by the systems and departments that had been bypassed.

Furthermore, the desire to even attempt a coup was—barring a few examples, such as the those orchestrated by Crimson Dawn, which will be discussed in a forthcoming chapter—highly unlikely because the system bred competition between various services and organizations rather than any desire for cooperation. Organizations tended to treat each other with varying degrees of suspicion or outright hostility, even within branches of the Imperial military or between Grand Moffs. While Palpatine nominally avoided getting involved in the minutiae of the Imperial state, when it came to funding for special projects, senior positions of leadership, or access to new technology, his decisions and input would have a great impact on the final outcome.

As a result, different branches and senior figures would compete and jockey with each other for the Emperor's favor. Grand Moff

Tarkin, as part of his competition with—and eventual victory over—Director Orson Krennic, ensured that distance was maintained between Krennic and the Emperor, even going so far as to ensure that Palpatine and Darth Vader did not attend the first test firing of the Death Star at Jedha.[2] While competing for control of the Death Star with Tarkin, Krennic was also trying to claim funding for the project against Grand Admiral Thrawn's TIE defender program.[3] Given that the Empire effectively controlled all industry and resources in the galaxy at this point, and even accepting the overwhelming expense of the Death Star, there should conceivably have been enough credits to go round. But it served Palpatine's purposes to have figures and projects such as these engage in direct competition with each other rather than forming any sort of cooperation. This meant that those within the Imperial system, particularly those within the upper echelons, were always working toward gaining Palpatine's favor rather than his throne. With the hierarchy working to solidify Palpatine's power rather than undermine it, the administration of the galaxy could be undertaken.

Orchestrating the State

Aside from the military—which will be discussed in another chapter—the two most important aspects of running the Imperial state were its security and its administrative bureaucracy. The organizations that took on these responsibilities were, to varying degrees, converted from previous entities under the Republic. However, as we might suspect, the new incarnations proved to have very different motivations and powers through which to achieve their assigned objectives.

[2] Imperial Archives, Section: Grand Moff Wilhuff Tarkin, File: Communications with Coruscant, Dispatch KH8217
[3] Imperial Archives, Section: Project Stardust, File: Funding. See also: Imperial Archives. Section: TIE Defender Program, File: Sev Tok Meeting

During the Clone Wars it was felt within some political circles that a movement to help mobilize the population of the Republic against the threat of the Separatists would help the military succeed in the actual conflict. As a result, the Commission for the Protection of the Republic (COMPOR) was founded with the aim of lobbying support for the government through various propaganda methods and other public relations campaigns. How successful COMPOR actually was in achieving its aims is difficult to ascertain, given that the Clone Wars were a largely rigged contest to begin with, though there are signs of its impact within the surviving records of the Population Observation program.[4] Regardless, they did invest significant amounts of credits and effort in publicly supporting Palpatine as supreme chancellor, which probably helped him in his overall aims. That alone should be reason to treat COMPOR's activities with a degree of suspicion. With the end of the conflict and the fall of the Republic, COMPOR did not disappear. Instead, it was absorbed by the new Imperial state and had its powers and mission heavily updated to reflect the change. From the ashes of COMPOR rose COMPNOR. While COMPOR had acted, ostensibly at least, to mobilize and motivate the population, COMPNOR would exist to control them.

Although it took time for the initial conversion from Republic to Empire and COMPOR to COMPNOR to take root, the end goal was for the full bureaucracy of the Imperial state to be placed under its control. Because of this, and through its control over the process of constructing and maintaining Imperial loyalty, COMPNOR grew to be a hugely powerful aspect of the state with the ability to reach into most forms of civilian life while also, to varying degrees, influencing military decisions and operations. As a result of its growth and activities the sheer number of files and datacards produced by COMPNOR during a standard year could feasibly have filled the Death Star. The fact

[4] Imperial Archives, Section: Galactic Republic, File: Population Observation

55

that even some of these records exist and are available to us is through the dedicated work of Amn Fos-er and the New Republic's Post-Imperial Administration and Ephemeral Preservation Network.

Observing the structure and layout of COMPNOR is a bewildering proposition in the aftermath of the Empire's fall and at the time it must have seemed thoroughly opaque. But there are ways to break down its operation to help us understand its role. All aspects of COMPNOR reported to a primary select committee. The membership of this body was unclear at the time and is no easier to discern now. Many records relating to COMPNOR were purged from Imperial archives as the Empire collapsed. Given that COMPNOR undertook such ongoing censorship as one of their many regular duties, it should come as no surprise that they were very good at covering their own tracks and disappearing back into the population at the end of the Galactic Civil War. Nonetheless there are some clues remaining that can help us gain an insight into the committee's membership and jurisdiction.

Most high-level communications out of COMPNOR have been removed from Imperial archives. However, within other holdings that did not exist on Coruscant there are records of figures like Grand Moff Tarkin communicating *to* COMPNOR.[5] A good number of these communications, though bland in content, were addressed to Crueya Vandron, Armand Isard, and Kinman Doriana. Vandron was one of the primary driving figures of the original COMPOR who then took an active leadership role in its successor, so it should come as no surprise to us that he was on the Select Committee, similarly Armand Isard served a spell as Director of COMPNOR so would inevitably be on the committee. However, Kinman Doriana is a much more interesting, and little known, figure. During the Republic he had served as an aide to Supreme Chancellor Palpatine but supposedly had little active influence or power

---

[5] Imperial Archives, Section: Grand Moff Wilhuff Tarkin, File: Communications with COMPNOR

within that position. That he now appears to have had a leadership position within COMPNOR suggests not only that his position with Palpatine needs to be reconsidered, but that the select committee had a direct line to Palpatine himself, thereby circumventing other more established Imperial advisors like Mas Amedda and Sly Moore.[6] Perhaps in time the other members of the select committee will become apparent—and it seems reasonable to suspect that Tarkin may also have had a role within it—but the identification of these figures helps us understand that decisions taken by the committee were not entirely done in isolation from Palpatine's wishes.

Beneath this committee sat the various departments, bureaus, and coalitions of COMPNOR. These were the means through which COMPNOR actively orchestrated the galaxy and influenced daily life within it. The Sub-Adult Group (usually contracted into SAGroup) was empowered with influencing the education, motivation, recreation, and recruitment of children across the Empire. Because the indoctrination of those too young to remember the Republic was considered crucial to the Empire's long-term survival, SAGroup was truly vast in size and had offshoots in almost every star system within Imperial space via the Sector SAGroup sub-divisions under its control. The SAGroup set baseline standards and curriculums for education across the galaxy to ensure that children, often specifically human children, would absorb approved lessons, histories, and understandings about the galaxy. Outside of school they would interact with approved sporting activities while also being covertly prepared for service to the Empire through prescribed loyalty programs. The emergence of the—now infamous— Imperial kinder-blocks on some worlds, which served as both housing and educational compounds where the Empire could raise a new generation of loyalists, is a further sign of the insidious nature of the overarching project. Given the huge reach and impact of the SAGroup

[6] Both of whom will be discussed in greater detail in Chapter Ten.

on the youngest generations of the Empire, I cannot help but wonder if the New Republic did enough to undo the damage caused to them through Imperial indoctrination. Certainly, when facing the forces of the First Order, my most abiding impression was of the shocking youth of its personnel, and the tragedy of young lives cut short.

Set alongside the SAGroup was the Coalition for Progress, which in many ways fulfilled similar roles and responsibilities relating to the adult population of the galaxy. Initially one of the smallest groups within COMPNOR, Progress—as the name was often shortened to—was sometimes greeted with a degree of trepidation by Imperial citizens and planetary governors.[7] Much of this stemmed from the actions of the group within Progress designated to deal with art and culture. Progress created a very narrow definition regarding acceptable art, music, or performances that could be held or showcased in public.

The result was a funding collapse in artistic pursuits and the black-listing of some extremely high-profile artists, performers, and musicians who fell afoul of the new regulations. This included some of the leading gonk-rock groups of Bormea sector, who regularly had their venues closed or raided, and the overtly anti-Imperial band Red Shift Limit.[8] Furthermore a musician from Naboo named Palo Jemabie was imprisoned at a labor camp by the Empire for a musical performance described—without detail—by his criminal record as "deviant."[9] This situation was particularly complicated as various planetary governors had previously been patrons and supporters of those who were now banned and could no longer enjoy their work. The internecine power

[7] Archives for numerous Imperial systems contain complaints from citizens regarding interactions with the Coalition of Progress and communication records between planetary governors and the regional Moffs of several sectors show a level of exasperation with their activities.
[8] Although this merely helped increase the underground appeal of these groups.
[9] Imperial Archives, Section: Criminal Records—Naboo, File: Trial Proceedings TR988713B

struggle between localized authorities and Progress over this matter was an ongoing theme through much of the Empire's lifespan. Despite this, there were some notable winners from the approval process for art. Grand Admiral Balanhai Savit's family were noted musicians and he was a skilled composer in his own right, having come to Palpatine's attention with his grand opera *To the Stars*.[10] He would later also compose a grand Imperial fanfare that became widely used in the navy, enduring even after Savit was seemingly arrested for treason. Ordinarily such a fate would lead to his music being banned but it seems that given his political connections and the Empire wanting to avoid publicizing such a crime from a ranking officer, Savit's removal was ascribed to poor health.[11]

Aside from Art, the Coalition for Progress also had departments named Science, Justice, Commerce, and Education, each with jurisdiction across the galaxy. It has been assumed that each of these aspects was largely self-explanatory, but this is only true up to a point. Science, Justice, and Education were all of course interested in their designated sectors, but they had wider remits than might be supposed. Science, for instance, was also tasked with managing the tensions between academics and other institutions such as the Imperial Military Department of Advanced Weapons Research, who believed that all ongoing research should be catered toward weapons development. Similarly, Education was not designed to carry out active teaching but instead to try and bring various schools, colleges, and universities across the galaxy into line with recommended Imperial curriculums and research topics. Even this proved a balancing act at times, given the tendency of academics—myself included—to disappear down tangents while undertaking work when the outcomes are unclear at the start. Both Justice and Commerce

---

[10] Details drawn from the *Coruscant Review of Music #7198*
[11] Imperial Archives, Section: Imperial Navy, Subsection: Grand Admiral Balanhai Savit, File: Arrest Warrant and Public Briefing Documents

were similarly charged with establishing acceptable galactic norms for the economy and legal systems that ensured Imperial superiority in ways that will be discussed in forthcoming chapters.

The Coalition for Improvements was tasked with bringing existing planetary infrastructure and operations into line with prescribed Imperial requirements. This seems benign on the surface, but the reality was more nefarious. The Department of Modification and Redesign ensured the advancement of officials across the galaxy based upon their loyalty to Imperial ideals and the degree to which they were willing to promote it at the expense of personal ties. Furthermore, at various points in the Empire's reign, it would look to either relocate or forcibly deport various populations or species from worlds that required repurposing for Imperial use, and such orders often originated with the Coalition for Improvements.

To help enforce these "improvements" and to ensure general conformity with COMPNOR edicts across the Empire, CompForce was effectively the military wing of the organization. The personnel who operated within CompForce were prized for their devotion to Palpatine above all else and many of the loyalty officers who served throughout the Imperial military were initially recruited and trained within CompForce. They largely operated outside of the existing military chains of command, which provided an ongoing source of tension within the Empire's armed forces toward these agents who were generally treated as unwelcome spies within regular units. For their part, CompForce and other COMPNOR agents viewed their role as absolutely crucial to the safety and stability of the Empire, as defined by perhaps the most infamous aspect of the organization—the ISB.

Security and Intelligence

The ISB is one of the most well-known, and feared, aspects of the Empire's state apparatus. The arrival of white-jacketed operatives was often enough to cause concerned ripples within Imperial institutions and trigger contingency plans within rebel operations—it was common knowledge that an arrest by the ISB was likely to end in torture and execution.[12] The ISB sat within COMPNOR and often drew upon the military forces available to it within CompForce. However, it was also, in some ways, a heavily misunderstood organization, even by some of its own agents. The ISB Mission Statement outlined that the organization's chief purpose was "to further security objectives by collecting intelligence, providing useful analysis, and conducting effective covert action".[13] Despite this, Major Lio Partagaz, who held significant power on the ISB Board, was known to disagree with this description entirely and posited that the ISB should be understood as a healthcare organization that looked for symptoms of disease within the Imperial system.[14] The ISB conducted widescale intelligence gathering throughout the Imperial state in order to spot the emerging symptoms of rebellion or corruption. In keeping with the convoluted nature of COMPNOR's leadership structure it is not entirely clear who was actually in charge of the ISB, with even former ISB agent Alexsandr Kallus unsure as to who operated at the top of the hierarchy.[15] However, Colonel Wulff Yularen was the most obvious leadership figure and seemingly had a direct line to Emperor Palpatine himself.[16]

In the years leading up to the Battle of Yavin, the ISB was one of the strongest and most politically secure agencies operating within the Empire. Because of this, at moments of crisis or high rebel activity, the

---

[12] Rebel Alliance Archives, Section: Mission Parameters, File: Response to ISB Operations
[13] Imperial Archives, Section: Imperial Security Bureau, File: Mission Statement and Regulations
[14] Imperial Archives, Section: Imperial Security Bureau. File: Board Briefing 19826
[15] Rebel Alliance Archives, Section: Defections & Debriefings, File: Alexsandr Kallus
[16] Imperial Archives, Section: Imperial Security Bureau, File: Aldhani Response Briefing

ISB was often tasked with leading the response and drawing upon Imperial resources to do so. ISB agents were able to commandeer naval assets, including Star Destroyers, if given the right authorization, and were often on the front lines of the earliest stages of what became the Galactic Civil War. However, the lead up to the destruction of the Death Star at Yavin appears to have been the zenith of the ISB's political power within the Empire. Colonel Wulff Yularen himself was on board the battle station when it was destroyed and, as a result, the ISB lost its most prominent leader. Beyond this the regularity with which the white jackets appeared within Imperial military operations and responses against the Rebel Alliance began to fall dramatically. Rebel soldiers themselves noted the sharp decline of ISB agents in the field.[17] It is not clear exactly what happened to the ISB for it to be sublimated to other organizations either within COMPNOR or the wider Imperial system. Some aspects still endured, principally the much-hated Imperial loyalty officers who continued to operate within the military until the war's conclusion. But it may be that following the destruction of the Death Star, the ISB was assigned much of the blame for not rooting out the rebel cells and agents responsible for the attack on Scarif that granted the Rebel Alliance the Death Star plans. Furthermore, the change in Imperial strategy after the Battle of Yavin placed a great deal of power and responsibility within the hands of the military, who were likely not minded to welcome the interference of a "political" body like the ISB, especially after their recent failures. Many of the records relating to the ISB beyond this point within surviving Imperial archives are either missing or too heavily encrypted to access, but ongoing efforts may produce more useful conclusions in the future.

Set aside from the activities of the ISB, was the work of Imperial military intelligence—formally referred to as the Ubiqtorate. In

---

[17] Rebel Alliance Archives, Section: Military Debriefings, File: ISB Activities

contrast to the ISB—which took a broad approach to the entirety of the Imperial state—military intelligence instead focused purely on matters relating to the ongoing war effort. While the ISB seemingly found themselves saddled with the blame for the Death Star's destruction, military intelligence instead coordinated the efforts to locate rebel bases of operations and military strength. Records show that they worked closely with the Imperial Army and Navy in a far more complementary and cooperative way than the ISB or COMPNOR tended to do. Many of the Imperial military's strategies and doctrines—which will be discussed in future chapters—had their roots in analysis and intelligence gathering work undertaken by Ubiqtorate agents. One of the greatest Imperial successes of the Galactic Civil War came via the destruction of a significant rebel convoy in the Derra system and this was a direct outcome of Ubiqtorate operations.[18] Similarly, the decision to seed the Outer Rim with Imperial probe droids, which eventually led to the discovery and destruction of the rebel base on Hoth, was pioneered by military intelligence and its success saw the architect, Major Roj Ohjon, promoted to colonel and reassigned to a new role on Coruscant.[19]

The various intricacies of the Imperial state can seem convoluted and cumbersome for those of us looking back at it, decades later. But one of the key things we should take from examining it is the fact that it did appear to work. Those Imperial civil servants who were taken into the New Republic Amnesty Program after the Galactic Civil War would often speak of the machinery of maintaining the Imperial state with a mixture of wonder and bewilderment. One of the reasons why the New Republic would eventually move some operations back to Coruscant after the war was because the world was already designed to handle and

[18] This operation will be discussed in greater detail in Chapter Eighteen.
[19] Imperial Archives, Section: Imperial Ubiqtorate, File: Promotion and transfer order #1662290

administer the galaxy's infrastructure. There can, however, be a tendency to view all the various committees and COMPNOR divisions as almost theoretical entities. They existed on datacards, but what impact did they actually have? To understand how the theory of Imperial state operation interacted with the reality of everyday life, we must now shift our attention to Imperial society itself.

Chapter 5

Imperial Society

Given the size and spread of the Galactic Empire, with its countless worlds, systems, and species, it would be wrong to suggest there was any singular experience of life under Imperial control. However, that is not to say that the Empire did not attempt to construct, or enforce, various societal norms or that—particularly for humans in the Core Worlds—there were not notable similarities in how everyday life was experienced within the Empire. Given the controls instituted by various Imperial governors, drawing upon pre-approved COMPNOR guidance and norms, it is possible to see how the Empire wished their society to be constructed and common themes regarding the way it was to be orchestrated.

The application of Imperial hierarchies onto civilian life exacerbated already existing inequalities within the galaxy's population. Under the Empire the class system within the Core Worlds was strengthened so that the wealthiest individuals in the galaxy became further enriched through their proximity to, and cooperation with, Imperial authorities. These same Core Worlds that had long possessed power, privilege, and influence beyond that of the Mid or Outer Rim systems, found their positions strengthened even as they were squeezed by Palpatine's Empire. For those living on the edges of the Empire, or on worlds that were annexed and conquered, their interaction with Imperial forces would be very different.

However, the hierarchies and systems of control that worked within the Empire were complicated by the fact that civilians across the galaxy bought into them and supported Imperial operations. While the Empire intended to be an oppressive regime, it would not have lasted as long as it did if there was not at least some popular support for it from those who were being ruled. The reasons for this support were multifaceted, but it would be wrong, and dangerous, to overlook the fact that there were not inconsiderable numbers of beings within the Empire who were at the very least content with the current government and, among those, a significant number who were vociferous in their support of Palpatine. Some of this can be ascribed to the intensive propaganda campaigns carried out by either COMPNOR or organized by figures such as Pitina Mar-Mas Voor or Pollux Hax. But there is only so much that propaganda can achieve in isolation. Understanding the ways in which the Empire held either legitimacy or support on worlds—particularly in the Core—is an important aspect of understanding not just how the eventual Galactic Civil War would take place, but why it took so many years to ignite.

Wealth and Power

While the inner workings of the Imperial economy will be discussed in greater detail in the next chapter, it is important to understand the role that wealth played in insulating some of the richest people in the galaxy from interference by the Empire. The richest members of the upper echelons of Imperial society generally, but not exclusively, split between those who were the inheritors of longstanding wealth and aristocratic positions, and various industrialists who had further enhanced their power and prestige through Imperial contracts.

Even before the rise of the Empire, the House of Tagge was one of the galaxy's longest running—and most powerful—noble families, controlling a significant swathe of space in its own right. Despite some members of the House having supported the Separatists during the Clone Wars the Empire did not attempt to dismantle it—instead they incorporated the entire faction into the Imperial elite and Palpatine's extended court. Cassio Tagge served within the ranks of the Imperial military, rising to the rank of grand general, where he briefly served as supreme commander of all Imperial military forces after the Battle of Yavin.[1] The Tagge family remained loyal and, importantly, financially generous supporters of Palpatine's rule throughout his reign. Offshoots of the family had connections with, or ownership of, industrial centers and corporations that were given preferential access to Imperial military contracts. The Tagges, though a very public and famous example, were not alone in their secure and luxurious position at the top of Imperial society. The likes of the Kuati nobility and the Sienar family also heavily prospered under the Empire through both their existing positions and by ensuring that their work benefited the expanding Imperial military, who were a constant source of ongoing funding.

It might be thought that the various aristocratic or industrial superpowers that existed at the death of the Republic may have been ripe targets for Imperial nationalization or asset seizing. Certainly, as will be discussed in the next chapter, some industrial companies had an uneasy relationship with central Imperial authorities and had their operations seized as a result. But by and large the industrial elite maintained their positions within the Empire and grew wealthier because of Imperial policies. It is possible that the Empire—certainly in its earliest years—did not have the stability to try and engage in political or economic conflict with the galaxy's wealthiest beings, given that their private funds could easily be used to finance the Empire's enemies. As a result, the Empire appears to have found creative legislative approaches to keeping the rich onside. Much of the Imperial tax system

[1] Imperial Archives, Section: Imperial Military, File: Grand General Cassio Tagge—Biography

was designed to funnel money and resources from the Outer Rim back toward the Core Worlds. Most of this would then land in Imperial coffers to finance Palpatine's planned military endeavors and construction projects like the Death Star. However, the wealthy had long mastered the art of finding loopholes within Republic tax legislation—it was no great stretch for them to do the same with Imperial ones. In many ways it was easier. The Republic at least attempted to maintain the appearance of being opposed to outright corruption. Everyone within the Empire knew that the right bribe at the right time could open doors or close unwelcome investigations. It would appear that actually circumventing the tax system entirely and making what were sometimes termed "loyalty donations" either to Palpatine himself or to noted Imperial officers and officials was the best way for the rich to maintain their wealth.[2] A form of patronage therefore existed within the Imperial hierarchy where wealthy families or companies would effectively sponsor the careers of promising young officers, or pay for the construction of new naval vessels, in exchange for highly preferential treatment from the state.

It might be thought that, given the close ties between the wealthy elite and Palpatine's Empire, that some form of investigations and prosecutions would have taken place following the Galactic Civil War. But it seems that the same wealth that insulated the likes of the Tagges from the Empire worked just as well against the New Republic. Notable figures who had prospered under Palpatine, such as Wayulia Tagge-Simoni, were still active in galactic affairs and politics right up to the recent First Order-Resistance conflict. Although some of Palpatine's wealthiest backers—such as the Strok family, who made numerous political donations during the Republic and the earliest years of the Empire while also fulfilling contracts for hyperdrives—disappeared after the Galactic

---

[2] Records for this sort of activity can be found in the following, imaginatively titled, location: Imperial Archives, Section: Revenue and Taxation, File: Financial Backers of Strong Character.

Civil War, many of the richest denizens of Coruscant do not appear to have been particularly affected by the fall of the Empire. Many treated the new government as just a "change in management," and various financial "rich lists" show very little difference in status following the establishment of the New Republic.[3] What is concerning is that both General Finn and Commander Rose Tico reported, following a mission to Canto Bight, that many of the wealthiest individuals in the galaxy were recently supplying both the First Order and the Resistance through overtly cynical war profiteering.[4] Given that there are so many who have lost everything during the recent conflicts, the fact that there are those who have been enhanced by them should not be overlooked by whatever government is now constructed.

Constructing Complicity

Outside of the protective bubble created by extreme wealth, most of those living under Imperial rule had very different levels of interaction with the state. As will be examined in forthcoming chapters, the further away from the Core Worlds you traveled the more overtly oppressive the Imperial regime became and the line between being governed and being conquered blurred. Very little time or resources were spent in the Outer Rim attempting to create Imperial loyalty through popular support or consent when the Imperial armed forces could achieve compliance through subjugation. Some of the established Imperial protocols designed to maintain, at the very least, a pliable population would make it to the Outer Rim, but the primary approach taken by the Empire to these worlds on the edges of the galaxy was to restrict opportunity to the extent that participation in the Imperial system was the only way to survive. In this way, the same approach taken by the Empire with

[3] See back issues of the "Profile" section in *Coruscanti Society*.
[4] Resistance Archives, Section: Intelligence, File: Canto Bight Debriefing

the Imperial Senate, was applied to significant parts of the population; they too would be forced or tricked into complying with the new order.

Those who lived on the Outer Rim had always been excluded from the bright lights and opportunities that existed in the Core Worlds. Frontier life in the Republic had always been restrictive and it only became more so under the Empire. Opportunities and funding for education, travel, and many alternative careers were often controlled by planetary governors on a case-by-case basis to force their population down particular avenues that benefited the Empire. In the Pressylla system, for example, Governor Hast Ulim closed many industries to ensure that the now unemployed civilian population would enter the strategically important mines as the only employment option.[5] Such arrangements appear to have been extremely common across the Outer Rim Territories. Aside from this form of highly selective industrial employment, the other ongoing opportunity in these systems was through joining the Imperial military and academies. In many ways the two options worked perfectly hand in hand; civilians could either undertake—often dangerous—manual labor for the Empire or they could enter its armed forces. Either choice was beneficial to the state. You would struggle to find a more significant hero of the Rebel Alliance than Luke Skywalker but even he, while growing up on Tatooine, felt so trapped by the life there that he was eager to join the Imperial Academy to escape it.[6] Skywalker would end up joining the Rebellion before entering Imperial service, but that option was likely not open to many of the Imperial recruits drawn from the galaxy's edges.

In contrast to the process of subjugation and selective restrictions imposed on the Outer Rim, in the Core Worlds the Empire enacted a policy that was, informally, referred to as "escalating normality."[7]

[5] Pressylla Archives, Section: Industry, File: Mining Bill
[6] Rebel Alliance Archives, Section: Luke Skywalker, File: Tatooine years
[7] Imperial Archives, Section: Core Worlds, File: Public Order Policies

This approach was designed during the Empire's early years to allow for the state to increase its involvement in civilian life slowly over time, in order for the changes to be scarcely noticeable to ordinary people who embraced the status quo. Surviving ISB documents suggest that it was modeled on biological lessons where the temperature is slowly raised in the tanks of Klatooinian paddy frogs who do not notice they are being boiled to death.[8] Such an approach from the Empire required patience but also gave the new Imperial state time to solidify its control and powers without having to worry about sudden spontaneous uprisings within the Core Worlds from populations who found themselves squeezed too quickly. As time went on the level of Imperial control in the Core would increase, but for years conspicuous signs of military occupation such as existed on the Outer Rim would have been unthinkable in the galaxy's heart. While growing up on Alderaan, a key Core World within the Empire, Princess Leia Organa reflected on the fact that there was no Imperial military presence on the planet at all.[9] By removing the Imperial military from the equation on Core Worlds like Alderaan, especially during times when such a presence could not easily be spared, the Empire avoided the overt appearance of ruling these worlds, but this meant it also had to find more inventive approaches to inspiring either loyalty or obedience.

Much of the work undertaken on the Core Worlds to construct a loyal base of civilians was organized by COMPNOR with particular emphasis on both the SAGroup and the Coalition for Progress, as discussed in the previous chapter. Together these bureaus worked to create general and approved forms of Imperial education and culture that could then be applied across the Core by various Moffs or planetary governors who also had a relatively free hand in adapting the guidance

[8] Imperial Archives, Section: ISB, File: Systems of control
[9] Senator Leia Organa, personal writings: *Lessons from serving in Palpatine's Senate*

for their own systems and sectors. Educational emphasis was placed on the justified existence of the Empire and the general heroic nature of Palpatine himself in saving the galaxy from both the horrors of the Clone Wars and the failures of the Republic.[10] Propaganda imagery was also developed along the same lines, particularly while the Empire was still solidifying its power.

More interesting than the obvious and overt forms of propaganda are the ways in which the Empire sought to recruit high-profile figures to help sell the message. The SAGRecreation group in particular was highly adept at identifying potential role models within various spheres of sport and culture who might appeal to younger citizens. Grav-ball already had an existing widespread appeal in the galaxy, but the Empire took the extra step of incorporating it into various military academies and recruiting some of its most famous stars as examples of what both physical prowess and loyalty to the Empire could mean. Broadcasts of grav-ball tournaments on the holonet were often accompanied by recruitment messages that featured popular players, and Grand Moff Tarkin was sometimes seen in the crowd for games that took place on Coruscant, though it remains unclear whether he actually had any interest in the sport.[11] By positioning these young, physically fit, and highly charismatic athletes as a prominent part of Imperial recruitment and culture, COMPNOR was able to create an image of the ideal Imperial citizen without ever having to overtly define it themselves. However, the process of elevating these figures to prominence was not without some risks. Edi Myrtaan, a keeper for the Coruscant Emeralds, had a significant fan following and appeared in numerous Imperial recruitment materials before one day completely disappearing. It was only when he resurfaced as part of a rebel cell on Sullust that it became clear he had defected right

---

[10] Imperial Archives, Section: COMPNOR, File: SAGEducation Guidance
[11] See the records for *Grav-ball's Greatest Games: Coruscant League.*

under the nose of the Empire, and rebel propaganda quickly adapted to make use of him.[12]

The holonet, and the ability for the Rebel Alliance to slice into it and broadcast their own propaganda, was an ongoing problem for the Empire. The system that had been bequeathed to the Empire by the Republic was extremely expensive to run and allowed, in theory, broadcasts to be made of practically any content, thereby circumventing the censorship laws the Empire was busy constructing. The initial solution was for Imperial officials, generally COMPNOR agents, to restrict broadcasting access to specific system and sector hubs. This therefore ensured that only pre-approved messages could be transmitted around the galaxy and that all news broadcasts would be screened by the Empire. Any attempts to create alternative news systems or publications was explicitly illegal. The ex-Imperial TIE fighter pilot Thane Kyrell witnessed stormtroopers imprisoning civilians indefinitely on Zeitooine for the crime of creating independent publications in the aftermath of the Battle of Yavin.[13] While Imperial attempts to restrict the holonet were largely successful, there were a number of instances of rebel cells accessing the system on a planetary level, as was the case on Lothal.[14] Such attempts to hijack the holonet were often met with fierce crackdowns by Imperial forces, but the Rebel Alliance would consider it a risk worth taking if it helped to undercut the Empire's ongoing propaganda reporting.

As with their approach to sport stars, the Empire homed in on various journalists who would act as the face and voice of Palpatine's regime. Regular broadcasts of the HoloNet News (HNN) produced a carefully constructed vision of the Empire as both a peaceful and stable state while, seemingly contradictorily, perpetually under threat from separatists, extremists, and rebel "terrorists." A degree of mental

[12] Rebel Alliance Archives, Section: Personnel, File: Edi Myrtaan
[13] Rebel Alliance Archives, Section: Defections & Debriefings, File: Thane Kyrell
[14] Rebel Alliance Archives, Section: Resistance Cells, File: Spectre—Lothal

gymnastics was required to have these two aspects exist in cooperation with each other but, crucially, the gravest threats were always reported as existing out on the fringes of the Empire. It was there that the most disruptive elements were said to be gathering their power and biding their time to plunge the galaxy back into the same sort of conflict that Palpatine had saved it from. Imperial journalists therefore pushed this message in broadcasts from war-torn locations such as Kashyyyk and Mimban to explain why Imperial military action was so necessary to maintain the safety of civilians back home. Some of these reporters, like Ilb Oyec, were little more than polemicists for the Empire who were more than happy to provide positive coverage of unfolding atrocities and genocides.[15] However, some reporters began to sour on the lies of the Empire as they became further exposed to them. Corwi Selgrothe gained fame as a journalist for the Rebel Alliance—particularly with her reporting from Yavin and Hoth—after she defected from her HNN position in response to the Ghorman Massacre.

There can be a tendency to believe that because of the reality of the Imperial state and its ongoing crimes and atrocities that the loyalty of its citizens must have been maintained purely by force or coercion. However, this is not entirely accurate. While many of the controls and propaganda attempts instituted by the Empire were designed to foster ongoing support and acceptance of Imperial rule, one of the most difficult aspects of understanding the Imperial state is acknowledging that much of its popular support appears to have been organically achieved.

Supporting the Empire

On the Core Worlds in particular, as has already been noted, Imperial military presence was kept at a minimum. Instead, the inbuilt Imperial

[15] New Republic Archives, Section: Post-war Tribunals, File: Ilb Oyec

class system helped divide civilians according to their wealth, background and, often, species. The further down the rungs of Imperial social hierarchy you got, the less the Empire cared about the disruption of your day-to-day life, with many of the poorest civilians being directed to manual labor positions or recruitment in the Imperial military. In many ways the support of the galaxy's working class was seen as irrelevant. However, despite the impact it was having on their lives, there were undoubtedly many among the less wealthy population who supported Palpatine and the Empire.

We need to understand the apparent contradictions that exist within the broadly defined groups of civilians who supported Imperial rule. In many ways these were seemingly good people. They loved their families. They worked hard at their jobs. They looked out for their neighbors. However, according to the surviving records of the ISB, they also regularly informed upon each other.[16] Sometimes these reports to the Imperial authorities—which no longer provide us with the identities of the informants—could be for serious infractions of the law and potentially seditious behavior. Sometimes they could be for the most mundane or petty reasons. It didn't matter. ISB agents or local security forces often followed up on them regardless. The informants must have seen their neighbors taken away, recognized when they didn't come back, and then welcomed the new families who moved into the vacant properties.

Despite the benefits of maintaining popularity within the ordinary masses, the support that the Empire was most keen to secure, and seemingly successful at gaining, was that of the comfortably wealthy inhabitants of the Core Worlds. Those employed in relatively well-paying jobs. Those who owned property. Those who had families and

[16] Imperial Archives, Section: ISB, File: Community Reports* *Many of these reports have been censored, redacted, or deleted since the fall of the Empire. However even the now empty records show that the system of civilian informants was vast.

children. These were the groups who had felt their lives had been overly disrupted by the high taxes and rationing of the Clone Wars. The Empire provided a form of security against the chaos that had recently engulfed them. In response it appears that many were prepared to turn a blind eye to the consequences the Empire inflicted upon others in exchange for their own personal prosperity. While, as will be discussed in a forthcoming chapter, the Empire often favored humans, they were not the only ones who embraced the comfort of Imperial rule in the Core.

One aspect of Imperial society that was not fully reckoned with after the Galactic Civil War—when the New Republic began its reconciliation movement—was the fact that complicity with the state was not just undertaken by those in military uniforms. Depending on age and species, many of our parents or grandparents were alive during Palpatine's reign. Not all of them were secretly rebel sympathizers plotting the downfall of the state. Many of them were content, model civilians. They flew Imperial flags on their property. They celebrated Empire Day. They voluntarily praised Palpatine and embraced his New Order. Not all their actions can be explained away by fear. They embraced a society that had seemingly been designed expressly for them, without either realizing or caring that if they were not paying the price for it then somebody else was.

When the Galactic Civil War came it split families in half. There were those who gravitated to the Rebel Alliance because they could not tolerate the injustices of the Empire and the way it casually and callously took the lives of its own citizens and opponents. But there were also those who stayed behind. Those who enjoyed the Imperial way of life. Who were happy to sacrifice some seemingly theoretical liberties if it meant they could live in comfort and security. It's one of the reasons the Empire spent significant resources on ensuring that higher end food stores were well-supplied even if it meant farming worlds on the Mid or Outer Rim were forced to operate under crippling quotas. It's why the mass transportation system on Coruscant was always so well-maintained and regulated, although often by forced laborers operating out of sight. If the obvious symbols of a functional state were in effect, then people would be willing to ignore how it was constructed. Over time there would come to be splits within some civilian families. Much of it could be generational, with older members who had lived through the previous conflict keen to maintain what seemed to be a peaceful life, while younger members balked at the reality of the society they existed within. But this was not universally the case. Anyone could be a loyalist in the same way that anyone could become a rebel. The divisions the Galactic Civil War caused within these families were not easily healed once peace came. You did not have to put on stormtrooper armor or a military uniform to play a part in the Empire's war effort. I can only wonder at how many children or grandchildren were discouraged from asking their elders about what they did in the Galactic Civil War because the truthful answer would outline how they had stayed at home, consented, and collaborated. I can certainly recall older members of my own family who would, in quiet and unguarded moments, reflect after the war on how much better, easier, or simpler things had been before. I ignored them when younger but now, as I have become a historian, I often wonder when exactly these simpler times were under the Empire? How were they better? Simpler for who?

Given how much of the galaxy the First Order recently ruled, how many of our fellow citizens embraced this new regime as it was also killing others? Were those who had contentedly existed under Palpatine, similarly happy to welcome Supreme Leader Kylo Ren? Did the broadcast of what appeared to be Palpatine's voice from Exegol provoke happiness in some of them, or even relief? Those who felt that the New Republic had somehow gone too far in dismantling the Imperial state. In redistributing power away from central figures out into worlds and species that had previously been held down by Imperial authority. How do we reconcile the fact that Palpatine, the Empire, and the First Order were not rejected out of hand by all of us? Evidently there were some who never rejected it and who welcomed it back when given the chance. How can we stop the Empire from continually haunting our galaxy when the ghosts of its acceptance exist in our own homes, our own families, and refuse to stay buried?

Chapter 6

Economy and Industry

To achieve their plans of border expansion and a greatly increased military, the Empire needed to effectively assume control of major industrial output across the galaxy and maintain a tight grip on the economy. The Republic had been able to produce ships and military materiel reasonably quickly during the Clone Wars, after the likes of Kuat Drive Yards (KDY) had been awarded major contracts and begun to utilize their considerable resources in service of the state. Such organizations, and their offshoots, would gain increased importance as the Empire solidified its control of the galaxy.

During the Clone Wars the various major banks were courted by both the Republic and the Separatists. Groups like the InterGalactic Banking Clan were early partners with the Confederacy of Independent Systems but, even though the galaxy was at war, also did business with the Republic (although charging them with extremely high interest rates for all borrowings). At the war's conclusion and the defeat of the Separatists, banking organizations that had been playing both sides against each other found themselves suddenly confronted by an Empire that did not exhibit the same unwillingness to control them as the Republic had done in peace time. Furthermore, the damage that high interest rates had caused during the war, particularly to civilians, meant there was very little popular sympathy for the banks when the Empire began to either place them under stringent controls or take full control of them through the process of Imperialization.

The Empire was not, however, only interested in major banking or industrial organizations. Imperial laws—as we will see in a future chapter—were often designed to give maximum flexibility to officials, allowing for the seizure and state control of effectively any business or financial center across the galaxy if it was viewed as advantageous to the Empire, or if its seizure could be used as a punitive measure on the owners or wider population. This effectively meant that sudden asset seizure hung like a specter for business owners across the galaxy and compelled them to make their services available to the Empire at even the most imbalanced levels of compensation, lest they be stripped of their control.

In some industries and sectors the Empire installed corporate overseers who would orchestrate their day to day running and ensure, sometimes through force and intimidation, that Imperial quotas and outputs—as dictated by the Imperial Bureau of Standards on Coruscant—were regularly met.[1] Being able to force people or organizations to adhere to Imperial requirements, orders, and standards voluntarily in fear of being placed fully under the Empire's control was one of the state's favored methods of motivation. Groups like Preox-Morlana and the Mining Guild were often so scared at the thought of having their organizations dissolved and subsumed fully into the Empire that they would, at times, appear more brutal in their management of sectors than the Empire could have been, given the military resources required to replace them. As with many other aspects of the galaxy's infrastructure, given time the Empire likely intended to take full control of most industrial and economic sectors, but outsourcing tyranny to those willing to obey orders and impose restrictions on others to ensure compliance was extremely useful in the state's early, comparatively vulnerable years.

[1] Imperial Archives, Section: Imperial Bureau of Standards, File: Quotas and Production Criteria

Building for the Empire

As mentioned in the previous chapter, there were certain industrial conglomerates who prospered under the Galactic Empire. It is difficult to think of organizations who benefited more from close Imperial ties than the arms manufacturers Kuat Drive Yards and Sienar Fleet Systems. While neither company was fully absorbed by the state's Imperialization process, they were viewed as effectively being too important to either fail or be left uncontrolled. As a result, both were the recipients of enormous military contracts to ensure the expansion of the Imperial armed forces and tied their long-term profitability to the survival of the Empire. The ongoing requirements for new Star Destroyers, support ships, and various generations of TIE fighters meant that huge amounts of money were transferred from the Empire into the coffers of its primary shipbuilding partners. The figures at the top of these organizations spent years enjoying the benefits of Imperial support. Although Raith Sienar was something of a reclusive figure who seemingly preferred work to the pleasures offered by the Empire, that was not true for everyone working at his company.[2] The various Sienar Fleet Systems' chief engineers and financial officers were regularly spotted at major social events on Coruscant and were highly enmeshed within the Imperial nobility.[3] Connections were even more pronounced at Kuat Drive Yards. Individual control of the company was passed along through a mix of hereditary bloodline and corporate approval. The person nominally at the head of KDY was, confusingly, generally referred to as Kuat of Kuat.[4] However, because of the size and complexity of the contracts awarded to KDY by the Empire, the combined senior executives of the company probably numbered in the hundreds. Many of these were also regular attendees at Imperial events and galas, and it can be surmised from surviving

[2] Imperial Archives, Section: Sienar Fleet Systems, File: Raith Sienar
[3] See *Coruscanti Society* #3582's section on "The Bright Lights of Sienar."
[4] Imperial Archives, Section: Kuat Drive Yards, File: Kuat of Kuat

Imperial financial investigations that the transfer of wealth in both directions between the Empire and KDY was not always restricted to just legitimate business.[5] By and large it seems that COMPNOR and the ISB were content to turn a blind eye to this level of corruption if it was not directly impacting the Empire's interests or KDY's ability to fulfill their contracts.

So intensive were the Empire's requirements of KDY that the main company spawned around half a dozen subsidiary organizations devoted to specific construction projects. Across its many branches KDY constructed everything from huge Star Destroyers and bespoke starfighters, all the way down to Imperial walkers, while still maintaining a division—Kuat Vehicles—expressly for civilian contracts.[6] With individual Sector Moffs and regional governors able to dictate priority orders, it is surprisingly difficult to determine exactly how many Star Destroyers of varying size and class KDY produced during the Empire's reign. Conservatively the number should likely be considered in the thousands, but surviving Kuati records are unclear as to how many were actually built and how many were only planned or existed only in the records, possibly as the result of acts of embezzlement.[7] Even comparing the KDY build records with the rosters held at various Imperial bases is not particularly instructive. Some Star Destroyers appear as multiple entries in the same base's records while some ships that were confirmed to have been built—and participated in combat with the Rebel Alliance— do not appear in any Imperial records at all.[8] Furthermore, ships of different classes appear with the same name in different Imperial bases. There is also no clear indication as to how many Super Star Destroyers were built in comparison to numbers ordered or planned for, and the design specifications regarding their planned size appear to vary across

---

[5] Imperial Archives, Section: Kuat Drive Yards, File: Accounting Investigations
[6] Kuat Archives, Section: Structure and Organization, File: Subsidiaries
[7] Kuat Archives, Section: Imperial Contracts, File: Production Records
[8] Records drawn from Yaga Minor Ubiqtorate Base, Carida, and Corellia

KDY records with no explanation given.[9] Alliance combat reports suggest that at least a dozen such vessels existed in the Imperial fleet, representing an enormous allocation of resources.[10]

Yet the vast resources required to construct so many different types of vessels and Imperial military equipment were dwarfed by the requirements for constructing the two Death Star superweapons. We currently know precious little about the actual construction process of the first Death Star, aside from what can be pieced together from surviving records in Imperial archives. The records at the Imperial vault facility on Scarif were destroyed during the battle there, so they are no longer available to us. It appears that at least some of the construction either of the weapon itself or its prototype was undertaken in or near Geonosis, with the final construction likely to have taken place above Scarif itself.[11] Given the circumstances surrounding the Battle of Endor there is obviously much more known about the construction of the second Death Star in orbit above the Forest Moon. While the initial plans and designs of both battle stations were undertaken by the likes of the Imperial Military Department of Advanced Weapons Research, overseen by both Director Orson Krennic and Grand Moff Tarkin—with scientist Galen Erso vital for the final design of the primary armament—it is also obvious that both KDY and Sienar were heavily involved in the construction of the weapons. These were the only two military development companies that could undertake the scale of the work. However, it was not simply expertise or industrial workforce that could bring an idea like the Death Star into reality. To fulfill its plans the Empire needed resources. Huge quantities of them. This would be the demand handed out to the rest of the galaxy.

---

[9] Kuat Archives, Section: Imperial Contracts, File: *Executor*-class
[10] Rebel Alliance Archives, Section: Intelligence Operations, File: Imperial Naval Strength—Super Star Destroyer Estimations
[11] Imperial Archives, Section: Project Stardust, File: Construction

Fueling the Machine

The Empire had an almost insatiable appetite for resources. The need to meet the demands of planned military production meant that the expansion of the Empire's borders stemmed as much from manufacturing requirements as from an ideological desire to conquer its near neighbors.

The need for ongoing sources of raw materials led to very targeted expansion toward legacy worlds such as Samovar and Wadi Raffa. These legacy worlds had previously been under legislative protection in the Galactic Republic because of the importance and beauty of their natural environments.[12] However, it had also long been suspected that such systems held important natural resources and mineral deposits. Once the Republic had fallen, the Empire used a variety of nefarious methods—which will be explained further in a forthcoming chapter—for annexing the planets and stripping them of their legal protection. Within short order, contracts were awarded to favored Imperial companies to begin the mining and extraction of various minerals, but in particular doonium and dolovite—both of which would be crucial in the construction of the first Death Star.

The Empire cast a wide net in identifying possible locations for industrial exploitation. Efficiency was seen as being of paramount importance. The safety of the workers and the protection of planetary habitats was not. As might be expected, all forms of trade and workers' unions were dismantled and made illegal, while most laws and regulations that had governed worker safety in the Republic were stripped away. To ensure that quotas were met, the Empire made use of various officials to oversee production. Perhaps the most notorious of these was Count Denetrius Vidian who was known for his high efficiency standards and often brutal methods of achieving them. Much of Vidian's early life is unclear though he had risen to a significant position of power in the Republic and swiftly embraced the opportunities offered by the

---

[12] Imperial Archives, Section: Galactic Republic, File: Legacy World Legislation

Empire. He had apparently been exposed to a flesh-eating illness known as Shilmer's syndrome, which had a devastating impact on his body.[13] As a result he wore a cybernetic support suit that, while less intimidating than Darth Vader's, helped solidify his fearsome reputation. Vidian would often be sent by the Empire to bring struggling systems or mining operations back on schedule through whatever means were necessary. Shortly before his death, Vidian was undertaking an operation in the Gorse system where he apparently intended to destroy the nearby moon of Cynda in order to extract thorilide crystals that could be used in turbolasers.[14] Although the attempt failed, and Vidian was charged with various crimes against the Empire before he was killed, it does serve as a useful example as to the lengths Imperial officials and forces would go to in order to gather the materials they needed.[15]

Major industrial centers opened across the galaxy and most of these worlds would suffer greatly from Imperial activity. On Lothal, in order to gather the resources required to supply the nascent TIE defender factory, the Empire had the mining guild deploy huge roaming ore crawlers on the planet's surface.[16] These machines, dubbed "World Devastators" by locals who had seen them in action, moved on enormous repulsorlift legs and stripped resources from the ground beneath them. Within the crawler itself, raw materials would be partially refined ready for use in Imperial factories. The process was hugely damaging to the planet's surface and resulted in significant amounts of pollution being released into the atmosphere. It took years for the ecosystem to be restored and repaired after Lothal's liberation from Imperial control.[17]

---

[13] Imperial Archives, Section Count Denetrius Vidian, File: Physiology
[14] Imperial Archives, Section Count Denetrius Vidian, File: Gorse & Cynda
[15] Imperial Archives, Section Count Denetrius Vidian, File: Commander Rae Sloane Report* *Dated from 11 BBY
[16] Post-Imperial Lothal Archives, Section: Imperial Operations, File: Resource Extraction
[17] Post-Imperial Lothal Archives, Section: Ecosystem, File: Repair and Reconstruction Activities

Lothal was not alone in suffering the destruction of its natural habitats. Reuss VIII had previously been a major farming and agricultural world during the Republic but, under Imperial control, had its fields brutally harvested and, once the soil was depleted, industrial factories installed in their place. The factories were used to process, refine, and smelt some of the most dangerous chemicals and minerals that could be found in the galaxy. As a result, the pollution from these plants was extreme and, over time, the atmosphere became increasingly poisonous, with the emergence of acid rain causing further damage. Similar factory construction and mining processes undertaken on Malador—around the date 14 BBY—left the atmosphere effectively unbreathable, and the wealthiest inhabitants of the planet abandoned it. The Empire outsourced the mining of the hyperbarides beneath the crust of Goroth Prime to various subsidiary organizations in 10 BBY. The minerals themselves were highly radioactive and the use of native Gorothites as forced labor led to many of them being horribly exposed. The damage both to them and the planet was disastrous.

The Empire cast a wide net for raw and precious materials alike. Anything valuable that could be dragged from beneath the surface of a world could be made to serve or benefit the Empire in some ways. For some of these resources, like the highly prized beskar of Mandalore, the Empire took to stamping the Imperial seal directly upon processed bars. This was partly in case of theft or piracy—it became very difficult for thieves to argue that they'd come across the material naturally if the Empire's symbol was on it. But the act also served another purpose—to remind those whose worlds had been pillaged that what was once theirs was now the property of the Empire.

There was one rare material that was particularly vital to the Empire. In order to gather the kyber crystals necessary for the superlasers of both Death Star battle stations, the Empire instigated a highly complex, but brutally destructive, series of mining operations on the sacred worlds of Jedha and Ilum. Part of this was likely also motivated out of a desire to either control or destroy the cultural history and legacy of the Jedi Order, but the need for these crystals, and the measures used to retrieve them, were tremendously damaging to both planets, even before Jedha City was destroyed by the Death Star. Ilum itself was subsequently removed from most galactic maps and it is only recently that we discovered the First Order had converted the world into the superweapon known as Starkiller Base.

It might be thought that worlds with close ties to high-ranking officials within the Empire would be spared most of the dangers of industrial extraction, but this was not universally the case. Mas Amedda was probably one of the most recognizable and powerful figures within Palpatine's Empire. He had originally joined the Republic Senate as a representative of his homeworld Champala. Whatever allegiance he had once held to that planet and system of government appear to have evaporated over time as he came to fully support Palpatine in his rule as Emperor. Champala had once been considered a popular resort world for the galaxy's wealthy elite, noted for its oceans and vibrant aquatic species. However, under Imperial control—even as early as 18 BBY—Champala became the home of dual, competing, industries. The oceans were significantly overfished by the Imperial Champalan Marine Resource Collective while the landmasses were extensively drilled by the Champalan Imperial Mineral Extraction Initiative in order to mine various fossilized resources. Together both companies poisoned the land and the seas of Champala while also squabbling over which had priority for the few spaceports, which became congested and polluted. Why exactly Mas Amedda allowed for his own planet and people to be the victims of such corporate destruction might seem unclear, but he later admitted under New Republic interrogation that he had accepted ongoing bribes from both companies as well as significant percentages of their trading profits.[18]

---

[18] New Republic Archives, Section: Imperial Prisoners, File: Mas Amedda, Interrogation Note #254

Extracting and refining minerals was—while important—only part of the industrial process the Empire required in order to fulfill its ambitions. The transportation of these resources around the galaxy was also necessary and required significant haulage capability. The Empire could have put military vessels to work carrying these resources, and did exactly that for the strategically vital kyber crystal transfers, but even the vast Imperial fleet would struggle to undertake convoy duties while also expanding the Empire's borders and dealing with pockets of resistance. As with the actual extraction of resources, the Empire outsourced much of the transportation to subsidiaries. However, where needed, they were also willing to seize existing shipping assets, particularly near valuable resource deposits or major trade hubs. The requirement for increasing supply runs to the Imperial fleet on deployment in the Outer Rim beyond Darkknell led to Imperial authorities taking control of various civilian shipping businesses and vessels in the vicinity.[19] The Empire was not hesitant in taking control of other operations if needed. Following a failed attempt in 5 BBY to capture the rebel agent Cassian Andor on Ferrix by officers of Preox-Morlana's corporate militia, the ISB arrested much of the upper echelon of the organization and stripped them of responsibility for the system.[20] In short order the planet, which was a useful trade hub and site of various industries, was fully occupied by Imperial forces. Similarly, Darth Vader authorized the full annexation of Cloud City—a tibanna gas mining facility in the atmosphere above Bespin—shortly after the Battle of Hoth. This was at least partially motivated by the capture of leading Rebel Alliance figures there, but General Lando Calrissian, who formerly served as Cloud City's administrator, believes that Vader intended to take over the facility regardless.[21]

[19] Imperial Archives, Section: Shipping and Transportation Seizures, File: Twin Suns Transport Services
[20] Imperial Archives, Section: ISB, File: Ferrix occupation
[21] Rebel Alliance Archives, Section: Lando Calrissian, File: Cloud City

For those businesses who found themselves absorbed into the Empire, there was no compensation for their loss of autonomy or livelihoods. The various subsidiary organizations that the Empire outsourced much of its work to were given reasonably lucrative contracts though it is unclear how much of that money made its way to the actual workers or if it ended up being kept by executives on Coruscant. Given that the Empire held an absolute monopoly on mass industry across the galaxy it was not as if workers could easily complain or find alternative employment elsewhere. But, while some businesses looked to supplant their labor force with droids, those on Imperial contracts—and those who worked directly for the Empire itself—did still require some form of payment. Their employers may not have given any specific consideration to the well-being of their staff but on a basic level it was accepted that starving workers were bad for productivity.[22] To pay for all its undertakings, projects, and expansions, the Empire would need more than just control of the means of production.

Footing the Bill

As previously mentioned, the end of the Clone Wars left many banks and financial institutions around the galaxy in highly precarious and vulnerable positions. Those who had sided with the Republic in the conflict now found themselves under the control of the Empire. Those who had been financing the Separatists were effectively conquered as prizes of war, with very little sympathy from the galaxy's wider population. Control of these institutions allowed the Empire to have almost total control of monetary transactions, trade, and capital across the galaxy.

Almost immediately the Republic Credit was phased out as a currency and replaced by the new Imperial version. The physical coins and

[22] Imperial Archives, Section: Imperial Bureau of Standards, File: Worker Productivity Study #TJ8210

chits bore the symbol of the new regime and were minted in huge quantities on worlds such as Muunilinst. However, while the Republic had had its own currency it had also allowed for worlds, particularly those on the Outer Rim, to maintain their own native monetary systems as well. The Empire did not. Given the time it took to produce the new forms of currency and then make them available on all Imperial worlds across the galaxy, there were significant delays in supplying distant systems with their new finances. Despite this, some particularly zealous governors, such as Moff Iraydion of the Belderone sector saw an opportunity to solidify Imperial control of their systems by banning Republic credits and any equivalent local currency.[23] Almost overnight residents of some of Iraydion's worlds effectively discovered that they were bankrupt. All their existing savings and wealth were rendered obsolete, shops would not accept—for fear of punishment from the security forces— newly declared illegal currencies in exchange for even basic items like food, and most businesses could no longer pay their own workers. The arrival of Imperial credits led to issues of price inflation given the scarcity of legal tender. The result of this localized financial collapse was a significant part of the population joining Imperial service, either through military recruitment or heading into industrial jobs that could at least guarantee a usable currency. Both outcomes were ultimately beneficial to the Empire as alternative employment sectors collapsed leaving people to depend on the state for survival. A desperation that made them far more pliable in becoming complicit with the regime.

The Empire generated much of its own revenue through systems of taxation. There were standard Imperial taxes that were levied across all worlds and sectors, while planetary governors and local officials could also impose their own taxes upon the worlds under their control. If the money was paid regularly and on time, the Empire did not give much in the way of consideration as to the burdens placed upon

[23] Imperial Archives, Section: Belderone Sector, File: Financial controls

each world. Taxation also provided the Empire with further opportunity for punitive measures. Following the theft of an Imperial payroll on Aldhani in 5 BBY, the ISB ordered that new taxes would be implemented galaxy wide. These new measures included a tax five times the amount stolen from Aldhani for any planets or systems that were found to be harboring "partisan activities."[24] The definition of "partisan activities" could be so broad as to mean effectively any form of resistance to Imperial rule.[25] As a result, the Empire was able to justify the further transfer of wealth into its own accounts while also using economics as a means through which to throttle planets viewed as being in any way rebellious.

In many ways this perhaps gives the best representation of the Empire's plans and intentions for the galaxy and the ways in which it viewed the general population. The amount of money that the Empire gathered into itself while it ruled the galaxy is truly astronomical. The wealth and resources and prosperity dragged from outlying worlds allowed the galaxy's rulers on Coruscant to enjoy opulent lifestyles, while also ensuring that the Star Destroyers and stormtrooper legions that the totalitarian system relied upon would continue to be funded. In essence, the galaxy paid for its own subjugation. The infrastructure required to achieve this was vast. Spaceports were expanded to cope with the increase of haulage traffic, planetary infrastructure was massively improved to allow for largescale transportation from remote areas, and additional hyperspace beacons were deployed to allow for easier navigation between isolated systems. But none of these changes were employed to enhance the lives of ordinary people. All of it was extractive. Taxes and valuable minerals were all perceived as being the property of the Empire. Economics was a weapon to be used against the

---

[24] Imperial Archives, Section: Imperial Security Bureau, File: Aldhani Response Briefing
[25] This will be discussed in greater detail in Chapter Eleven.

populations of worlds that were being dismantled around them. Some of the Empire's fiercest defenders, figures such as Lenang O'Pali who continued to act as polemicists for the Empire long after it had fallen, point toward the industrial and transportation networks created during these years as "things built by the Empire to benefit the populations of Imperial worlds."[26] But it takes a very creative definition to consider that any of these things were built by the Empire. Imperial officials did not do the labor. They did not do the mining. Wookiees in stun cuffs toiling in forced labor camps and impoverished populations digging for doonium deep beneath the surface of Outer Rim worlds were not "the Empire." The systems they were creating were not for the benefit of ordinary people either. Armed convoys taking resources toward the Core were not pleasure cruises. Low-paying jobs did not allow civilians to take exotic excursions on the new hyperlanes. And weapons factories spewing toxins into the atmosphere did not enrich their sick, impoverished workers.

The Empire sat at the center of the galaxy like an enormous black hole—forever sucking wealth and resources inward. Coruscant glittered while those at the edges suffered. Worlds who had nothing left to give were abandoned to their fate and allowed to go dark. This is how Palpatine and his many advisors viewed the natural hierarchy of their New Order. Now that we understand how they planned to maintain, consolidate, and exploit it, we must also come to examine how they planned to expand it.

[26] Lenang O'Pali, public lecture on Eriadu: *A Call to Empire: The Failings of the New Republic*

Part Two

EXPANSION AND OPPRESSION

Chapter 7

Imperial Expansion and Strategy

Having gained control of the territory that had previously comprised the Galactic Republic and begun to strengthen its grip over these worlds, the Empire moved into an expansionist phase. The new regime's desire to push outward its own borders likely had several aspects to it. Whether it was the need for greater resources to power the major construction projects it planned to undertake, the need to find additional workers and taxes to help construct and finance the state, or just Palpatine's desire to rule over—and therefore control—every world, the outcome was largely the same. Where the Republic had sought to entice new member systems to join its ranks through diplomacy, the Empire would seek to conquer them by force.

The Imperial approaches taken to annex its near neighbors would differ slightly from system to system. Though it sought to build up its military forces through the creation and deployment of its new Star Destroyers and the recently recruited stormtroopers, they could not be in all places at once. Furthermore, given the ongoing influence of the Senate, the military had to walk a fine line between fulfilling the Empire's expansionist objectives and appearing to be overly aggressive in a manner that might have difficult political ramifications. Therefore, in order to balance these two competing considerations, the Emperor placed responsibility for the Outer Rim expansions into the hands of someone he could trust: Wilhuff Tarkin.

Tarkin, as will be discussed in more detail in forthcoming chapters, had both the ruthlessness and the strategic instincts that made him invaluable to a man like Palpatine. He was brutal enough to utilize all the available Imperial military resources in targeted campaigns, imaginative enough to find alternative pathways to full military conquest, and connected enough to the Imperial Senate to navigate the political pitfalls. In many ways we should consider him one of the prime architects of the Empire's successful ascendence. To understand how the Empire grew to its largest size, we must examine the different ways Tarkin and others found to absorb previously unaligned systems.

Separatist Legacies

Some of the earliest moves made by the Empire to secure new worlds were against systems that were nominally already part of the Galactic Republic, but which existed within very specific legal protections. Across the galaxy, "Legacy worlds" existed that were famed for their natural beauty or the rarity of certain species of plants or animals. Over hundreds of years the Republic had granted these worlds legislative status and guarantees to ensure that they could not be pillaged for the resources that also existed alongside their natural wonders. Where the Republic had seen such laws as necessary for the longevity of a diverse galaxy, the Empire saw them as an obstacle to progress. However, these legal protections could not just be summarily stripped from Legacy worlds without just cause. The Senate would surely protest. Instead, sufficiently good reasons would have to be manufactured. The solution was to be found in the remnants of the defeated Separatist army.

It is unclear who crafted the initial plan to circumvent the protections of Legacy worlds. Various accounts and records mention both Grand Moff Tarkin and Director Orson Krennic, though the pair of them actively cooperating on something seems unlikely given their mutual dislike.[1] Regardless, the plan itself was as inventive as it was cynical. The end of the Clone Wars had left the Empire in possession of huge swathes of weapons and other military materiel seized from the defeated Separatists. Much of it was either of no interest to the new Imperial state or was effectively useless anyway. Battle droids with no command signal to operate them, heavy weapons that would soon be obsolete as a result of Imperial military advancements, millions of pistols and blasters that were uncomfortable to use for human hands. While these weapons had little active military value, they could still be used to serve the Empire. In short order, Imperial patrols began to "discover" caches of Separatist weapons on various Legacy worlds like Samovar and Wadi Raffa. These discoveries were quickly reported to the Imperial Senate and were greeted with outrage. Not only did it appear that these systems had covertly aligned with the Separatists during the recent war, but they had used their Legacy status to act as a shield behind which they could hide stockpiles of ordnance. These weapons and munitions had not been surrendered at the end of the conflict and Imperial forces could only assume were intended to be used in future military activities against the Empire. Given such obviously treasonous acts, the Empire and Senate had no choice but to strip these Legacy worlds of their legal protections.[2]

The case against these Legacy worlds was, of course, a lie created by high-ranking Imperial officials. It was they who had hired various smugglers to sneak the weapons into each of their targeted worlds and have them deposited somewhere easily findable for the seemingly random Imperial patrols that would shortly follow. It seems highly implausible that there were not some in the Imperial Senate who recognized this sham for what it was. But set against the specter of a return to the violence and destruction of the Clone Wars, many senators were

---

[1] Imperial Archives, Section: Expansion, File: Legacy worlds—Breaches of Imperial Regulations
[2] Imperial Senate Proceedings, File DW851.17

willing to accept it at face value. Shortly after Legacy status was revoked, the Imperial military began occupation proceedings, and each world was quickly designated for full scale mining operations.

So successful was the plan to plant illegal weapons on worlds targeted for Imperial annexation, that it was swiftly expanded beyond just the Legacy systems into those that had remained neutral during the Clone Wars and had not been members of the fallen Republic. If anyone within the Senate bothered to give an overview of the reports to see that weapons with the same distinguishing features and serial numbers were reappearing repeatedly on different planets, they did not raise it as an issue. We can see from the Imperial archives that, had they done so, the pre-planned response would have been to suggest that Separatist sympathizers had infiltrated parts of the Imperial military, resulting in a further purge of personnel viewed as having suspect loyalties.[3] It was only when this tactic was attempted in the neutral Salient system that it began to encounter resistance.

Once again smugglers had been employed to deposit the weapons, but it appears as though they betrayed the Empire by warning the Salient authorities in advance and coordinating with noted rebel fighters like Saw Gerrera. When Tarkin arrived in his Star Destroyer *Executrix* he was met with a situation that rapidly devolved into an ongoing and grueling battle where much of the system's infrastructure was destroyed.[4] Stripped of the administrative excuse of illegal weapons, Tarkin resorted to a punitive campaign of invasion and occupation to subdue Salient and send a message to other neutral systems who may have been tempted to resist Imperial occupation. The Salient affair also brought an end to the policy of expansion by subterfuge. It had largely served its original purpose and, if it was going to result in fighting anyway, Tarkin and others counseled it was best to approach such

[3] Imperial Archives, Section: Expansion, File: Separatist Caches—Response #21-87
[4] Imperial Archives, Section: Grand Moff Wilhuff Tarkin, File: Salient Campaign

systems with overwhelming force to either prompt an immediate surrender—or win any subsequent battles swiftly—and send a message out to their neighbors. This approach would eventually crystalize into what would collectively become known as the Tarkin Doctrine of "ruling through fear of force rather than force itself."[5] Before that could be fully implemented, the Empire needed to deal with additional developing problems.

Imperial Borders

The Galactic Republic had, at various times in its history, incentivized civilians to move from the Core Worlds to the galactic frontier and Outer Rim, where they were often equipped with ongoing supplies and assistance.[6] There were various reasons for this. By relocating parts of the population, they freed up space in systems where cities were becoming overcrowded or lacked space for further expansion. Additionally, for the selected worlds that were uninhabited, the Republic was able to begin the process of colonization by those dedicated to seeing the process through. For worlds that already had inhabitants, the new arrivals would serve as strong proponents for the Republic and, it was hoped, eventually lead toward an application for membership. When you also consider that these colonists agreed to supply the Republic a percentage of any resources they mined or gathered, then it was a very good deal all round.

The Empire did not care about such deals, though as was typical of them, where the Republic had seen an opportunity for peaceful enlargement, the new state saw a system to be weaponized. As it completed its annexation of the various Legacy worlds around the galaxy, questions

[5] Imperial Archives, Section: Grand Moff Wilhuff Tarkin, File: Tarkin Doctrine
[6] Imperial Archives, Section: Galactic Republic, File: Republic Ministry of Economic Development—"Homestead Act"

began to arise regarding the future expansion opportunities for the new state. Given Imperial requirements for ongoing growth and constant resource extraction, it was only a matter of time before it began to push its borders outward. But there were also issues regarding internal stability that meant some expansion would have to be slowed. Furthermore, the Empire was developing a population problem of its own, by way of seizing new inhabited planets where the resources on the world were highly desirable, but the population was not. Civilians who had been evicted from their homes by Imperial officials needed somewhere to go. Not all these undesirables could be sent to the various labor camps that were beginning to appear across the galaxy, lest they be overwhelmed.

It appears that it was Grand Moff Tarkin who proposed a solution to this issue.[7] Where once civilians had left the Republic to become residents on remote worlds through choice, the Empire simply deported them. Huge transport ships, organized by the Coalition for Improvements, landed on various planets across the Outer Rim that had not yet been absorbed by the Empire, disgorged their civilian cargo, and left. Senate approval for the measure was secured through a mix of Imperial promises to relocate all civilians who had lost their homes through "unavoidable but regrettable Imperial activities" and the reluctance of many Core World senators for their planets to take on additional refugees so soon after the end of the Clone Wars.[8] There were various benefits to this new arrangement. Previously these emigrants would have brought stories about the benefits of the Republic with them. Now they brought stories and fears that the Empire would surely, at some point in the future, return to conquer these worlds. For now, the Empire managed to rid themselves of civilians they had no use for, who would help instill in their new homes the dangers of resisting Imperial rule. In

[7] Imperial Archives, Section: Grand Moff Wilhuff Tarkin, File: Population Relocation
[8] Imperial Archives, Section: Mas Amedda, File: Imperial Relocation Speech

theory, though this did not always prove successful, these refugees would also serve to undercut the existing societies on each new world. The inhabitants soon found they had to compete for resources with these new arrivals who grouped together in so-called "Tarkin towns." Conflicts between these groups could help ensure that the population would be sufficiently divided enough to not muster much of a defense when the Empire did return. In this way the Imperial state was able to colonize and slowly conquer some Outer Rim worlds in installments.

As a result of this approach to the worlds right on the borders of the Galactic Empire, some systems ended up inhabiting an ill-defined space between being absorbed and colonized and maintaining some form of independent autonomy. Tatooine—the home planet of Luke Skywalker—is a prime example of this. It was a world that existed outside of the Republic, while the Republic still stood, and was largely controlled by a representative of the Hutt Cartel. In the years leading up to the Battle of Yavin, Tatooine retained aspects of independence from the Empire, something the residents were apparently highly defensive of, but over time Imperial patrols in the space around the planet and in some of the major cities began to increase. Despite the fact the Empire did not have any specific claim to the planet, there were recruitment offices on the world and its inhabitants were able to apply to join the Imperial Academy, as Luke Skywalker intended to do. Tatooine, and other worlds along the borderline of the Empire's territory, remained locked in this dual existence of being partially occupied and colonized without being formally conquered, for much of the Empire's existence.

This status had benefits for both the Empire and individual systems. While worlds like Tatooine had to deal with living alongside a highly belligerent neighbor they also avoided some of the worst aspects of life under the Empire including the war crimes and genocides that, as we will see, became increasingly commonplace in the Outer Rim. For the Empire itself, it was absolved from actually administering borderland worlds, particularly those that were already under the control of noted crime lords, while still being able to draw new recruits from them and—in some places—use Imperial patrols to take a cut of any trade profits. There were other worlds that existed alongside the Empire which were far less fortunate.

Expansion by Force

While there is an understandable tendency to view the Empire's military endeavors entirely through the sphere of the Galactic Civil War—a topic we shall also be examining in this study—that does, to an extent, distract from the fact that the Empire had effectively been at war for years even before a structured Rebel Alliance came into existence. Along the Outer Rim and on worlds in the Expansion Region, the Empire dispensed with any attempts to covertly conquer or administratively colonize star systems and, instead, resorted to overwhelming military force. During this period the line between Imperial expansion and ongoing pacification activities becomes heavily blurred, but both should still be considered as furthering the Empire's overarching goal of securing additional territory for itself.

Furthermore, there were additional, more cynical, reasons behind the Empire's desire to use force on some worlds, especially those that sat within territory that was nominally controlled by the Republic but had, for whatever reason, remained neutral during the Clone Wars. If Tarkin's emerging doctrine of using fear to maintain Imperial control was going to work, the Empire would have to provide examples of what to be afraid of. Worlds like Ryloth and Mimban provided useful opportunities for this point to be made. The way that the Twi'leks of Ryloth had resisted the Separatist invasions during the Clone Wars had been of great benefit to the Republic. Under the Empire this same warrior culture and desire to avoid occupation made them an unacceptable liability. Imperial forces attempted to violently disarm the militia of Ryloth in order to guarantee the safety of the new doonium refinery that was being constructed on the surface. However, resistance to the Emperor's rule remained, under the guise of the Free Ryloth Movement operated by General Cham Syndulla. For years Palpatine's oppressive regime attempted to deal with ongoing guerrilla warfare on Ryloth, fighting against insurgents who operated in the many caves and valleys that crisscrossed the planet's surface. The Empire generally made use of airpower, deploying TIE bombers to try and either flush out the insurgents or collapse their underground bases. The bombing runs varied in effectiveness, and it wasn't until Grand Admiral Thrawn took command of the operations on Ryloth that notable successes were achieved.

However, that is not to say there were no other benefits to the Empire for having combat drawn out on Ryloth. With the Grand Army of the Republic being disbanded by the new regime, most military personnel were ordinary civilians who either volunteered or were conscripted into service. These forces needed to be blooded in combat to gauge their effectiveness while also providing the Empire opportunities to test out various battle strategies. Ryloth was an excellent contender for the Empire to use as a form of military laboratory given that the enemy there showed no signs of surrendering, meaning that the fight could continue long enough for Imperial forces to test out new weapons and combat tactics.[9] The fact that the insurgents on Ryloth were committed to violent resistance also made it easier for the Empire to justify its increasing military presence there to the Senate. While there was a danger that the rest of the galaxy would see the Twi'leks continuing to fight and resist the Empire, it was offset by the fact that the Imperial determination to wage war against them would also send a message regarding their own resolve. We can only wonder how many other planets looked at Ryloth and decided they did not wish to become a perpetual ruined battlefield.

[9] Imperial Archives, Section: Expansion, File: Ryloth Campaign

While Syndulla's homeworld served as an opportunity for the Empire to perfect some of its military strategies, operations on Mimban brought different benefits. Like Ryloth, Mimban had seen heavy combat during the Clone Wars with the Mimbanese Liberation Army undertaking battles against the invading Separatists. Mimban also had considerable natural resources that had first made it a target for the Separatists, and then the Empire. The plentiful deposits of hyperbarides—crucial components of turbolaser production—made the planet a highly tempting target, but the Liberation Army were no more willing to allow the Empire to conquer them than they had been the Separatists. Once again, the Empire deployed extensive military forces to the campaign. Star Destroyers, TIE fighters, and various ground forces were all committed to the operation. The planet's climate made it a very difficult environment to wage war in. The heavily ionized atmosphere meant that conditions were almost perpetually misty and the surface quickly became almost impassably muddy. For Imperial soldiers, generally referred to as "mudtroopers," the conditions were hellishly difficult. The indigenous combatants were well acquainted with their own battle-grounds and would attack out of the mists using camouflage and secret tunnels, making every battle a grueling and attritional slog.

As it turns out, that was exactly what the Empire was hoping for. As with Ryloth, the Mimbanese campaign allowed for Imperial forces to be trained directly in combat, which helped prepare the military for the battles yet to come. But more important were the legislative and funding opportunities the campaigns presented. While the Empire planned a substantial military expansion, the construction of new capital ships and fighter squadrons, and the recruiting of new legions of stormtroopers, was expensive. Though the Empire might control the taxation of the galaxy, the spending of that money had, to varying degrees, to go through Senate oversight. Trying to gain approval for additional military expenditure was difficult when the Empire was nominally at peace. However, being able to point to the campaign on Mimban and suggest it was dragging on simply because the Empire lacked the resources to decisively win the battle was a far more compelling argument. As a result, it seems highly plausible that General Ire Falk, the commanding officer on Mimban, was under instructions to ensure that the battle was drawn out for as long as necessary.[10] This allowed the Empire to submit ongoing military requisition bills to the Senate which would enable them to massively increase their armed forces.[11]

The examples listed in this chapter are selected to provide useful insights into some of the strategies and approaches the Empire took toward its expansion policies. While it is certainly true that Grand Moff Tarkin had a great deal of control over the general principles and strategies of expansion, he could not provide direct oversight of every planet or operation. There were few within the Empire's ranks who possessed both his strategic mind and political instincts, and while he may have presented the overall plans to the various Imperial officers who were tasked with carrying them out, the actual practicalities could often sacrifice even Tarkin's considered finesse in favor of overwhelming brute force. It would be easy to assume that the Empire's violent attempts to expand its own territory were not part of some sophisticated plan. But Tarkin knew that they could not push outward everywhere at once. Expansion had to be carefully managed to be effective. Furthermore, the rest of the galaxy had to take various instructive lessons from the ways in which the Empire approached unwilling systems or the instances in which it deployed violence.

This concept was right at the heart of Tarkin's emerging doctrine regarding the importance of instilling fear within the Imperial population, and especially those outside the Core Worlds. If necessary, the Empire would not be afraid to resort to military force to achieve its

[10] Imperial Archives, Section: Grand Moff Wilhuff Tarkin, File: Communications to General Falk
[11] Imperial Archives, Section: Military Requisition Bills, File: Mimban Campaign

goals, but it was far more efficient if worlds and civilians knew what such a response looked like and therefore would go to any lengths to avoid being the victims of it. Tarkin needed Imperial violence to be both destructive and instructive. Therefore, every turbolaser barrage or orbital bombardment became a lesson that existed in perpetuity. This desire to send a message to civilians was not just restricted to the Empire's expansion policy either. It was—as we shall see—present in the ways in which the Imperial state sought to implement and inflict its own prejudices and bigotries upon the galaxy.

Chapter 8

The Imperial Military

For many beings across the galaxy, symbols of the Imperial state such as the Senate or even the Emperor himself were largely theoretical. Their day-to-day interactions with the Empire did not come in the form of distant representatives or the ruler of the Imperial palace. Instead, they existed through the presence of the Imperial military. Palpatine and his myriad advisors chose the many ways that he would be represented to his subjects—faceless stormtroopers and imposing Star Destroyers were perhaps the most instructive way that his intentions were indicated.

Since the end of the Galactic Civil War there have been a variety of attempts to try and explain and contextualize the way the Empire's armed forces operated and how they were structured. The permanent exhibit on "The Empire at War" curated by Samjo Li at the Museum for Galactic Conflict on Coruscant is an excellent example of how such a huge topic can be distilled for a civilian audience. There can often be a tension between the desire of, at least some of the public audience, to get up close to famous (or infamous) weapons of war like TIE fighters or stormtrooper armor, and the need for museums and historians to explain the context of these objects and the ways in which they are not neutral or set apart from the crimes and horrors they carried out. As will be mentioned in a later chapter, there remained under the New Republic groups who idolized the Imperial aesthetic and tried to present a "clean" version of the Imperial military, which championed their training and military effectiveness while ignoring their war crimes and atrocities. This should not be allowed to stand unopposed. There remains room to further explore how the largest armed forces the galaxy has ever known were organized, trained, and deployed while also making clear exactly what they were intended to achieve.

There can be an understandable tendency to look at the vast legions of anonymous soldiers and the terrifying arrays of starships and believe that the Empire's military was all part of one enormous uniform whole. But that is not entirely the case. There was a surprising amount of variation and specialization built into the multiple military branches that made up the Empire. In fact, these variations serve to highlight some of the strange and inexplicable ways in which the Imperial military hobbled itself by refusing to adapt or deploy the best forces as required by circumstance during the Galactic Civil War. There may never have been a more lopsided conflict in history than that between the Empire and the Rebel Alliance. As we shall see in subsequent chapters, there are clear reasons behind the Empire's failure to successfully defeat their opposition. But to understand those lessons we must also understand how this enormous military force was intended to operate.

Origins

With all armed services, including that which (until recently) comprised the New Republic's military, there are distinct rivalries between the various branches. Despite this it seems obvious to look back at the Empire and declare that the Imperial Navy was the most important aspect of the military. While the army and the starfighter corps were both distinctive branches that could, and would, operate independently at times, the fleet of capital ships was the lynchpin around which the entirety of the military force was built.

Chapter 1: The Emperor

Supreme Chancellor Palpatine at the "Liberation Day" Parade on Naboo. Image from the *Theed Daily News*.

Republic HoloNet News: Senate Feed record of Senator Palpatine.

The "Declaration of Empire" speech by Emperor Palpatine, preserved and rebroadcast by Imperial authorities.

Bas relief from Supreme Chancellor Palpatine's Chambers. Image #R187.

Chapter 2: The Clone Wars

Republic HoloNet News image of the Grand Army of the Republic deploying from Coruscant.

Chapter 3: The Imperial Senate

Senators Mon Mothma and Bail Organa.

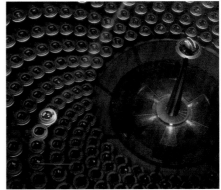

Image taken from the Imperial security feed of the Senate arena.

Senator Mon Mothma during the Ghorman Debates.

Chapter 4: The New Order

ISB Headquarters, Coruscant.

Colonel Wullf Yularen. Image published posthumously in his obituary.

Only existent image of an ISB briefing. Image secretly captured by covert rebel asset.

Chapter 5: Imperial Society

Imperial stormtroopers on patrol on Jedha. Image from Imperial Training Protocol 1756b.

"Join the Imperial Army" recruitment poster.

Chapter 6: Economy and Industry

Salvage yard on Ferrix. Image from Preox-Morlana records seized by the Empire.

Imperial Bureau of Standards, Coruscant.

Chapter 7: Expansion and Strategy

Forward Outpost B916, Mimban. Imperial Army records.

Mudtroopers in Mimbanese trenches. Imperial Army records.

Destroyed materiel on Mimban. Image from a military requisition bill to the Senate

Chapter 8: The Imperial Military

Imperial Star Destroyer profile from Kuat Drive Yards schematics.

Imperial stormtroopers in standard deployment gear, Imperial Army records.

TIE fighter training simulation pod at Skystrike Academy.

Imperial snowtroopers in combat on Hoth. Image presented to the Joint Chiefs.

Chapter 9: Key Imperial Figures

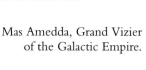

Supposedly an image of the Joint Chiefs aboard the Death Star. Image source is unknown.

Mas Amedda, Grand Vizier of the Galactic Empire.

Grand Moff Wilhuff Tarkin. Image taken aboard the Death Star.

Emperor Palpatine, Darth Vader and several dignitaries aboard the second Death Star. Image taken by Royal Guard security detail.

Chapter 10: The Inquisitorious

Inquisitors on Tatooine. Image reproduced by *Mos Eisley Chronicle* #27635.

An Inquisitor on Tatooine. When shown this image, General Leia Organa seemed to recognize this woman.

Chapter 11: Crime and Punishment

Preox-Morlana Enforcement Officers. Image from records seized by the Empire.

Prison complex on Narkina 5.

Courthouse on Niamos. Image from
Coalition of Progress files.

Imperial prison labor.
Image from surveillance
cameras at the Narkina 5
prison complex.

Imperial military
deployment in
response to riot on
Ferrix. Sourced
from ISB records.

Chapter 12: Prejudice and Discrimination

Wookiee-sized stun cuffs
and restraints.

Aldera, the capital city of Alderaan.
Personal image kept by Leia Organa.

Destruction of Jedha City. Test imagery
of Death Star firing, recorded by nearby
ISD *Dauntless*.

Indigenous inhabitants of Aldhani prior to
their relocation. Image held by the ISB.

Strip Mining on Kenari. Image taken
by Imperial authorities before an
"emergency evacuation."

As with many other tools used by the Empire, the fleet evolved from the one created and utilized by the Republic during the Clone Wars. Given that the Republic had effectively been a state that existed without a standing army or military, everything needed for the Clone Wars had to be constructed from the ground up, including new terminology. Kuat Drive Yards had been responsible for designing and building the *Venator*-class Star Destroyers that the Republic used widely throughout the conflict and as previously discussed, maintained these industrial contracts with the Empire. While the idea of a "Star Destroyer" is incredibly commonplace to us now, before the Clone Wars even the concept of such a vessel class would have seemed unthinkable to many. The architects of the Anaxes War College System had to create an entire classification structure to standardize ship types both for industrial designers and for fleet personnel to refer to in tactics and strategy.[1]

Though the Venator served the Republic's purposes well during the Clone Wars there were definite limitations to its design and image that made it unsuitable for the Empire. The dual bridge design of the ship, with one of the towers controlling starfighter operations and the other the ship's helm, allowed for a degree of contingency given the unpredictability of battle, but having them both within a single structure would have greatly improved efficiency and communication speed. Furthermore, its official name was not nearly foreboding enough for Imperial purposes, not to mention the ship had popularly been referred to as the "Jedi cruiser" during the conflict. Given the nature of Order 66 and the Great Jedi Purge, the Empire had no wish to continue utilizing tools associated with a hated enemy. Despite these perceived drawbacks, the Venator generally acquitted itself well in combat. The Battle of Coruscant toward the end of the war was one of the largest fleet battles in history, and the Venator proved to be a stable and flexible weapons platform in such an

---

[1] Anaxes War College Archives, Section: Anaxes War College System, File: Classifications and Criteria—Amendment Request #TAJ8265 "Star Destroyers"

encounter. Some of these benefits can be attributed to the theory behind its use. While the Separatist ships used, as with most of their military, a variety of droid controls for gunnery calculations, the Republic had taken an approach based far more on sentient recognition. Much of the Republic's gunnery doctrine was constructed by Commander Seoln Kaytee. Her approach emphasized the importance of gunnery teams coordinating leading shots and timed barrages to strip away enemy shield segments, as opposed to the droid approach, which could be more surgical but tended to misread subtle signs of impending shield or hull collapse that were more easily noticed by sentient observers. The Empire took this doctrine onboard—even while automating some of it—when creating their next generation of warship.[2]

The new *Imperator*-class Star Destroyer began to exit KDY facilities toward the very end of the Clone Wars. Noticeably larger and more heavily armed than the Venator, this new ship saw only very limited service before the war ended. But as far as the newly declared Empire was concerned, it represented the future. An immediate name change saw the Imperator re-christened as the *Imperial*-class Star Destroyer. Interestingly, surviving records from KDY are remarkably reticent on when they were first informed of the forthcoming name change, raising the question of whether they were already aware of what was about to happen on a galactic geopolitical level.[3] Regardless, these new *Imperial*-class Star Destroyers would soon become one of the most obvious public symbols of the Empire.

Alongside them, both the stormtroopers of the army and the TIE fighters of the starfighter corps would also become indelibly linked to the military power of the Empire. Both forces evolved out of the systems in place within the Republic during the Clone Wars. All military branches faced issues regarding the phasing out of clones and the need

[2] Imperial Archives, Section: Galactic Republic, File: Capital Ship Doctrines
[3] Kuat Archives, Section: *Imperator*-class Star Destroyer, File: Renaming Protocol*
*File Redacted

to recruit or conscript replacements. For the army virtually the entirety of the fighting infantry would need to be replaced with new personnel after Emperor Palpatine's introduction of the Imperial Stormtrooper Program.[4] While we now consider the Imperial stormtrooper to have effectively been ever-present within the ranks of the military and on thousands of different worlds within the Empire, there was a time when they were relatively scarce. Stormtroopers were initially intended to be the elite corps of the new Imperial military. However, training new recruits, as we will see, took a good deal of time. Ordinary civilians lacked the instincts and abilities that were included within clones from the point of their creation. For many years, while stormtroopers remained relatively few in number, the Empire made use of other forms of infantry, such as regular army troopers or specialized variants. This included the mudtroopers who slogged their way across Mimban.

Conflicts and crises had to escalate through numerous levels of the military's internal ranking criteria before they would be considered serious enough to justify stormtrooper deployment. Members of the ISB could request stormtroopers where necessary but—as seen in the Imperial forces deployed against an unfolding riot on the remote planet Ferrix—even as late as five years before the Battle of Yavin, there remained a divide between security forces, regular army troopers, and stormtroopers.[5] By the time of the Galactic Civil War, however, stormtroopers had been almost entirely incorporated as the primary infantry of the Empire and were regularly deployed to systems across the galaxy, while also manning countless starships of the Imperial Navy. Alongside them came the various TIE fighter variants of the Imperial Starfighter Corps manufactured by Sienar Fleet Systems. The main benefit of the TIE fighter was that it could be produced easily and in

[4] Imperial Archives, Section: Military Expansion, File: Stormtrooper Program
[5] Imperial Archives, Section: ISB, File: Ferrix occupation: ground forces contingent

huge numbers. In fairly short order the Empire was able to phase out the V-wings that had become a staple of the Republic.

However, across all branches of the Imperial military the need to recruit and train new personnel would require an expansion of training infrastructure and an overhaul of the ranking system. The Empire may have been planning a significant increase of its armed forces, but this would pose questions over who was to command it.

Command and Structure

The Imperial Navy borrowed some of the rank structures and systems of the Republic as a starting point but generally prized discipline and loyalty above ingenuity. The Empire's decision to retire the clone army did not just affect ground forces. While a number of larger capital ships within the "home fleet" that protected the Core Worlds during the conflict had a mix of clone and human personnel, these examples were not the norm. Many ships were still crewed almost entirely by clones, and they would all need to be replaced with suitably trained alternatives. Furthermore, the Empire initiated several purges of military figures who were deemed as either politically suspect or were alleged to be harboring Jedi sympathizers. Most Star Destroyers were generally commanded by an officer with the rank of captain or above. At the top of the new fleet structure was the rank of grand admiral, a position believed to be held by only twelve officers—some of whom will be discussed in a forthcoming chapter—who were generally recognized as having superior abilities in tactics or strategy.

By contrast, the highest rank of the Imperial Army was the position of grand general, which appears to have been created only after heavy petitioning by army officials to try and grant their service a similar measure of prestige as the navy.[6] The officers who were granted the

[6] Imperial Archives, Section: Imperial Army, File: Rank structure petitions

newly created position appeared to have been a mix between those with military prowess and those with political connections. Cassio Tagge is the most well-known figure to achieve the rank after he was granted control of the entirety of the Imperial military following the Battle of Yavin. Grand General Ormeddon was often deployed by either the military or Palpatine himself as a "fixer" for dealing with disruptions to Imperial supply lines.[7] However, on the other end of the spectrum were men like Grand General Levinous who was often mockingly referred to as a "holotable officer," given that he never left Coruscant or even appeared in the same sector as an ongoing military campaign. His rank seemed to be almost entirely attributable to his ties to Mas Amedda, as he was a major shareholder of the Champalan Imperial Mineral Extraction Initiative. That figures like Levinous were granted the most prestigious rank in the Imperial Army while others like General Maximilian Veers were not, is an indication of how counterproductive the decision-making process within the Imperial military could be.

By contrast to the army and the navy, the Imperial Starfighter Corps was viewed as being noticeably less prestigious but did have a greater romantic mystique attached to it. Furthermore, the process of reaching the rank of wing commander or general actually required a great deal more skill and ability than can definitively be said for the army or navy equivalents. Political connections could be very useful, but they would not provide someone with the skills to pilot a TIE fighter and survive combat operations in microgravity. As a result, it was a far more dangerous branch of the military for those who had political ambitions to consider.

Though the navy was by far the most prestigious aspect of the Imperial military, it was necessary for the three branches to work together both in specific combat operations and also more generally in

---

[7] Imperial Archives, Section: Imperial Army Personnel, File: Grand General Ormeddon—Service Record

matters of wider strategy. Outside of a few specific instances, such as following the Battle of Yavin when Grand General Tagge took full control, it is surprisingly difficult to place a single individual at the top of the Empire's military forces. Instead, strategy appears to have been directed by a committee featuring a variety of representatives from the Imperial military and relevant Imperial agencies such as the ISB. This group was collectively referred to as the Joint Chiefs of the Imperial Military and would liaise with both the supreme commander of the Imperial military—should one exist—and the senior figures of Imperial High Command (IHC), who had a general overview of ongoing operations and reported directly to Emperor Palpatine. The system was, as is traditional for the Empire, extremely complicated and convoluted. This was probably by design to prevent any single figure from seizing control of the Imperial military and threatening Palpatine with a coup.

Membership of the joint chiefs seems to have been a mix of permanent representatives and rotating high-ranking officers. One of the earliest meetings of what would shortly become the joint chiefs appears to have taken place at a summit regarding the future of the Imperial military organized by Grand Moff Tarkin on Eriadu within a year of the Empire's formation. In attendance were Tarkin himself, effectively acting as chair, Admiral Barton Coburn, Commander Orson Krennic, General Hurst Romodi, and Chief Scientist Royce Hemlock.[8] Tarkin seems to have been an ever-present leader of the joint chiefs up to his death at Yavin. Alongside him appears to be a veritable "who's who" of leading Imperial figures in the years before Yavin. From the military itself, Conan Motti, Cassio Tagge, Jhared Montferrat, Kendal Ozzel, and Tiaan Jerjerrod all appeared while serving at various ranks. COMPNOR appears to have been represented at least partially by Armand Isard, while the ISB appeared through Deputy Director Harus Ison and

[8] Imperial Archives, Section: Joint Chiefs of the Imperial Military, File: Summit on Eriadu Attendance List

Colonel Wullf Yularen. Vice Admirals Rancit and Screed represented the interests of naval Intelligence.[9]

As the Empire solidified its control over the galaxy, the figures who served on the joint chiefs held a tremendous amount of power and influence over Imperial military policy and strategy. Decisions regarding expansion and annexation, and orders to use military force against civilian targets, often originated there. This meant that the destruction of the Death Star, with many members of the joint chiefs aboard, was an absolute catastrophe for the Imperial military. Leading—and already noted—figures such as Tarkin, Motti, Yularen, and Romodi were all killed onboard the Death Star, along with others such as General Trech Molock, Officer Siward Cass, and Chief Moradmin Bast.[10] Coming so quickly after the disastrous Battle of Lothal, where much of the 7th Fleet had been lost along with Grand Admiral Thrawn, and the death of Commander Krennic at Scarif, the Empire suddenly found itself shorn of leading military figures and commanders.

It seems to be for this reason that Cassio Tagge, who had left the Death Star shortly before the Battle of Yavin, was promoted to grand general and supreme commander of the Imperial military, as there were precious few obvious alternatives left available, while the joint chiefs was restructured with surviving members and new additions. Many Star Destroyer captains who had seen combat, or displayed notable abilities against what had become the Rebel Alliance, found themselves promoted up several rungs of the Imperial Navy hierarchy in an attempt to plug gaps caused by the recent losses.[11] Though Tagge would not survive long enough to see it, the joint chiefs would be reconstructed using

[9] Imperial Archives, Section: Joint Chiefs of the Imperial Military, File: Membership Records
[10] Imperial Archives, Section: Joint Chiefs of the Imperial Military, File: Death Star Summit
[11] Imperial Archives, Section: Imperial Military, File: Post-Yavin Emergency Promotions

the likes of Admirals Ozzel and Montferrat, alongside Moff Jerjerrod, given that they all already understood the role. By the time of the Battle of Endor, Admirals Firmus Piett and Rae Sloane, Generals Veers and Falk, and Vice Admiral Corf Ferno had all appeared within the ranks of the joint chiefs.[12] However, while records for some of these meetings are lacking, there appear to have been fairly serious ideological and doctrinal differences between this latter wave of officers. Without the overarching leadership of a man like Tarkin, several factions appear to have grown up, particularly within the Imperial Navy, regarding the best way to fight the rebels. These specifically can be understood as the "Overwhelming Force" and "Surgical Strikes" lobbies. As we will see in a forthcoming chapter, the arguments between them would have huge impacts on how the Empire waged the Galactic Civil War.

While leading figures within the Imperial military would vie for control of strategy, beneath them lay the difficulties and problems of training huge numbers of soldiers, pilots, and officers for the various types of conflict facing the Empire.

Training and Specialization

Much of the ordinary Imperial military were trained at the huge academy that sprawled across the surface of Carida. There new recruits would be taught the basics in marksmanship and combat tactics for both planetary encounters and boarding actions. They would be instructed on the operation and maintenance of stormtrooper armor and weaponry. Most importantly, through a series of lectures and drills, they were taught absolute obedience to orders and the importance of complete loyalty to the Emperor.[13] It was, as ever, important for the

[12] Imperial Archives, Section: Joint Chiefs of the Imperial Military, File: Membership List* * Emergency Reconstruction
[13] Imperial Archives, Section: Carida Military Academy, File: Training Protocols—Intensive Loyalty Program

soldiers of the Empire to be as amenable to instructions as possible to ensure both their devotion and willingness to be complicit in Imperial crimes. Similar instructions were provided to recruits at naval and starfighter training institutions across the galaxy, in addition to their more specific technical lessons regarding the operation of capital ships or starfighters.

Ordinary training proved to be a fairly generic experience, but the options available for those who wished to enter the officer corps were much more varied. Although there were undoubtedly many highly capable military officers within the ranks of the Empire there were also plenty of limited, unimaginative, political appointees as well. The prime beneficiary of this imbalance of ability within the Imperial military hierarchy would eventually be the Rebel Alliance.[14] There are whole spheres of military history and analysis dedicated to defining what makes a good officer or leader, which I will not attempt to rewrite here. But what is clear from looking at the Imperial military is that while certain principles held universally true—specifically, demonstrable loyalty to the Emperor and the New Order—the actual details of training could differ notably depending on where training was undertaken.

There were numerous officer academy options available as the Empire developed in the years before Yavin, but the two most prestigious were generally considered to be the Royal Imperial Academy on Coruscant and the Eriadu Officer's Academy that had been reformed by Grand Moff Tarkin. While many of the Empire's new wave of officers were trained in these institutions, they were not necessarily home to the best instructors or recruits. Certainly, after Tarkin's death, the academies on Eriadu and Phelarion became home to a great number of the children of Coruscant's wealthy elite, who wanted the honor attached to

[14] Rebel Alliance Archives, Section: Military Intelligence, File: Shortcomings in the Imperial Training Program* *This file appears to have been authored by a Commander Lefix Rovey and goes into great detail regarding ways of exploiting gaps in Imperial military instruction.

Tarkin's memory and reputation but who displayed none of his military instincts. Instructors on Coruscant often possessed a mix of abilities and skills. For every instructor who had undergone recent military service and was able to apply relevant lessons, was another who thought that everything a recruit needed to know could be discerned from obscure Clone Wars battles or even the High Republic's struggles against the Nihil.[15]

Looking further afield it is possible to see that some of the most potentially useful innovations were taking place at lesser-known centers, closer to some of the combat zones that officers would actually serve in. The Imperial Military Academy on Corulag appears to have produced a number of well-regarded Imperial graduates. Much of this appears to be rooted in their tendency to pair training instructors based on their complementary abilities. For example, Commandant Angor was noted for his relevant and robust combat strategy classes, and often worked closely with Commandant Bedgar who instructed officer cadets on the intricacies of military administration.[16] Together the pair were able to produce well-rounded officers who could both act in combat and undertake the bureaucracy that was inherent in leadership positions. Meanwhile, amid the slightly outdated tendencies of some instructors at the Imperial Academy on Alsakan, Major Urkhaste's lessons on defensive tactics and deployments were apparently legendary.[17] Although tensions between able officers and political appointees would hobble the Empire for much of its lifespan, there were clearly commanders, as the Rebel Alliance can attest, who provided their enemies with plenty of problems on the battlefield.

[15] Imperial Archives, Section: Coruscant Royal Imperial Academy, File: Military History Curriculum—Class YE177
[16] Imperial Archives, Section: Corulag Imperial Military Academy, File: Combined Officer's Curriculum 27
[17] Imperial Archives, Section Alsakan Imperial Academy, File: Lecture Series—Principles and Precepts of Defensive Fortifications

Under the Republic, clone soldiers had been renowned for personalizing their armor and units with different symbols and slogans. Such individuality was heavily frowned upon within the ranks of the Imperial military. Despite that, it was not entirely unheard of for different squadrons or stormtrooper battalions to have their own traditions and approaches. The 209th Stormtrooper Division was stationed on Naboo for much of the Empire's existence. Because of their proximity to Palpatine's own secluded retreat on the world, many within the Imperial military viewed a position with the 209th to be a fast track into the Imperial Royal Guard. Whether that is actually true or not is difficult to ascertain, given the absence of reliable records relating to Palpatine's red-robed defenders. Nonetheless, a transfer to the 209th was often referred to as a "Crimson Order" and they were, as a result, highly prized.[18]

Despite examples like the above, members of the Imperial military, particularly its ground forces, have largely been regarded as faceless figures who perpetuated numerous war crimes and atrocities across myriad worlds. Because of this there can be a tendency to lump them all together. But doing so actually overlooks the level of specialization and variety that appeared within the military. For such a totalitarian state, the Empire's armed forces, at times, displayed an interesting level of adaptability regarding the various threats it faced and locations it anticipated having to use its might. While stormtroopers were the standard form of infantry, there were any number of slight variations on the theme, with "snowtroopers" and "sandtroopers," for example, undergoing different training and utilizing separate armor and equipment for operating in cold or desert climates respectively. To list all the types of stormtrooper variants here would take a considerable amount of time, but just the existence of such soldiers shows the considerations the Empire undertook in applying the right tools for the job. This is not

[18] Imperial Military Archives, Section: Military Deployments, File: 209th Stormtrooper Division

counting the more specialized units either, such as the infamous death troopers who were trained in additional combat skills and often accompanied senior military figures in the field.

Given that the Imperial military had no issue creating specializations like the ones described, it makes some of their other decisions far more perplexing. The sensors and controls within stormtrooper helmets provided various battlefield advantages to their wearers and in some cases the armor would turn a potentially deadly shot into just a seriously wounding one, but the Empire does not appear to have undertaken much in the way of research and development to improve the armor worn by its primary infantry. As we will see in a future chapter, this shortsightedness was replicated in starfighter and capital ship designs and advances, and it is unclear whether it stemmed from a callousness toward their own personnel, given the Empire's overwhelming advantage in numbers, or from various military branches fighting over the same sources of funding, and different commanding officers clashing over what research was deemed important enough to pursue.

The tensions within different branches of the Imperial military, divisions and disagreements over how best to utilize or deploy its forces, and the limitations of various parts of key military hardware would all combine to dramatically complicate its ability to wage war. Though the massed forces of the Empire's military were a truly terrifying entity capable of subjugating huge swathes of the galaxy, it was not an agile or particularly intuitive organization. Too often it found itself hobbled by the weaknesses and limitations of its leaders.

Chapter 9

Key Imperial Figures

As has already been established, Palpatine did not organize or orchestrate his Empire alone. In fact, quite the contrary. In many ways he appeared to have had very little interest or involvement with the day-to-day running of the regime at all. As such, we should reconsider much of what we once accepted about the nature of the Empire's inner workings. Palpatine undoubtedly made both his general and specific wishes known to his servants and underlings, but he would not be the one who either realized them or carried them out.

Therefore, to understand how the Empire functioned and who gave and carried out the orders that directed its military and political aspects, we must also understand the identities, personalities, and motives of those who operated below Palpatine. The Empire was both a political and a military institution, and Palpatine divested power to figures in both fields to ensure his Empire functioned in the ways he desired. Some of these figures may be familiar to the galaxy at large, while others may not. But given the nature of this study, and the additional materials that have become available to us recently and, more generally speaking, since the end of the Galactic Civil War, it is useful to reconsider some of the popularly held beliefs about them. It may be that what we had once accepted about Palpatine's political and military officials might now be flawed, or subject to revision in light of new information.

An indicative example of this is a figure who, while very well known to us now and highly feared during the Galactic Civil War, seemingly existed for much of the Imperial era in a strangely detached hierarchy—one that was confusing even to those who knew of him, and for a long time that was a very select group indeed.

The Emperor's Enforcer

For a figure who has only grown in infamy and public recognition, particularly after the much-publicized revelation regarding his relationship toward Leia Organa and Luke Skywalker, Darth Vader remains perhaps one of the great enigmas of Palpatine's Empire. Though he rose in prominence and military importance following the Battle of Yavin, there are significant periods of time where it is very difficult to ascertain exactly what role Vader played within the Imperial hierarchy, or what he was actually doing. Perhaps most intriguing of all is the fact that, for years after the Empire was founded, there is very little evidence to suggest that anyone outside of a handful of selected Imperial officials even knew of his existence at all.

Perhaps we should begin by re-establishing what we know of Darth Vader's actual background. The aforementioned exposure of recordings by Senator Ransolm Casterfo in the New Republic Senate regarding Darth Vader's true identity, and the fact that he was the father of Luke Skywalker and Leia Organa, has helped fill in substantial missing gaps both in Vader's background and also the biographies of his offspring.[1] Furthermore, documents recovered from the ongoing excavations of Exegol—combined with the work by Kitrin Braves—have provided additional insight into how the Jedi Knight Anakin Skywalker—a man that surviving HoloNet News coverage from the Clone Wars informs us was once nicknamed "the hero with no fear"—was transformed

[1] New Republic Senate Proceedings #HT57196

into a Sith Lord.[2] From these records it appears that Palpatine, acting in his role as Darth Sidious, had long been preparing Anakin Skywalker for the moment he would attempt to recruit him as his Sith apprentice. Abandoning his former name and identity, Darth Vader played a key role in the initial attack on the Jedi Temple that heralded the beginning of Order 66.[3]

However, something catastrophic appears to have happened to Vader between the end of the Clone Wars and his emergence within the new Galactic Empire. Gone was the young man who had adorned holo-net screens throughout the Clone Wars. In his place was the imposing, black-clad figure who would eventually strike fear in the hearts of many. It is unclear exactly what types of injuries Vader sustained that required him to don an armored suit that evidently also acted as a life support machine. Following the Battle of Endor, Luke Skywalker reported that Vader's skin appeared to bear the scars of serious burns, but when and where such an event happened, and the details for it, remain a mystery.[4] What we can tell from the Exegol records uncovered so far, however, is that the version of Darth Vader that Palpatine ended up with was not the one he had initially intended.[5]

What is also obvious, and of relevance to this study, is that there were clearly those alive at the end of the Clone Wars who were aware that Anakin Skywalker had become Darth Vader. What is additionally interesting and important is that, for years, those same people appear to have been operating under the belief that Vader was dead. His survival and ongoing existence within the Imperial hierarchy must have been one of Palpatine's most closely guarded secrets. This series of events may seem difficult for us to believe now, but there is evidence to support it.

---

[2] Republic HoloNet News Core Edition 15:01:03
[3] Exegol Excavation Project, Section: Sith Lords, Files: Darth Vader
[4] Rebel Alliance Archives, Section: Luke Skywalker, File: Debriefing after the Battle of Endor
[5] Exegol Excavation Project, Section: Sith Lords, Files: Darth Vader

Bail Organa—Leia's adoptive father—was clearly one of those who knew about the link between Anakin Skywalker and Darth Vader. The recording played by Casterfo proves this. However, it is equally clear from Leia's own reflections on an incident in her youth, when she was kidnapped by agents of the Inquisitorius, that it was she who informed her father of a man named Darth Vader, and not the other way round.[6] By this point, the Empire had existed for around nine years. Bail Organa had served in the Imperial Senate for the duration of that period and for years beforehand. Given his role in forming the Rebel Alliance he was likely one of the most well-informed and connected individuals regarding the realities of Imperial rule in the galaxy. He would, presumably, have been incredibly watchful for even the merest hint of anything related to Anakin Skywalker or his persona as Darth Vader, lest it threaten his adopted daughter's safety and security. And yet he did not know.

This fact alone should give us all pause for thought regarding the role Vader was playing in the Galactic Empire, certainly during its earliest years. If leading members of the Imperial Senate were oblivious to his existence (or survival in Bail Organa's case), then whatever his activities, they were clearly being carried out in secret. There are suggestions in the Exegol records that Palpatine tasked Vader with the collection of various items of Sith history or arcana, and perhaps this is how he spent his first years in service to the Emperor while building up his powers and strength.[7] As a forthcoming chapter will explore, Vader also maintained a strict control of the Inquisitorius and could, feasibly, have been considered merely a more powerful senior Inquisitor by those who were unaware as to his actual nature. Given the number of executions attributed to, or rumored to have been carried out by, Darth Vader it is also

---

[6] Senator Leia Organa, personal writings (sealed until after the fall of the Empire): *Growing up in the Alderaanian Court*
[7] Exegol Excavation Project, Section: Artifacts, Files: Location and collection

possible that for a time he existed within the Imperial system almost as the type of specter usually reserved for children's stories. A cautionary tale for those who served the Emperor about who they would face should they fail in their duties. Despite this there were definitely high-ranking officials, such as Mas Amedda, within the Empire who were aware of Darth Vader and his importance to the Emperor, even outside of traditional hierarchy.

Given Vader's reputation and the level of power and authority that is now ascribed to him, his relationship with Tarkin is particularly interesting. As early as a year into the Empire's reign, Tarkin—before his promotion to Grand Moff—and Vader cooperated in an attack on Mon Cala, meaning Tarkin may have been one of the first senior military officers to interact with this mysterious figure.[8] While in captivity on the Death Star, Princess Leia reported that Vader appeared to be very much subservient to Tarkin in the station's command structure. The phrase she recalled using at the time was that Tarkin was "holding Vader's leash."[9] The fact that she was able to speak obviously about Vader's reputation by this point indicates to us that he had clearly developed more of a public profile within the Senate, probably as a result of the emerging threat of the Rebel Alliance and Vader's role in dealing with it. It also suggests that Tarkin outranked Vader in the formal hierarchy and that the Sith's presence was as an overseer or representative of the Emperor, but one who bowed to Tarkin's jurisdiction.

This should make us wonder how exactly other military officers received this mystical representative of the Emperor. There was a certain level of arrogance within the upper echelons of the Imperial military, especially before the full onset of the Galactic Civil War. With a number of these officers having achieved their ranks courtesy of social class or private wealth, and with others having placed their faith

[8] Imperial Archives, Section: Military Operations, File: Invasion of Mon Cala
[9] Rebel Alliance Archives, Section: Leia Organa, File: Death Star Debriefing

in technology and Imperial science, Vader must have seemed an odd, anachronistic figure at times, with his Force abilities being linked to a period already being considered as ancient history. It is hard to imagine a man like Admiral Motti—who was renowned as being sneeringly dismissive of those he judged inferior—having much time for someone who did not appear within traditional rank structures and yet demanded obedience. The records for the summit of the Joint Chiefs of the Imperial Military on the Death Star before the destruction of Alderaan reference a "difference of strategic opinion" between Motti and Vader.[10] There is also an almost entirely redacted incident report within the Imperial Archives submitted by Admiral Motti immediately after that summit took place, presumably about something that happened to him during it.[11] While we can only speculate as to the nature of the disagreement between Vader and Motti, it must have been fascinating to watch.

The subsequent destruction of the Death Star and the termination of the likes of Tarkin and Motti had a wide-ranging impact on the Empire but also, seemingly, on Darth Vader. He might have been considered a leading contender for control of the military given the command vacuum. But whether he was being punished by the Emperor or was still kept out of the military sphere, it seems that he was placed subservient to Grand General Cassio Tagge for a time. Given our knowledge that, upon later being placed above the grand general in the rank structure, Vader immediately had him executed, it seems he was not as willing to work beneath Tagge as he had been with Tarkin.[12] Even when given command of his own Super Star Destroyer, the *Executor*, and the

[10] Imperial Archives, Section: Joint Chiefs of the Imperial Military, File: Death Star Summit
[11] Imperial Archives, Section: Joint Chiefs of the Imperial Military, File: Admiral Motti Incident Report
[12] Imperial Archives, Section: Imperial Military, File: Grand General Cassio Tagge—Unedited obituary

vaunted Death Squadron task force, it still does not appear clear exactly what Vader's position within the military sphere was.

There has been a tendency in the years since the Empire's fall to look at Vader's personal fleet and his presence at various battles and consider him to be the supreme commander of Imperial military forces. But I'm unsure if the evidence backs this assertion up. The joint chiefs still had oversight of strategy and command, though Vader was clearly in control of his own forces and could overrule military officers and requisition their forces if needed. As we will see from the Battle of Hoth, Vader appeared so uninterested in wider strategic aims that he would abandon existing plans simply to pursue his own agenda. As a result, his methods and approaches caused some serious issues within an Imperial military that struggled to find a unified way of dealing with Vader while also preserving their own forces, autonomy, and lives. It certainly was not an institution that prized imagination in its officers, and Darth Vader represented an anomaly to many who did not understand quite how he fit into the existing system or why the Emperor placed so much value upon him.

What we should take from this initial examination of Vader, which shall be further explored in future chapters, is that in many ways Vader appears to have been an anomaly. He either operated in secret, presumably following direct orders from Palpatine, or, when in military roles, he seemingly had full jurisdiction over whatever he required. At times Vader's fortunes appear to have fluctuated and he may have fallen from favor with Palpatine following the debacle at the Battle of Yavin. But he fiercely guarded his own status relative to those around him. In short: the Emperor could challenge or criticize Vader, but he would not allow others to do so. This appears to be the norm for relations between Sith masters and their apprentices. But it also means that while Vader had significant power and prestige, he was not running the Empire in any meaningful way. As a consequence, we should turn our attention to those who were.

Palpatine's Political Advisors

Although Palpatine was not invested in having hands-on control of the running of his Empire, it is important to acknowledge that it was his political skills and abilities that had helped place him on the throne. While he outsourced the majority of the political duties to assorted figureheads and underlings, we should wonder quite how involved Palpatine was with some of the tricks and traps that snared various senators. Those he charged with running the Empire had specific skills that suited their task, but it is hard to argue that any of them possessed Palpatine's rounded political instincts.

The most public face of Palpatine's political regime was Grand Vizier Mas Amedda. In the Galactic Republic, Amedda had been the senator for Champala before rising to the position of Speaker of the Senate to Chancellor Finis Valorum. It is unclear exactly at what point in his career that Amedda began collaborating with Palpatine or when he was informed of his Sith identity. Amedda was notably reticent on all these points during interrogations by New Republic officials.[13] What is obvious is that the knowledge that Palpatine was also Darth Sidious did not prevent Amedda from serving him diligently as his primary political figure. While Palpatine's appearances in the Senate became increasingly rare following the declaration of Empire, Mas Amedda remained a focal point and figurehead for the running of the state and was apparently content to be the public face for many of the Empire's activities. Within days of the Empire's birth, it was Mas Amedda who gave a speech on the steps of the former Jedi Temple—soon to be the Imperial Palace—where numerous lightsabers collected from murdered Jedi were burned in a furnace to celebrate how Palpatine had "saved" the galaxy "from their treachery."[14]

What is interesting about Mas Amedda is that the degree of power he came to wield in the Empire seems now to have been utterly

[13] New Republic Archives, Section: Imperial Prisoners, File: Mas Amedda
[14] Imperial Archives, Section: Grand Vizier Mas Amedda, File: Jedi Temple Speech

disproportionate to his actual abilities and status. It was also wildly divergent from overarching Imperial ideology regarding the apparent inferiority of non-human species. That one of the most powerful beings in the galaxy, one who effectively ran the political side of the Empire for Palpatine, was a non-human must have seemed almost heretical to some leading Imperial officials. For years Amedda served as Palpatine's eyes and ears in the Senate and his voice further afield. It was he who would summon military figures, Moffs, and sector governors to meet with the Emperor on Coruscant. It was he who announced new laws on the Senate floor and passed on information to either the ISB or COMPNOR regarding those with suspect loyalty. It was widely thought both through the military and political wings of the Empire that attracting Amedda's attention was the same as attracting the Emperor's. Meaning that, following Palpatine's death at Endor, Mas Amedda should, theoretically, have been the obvious political candidate to replace him. However, as will be discussed in greater detail in a forthcoming chapter, we know now that stripped of the Emperor's backing, Amedda had very little actual power or support at all and was reduced to a mere figurehead in possession of Coruscant before his eventual surrender. Part of this fall may well be traced back to his non-human roots. It does not seem implausible that the same Imperials who had tolerated him while Palpatine was alive now balked at taking orders from him once the Emperor was supposedly dead. Given what we know now about Palpatine's apparent plans on Exegol it also seems inconceivable that Mas Amedda was not aware of the construction project there, and highly likely he had witnessed it firsthand. That New Republic interrogators failed to get this information from him represents one of the most staggering intelligence failures of the post-war period.

Mas Amedda, for all of his proximity to power, did not run the political operations of the Empire alone. Palpatine had gathered other advisors, ministers, and aides around himself. Sly Moore had been Palpatine's chief of staff while he served as Supreme Chancellor of the Republic, and she maintained her proximity to him as an aide and advisor under the Empire. Given her Umbaran heritage, and the apparent anti-"alien" sentiments of much of the Imperial regime, it seems likely that she—like Mas Amedda—was providing Palpatine with notable service that guaranteed her position. It is also possible that she served as a spy for Palpatine within the upper echelons of Imperial society. There have been long-standing rumors that she possessed some sort of fledgling Force abilities that may have provided her with insight into the motives of others, but these remain unconfirmed. Surviving communication records from the Empire do show that she was the recipient of several dinner invitations on behalf of Mon Mothma's husband Perrin.[15] Given the political enmity between the two women, this seems like a bold move to bring them into closer proximity. Like many who served in the Empire's corridors of power, Moore's ultimate fate after the Galactic Civil War remains unclear, with New Republic intelligence following up on numerous rumors in the years since Endor without locating anything definitive.

Alongside Moore and Mas Amedda were the various figures who populated the Imperial Ruling Council. Men like Sate Pestage, Sim Aloo, and Janus Greejatus served upon this body, which seemingly organized and orchestrated the vast Imperial bureaucracy, serving as both a buffer and filter mechanism to manage the vast quantities of information produced by the Empire before important matters were sent to the Emperor. Given the nature of the Imperial state and the importance Palpatine placed on rivalry between different branches and personnel it should come as no surprise that the members of the ruling

---

[15] Imperial Archives, Section: Sly Moore, File: Communications from Perrin Fertha

council all apparently had an enduring dislike of each other.[16] The closer to Palpatine these men could stay, the more power and influence they were viewed to possess. As a result, on the incredibly rare occasions that Palpatine left Coruscant, some of these figures would inevitably accompany him. This was certainly the case with Palpatine's visit to the second Death Star at Endor, but this voyage ended up costing several of his advisors their lives when the battle station was destroyed shortly afterward.

Below the ruling council lay the various ministries and bureaus that actually carried out much of the work within the Empire. Palpatine identified the most important of these, for different reasons, as the Coalition for Progress—in charge of propaganda operations—and the Ministry of Antiquity, and subsequently entrusted them to some of his most skilled underlings. The Coalition for Progress was, for many years, run by Minister Pitina Mar-Mas Voor, with input from Pollux Hax. Pitina Mar-Mas Voor came to prominence initially through her marriage to a trusted Imperial senator who appears to have played a significant role in the ordering of Imperial genocides. Following his suicide, rumors in the Imperial court placed the blame for it on Pitina's influence, as she effectively inherited his position and wealth. The knowledge she already possessed regarding the realities of Imperial atrocities and the ability she had supposedly shown in falsifying the official documents of her late husband, meant she was well-placed to begin to restructure the Empire's public face. Pollux Hax was probably one of the most ideologically fanatical and morally bereft individuals operating within the Empire and there are few instances of Imperial

---

[16] Imperial archives appear to have been scrubbed clear of many details relating to the cadre of advisors who worked closely with the Emperor. It is not even entirely clear which ones were aboard the second Death Star when it was destroyed. However, the archives of the Rebel Alliance do contain a rundown of the principal figures based on Mon Mothma's recollections and experiences with them: Rebel Alliance Archives, Section: The Emperor's Court, File: Palpatine's Advisors.

brutality that he didn't attempt to justify as a necessity for the security of the state.

Between the pair of them, they crafted most of the official messages published and disseminated by the Empire and also effectively censored the content of the HoloNet News Network. The ability to control information across the Empire and even from system to system was invaluable in providing security for the fledgling Imperial state. However, as previously noted, Pitina Mar-Mas Voor struggled to reconcile the public image she was trying to build with the worst traits of Palpatine himself. She was eventually caught on an illicit holonet broadcast criticizing the way the Emperor conducted his own affairs, thereby undercutting the message of peaceful security that the Coalition for Progress was trying to produce and, as a result, was executed by Darth Vader. Without her knowledge and experience, however, the Empire struggled to set a cohesive tone during the latter part of the Galactic Civil War as it became increasingly clear that the conflict was not being won anywhere near as decisively as had initially been claimed.

The Ministry for Antiquity, by comparison, had very little input or activities relating to the actual management of the Empire. Instead, founded under the control of Minister Veris Hydan, it was concerned with the locating and collecting of various artifacts that were of importance to Emperor Palpatine himself. Hydan was a noted scholar of both the ancient Jedi and the Sith. Some of his works are still in circulation and regrettably have been referenced in my own writings on the topics. His knowledge and ability to both identify relevant ancient objects and discern their functions must have been invaluable to the Emperor. I have noted from my own studies the extent to which ancient sites mentioned within surviving literature of their time already appeared to have been pillaged by the time I arrived with my researcher colleagues. It seems likely that at least some of these excavations were undertaken by Veris Hydan. As we continue to excavate the stores on Exegol it may become possible to cross-reference the objects there with historical texts. The ministry continued to function even after Hydan's death on Lothal prior to the Battle of Yavin, before dissolving in the aftermath of the Battle of Endor.[17]

While the political aspects of the Empire remain difficult to fully unravel from the mix of rumor and paranoid obliqueness that seemed to characterize many of its key players, it was not the only realm in which individuals enacted the Emperor's will. Where some within the Imperial system would use words or propaganda posters to advance the Empire, others would prove to be much more direct.

Orchestrating the War Machine

Over the course of this chapter we have already examined various key political operators like Mas Amedda and Sly Moore alongside the enigmatic figure of Darth Vader. All of these individuals clearly held considerable power both individually and within the system that they operated. With Darth Vader his power both transcended the rigid Imperial structure and defied easy definitions. However, I would argue that a close examination of the Empire in the years leading up to Yavin indicate that none of them was as crucial or powerful as Grand Moff Tarkin. There is an argument to be made that, given the Emperor's absence from most aspects of the Imperial operation, it may well have been Tarkin more than anyone else who was actually organizing and running the most important aspects of the state. Having been born and raised on Eriadu, Tarkin served with distinction in the Republic's military during the Clone Wars.[18] It was here that he began to forge ties with Palpatine who, we can only presume, saw a kindred spirit in him. In service to the Empire, Tarkin had a myriad of different responsibilities and duties, which included oversight of the Death Star's construction

[17] Imperial Archives, Section: Ministry of Antiquities, File: Minister Veris Hydan
[18] Imperial Archives, Section: Grand Moff Wilhuff Tarkin, File: Life and Career

and, eventually, command of the battle station once he had wrested it from Director Orson Krennic.

Such was Tarkin's importance and influence on the Empire that it may be necessary to reconsider the existing evaluation of the Battle of Yavin. Aside from the rebels preventing the obliteration of their base, killing Tarkin might actually have been the most significant outcome of that battle, rather than the destruction of the Death Star. As would be shown in time, the Emperor could always order the construction of replacement—bigger and better—Death Stars. Palpatine could not create another Tarkin. Already throughout this study, it is clear the extent to which Tarkin's fingerprints are all over various Imperial expansion policies, military reorganizations, and targeted atrocities. There may never have been someone as useful and important to Palpatine as Tarkin across the entire duration of the Empire, and I include Darth Vader in that assessment. While Tarkin's doctrine regarding the importance of fear—to be discussed in a forthcoming chapter—may have proved counterproductive by invigorating the Rebel Alliance, there was no other figure within the military at the time who possessed his strategic vision. His death, and those of the other joint chiefs still onboard the Death Star, did not simply open a vacuum in the rank hierarchy, but also one of cohesive military strategy and direction. As a result, the senior officers of the Empire would fight it out among themselves for the best course of action while the Galactic Civil War was unfolding around them. Similarly, the fortunes of the ISB seemingly fluctuated in the years after the Battle of Yavin. Some of this can likely be apportioned to the loss of Colonel Wullf Yularen, who had served as an admiral in the Republic Navy during the Clone Wars but had also tied himself closely to Palpatine's new regime, and helped to institute many of the most brutal Imperial laws. His loss, and the impact on the ISB, were an additional difficulty for an Empire at war.

Tarkin's loss—and the deaths of Yularen and other officials onboard the Death Star—exacerbated the recent disappearance of Grand

Admiral Thrawn following his catastrophic defeat at Lothal. Thrawn himself is likely one of the most studied and biographized Imperial figures to have ever existed, so there is little to be gained in going over all his exploits here and risk boring the reader with information they are already heavily acquainted with.[19] But Thrawn embodied an emerging split within Imperial command regarding the best strategy to combat the Rebel Alliance. His lobbying for more advanced starfighters like his TIE defender project were at odds with those who believed deploying greater firepower, either through Star Destroyers or the Death Star, was the solution. While Thrawn appears to have been in possession of remarkable military abilities—and commanded considerable loyalty from his subordinates—he was not a man without shortcomings. Some of these will be discussed in relation to specific battles in a forthcoming chapter, but there has been plenty of evidence collected over the years to highlight his inability to cope with political intrigue.[20] Furthermore, for all of his perceived sophistication—apparently his analysis of artwork gave him insights into the tactics and tendencies of his opponents—he had no qualms in bombarding civilian targets on Lothal or causing significantly high casualties at Batonn and, as a result, should not be thought of as any more civilized in his approach to war than any other Imperial officer.[21]

Cassio Tagge, as has been mentioned before, was one of the primary beneficiaries of the Death Star's destruction—both through his elevation to grand general but also in that he had a window of opportunity to apply his belief that the future of the Imperial military should be embodied in the fleet rather than terror weapons. Whether his strategy

---

[19] However, I do strongly recommend the analysis of him by Gre Halhg in her groundbreaking study *Artistically Done: The Life and Times of Grand Admiral Thrawn*.

[20] Imperial Archives, Section: Grand Admiral Thrawn, File: Political Controversies

[21] See; Post-Imperial Lothal Archives, Section: Imperial Occupation, File: Grand Admiral Thrawn's bombardment, and; Batonn Archives, Section: Battle of Batonn, File: Casualty Estimates

would have had a long-term impact on waging the Galactic Civil War is unclear. Following an apparent attempt to seize control of the Super Star Destroyer *Executor* by a seemingly rogue Imperial scientist called Cylo, Tagge fell from the Emperor's favor.[22] He was subsequently replaced and then executed by Darth Vader.

Into this vacuum other military figures also rose to prominence. Kendal Ozzel served, for a time, as the admiral commanding Vader's Death Squadron before he too was executed for his failure just prior to the Battle of Hoth.[23] Captain Firmus Piett—seemingly both a more capable and less objectionable officer—was elevated to the rank of admiral in his place, a position he served in until his death aboard the *Executor* at Endor. General Maximilian Veers commanded the ground forces at Hoth and his tactics for the deployment of armored vehicles had a profound influence on the Imperial Army doctrine, despite the grievous injuries he suffered in that battle. Moff Tiaan Jerjerrod was tasked with overseeing the construction of the second Death Star above Endor. However, for all his administrative abilities, he was not another Tarkin, and lacked many of the deceased Grand Moff's abilities. As a future chapter will discuss, Jerjerrod's lack of Tarkin-like personality may have been one of the reasons behind his appointment.

Many of the figures mentioned in this chapter have appeared already in this study and will likely do so again in forthcoming sections. Given the Emperor's desire to centralize absolute power but delegate responsibility, it should be no surprise that the various aspects and areas of the Empire required different types of management and leadership. However, there is an issue in concluding that responsibility for the Empire and its crimes should be limited just to those in overt positions of power. Tarkin, for example, gave a great many orders that resulted in widespread death and destruction. But he did not commit the acts

---

[22] Imperial Archives, File: *Executor*, Section: Cylo Hijacking
[23] Imperial Archives, Section: Admiral Kendal Ozzel, File: Execution

themselves. The Empire was determined that both consent and culpability should be shared among those in Imperial uniform. If Tarkin had survived the Galactic Civil War he would undoubtedly have faced a New Republic tribunal. But we should not ignore the fact that much of the Empire's evil did not take place in the towers of Coruscant, just as the Rebel Alliance was more than just Princess Leia and Mon Mothma's leadership. We should not overlook the activities of those at the very grassroots of galactic society. Just as anyone could potentially be a hero in the Rebellion, so too could anyone be a monster in Palpatine's Empire.

Chapter 10

The Inquisitorius

The Galactic Empire had no shortage of enemies whether they were imagined, purposely stirred up to justify further oppression, or emerged organically in the face of Imperial tyranny. But certainly during the earliest years of the Galactic Empire, there was one enemy above all others that motivated the various military and political wings of the state into ongoing vigilance and action. Perhaps even more than the, largely manufactured, ongoing threat of "Separatists," the remnants of the Jedi Order provoked constant Imperial intervention.

The Imperial quest to both demonize the Jedi and complete their eradication had to walk a very careful line. The Empire needed to convince a population, which until relatively recently had been broadly supportive of the Jedi, that the Order was a treasonous front that needed to be purged. To achieve this the Jedi had to appear simultaneously as a grave threat to the Empire *and* something that should be forgotten about as quickly as possible. An enemy that was both real and present but also that should be consigned to Imperial history books. An enemy that was, somehow, both strong and weak at the same time. To accomplish their goal, the Empire would have to battle the remaining Jedi survivors not just on whatever worlds they had come to hide upon, but also within the minds and the homes of the general population.

Some scholars have previously wondered why the Empire devoted so many resources to completing the Great Jedi Purge, when there were more pressing military matters to attend to in the opening years of the Imperial regime.[1] This is a reasonable question to ask but I feel it misunderstands slightly the nature of the Emperor's thought process. Like the previously mentioned distinction between the Clone Wars objectives of the Republic and those of Palpatine, here too I believe a divergence should be recognized and understood. Palpatine was clearly content to allow the Imperial military to secure his Empire through whatever methods seemed the most appropriate. But his real concern, the enemy who he felt could threaten him specifically, were not the Wookiees on Kashyyyk or the Twi'leks on Ryloth. It was the Jedi. This fear must have only grown after Yoda's attack on the Emperor shortly after the new state had been proclaimed.[2] That he had come so close to death within hours of seemingly achieving his goals must have been very unsettling to Palpatine. If he, and his long-term plans for immortality, were to be kept safe and secure, then there could be no repeats.

As a result, we should not just consider the Inquisitors themselves to be the sole agents of eradication that Palpatine set against the Jedi. The very nature of the Great Jedi Purge required the weaponization of significant parts of both the Imperial military machine and Imperial society more broadly. For every specialist purge trooper that was recruited and trained, an Imperial citizen had to learn firstly to fear and hate the Jedi, and then to report any rumors about them. Blasters would not be enough to win this war. The hearts and minds of ordinary people would have to be utilized against the supposed "Jedi menace."

---

[1] See, for example, Ril Shiwer's *After Order 66: The Empire's War on the Jedi Order*
[2] Imperial Archives, Section: Emperor Palpatine, File: Jedi Assassination Attempts—Yoda

The Perpetual Enemy

We should not underestimate quite how dramatic a shift in public opinion was seemingly required as the Republic fell and transitioned into the Empire. While, as has been previously mentioned, popular support for the Jedi as an institution had begun to ebb as the war dragged on and they were viewed as being at least partially responsible for it, individual Jedi were still being heralded as heroes mere days before Order 66 was enacted and their "treason" exposed. The vast majority of the galaxy's population had never met a Jedi—and almost certainly never would— and did not really understand anything about their powers. However, similar things were true about their elected representatives in the Republic and Imperial Senates. Lack of contact with individuals of the wider group did not mean that they did not exist within wider public understanding or even within popular culture. The people of the Republic and then the Empire had understood that the Jedi existed and broadly what their supposed merits and purposes were. Not only would the established "facts" about the Jedi need to be undone, but all references to them would have to be rooted out of Imperial society.

The latter of these two goals was perhaps the most difficult. While COMPNOR and the ISB would be able to utilize various assets for the task, there was a huge amount of material that needed to be screened, censored, or banned. Agents of the Empire swiftly homed in on the easiest way of getting the wider message across. The Republic had long been teaching children, especially those in the Core Worlds, about both the structures and benefits of democracy and the beneficial role played by the Jedi Order. Such lessons were immediately removed from the curriculum and access to datafiles on the Order were blocked in most libraries.[3] This, however, was only a partial solution. Many children had grown up watching holodramas about heroic Jedi Knights. While these had obviously been banned immediately, they could not be so easily forgotten. Nor

[3] Imperial Archives, Section: COMPNOR, File: Censorship of Jedi material

could the pictures and toys that existed in many homes. As parents grappled with the dramatic fall of the Jedi, many younger children did not fully understand what had happened. Some still liked to play with fake lightsabers in the streets of various planets. This was unacceptable.

In the Recopi system, Governor Drelishav coordinated with the ISB and decided that the easiest way to deal with this trend was an implied threat of overt brutality toward any who appeared in the least bit sympathetic to the Jedi, no matter their age. In response, toy lightsabers, fake Jedi robes, and anything that could be construed as such were secretly destroyed in millions of homes. Stripped of the opportunity to play as Jedi and rapidly educated in schools as to the real dangers that the Order had posed, children began to forget about the Jedi altogether.

This approach, generally, was not going to work across the galaxy though. Some worlds had constructed statues of famous Jedi that had emerged from their population. There were streets and buildings named after them. These would inevitably be torn down and renamed but their absence could prompt memories of what had once existed in those spaces, and this did not serve Imperial purposes at all. Some local governors and Moffs took the decision to remake the rubble of destroyed statues into new ones of Emperor Palpatine. While this might seem to be an ostentatious policy, it did hint at a wider strategy that would prove effective. Taking their cue from Palpatine's retelling of the assassination attempt that had left him badly disfigured, the Empire looked to position the Jedi in direct opposition to a man who had eclipsed them in popularity at the end of the Clone Wars. The Jedi were not just an evil that threatened the wider peace and stability of the Imperial state—they had tried to kill Palpatine. This was a line that could be easily repeated and accepted. The absence of any Jedi to argue against it obviously helped, but there could be no easy way to reconcile the Jedi's assumed goodness with the evil they had inflicted upon the man who saved the galaxy from war.

Imperial propaganda messaging, at least as far as the Core Worlds were concerned, was clear that Palpatine *was* the Empire. The attack on him had been a grand betrayal of all. Palpatine's near-death experience had been personal not just to him, but to the galaxy as a whole. Mas Amedda's speech on the steps of the abandoned Jedi Temple while orchestrating a mass burning of lightsabers had set the political tone for the drive to paint the Jedi as villains, but more was still needed. To hammer this message home the Coalition for Progress created brand new holodramas like *The Last Betrayal*, where earnest Imperial officials and officers were attacked or undermined by shadowy robed figures. Others such as *Disorders of Magnitude* depicted crazed idealogues who claimed to possess "magic powers" and sought to indoctrinate children and twist them against their parents. Even long running shows like *Hyperspace Daze* were forced to dramatically rewrite their plots and characters to deal with the new reality.[4] Without explicitly identifying "the Jedi" as either the nefarious villains or the cause of various ills, the shared reference points still struck a mark with the audience. When placed alongside the more violent methods of forcing any aspect of Jedi culture underground, the reeducation of children, and the need to embrace Palpatine as a savior, it was not long before fond memories of the Jedi began to die out across the galaxy.

But while killing these memories was a necessary starting point in winning the "home front" of this war against the Jedi, it was not enough in isolation. Killing their memory was one thing. Now the Empire needed to kill the survivors and erase their legacy.

Brothers and Sisters

As much as the Emperor may have wished it, it was unrealistic to expect every Jedi to be killed during Order 66. While many hundreds or

---

[4] Imperial Archives, Section: COMPNOR, File: Coalition for Progress—Anti-Jedi Propaganda

thousands were killed by their own clone troopers, some defeated their former allies and escaped, while others existed out in the wilds of the galaxy without clone troopers in close proximity who could carry out the execution order. From the many Jedi who had existed only hours before, the last few survivors, barely a fraction of the total, escaped death and disappeared into the general population. They—and, according to one rebel cell, other surviving Force users like Maul—would have to be found and eliminated.[5] For this task Palpatine unleashed his own collection of Force-wielding assassins. They were the Inquisitors and they answered to Darth Vader.

As odd as it may seem now, there is reason to believe that the Inquisitors were actually more well-known and recognized by both civilians and Imperial officials than Darth Vader was. As we have already examined, Vader's existence was shrouded in secrecy for years, but this was not the case with the Inquisitorius. With their bespoke black armor and lightsabers that could be configured to various forms, the Inquisitors were certainly a distinctive group. Even for worlds that existed outside of Imperial borders, the dark-side warriors were infamous enough to provoke a reaction, as noted in surviving news reports from Tatooine about the arrival of Inquisitors to hunt for, and eventually kill, a Jedi hiding near Anchorhead ten years after the Empire's formation.[6]

Trying to piece together information about the Inquisitors so many years after the fall of the Empire is a challenge. Their apparent success in rooting out Jedi who had survived Order 66 is likely attributable partially to their skills and partly to their fearsome reputation. But these same aspects make it difficult to discern fact from fiction and we are forced to make several educated assumptions. Considering the

[5] Rebel Alliance Archives, Section: Resistance Cells, File:
Spectre—Inquisitors—Maul
[6] *Anchorhead Chronicle* #27635

precedent Palpatine himself set in recruiting apprentices who had once been Jedi, it seems safe to accept that a number of the Inquisitors were also drawn from the Jedi Order. Why exactly these individuals chose to abandon the Order and become tools of the Empire is unclear. Some perhaps had become disenchanted with the Jedi and the Republic as the Clone Wars had dragged on, though how Palpatine was able to identify those who held these beliefs and were willing to embrace the dark side of the Force is unknown. Other rumors persisted that captured Jedi were tortured and broken until they willingly acquiesced, though this too is impossible to verify. Likely apocryphal stories spread during the early years of the Empire about the Inquisitors, some suggesting they'd once been the Jedi Council, others that one of the Inquisitors had been a twin who murdered their Jedi sibling to prove their allegiance. While almost certainly untrue, these stories helped stir up fear and foreboding regarding the Inquisitorius and were likely permitted to spread because of it.

Similarly difficult to ascertain is exactly how many Inquisitors there were and where their base was. Current estimates, based on surviving records of Imperial officials interacting with the Inquisitorius suggest that there may have been over a dozen individuals of different species operating at any given time.[7] Of these individuals we really only know the codenames they went by rather than their real identities. Even these codenames were based around a strange system of numbers and relationships, with Inquisitors answering to titles like "Ninth Sister" or "Third Brother." Only the Grand Inquisitor, the Umbaran who stood at the top of their hierarchy, differed from this naming convention. As for their headquarters, for a time at least the Inquisitorius was based on Coruscant. However, following what appears to have been a chaotic chase through the city featuring several Inquisitors and Darth Vader that resulted in the death of Maklooq, an Imperial senator from

[7] Imperial Archives, Section: The Inquisitorius, File: Debriefing reports

Malastare, it seems they were ordered offworld.[8] Requisition records suggest, in response to the Coruscant incident, a fortress in the Mustafar system was purposely designed for them. Leia Organa's childhood recollections of having briefly been held as a prisoner on this base strongly suggest it was located on the ocean moon of Nur.[9] This is further supported by records showing that large amounts of equipment destined for this fortress needed to be waterproofed. However, given the number of transparisteel viewport panes that were constantly being requested as replacements, it's possible there may have been flaws in the overall design.[10] Furthermore, there had long been rumors and whispers about the Mustafar system as a "place the Jedi go to die" and there are also records that further suggest that Darth Vader had a presence within the system.[11]

The Inquisitorius also appears to have existed outside of any form of Senate oversight or controls from the political wing of the Empire. Two years after the Empire had been declared, the Barabel Senator Sanver was found to have secreted three fugitive Padawans in his private quarters.[12] Barabel culture had long revered the Jedi and it should be no surprise that this carried over into sheltering survivors from Order 66. When this deception was discovered, Sanver and the three Knights were swiftly executed by the Inquisitorius, but Palpatine seized on this event to detach all anti-Jedi operations from the political wing of his Empire.[13] This incident also helped sow further seeds of doubt regarding whether non-humans were truly loyal to the Empire at all. Freed from any of the political shackles of the Empire, the Inquisitorius was in a

---

[8] Imperial Archives, Section: The Inquisitorius, File: Coruscant Incident—Senator Maklooq
[9] Senator Leia Organa, personal writings (sealed until after the fall of the Empire): *Growing up in the Alderaanian Court*
[10] Imperial Archives, Section: The Inquisitorius, File: Requisitions
[11] Imperial Archives, Section: Darth Vader, File: Mustafar
[12] Imperial Archives, Section: The Inquisitorius, File: Senator Sanver
[13] Imperial Senate Proceedings, File 141.5

position to effectively act anywhere in the galaxy without requiring authorization from anyone other than Darth Vader and the Grand Inquisitor. In the earliest years of the Empire a program was initiated where civilians could submit tips and snippets of information on Jedi survivors in exchange for a variety of rewards.[14] These reports were directed straight to the Inquisitorius. It is debatable how many of the stories on the Core Worlds were ever based on anything real, but the existence of the program probably helped foster a sense of civic responsibility within the Imperial population. In the Mid and Outer Rim however, on systems where a Jedi could disappear into obscurity, the stories were likely given much more credibility.

The Spectre Cell of the Rebel Alliance, who were an extended part of Phoenix Squadron, noted numerous confrontations with Inquisitors both on Lothal and other worlds and were, in fact, ultimately responsible for the death of the Grand Inquisitor above Mustafar.[15] Other stories and reports on the Inquisitorius place them on numerous worlds and systems across the Mid and Outer Rim but it is very difficult trying to uncover which of these worlds, if any, were home to hidden Jedi. For every rumor or story of an Inquisitor fighting a Jedi in the backstreets of some abandoned remote world, there are also others suggesting they were ransacking museums, archives, and other similar locations on the hunt for Jedi antiquities. Whether they took these objects for themselves or delivered them to Darth Vader is unclear, but we can likely attribute the ongoing act of erasing the Jedi's heritage to the actions of the Inquisitors.

These warriors did not act alone in their operations either. Alongside the more generic stormtroopers that were being trained up within the Imperial military came variations that were specifically aimed at combating Jedi. The purge troopers were the most prominent among these.

---

[14] Imperial Archives, Section: The Inquisitorius, File: Informant Protocol
[15] Rebel Alliance Archives, Section: Resistance Cells, File: Spectre—Inquisitors

Often armed with electrostaffs or similar melee weapons, these soldiers were trained to counter recognized Jedi fighting styles, while wearing armor with some built-in resistance to lightsabers. It was unlikely that they would be capable of dealing with a Jedi at the peak of their powers, but many of the survivors of Order 66 had allowed their Force abilities to wane and atrophy during their time in hiding, which meant they were out of practice and ill-suited to dealing with such determined enemies. Even if the purge troopers were unable to dispatch a Jedi adversary, they would likely wear them out or injure them and allow for an Inquisitor to swoop in and deliver the killing blows.

When it comes to trying to identify specific Inquisitors and their actions, the Grand Inquisitor himself is an interesting case study as we know perhaps a little bit more about him than any of the others. The Spectres reported various confrontations with him where it became clear that he had deeply studied the fighting styles of different Jedi and could identify former Padawans based on their masters' quirks. He also utilized the mummified and embalmed corpse of Jedi Master Luminara Unduli to bait Jedi exiles into a rescue attempt that would cost them their lives. While it failed to work on the Spectres at Stygeon Prime it was implied to have worked numerous times in the past.[16] Former Jedi Kanan Jarrus, who led the Spectres and had abandoned his previous identity of Caleb Dume, once reported having experienced a form of Force vision that suggested the Grand Inquisitor may have once been one of the Temple Guards on Coruscant, though there is no way to assess such a thing for accuracy.[17] My own research has shown numerous references throughout the centuries to visions and dreams provoked by the Force and trying to gauge their real meaning was a fraught process even for the Jedi and an impossible one for the rest of us. What is

[16] Rebel Alliance Archives, Section: Resistance Cells, File: Spectre—Stygeon Prime
[17] Rebel Alliance Archives, Section: Resistance Cells, File: Spectre—Grand Inquisitor

most interesting about the Grand Inquisitor is the manner of his death. Following an attempt onboard Grand Moff Tarkin's Star Destroyer firstly to torture Kanan Jarrus into submission and then to kill his apprentice Ezra Bridger, the Grand Inquisitor was defeated in a duel by Jarrus. However, rather than surrender he voluntarily fell to his death after suggesting it was the less frightening option. Given that Darth Vader was shortly dispatched to Lothal to deal with the Jedi within this rebel cell, it seems likely he was referring to him. It also suggests the level of danger inherent within the ranks of the Inquisitorius and the price failure could bring.

We may never really know how many Jedi the Inquisitors hunted down in the early years of the Empire. The war waged against these survivors by the regime was so devoted and so thorough that even the few Jedi who escaped Imperial notice remain reluctant to step back out of the shadows. However, as the Jedi were driven nearly to the point of extinction, it appears that the Inquisitorius was also entering its final stages.

Beyond the Purge

Though it is impossible to accurately judge the number of Jedi who became victims of the Inquisitorius, it is nonetheless clear the Inquisitors were highly successful in their assigned task. Whatever the number of Jedi who survived Order 66, it is obvious that they were unable to mount anything approaching a combined or coordinated response to Palpatine's rule of the galaxy and much of this can probably be ascribed to the actions of Darth Vader and his agents. With the numbers of fugitive Jedi beginning to decrease and many of the trails for them going cold, it is possible that at this point the Inquisitors became victims of their own success.

Having been so active in the years before the Galactic Civil War, the Inquisitors appear to have disappeared entirely by the time of the Battle of Yavin. The reasons for this are unclear. It's possible that as their numbers thinned—the Spectres alone can account for the deaths of four separate Inquisitors—the Empire was unable to replace them because of the lack of viable Force users and the group died out. However, I feel that this is probably an unlikely eventual fate for the Inquisitors. The excavations on Exegol have found a few references to the group within what appear to be recollections by Palpatine where he states that they had become "obsolete."[18] If this is the case then it seems plausible that Palpatine had the remaining Inquisitors dealt with. For all their power I do not expect many of them could have survived an encounter with Darth Vader.

The reasons behind their potential obsolescence should be of interest to us. Certainly, the lack of viable Jedi targets limited their ongoing value to the Empire. Surviving Inquisitors with nothing to do were little more than a drain on Imperial resources, but those who could threaten Vader's own plans were likely to be viewed as a liability and swiftly dealt with. The disappearance of the Inquisitorius as an active component of the Empire has left us with many more questions than answers. Given that the exact number of Inquisitors is still undetermined, we cannot be sure if any survived the fall of the Empire. However, security recordings of an encounter at the Santhe Shipyards on Corellia attended by General Hera Syndulla of the New Republic and Ahsoka Tano—previously a Jedi herself—show an individual who appeared to be an Inquisitor, despite it taking place some years after the end of the Galactic Civil War.[19]

As the Inquisitors and their actions faded from memory, there was a subset within the New Republic who already cherished Imperial uniforms and artifacts, a group—as will be discussed in detail in a future chapter—that came to vaguely romanticize the Inquisitorius. The armor

[18] Exegol Excavation Project, Section: Warriors of the Dark Side, Files: Inquisitorius* *Information retrieved from the Arcane Library
[19] New Republic Archives, Section: Corellia, File: Morgan Elspeth Conspiracy

and mystique of these Force users conjured up images of high stakes duels between them and surviving Jedi. I find these ideas problematic to say the least. Firstly because of what we already know about the Inquisitors and their dark side tendencies. But also because it overlooks a horrifying aspect of their mission for the Empire. As Jedi numbers dwindled, it would appear that many excursions and operations carried out by the Inquisitors were not devoted to exchanging lightsaber blows with renegade Jedi. Instead, they traveled to distant worlds and abducted children. The Spectres reported this happening on the planet Takobo, and there are reports and rumors of the same elsewhere.[20] What happened to those children taken and delivered to either Vader or the Emperor is unknown. Presumably they displayed some innate Force talents that made them desirable, but their ultimate fate remains a mystery. But we should recall those stories every time we hear the Inquisitorius being discussed, and we should remember that these were individuals twisted by the dark side of the Force who often, under the cover of night, murdered parents and stole away innocent children. If the Inquisitorius truly are gone, then we are all the better for it.

[20] Rebel Alliance Archives, Section: Resistance Cells, File: Spectre—Takobo

Chapter 11

Crime and Punishment

O fficials and leaders of the Empire put a great deal of weight and emphasis on the "order" it supposedly brought to the galaxy. Speaking in the aftermath of the Ghorman Massacre—which will be discussed in a forthcoming chapter—Pollux Hax, who could always be relied upon to deliver a quote justifying the unjustifiable, declared that "acceptance of Imperial law is the only way in which ordinary citizens can protect themselves from the dangers and violence of disorder."[1] In many ways Hax was correct in his assertion. For the various laws and legal systems created by the Empire were never designed or intended to be used in the service of justice. Instead, they were, like so many other tools, a weapon to be used against those who failed to comply with the required levels of obedience demanded by Imperial authorities.

By taking this as a starting point it becomes increasingly clear the extent to which the laws of the Empire existed not to protect its citizenry but rather to define the extent to which ordinary people had to accept Imperial rule. What is also interesting to note now, is the degree to which large swathes of citizens and civilians seemed to understand, on varying levels, the huge contradictions inherent within the Imperial legal system and the ways in which laws were applied brutally to some

---

[1] Pollux Hax, interview with Imperial HoloVision Broadcast #578841

and not at all to others. Accepting this situation allowed many civilians to live in relative stability. When you understood that the laws were not designed to bring about restitution, but instead would be applied in specific circumstances, then a strange form of predictability could be assigned to the Empire's justice system. By living lives that made allowance for the Empire's controlled hypocrisy, people could convince themselves that they were safe from it.

However, in reality, there was no stability, safety, or security to be found within Imperial laws. The Empire repeatedly changed the nature and reach of their own legal system to suit whatever circumstances, or threats, faced them. Those citizens who remained untouched were themselves only ever a short distance removed from finding themselves in breach of a law that had not previously existed. On Corellia there used to be a widespread ironic joke that "when crossing the major transport lanes, the direction you looked in first defined which laws you'd broken." The point of this comment was to explain that regardless of what you did you were always in breach of Imperial law. The seriousness of your possible sentence depended on little more than circumstance and Imperial capriciousness. When the Empire instituted its chain codes initiative where access to a wealth of public services required each individual to submit their biometric information to the Imperial state, many went along with it not realizing that the Empire was cataloguing its own population in order to track—among other things—their movements, their background, and their everyday activities. Many believed that such information was safe in the hands of their new benevolent government, but some would come to regret that when it was used against them in various trumped-up legal charges.

What further undercut the Empire's visage as a state determined to uphold the just rule of law, was the extent to which it was utterly riddled with corruption and close links to various serious underground crime syndicates. It might be assumed that the Empire would be unwilling to share control of the galaxy with the various underworld powers, and in some circumstances this was true. But the Empire was a truly corrupt entity from Palpatine all the way down. Such systems require partners and contacts who will do things in the shadows that Imperial officials are reluctant to do in daylight. This association was predicated on the exchange of power, survival, and money. Bribery was rife in the Empire, and many things were for sale for the right number of credits. Furthermore, individual Imperial officials would happily guarantee their own lives by supplying information when approached by representatives of Black Sun or the Pyke Syndicate. Similarly, those same criminal organizations would happily pay to turn the gaze of Imperial officers in other directions. This too had a certain stable predictability to it. The laws of the Empire were always in force and ready to be applied except for the times when they weren't. Being able to tell the difference was the key to living or dying.

Hierarchies of Control

As with many aspects of the Empire, there was a tiered system of legal restrictions and frameworks that applied across the galaxy. Virtually every populated system had its own laws, rules, and customs that existed to protect or dictate acceptable behaviors and norms within their own individual societies. These could differ dramatically from world to world and species to species and, by and large, as long as they did not directly impact or infringe on wider Imperial intentions, they were largely allowed to exist unchallenged. Above them, however, lay the more formalized and wide-ranging structure of Imperial law. This legislation was generally accepted to overrule any contradictory localized laws, though in the years following the Clone Wars when the Empire was solidifying its power, this was not always enforced.

As the Republic had previously noticed, governing the galaxy is not easy, particularly with such a disparate spread of worlds, sentient beings, and legal frameworks. The Empire needed to create a system that made clear which activities were overtly illegal and would not be tolerated, while also enforcing those laws in a way that didn't tie up the Imperial military and delay its expansion campaigns. The solution to this issue was, as is often the case with the Empire, an appropriate blend of ingenuity and cynicism. Effectively they subcontracted the work of enforcing laws to a variety of industrial and private security forces. These organizations would then do the active work of policing systems and sectors, freeing up Imperial soldiers who could then be used elsewhere.

While, by its nature, the Empire was never particularly keen on sharing power with other organizations there was a clear logic to allowing others to enforce Imperial laws. Firstly, as mentioned above, it solved a significant personnel crisis for them, particularly while phasing out the old clone soldiers in favor of the stormtroopers who would be trained in their place. But policing the galaxy did not just require active participants on the ground of each planet. A whole bureaucracy had to be created around it. As we have already seen, the Empire was not averse to bureaucracy and often attempted to hide some of its worst crimes and excesses between the lines of complicated regulatory frameworks, but there was a limit to what the fledgling system could sustain. By placing the responsibility on subsidiary organizations, the Empire forced them to be responsible for the administration, with only necessary reports making their way up to the Imperial level.

The bigger benefit, and the one that made the arrangement most appealing to the Empire, was the way in which it would divert the direction of resistance. It is rare even in the most pacifist communities, such as the Alderaanians or the Caamasi, that the enforcement of laws is universally accepted. Given that Imperial laws were not designed to safeguard the interests of the citizenry but rather secure the power of the state, there was little benevolence in evidence. As Imperial laws began to bite on various worlds, particularly outside of the Core, it was inevitable that people would begin to strain against them. But, because of the design of the system, they were not actively pushing back against the Empire itself but rather against the intermediary security forces who actually presided over them. By acting as a buffer between the population and the Empire, groups such as Preox-Morlana of the Corporate Authority or even CorSec from Corellia to a lesser extent, ensured that no damage would be done to the state by those who fought back against the enforcement of law. Of additional benefit, many of these private security forces were closely tied to Imperial industrial concerns, so were even more motivated to help ensure the smooth running of the wider infrastructure.

This balance between those being ruled and those enforcing the rules could be a fragile one. What helped maintain it was the shadow of further Imperial intervention. This was a fear not only felt by the population of these worlds but also by the organizations who ruled them. In many ways, as Grand Moff Tarkin would adapt with his infamous doctrine, this fear of Imperial involvement was far more effective than Imperial forces themselves could hope to be. Imperial training may have prepared stormtroopers for many things, but they were little more than a blunt instrument designed for subjugation rather than a more nuanced governing force. The fear of having them deployed to a system, tipping it from being governed into being occupied, could cool even the hottest of tempers among those who found themselves on the wrong end of shifting Imperial laws. Furthermore, the security forces themselves were equally keen to avoid active Imperial scrutiny or involvement in their affairs. Should the Empire see fit to take over day-to-day running of a system or sector, the knock-on effect could be severe. At the very least the budgets for the previous security forces would be slashed and their power substantially curtailed. If the failure to maintain order was viewed as being particularly egregious then brutal punishments or imprisonment for those officials responsible could follow. For years rumors circulated among some of these Imperial subsidiaries of a terrifying Imperial enforcer who could be drafted in during serious crises and who was renowned for not tolerating failure. Based on my wider research I have strong suspicions as to who that figure may have been.

It can perhaps then be said that the enforcement of law within the Empire operated on a structure of continual escalation that acted as both deterrent and violent response. Local planetary security forces sat at the bottom of this hierarchy and, as previously mentioned, generally dealt with matters deemed beneath the attention of any enforcement groups affiliated with the Empire. However, should serious crimes against Imperial law be committed then the larger security forces would become involved. These groups would often be incredibly overzealous in their policing, out of concern that the Empire would intervene and relieve them of duty, meaning that they could—in their own ways—be more brutal in the short term than the Empire would have been itself. However, not all criminal—or indeed rebellious—activity was halted at this point, and it becomes instructive to look at the likes of Lothal or Ferrix as test cases of how the Imperial system then began to function. If the situation on an Imperial planet became particularly unruly or criminal, it was only a matter of time before it drew the attention of the ISB. This was often the first step on the road to Imperial forces taking control of a planet to enforce the law themselves.

On Ferrix this came after what appears to have been a disastrous Preox-Morlana operation to capture the future rebel agent Cassian Andor, as well as a rebel-affiliated figure known to the Empire only as "Axis."[2] So badly did this raid go that those in charge were either relieved of duty or arrested, and the planet was fully absorbed and occupied by Imperial forces. As the threat of a possible rebel uprising grew over time, additional levels of the security hierarchy were triggered and, eventually, stormtroopers and other military personnel were deployed across the planet shortly before it was the site of a riot. On Lothal the opening stages of Imperial escalation were very similar. The ISB agent Alexsandr

[2] Rebel Alliance Archives, Section: Cassian Andor, File: Ferrix #GN12

Kallus was tasked with dealing with an active rebellious presence on the planet that had been eluding local security forces. However, upon discovering the nature of the rebels, Kallus triggered a different branch of the Imperial response network.[3] Once it was established that a Jedi was among the fugitives, word was swiftly sent to the Inquisitorius and the Grand Inquisitor himself was dispatched to deal with the problem. From here the escalation intensified with additional Imperial forces— both army and navy—being re-routed to the system before it was eventually brought to Grand Moff Tarkin's attention and then subsequently Darth Vader's. It was only when the threat of this rebel group was perceived to have been eliminated, that Lothal moved sideways to being under military control and Grand Admiral Thrawn began his TIE defender operation there.

In this sense the Imperial legal response was surprisingly flexible. As long as they did not have to react to serious situations all across the galaxy, they could leave designated forces in charge of systems and sectors and only dispatch additional military resources to worlds if they began to show serious warning signs via the ISB. It also provided the stability mentioned at the beginning of this chapter for the local populations who had a general understanding of what could happen should severe lawlessness break out. What is also interesting when considering the ways in which Imperial forces ruled over the galaxy was the extent to which it was based on the expectation or appearance of strength rather than the reality of it. The galaxy is a big place, and the Empire was often spread thinly across many worlds. Garrisons would sometimes run at reduced strength or prisons would be manned by the bare minimum number of guards. The Empire would mask any shortfalls behind the widely held belief that the state was possessed of plentiful resources. The combined beliefs within the population that the Empire

[3] Rebel Alliance Archives, Section: Defections & Debriefings, File: Alexsandr Kallus #PF23

was as strong as appearances suggested and that following the rules would keep them safe regardless, allowed Imperial rule to solidify through a peculiar form of consent. This was complicated, however, by the Imperial tendency to change both the law and its assigned punishment.

The Rules of Law

The Galactic Empire operated a classification system to define its own laws and the severity of the crime involved with breaking them. As previously mentioned, these laws would override any local legislation and customs to ensure that Imperial interests were always primary. It would also mean that, even in instances such as murder, if the crime was not perpetrated against, for example, an Imperial official, it might not necessarily attract the Empire's attention. Prisons on many planets were filled with their own domestic criminals, including murderers, who had not actively committed a crime against the Empire and so were tried and incarcerated by local judges. This is not to say that Imperial law enforcement would turn a blind eye to all crimes. It was never easy to tell what the Empire would care about in any given situation, just that breaking a local law would not necessarily see someone doing a long stint on Garen IV or similar prison worlds.

The Imperial Legal Code was essentially composed of five major forms of illegal activity—albeit with many subsections and clarifications.[4] It would be wrong to say that a Class Five infraction, at the bottom of the scale, was not a serious crime. As mentioned above, the Empire did not tolerate lawbreaking and, for example, vandalizing or putting graffiti on Imperial property could quite easily land the perpetrator a lengthy prison sentence. Some Imperial Moffs or planetary governors could be intensely draconian in how they interpreted a crime

[4] Imperial Archives, Section: Legislation, File: Imperial Penal Code

against the Empire. Following a speeder crash on Ringo Vinda, Governor Harkell sentenced the perpetrators to six months imprisonment for careless driving plus an additional ten years because the crash had damaged a bust of Emperor Palpatine, which he considered to be a serious crime against the Empire.[5] This helps us understand a little bit about how loosely defined an Imperial crime could be.

However, at the top of the legal code sat the Class One infractions that were almost guaranteed to provoke harsh responses, sentencing and, at times, wider repercussions. Coming under the heading of a Class One offense were things such as fomenting rebellion, active sedition, assassination attempts against senior Imperials, or active piracy. The last of these might seem like a slightly odd inclusion particularly given, as we will shortly see, the fact that the Empire was not above working with the type of criminal enterprises that also undertook piracy. But unsupervised and unapproved piracy would often take place in Imperial shipping lanes, as these were the routes with the highest chance of landing a suitable ship and for that vessel to be carrying a cargo worth stealing. Therefore, stealing from the Empire, particularly when they were constructing the Death Star and needed every resource they could gather, was a hugely serious matter. Stealing from the Empire was bad enough, but impacting its ability to build weapons and wage war even more so.

The Imperial response to a serious instance of lawlessness could be swift and brutal, but also highly instructive in helping us understand what they considered to be criminal activity and also how flexible some of their laws were for redefinition. Following the theft of a large amount of Imperial payroll on Aldhani, the event triggered many of the most serious flags within the aforementioned Imperial security hierarchy. The response to the theft was immediately organized by the ISB, who

[5] Ringo Vinda Archives, Section: Criminal Sentencing, File: Speeder accident #5744182

gained significant new powers of "surveillance, search, and seizure."[6] Furthermore, the Imperial reaction was not limited just to the scene of the crime. New laws were instituted, or existing ones edited, to place limits on indigenous rituals and levy significant new taxes on any world that was considered to be the home of partisans. This last aspect was left open to definition by any Imperial governors or Moffs. Additionally, it was decided that any crimes committed "with even indirect effect on the Empire" would now be recategorized as a Class One offense as part of the Public Order Resentencing Directive (PORD).[7] The PORD allowed these laws to be applied retroactively. There were many inmates of Imperial facilities who quickly discovered that their sentences had been extended because the crime they had been convicted for had been recategorized.

There is much that we can take from this example. Firstly, that the Empire did not feel particularly inclined to leave its own laws and legal statutes in a fixed form, when they could instead be adapted and applied effectively in whatever manner suited their purposes. To reiterate: the laws existed to serve the Empire, not protect the citizenry. Furthermore, given that we now know that the Aldhani raid was not some simple bank heist, but was part of the fledgling rebel movement, it is very interesting that the Empire viewed it as a criminal act of theft rather than one of insurrection. While the Rebel Alliance and its members were obviously in breach of any number of Imperial laws, for the Empire to treat them simply as "criminals" suggests they were very slow in understanding exactly what was happening in the galaxy they were trying to rule. As we will see in later chapters, though the early years of the Rebel Alliance were fraught with dangers and difficulties, it can also be said that the Empire's lack of recognition of the growing threat greatly

[6] Imperial Archives, Section: Imperial Security Bureau, File: Aldhani Response Briefing
[7] Imperial Archives, Section: Emergency Legislation, File: PORD

benefited the rebel cause. Furthermore, incarcerating rebels was risky in itself. Placing effective recruiters alongside prisoners who had no love for the Empire may have resulted in any number of inmates drifting toward the fledgling uprising. However, as far as the prison system was concerned, it is also apparent that the Empire was—at best—apathetic to the idea of releasing its convicts.

The Benefits of Crime

When the Republic fell to the Empire, the new state found itself in control of various types of prisons. It would also quickly begin to make plans for the construction of its own more bespoke facilities. Some of the larger supermax facilities, such as Selnesh, were home to a mix of serious criminals, murderers, and those who had been convicted of Class One offenses. Many of these inmates were highly dangerous—with the most serious individuals either kept in permanent isolation or scheduled for execution—and, as such, not really suited to what the Empire had in mind for its prison population. Instead, the Empire turned their eyes to more mid-level prisoners. Those who had been convicted for lengthy enough sentences to learn specific tasks, but who still had the hope of one day being released, pending their acceptance and obeyance of instructions. The Empire had long recognized the benefits of weaponizing an individual's hope against them.

Across its prison system, the Empire put inmates to work. Cassian Andor reported, having escaped from the facility on Narkina 5, that he had spent weeks—and other inmates years—building some form of mechanical joint system for the Empire, though it is unclear what these devices were ever used for.[8] The Empire, through representatives within the prisoner population itself, effectively challenged the inmates to ongoing competitions regarding their industrial outputs. The winners

[8] Rebel Alliance Archives, Section: Cassian Andor, File: Narkina 5 #2

would receive flavored food substances. The losers would undergo violent electric shock punishments. On Delrian, inmates were charged with installing electronic controls within durasteel cylinders which, when we now look at surviving records, were then sent to a different prison at Oovo 4 and used to restrain prisoners there.[9] On Jubilar the prisoners made the "toes" for AT-ST feet.[10] The Empire had an entirely captive labor force that existed outside of traditional labor camps, such as Wobani, which they could force to undertake any work they desired with little fear of resistance as long as the prisoners believed they were working toward their freedom. Many of them were, of course, deceived. The eventual prisoner riot on Narkina 5 and resultant escape attempts were motivated by the realization that nobody from that prison would ever be released. We can only guess how many other prisons and black sites across the Empire also operated under such rules.

Beyond the benefits of having an industrial aspect to their prison system, the Empire also managed to work alongside a variety of crime syndicates or enterprises to ensure profits could be made from illegal activities. Spice had legitimate medicinal properties but was also highly addictive and the use of it by civilians was deemed illegal within the Empire. However, that did not stop them from first excavating the substance for Imperial requirements from the infamous Kessel mines and then striking a deal with the Pyke Syndicate, for a substantial cut of the profits from black market sales, before later assuming full control of the output themselves.[11] Similarly, the galaxy's underworld often found ways to co-exist and profit from contracts with the Empire.[12] Darth Vader seemingly made liberal use of bounty hunters and other mercenaries

---

[9] Oovo 4 Prison—Recovered Archives, Section: Supplies, File: Delrian Cuffs
[10] Jubilar Prison Archives, Section: Industrial Output, File: Carida Contract #19
[11] Imperial Archives, Section: Kessel, File: Pyke Syndicate* *Information partially recovered from the databanks of the ISD *Deliberator* near the Kessel system in 6 ABY.
[12] Imperial Archives, Section: ISB, File: Bounty Hunters* *Elements within this file appear to have been created by Agent Andressa Divo.

over the years, and both the Hutt Cartel and Black Sun appeared to find ways to be useful enough to avoid being crushed by Imperial forces. This was not universally the case. There seem to have been plenty of smaller syndicates or gangs, such as the Bedlam Raiders who were in conflict with the Empire in the Outer Rim around a decade before the Battle of Yavin. The Empire would only tolerate—or turn a blind eye to—those organizations that did not directly threaten or hinder its own interests.

As the galaxy began to move closer to full-blown war, the line between useful ally and unnecessary enemy must have seemed like a very fine one for those who lived on the edge of the Empire's laws. Because, as we shall see, when Imperial officials decided groups or populations—no matter how large—were no longer required or welcome, they had no qualms about committing unspeakable acts.

Chapter 12

Prejudice and Discrimination

The ways in which the Galactic Empire sought to divide up the residents of the galaxy into different groups and categories—even as it oppressed them all—are both complicated and, from a certain point of view, incredibly simple. As mentioned in the previous chapter, the Imperial legal system did not exist to apply justice to everyone, but rather was flexible enough to give the Empire the space it required to act in whichever ways it chose.

Even before the rise of the Galactic Empire, the galaxy was not some utopian vision of equality and liberation, despite the best efforts and intentions of those who strove for change within a system seemingly designed to create inertia. Inhabitants of the Core Worlds had always looked down on those from the Outer Rim. Depending on circumstances, droids were treated as companions, possessions, or annoyances. Tensions had long existed between humans and those they deemed to be "aliens," and the Clone Wars, with the Separatist forces dominated by non-humans, only exacerbated this. Even within the many human worlds and populations that were spread across the galaxy there existed tensions that could be identified and exploited. Differences in heritage, class, territory, creed, and wealth could all be used to drive wedges between populations that should, on the surface, have been united. It is important to mention all these aspects now, in order to make a point that has also been raised in previous chapters: the Empire did not invent the prejudices it manipulated. It did not pit humans and non-humans against each other for the very first time. Neither did it create the issues between various groups of humans on specific worlds across the galaxy. It finely honed some and expanded upon others, but it did so with material and emotions that already existed within the population. This is partly what made it such an easy sell, particularly to humans on Core Worlds. The Empire did not need to convince many people to embrace its ideology, it just had to validate the prejudices they already held and grant them permission to act on them.

The outcome of the Empire's prejudices, its quest to drive divisions between different groups, to carve up the galaxy along lines of its own choosing, and to finally commit some of the most horrendous massacres and genocides imaginable will be discussed in the next chapter. But to fully recognize the end point of this process we must also recognize that Imperial crimes did not begin with Alderaan or a thousand other atrocities. There was a process that built over years of Imperial rule to reach those moments. If we cannot learn how to see those earliest moves when they play out again then we doom ourselves and the galaxy to relive their horrors.

To understand the ways in which the Empire decided who should be discriminated against, we must also understand who it believed to be superior. The Empire was based upon concepts of supremacy—though some of them may not have been quite what its citizens expected or understood. It is difficult to assign much in the way of ideology to Emperor Palpatine beyond the fact that he believed himself to be superior to everyone else in the galaxy. The structure of the Empire helped solidify this hierarchy, but the key point is that Palpatine disdained virtually everyone else alive: all were viewed as inferior. Presumably officers and other Imperial officials found ways to look past the fact that the man at the top of the Empire viewed them with contempt. But what they did not look past was the fact that he created the outlines of a top-down system that would greatly benefit them.

As has been previously noted, the Empire went to significant lengths to outline—or, more accurately, invent—the underlying heroic greatness of Emperor Palpatine. Much of the Imperial structure was based around the idea that only he could run the Empire. As a result, aspects of Palpatine provided a framework for others to co-opt. Palpatine was a human male who had risen to the pinnacle of galactic power and politics. For the most important—and therefore presumably the "best"—sentient being in the galaxy to be a male human suggested that there was an underlying aspect within all male humans that made them superior. This was eagerly seized upon by various Imperial officials and officers who were looking for a reason to create a human-centric and patriarchal aspect to Imperial organization.

This was manifested in ways that might seem unusual to us now. Much of the emphasis of the Imperial system was based upon Palpatine's species but there have been enough testimonies from ex-Imperial officers to suggest that Rae Sloane encountered prejudice throughout her career from Imperial officers who took a very literal interpretation of Palpatine's supposed superiority and looked down upon her because she was a woman.[1] That she rose to become a grand admiral is undoubtedly testament to her martial abilities rather than the flexibility of the Imperial system, and it seems unlikely she was alone in facing such issues from those within the Imperial hierarchy who felt emboldened to apply their own existing prejudices. Major Lio Partagaz of the ISB was apparently renowned for warning female supervisors that they would have to work even harder than their male compatriots to advance through the Imperial hierarchy.[2]

These were not the only forms of prejudice that existed within the Imperial system. While Palpatine's roots were on the Mid Rim world of

---

[1] New Republic Archives, Section: Imperial Prisoners, File: Interrogations 141, 227, 284, 310

[2] Imperial Archives, Section: Imperial Security Bureau. File: Major Lio Partagaz

Naboo, he had come to embody the prestige and privilege of Coruscant and the Core Worlds. The sense of superiority and nobility held by some of those who had grown up wealthy within the Core had been a sticking point for the rest of the galaxy for so long that there are entire collections of jokes based around the concept. But within the Imperial system it allowed some groups to ostensibly block and patronize their fellow officers who originated from further afield. Within the remaining writings of Grand Moff Tarkin are numerous references to Military Director Orson Krennic's supposed inferiority syndrome regarding the difference in social class between himself and those at the center of Palpatine's court. Tarkin also made various oblique references as to how best to provoke Krennic along those lines.[3] But Palpatine's species and gender were not the only examples that he provided to those looking to structure the Empire. What mattered most was a simple truth: power gave permission for oppression.

Imperial prejudice was not just restricted to biological beings. Even under the Republic there had long been split opinions as to the sentience or possible "rights" of droids—particularly within some of the wealthy aristocracy of the Core who seemed to view them as basically unpaid domestic servants. The huge numbers of battle droids that symbolized the Separatist military effort gave some cover for considering all droids to be either possessed of suspect loyalties or lesser than living beings. Under the Empire anti-droid prejudice intensified to the extent they were often viewed as tools comparable to a hydrospanner. But those of us who can count droids as dear friends and colleagues know that this constructed viewpoint of them is deeply prejudicial. I wonder how far the Rebel Alliance would have gotten in their war without the diligent, and often voluntary, service of various droids.

[3] Imperial Archives, Section: Grand Moff Wilhuff Tarkin, File: Reflections on Project Stardust & Director Orson Krennic

The Galactic Empire provided cover for those who bore virtually any conceivable prejudice. It did not matter if it did not exactly tie into specific Imperial policies, the very fact that it was a form of power that could be used against someone else made it viable. Furthermore, the whole machinery and apparatus of the Empire was predicated on the, often repeated, assertion that one of the reasons the Republic had failed was because of the many diverse voices, species, and interests that pulled it apart. Only the singular vision and voice of the Emperor could hope to moderate the desire of all species to further their own ends when they should instead focus on the longevity and success of the Empire. Those with hatred in their hearts, whether it be for all non-humans or just specific ones, for the young or the old, or the poor—all these people and their prejudices found a home within the Galactic Empire. We cannot view each and every one of these forms of bigotry as being separate from each other. Some were applied broadly across the Empire while others were localized and just applied by individual officers or bureaucrats, but they all formed part of a wider whole. This collective allowed the Empire to define what would be considered both natural and normal regarding how the galaxy would be restructured and ruled. In doing so, they provided us with some difficult but important lessons to learn.

The Problem with Humans

Many of the leaders and organizers of what became the Rebel Alliance were human. Humans, as a species, are an ancient spacefaring people. Wherever our true planets or systems of origin are, we have spread across the galaxy and, as a result, shaped galactic history in innumerable ways. The Empire tried hard to convince the galaxy that humans were the greatest of all the species. I refute that utterly, but it is perhaps fair to say that we are the most numerous. Humans are particularly well-represented within the Core Worlds and, as a result, were already in possession of a great deal of the galaxy's wealth and power even before the rise of the Empire. Whether directly or indirectly I, along with all other humans, have been the beneficiaries of the prestige and privilege that have been associated with my species. I am a human who served in the Resistance alongside many other humans. When it came to defeating the Empire, humans were well-represented within the ranks of the Rebel Alliance. Perhaps overrepresented in some cases. This has caused problems. Since the Galactic Civil War there has been a tendency to believe that non-humans owe humans something for their "liberation." This accusation is insidious and predicated on concepts of human superiority that are highly problematic. Firstly, it further divides those who have power (humans) from those who do not (non-humans) and forces the latter into a subservient position to the former. In doing so it also obscures perhaps the biggest and most important issue and question that surrounds this topic: what took humans—particularly those in the Core Worlds—so long to realize and care about what was happening under Imperial rule? Often, it appears, the answers revolve around convenience, complicity, and willful blindness.

Regardless of what Palpatine and those in positions of power within the Empire may have wanted, it was not possible for them to conquer and rule the entire galaxy all in one go. It took, as we have already discussed, years for the Empire to feel secure enough in its position to even do away with the Imperial Senate. This meant that changes and domination had to be instituted slowly, by incrementally increasing degrees, and this also brought about notable contradictions. To give an example, on Coruscant, Pollux Hax—one of Palpatine's most ideological and nefarious officials—was very open in explaining the benefits of "segregated areas of the cities" where non-humans were pushed together ostensibly to allow them to live their lives according to shared customs, but in practice to forcibly separate them from humans.[4] Hax would often point out that Coruscant had long been home to innumerable

---

[4] Pollux Hax, *An Imperial Guide to Coruscant*

species from across the galaxy and many gravitated toward their own kind and lived in close proximity together. During the Clone Wars, Coruscant had come to serve as a location for millions of beings fleeing the fighting. Hax argued that the Empire was justified in bringing these groups together into centralized locations to aid administration and for their own safety.

This process of driving non-human species on Coruscant into control zones was also taking place while non-humans sat in the Imperial Senate. It might be thought, understandably, that the contradiction between these two situations would prove to be a problem for the Empire, but it was actually incredibly useful. Imperial officials could point to non-human representation in the Senate as clear proof that there was no anti-alien prejudice within the regime and then follow it up by noting that "if so many aliens had problems with what they term 'human supremacy,' surely segregated communities are exactly what they really want!"[5] The hypocrisy did not burden the Empire because the blurring of lines provided them with an easy excuse and, just as importantly, they knew their audience. Propaganda regarding discrimination and prejudice was rarely aimed at non-humans. It was all designed and intended to be consumed by humans to help them rationalize what was going on around them. Too often we have heard that when it came to the Empire those humans living in the Core Worlds traded their rights for what appeared to be a peaceful and secure state. This is incorrect. They traded the rights of others for it.

I am not blind to the problems inherent in having a human write this study. There are huge issues with taking a human viewpoint on the systems of Imperial prejudice. Non-humans did not need to have the dangers of the Empire explained to them, they very quickly began to recognize what lay at the end of this hyperlane. For too long humans of

---

[5] Response from Commander Alod Zfal, COMPNOR: Coalition of Improvements to motion #DP6218b in the Imperial Senate

various worlds have congratulated ourselves for the actions and achievements of Leia Organa, or Mon Mothma, or Luke Skywalker. We have allowed their successes to mask our own inactivity. We have taken the fact that seemingly a high percentage of rebel fighters were humans to suggest that we were the ones who stepped up to save the galaxy, without recognizing that we were often the only ones who had the relative freedom to join in the first place. Comparatively, it was easier to disappear and join the Rebellion as a human on Commenor than it was to escape a forced labor camp as a Wookiee. If all the humans in the galaxy had revolted against Imperial rule, as some other species on their own worlds did, then the Empire would have become far harder to maintain. The answer therefore to the question of "what took humans so long to rise up?" is, sadly, "because they did not want to."

Structures of Oppression

Citizens and subjects of the Empire functioned by understanding that there were a variety of written and unwritten rules that governed their daily actions. Some were obvious, for example criticizing the Emperor in public was ill-advised. Others were more subtle or localized. The very concept of these rules provided both justification and cover for the Empire to spread its influence into all aspects of life in the galaxy and punish those deemed to be breaking them. It became very easy for people to look away when the Empire cracked down on specific groups because, clearly, they should simply have not broken the rules. Within this structure particular planets or regional governors might institute their own rules that were not widely reflected elsewhere in the Empire. Many of these rules were aimed at non-humans but this was not exclusively the case. The majority of those who existed under the Empire had their lives impacted in various ways, including humans. The Empire was designed to rule the galaxy so therefore everyone within it suffered to varying degrees. It is, however, instructive to see the moments when

Imperial officials went further beyond this, where they invested time and Imperial resources on pursuing specific or systemic prejudices.

Ideas and constructions of "normality" were very important to the Empire. By being able to position their policies as being either common sense or a reaction to those trying in some way—often through simply existing—to uproot the natural order of things, Imperial officials could push forward with whatever personal prejudices they wanted to impose alongside galaxy-wide diktats. In many ways the Empire was incredibly accommodating toward the prejudices of its officials. As long as someone was being oppressed it did not matter if it happened as part of standard policy or as an addition on the side. The Empire wanted its personnel to be complicit in varying forms of violence toward the population.

Talus in the Corellian system had, like the other nearby planets, a diverse mix of species inhabiting it. During the early years of the Empire, Imperial Planetary Governor Ili P'tan—a man who was ferociously xenophobic—took his lead from structures created by COMPNOR's SAGEducation division to reorganize teaching on his world. Given the number of non-human species who had participated in the Separatist cause, many humans on Core Worlds had already begun to view the "aliens" around them with a degree of suspicion or hostility. There had also long been tensions between humans, Selonians, and Drall in the Corellia system which Governor P'tan was keen to make use of. His plan was as cynical as it was inventive.

Firstly, to bring Talus in line with "wider galactic norms and standards" all teaching was to be delivered in Basic rather than translated into other languages. In the short-term, classrooms continued to contain a mix of species and non-human teachers still delivered lessons. Initially this seemed to allow for a sense of normality, but human parents noticed that both the individual and wider compiled class grades of children taught by teachers of a different species were beginning to fall. Additionally, classes that had pronounced mixes of human and non-human students began being held back after school as punishment for supposed "disruptive elements" within the group. As human parents began to question falling grades and seemingly unruly classes it did not take long for them to call upon schools to segregate their children away from the "aliens" who were apparently ruining their education.[6] Governor P'tan was only too happy to oblige.

Within weeks of the first petitions and news stories about the unfolding "crisis in combined education" on Talus, new laws were passed to ensure that human children were educated by themselves while "alien" children were brought together in much larger numbers to be taught separately.[7] The movement to separate human children from their friends was easily justifiable to an array of human parents. The importance of maintaining their children's education, the clear—but obviously manufactured—evidence that non-humans were an impediment to the real natural order, and the fact that none of this would have happened if those other species and races had just "followed the rules" were all ready-made excuses.

Records that have survived from the Talus educational archives show the extent to which the grades of human and non-human children were either manipulated or automated to ensure that human superiority appeared to be a matter of undeniable fact.[8] Meanwhile non-human children swiftly became seen as a drain on educational resources and a group who had been coddled by the previous government. A Selonian compatriot of mine at the Lerct Historical Institute, Professor Kavuss Boh, was only able to access higher education after the New Republic had come to power. She later discovered that her Imperial academic transcripts had been repeatedly altered by algorithm to drag down her test scores while comments were attached to them instructing that

---

[6] Talus Archives, Section: Education, File: Parental Petitions
[7] Talus Archives, Section: Education, File: Governor P'tan's Reforms
[8] Talus Archives, Section: Education, File: Imperial Algorithm X P 27

anyone who requested references for her should be told that she "was simply unable to compete with her human peers."[9]

However, discriminatory activity did not have to be formalized into specific policies. It could manifest in the most mundane ways. According to the rebel cell that operated on Lothal, stormtroopers regularly stole fruit and produce from market stalls operated by Rodians.[10] Similarly Imperial military personnel often performed shakedown raids on bars and cantinas on Eriadu that were frequented by non-humans.[11] Such instances were replicated on countless worlds around the galaxy and yet existed in the minds of some as almost purely anecdotal and all easily explained away as those victims having failed to observe the rules. But the officials and personnel of the Empire were not the only ones who took Imperial policy and prejudices as permission to pursue their own. On Taris, private landlords refused to rent property to those deemed "unacceptable."[12] The label was almost exclusively used for non-humans and resulted in many of them being forced out of the main city to live in the ruined starships that littered the swamplands beyond. Personal prejudices and Imperial ones often had an escalating effect on each other. There had long been lingering suspicions among some groups about the "acceptability" of relationships between different species or even with droids. There were some within the newly formed Empire who saw an opportunity to try and legislate some of these practices out of existence. On Denon, planetary officials used marriage licenses and other official registrations and forms firstly to restrict the rights and relationships of non-humans, before then gradually extending the same controls into the lives of humans as

[9] Talus Archives, Section: Education, File: Kavuss Boh—Alteration Recommendation
[10] Rebel Alliance Archives, Section: Resistance Cells, File: Spectre—Lothal
[11] Imperial Archives, Section: Eriadu, File: Standing Orders
[12] Imperial Archives, Section: Taris, File: Rental Legislation

well.[13] The need to maintain the cultural norm meant that each application of prejudice was merely a steppingstone on an evolving path rather than a destination of its own.

This raises some serious issues for trying to understand how quickly and easily the galaxy's population was able to accept the Empire's determination to drag them down a path of prejudice. During the Clone Wars there was significant public debate, often orchestrated by the Separatists, as to the morality of the use of clone troopers. While they may have appeared to be adults their actual ages put them as little more than children. The continued use of them by the Republic was often couched in pragmatic terms but the debates about the ethics of this did exist.[14] How could it be that within only a few years of those debates taking place, civilians were able to reconcile the concept that some species—such as Wookiees—who had long held visible roles in the Republic, were really "primitive" or subordinate after all? What could account for this acceptance? Similarly, as the Empire strengthened its grip on the galaxy the use of torture against its enemies, and enslavement of "lesser beings" become increasingly widespread. How do we reconcile the apparent tacit acceptance of this among the wider population? It is possible that many were unaware of the details, but it is not plausible to believe that ignorance was truly universal. Enough of the new Imperial changes happened in public. Trying to understand and answer why the civilians of the Empire were willing to, at the very least, turn a blind eye to things is not easy. But these questions should inform our understandings of what happened next and what we can still do to rectify matters.

---

[13] Imperial Archives, Section: Denon, File: Bureaucratic Restrictions
[14] The COMPOR sponsored poster *Support The Boys in White* by Hamma Elad was intended to try and counter criticisms of the Republic's use of clones, though even the word "boys" hinted at their status as possible children.

Damage and Restitution

As mentioned earlier in this chapter, those who were the primary victims of Imperial oppression recognized very quickly what was about to happen to them. While we will cover the full horrors of the genocidal activities of the Empire in a subsequent chapter it is still important to examine and acknowledge the difficulties faced by many different groups under Imperial rule.

One of the complicated aspects of Imperial-approved prejudice was the ways in which it could set oppressed groups against each other. While Trandoshans lost many of the rights they had previously held under the Republic, the knowledge that the Wookiees suffered even more greatly through Imperial occupation and enslavement was warmly greeted by many of the reptilians. Rather than consider how anti-alien sentiment impacted both their species, the opportunity to drive home their pre-existing rivalry deflected them away from the concept of a common foe.

Trandoshans did not simply suffer under the Empire because they were non-humans. They, much like Twi'leks, Rodians, and Gran were subject to a process of stereotyping that obscured significant aspects of their cultures and societies in favor of depicting them as criminals, gangsters, drug-dealers, or decadent workers. These stereotypes were reinforced by art, literature, and holodramas and became self-perpetuating within Imperial society, to the extent that individuals attempting to deviate from the prescribed norms for their species were viewed with suspicion by both officials and civilians. With many doors and opportunities closed to non-humans anyway, this further forced the members of many species deemed "unsavory" to enter into illicit activities simply to survive. In this way, Imperial prejudices became self-fulfilling, while serving as a pipeline that maintained the black market and criminal underworld that corrupted the galaxy— but which also provided the Empire with mercenaries and bounty hunters for hire.

What is interesting and important to note, however, is the extent to which those oppressed by the Empire were able to recognize each other. Mon Calamari, Sullustans, and Wookiees were all persecuted in different ways but could recognize in their own suffering the suffering of others. Such recognition bred sympathy and, eventually, cooperation. This may ironically have been one of the Empire's greatest miscalculations. To the extent that Imperial officials had considered the implications of their actions at all, the expectation was clearly that, under the pressure of the state, different species and groups would become isolated from each other and easier to manage. That is not what happened. A mixture of non-human species and those humans who existed at the edges of what was deemed "acceptable" by Imperial standards quickly realized that liberation for some was not liberation at all. Cooperation, collaboration, and shared empathy are the antidote to a system designed to destroy and constrict. Networks and safe houses for those fleeing persecution began to appear across the galaxy. Bothans forged false chain codes that were implanted into Aqualish by Nautolan doctors. Imminent Imperial raids and patrols were spotted and signaled ahead by different species to people they would never know or meet. Solidarity emerged from suppression.

How much did the Rebel Alliance owe to these informal networks? The safe hyperlanes and pipelines that were initially designed to help those fleeing enslavement? The safe houses and hidden stashes that allowed those on the run to remain hidden or the hungry to find food? In many ways the alliance aspect may have existed before the rebel part. Not codified or organized but sustained and nourished by those who looked around at their fellow citizens and through words or action said "I am sorry this is happening to you, it is not right, and you do not deserve it." While some humans took their time in recognizing the realities of the Empire, many species did not have that luxury. Of those, many risked—and gave—their lives to help others. They deserve better than to be told they should be grateful to those who have never had to worry about stun cuffs and slave collars.

Which brings us to the question of restitution. It is undeniable that humans generally fared much better under the Empire than other species and still retained much of their political power and presence after it fell. While there were certainly horrendous acts—Alderaan not least among them—inflicted upon the human population of the galaxy, there were clearly other worlds that were effectively destroyed and other species that were driven to the brink of extinction—or beyond. Having lost their own worlds, much of their property, their societal culture and wealth, and political power—what would meaningful compensation even look like? Much of the wealth of the Empire vanished through theft and embezzlement at the end of the Galactic Civil War. The arguments that followed often focused on reconciliation and rehabilitation rather than restitution, which was deemed to be "impossible".[15] But is that really true? Was there nothing that could be done then—or even now—for those who were harshest treated by Imperial rule? That all the crimes of the Empire, the pillaging of natural resources or the theft of cultural artifacts and memories—none of it can really be returned or repaid? I don't believe this to be true. By the time the Empire had fallen there was more misery and pain in the galaxy than could easily be solved. But those who were hardest hit needed a future that was more than refugee camps and platitudes. While some planets and people were able to rebuild themselves through industry or protected assets there were plenty who could not. The Empire had stripped their planets and funneled the material and profits away into the holdings and accounts of others. There was no ladder left to reclimb. Did the rest of the galaxy really do all it could to help them?

As Lelie Ruemerll argued in their wonderful study *The Long Shadow of the New Order*, this is not simply a problem of the past. Those who

---

[15] Some of this will be discussed in Chapter Twenty-Three.

were left bereft and devastated by the Empire are still suffering and now they have been joined by those persecuted by the First Order. As with the aftermath of the Empire there remain today lingering suspicions among some in the galaxy that those who bore the worst brunt of oppression had perhaps somehow deserved it, or brought it upon themselves. We should not replicate the prejudices and racisms of the Empire and First Order and allow their worst ideologies to survive their regime. If we allow yet more groups to be left in poverty and pain after this war, as we did the last, then we should hang our heads in shame. True freedom and liberation can only exist for all of us when none are left behind.

Chapter 13

Atrocities and Genocides

As we have seen in the preceding chapters, the Galactic Empire instituted and utilized a variety of measures and controls to maintain order across the galaxy. Many of these were predicated on the threat of force being used against dissidents, dissenters, and those who sought to resist or disrupt Imperial rule. It should come as no surprise—even to those with only the most passing knowledge of our recent past—that the Empire would employ violence to pursue its objectives. This chapter will predominantly focus on those actions undertaken during the period of Imperial rule itself. Attacks against the New Republic and the horrors of Operation Cinder will be dealt with in a subsequent chapter. The very fact that such a decision must be made indicates the scale of Imperial atrocities and genocides against the people of this galaxy. It is with no small amount of horror that I must also state that it is not possible to cover them all.

What is important to understand, as a foundational starting point, is the way violence was rationalized by the Empire and how it has come to be understood following its defeat. Often Imperial atrocities are considered to have served specific purposes, such as sending a wider message about the inevitable outcome of resistance. There is certainly some truth in this, Alderaan being a potential case in point. But to accept that this was the only real motivation for the Empire's atrocities, massacres, and genocides is to also fundamentally misunderstand how the Empire and

Imperial officials used the power they wielded. In all too many cases, episodes of mass killing were carried out not as part of a wider attempt to discourage opposition to the Empire, but simply because Imperial officials could order them, particularly in the Outer Rim, without any likelihood of chastisement from Coruscant. Those in command positions in the Empire used violence because they *could*. Massacres and genocides were both a means to an end, and also a recognized tool to be used as a solution for a multitude of problems. At times, what is striking about the Imperial use of violence and the decision-making process leading to genocide was the mundanity of it, the recognition within the system that it was just another instrument to be used. There was often no great overarching plan and no grand objective behind the atrocities that led to huge numbers dying. The Empire often evaluated the utility of the species and populations under its rule but was seemingly happy to kill both those they found useful and those they found useless should it be determined necessary, beneficial, or even expedient. Many of us have come to imagine that the reality of Imperial genocide was embodied by faceless stormtroopers and blaster rifles. That death was both decided and delivered in close proximity to the victims. But that is not really how it worked. Stormtroopers could be, and often were, violent toward civilians under their control. But they were trained to obey instructions and not go beyond that. That was a key aspect of Imperial military conditioning. It was Imperial officials on worlds like Coruscant who went to work and gave the orders that committed mass murder. They did it with a datapad or a commlink. And then—at the end of their day—they returned home to their families without giving it a second thought. The Empire and its personnel killed by memo and dispatch, and they did it from office buildings surrounded by their colleagues.

However, this is not to say that Imperial officials were orchestrating genocides in full public view from the moment of the Empire's inception. It would take time for the new state to reach this point. There were some controls imposed by centralized Imperial authority for fear of drawing the attention of the Imperial Senate. For the most part it was necessary for the worst acts of violence to take place beyond the Core Worlds. Certainly, during the earliest years of the Empire while the state was still strengthening its controls over the galaxy, the Imperial Senate could cause a great many problems if there were to be significant outrage at the use of widespread extrajudicial killings. The Empire's early solution to this was to, where possible, hide its massacres. This could take several forms. For example, having them take place on Outer Rim worlds remote enough that those in the Core essentially did not care, but where their targets' near neighbors got the intended message. Alternatively, they could be perpetrated in systems and sectors that had been designated as areas of expansion and annexation, where the Imperial fleet was actively operating and could therefore act as legitimizing cover. Even where significant loss of life could not be concealed, the cause of it could be rationalized away through carefully sculpted lies. This was the case with Jedha, where the first test firing of the Death Star's primary weapon was explained away as a mining disaster that had destabilized the moon's crust.[1]

What we should take from this is that, even before famous examples like Ghorman and Alderaan, the Empire was not averse to using violence to either spell out the consequences of resistance or simply to kill large numbers of sentient beings. However, being seen overtly doing so—in the earliest days of Imperial rule—was a problem. In time, the Galactic Civil War would give the Empire an excuse to drop even the minimal façade that existed before Alderaan. But for many years acts of extreme violence took place largely out of sight of the Core Worlds. The fact that such acts could not be witnessed, even if they were suspected, made it unlikely that any other Imperial subjects would either care about, or risk, questioning the methods of the state. As with the Imperial approach to discrimination, violent repercussions against entire species could be dismissed as the results of "breaking the rules." Such a line

[1] Imperial Senate Proceedings, File 8364.2

proved surprisingly, and sadly, durable even as the worst Imperial atrocities began to be made public.

However, even by the time of the destruction of Jedha and then Alderaan, the Empire had grown bolder and reached a point where it had ceased to actively cover up many of the atrocities being propagated. Instead, the strategy had evolved—as was noted by early theorists of what would become the Rebel Alliance—to recognize the inability of the wider galactic population and whatever Holonews networks that were not under full Imperial control, to process the sheer extent of horrors being inflicted at any given time.[2] The Empire calculated that they could overwhelm the people of the galaxy with stories of misery in the belief that many would desperately cling on to the notion that the victims had somehow brought it upon themselves by a failure to comply, while the rest would become cowed and pliable.

What is also important to understand is that, while the Empire did not want others to know of some of its worst actions, they did make sure to keep their own internal records. Some of these have survived to the present day and are still available to us. However, the rationale behind the Imperial record keeping, and what it deemed important enough to preserve, reflects its own ideology. Some of the details that follow are deeply shocking and deserve examination and recognition.

The Use of Violence

As has been noted in previous chapters, the Empire operated on a system of gradual escalation in the face of resistance or possible rebellion. While many of the steps on this process also included violence—the arrest and incarceration of suspected dissidents and their families for example—there were also levels above these that included the

[2] Rebel Alliance Archives, Section: Political Thought & Manifestos, File: Karis Nemik

widespread and indiscriminate use of lethal force. There are numerous notable examples of the Empire using violence on civilian populations, but it is useful to highlight those which can be considered as warnings or retributions and those which were simply a routine, if horrifying, decision taken by Imperial officials.

The planet Lothal saw several examples of this violence while under Imperial rule. Darth Vader ordered a refugee camp, nicknamed "Tarkintown" to be burned with no records remaining as to how many refugees were casualties.[3] This was, supposedly, designed to bring the local rebel cell out of hiding, but given Darth Vader's already noted predisposition to violence, there were likely less destructive ways to achieve the same thing. Grand Admiral Thrawn also brought his own Star Destroyer into Lothal's atmosphere and carried out a bombardment of civilian areas to force that same rebel group to surrender. Again, despite the planet's subsequent liberation, it is unclear how severe the civilian casualties were. The intended audience for both attacks on Lothal were the civilians living, and rebels operating, in the same system. The Empire had effectively already locked the planet down to avoid the insurrection there spreading, so there was no way that details of the events could spread off-world, either to serve as a threat to others or inspiration for similarly rebellious factions elsewhere.

In contrast, following the theft of Imperial payroll on Aldhani, the Empire deployed a Star Destroyer to the system to begin a process of retributory violence against the population, intending to send a wider message to the galaxy. The inhabitants of the world had already been subject to years of Imperial controls designed to suppress and disrupt their way of life. According to reports found within the ISB archives, Imperial forces on the planet were actively involved in the forcible

---

[3] This event has been recorded in both Imperial and Lothal archives and the differences between them are notable. Imperial Archives, Section: Lothal, File: Reprisal Activities. Post-Imperial Lothal Archives, Section: Imperial Occupation, File: Refugee Massacre.

relocation of native groups to make way for Imperial infrastructure. [4] These efforts were later extended to undermine native religious festivals and celebrations as well. The Imperial investigation into the payroll heist led to the planet Ferrix, where a funeral in one of the cities became an anti-Imperial demonstration and then subsequently a riot. In response, Imperial stormtroopers and army personnel opened fire on the crowd causing mass civilian fatalities. These cases serve as representative examples of activity that was routinely carried out under the Empire on planets across the galaxy but, predominantly, beyond the Core. What is important to note, however, is that while Lothal, Aldhani, and Ferrix experienced repression, these were predominantly human worlds. The Empire exhibited markedly less restraint in subjugating non-humans.

Following the end of the Clone Wars, the newly formed Galactic Empire attempted to secure its position and power in the short term with noted acts of violence. Under the orders of Grand Moff Tarkin—a man whose fingerprints are all over many of these atrocities—Vice Admiral Rampart forcibly interned and then deported the population of Kamino before destroying Tipoca City and its cloning facilities in a mass orbital bombardment. This was an attack intended to be carried out entirely in secret and was only brought to wider attention when a recording of it was played on the floor of the Imperial Senate.[5] What should have been a serious issue for the Empire was avoided when Palpatine was able to place the entirety of the blame upon Rampart's shoulders. Given that the whole Kaminoan operation was intended to be hidden from the Senate, it provides a useful insight into how readily Imperial officials reached for mass destruction in order to solve their problems.

While Kamino was meant to be kept hidden, the Imperial blockade of Kashyyyk was a far more public affair designed to instill fear in populations that were closely loyal to the fallen Republic or were viewed by

---

[4] Imperial Archives, Section: Imperial Security Bureau, File: Aldhani Protocols
[5] Imperial Senate Proceedings, File 19.6

Imperial officials as liable to rebel. Even before the Empire had been formally declared, clone troopers had seized control of aspects of Kashyyyk's infrastructure. Within days squadrons of the Imperial fleet effectively isolated the Wookiees' homeworld from the wider galaxy and staged multiple landings of troops onto the surface. The primary aim of these attacks was to conquer the planet, enslave its population, and then harvest its resources. The enslavement program was as cynical as it was brutal. Adult Wookiees were strong and had clear utility as workers. Some Imperial officers, however, viewed their children as either useful hostages to compel the adults to work or, depending on circumstances, a potential liability. As a species the Wookiees are known for their long lifespans. Adults can live for hundreds of years—making them very appealing as forced labor—but they also require significant food supplies, particularly when young, in order to grow and maintain productivity, something some Imperial officers seemed to believe was a waste of resources. It is here that complications begin to appear in the records of those Wookiees taken prisoner by the Empire. In some circumstances children were kept in proximity to their parents—but in separate holding cells—to force compliance.[6] Many of those who were still children when the Imperial forces arrived on Kashyyyk are conspicuously absent from later Imperial records.[7] What is clear is that Imperial labor camps and largescale construction projects heavily utilized Wookiee workers and that their safety and wellbeing was not foremost in the minds of overseeing officials.

Surviving Wookiees have passed along the details of the Imperial occupation of their world in various forms, but the most haunting of these is a 13-hour-long collective retelling that can be roughly translated into "The Day the Trees Fell." While many attempted to resist the

---

[6] Imperial Archives, Section: Forced Labor, File: Wookiee Protocols
[7] Imperial Archives, Section: Kashyyyk Occupation, File: Prisoner Numbers (Updated)

Empire—and fighting on the world continued for years—hundreds of thousands, if not millions, of Kashyyyk's inhabitants were either killed or sent into Imperial slavery. This attack on Kashyyyk was not hidden in the same way that Kamino or other atrocities were. At the time, Imperial propaganda worked hard to build an image of Kashyyyk and its Wookiee inhabitants as having been compromised at the end of the Clone Wars—partially through their close contact with the treasonous Jedi Order—and that they now represented a grave security threat to the new Empire.[8] Even when tinged with Imperial-approved propaganda, the reality of the situation was obvious enough to deliver a clear message regarding the new state of the galaxy.

The worlds of other non-humans also found themselves targeted by Imperial forces. Ryloth had already been badly hit during the Clone Wars, and given the proud warrior tradition that motivated some Twi'leks, the Empire viewed the world as a potential liability.[9] However, just as with Kashyyyk, the Empire was not content simply occupying the planet; they drove many inhabitants from their homes into the wilderness and attempted to systematically dismantle Twi'lek culture and history. Many of the attempts to conquer Ryloth were haphazard at best given the unsophisticated tactics of most Imperial officials, and TIE bombers were regularly used to bombard civilian targets across the planet's surface. However, Grand Admiral Thrawn was particularly adept at dealing with insurgencies and had largely suppressed much of the resistance on Ryloth in the years before Yavin. As with the Wookiees, forced labor was the destination for many Twi'leks who were captured by the Empire.

The brutal Imperial campaign on Mimban was designed not just to conquer the planet but, where possible, to destroy the native population.

---

[8] Imperial Archives, Section: Propaganda, File: Kashyyyk Justifications
[9] I strongly recommend the renowned Twi'lek historian Amiy Rua'chi's study *Twi'lek Culture and the History of Ryloth.*

Huge numbers of poorly trained "mudtroopers" of the Imperial Army were deployed to the planet alongside sizeable elements of the Imperial Navy to fully conquer the world for its rich resources. As previously noted, there remain strong suggestions that the Empire aimed to drag the campaign out for as long as possible to force further military requisition bills through the Senate. To achieve this, attacks on civilian Mimbanese targets were widespread in order to motivate the population to continue to fight a perpetually losing battle, rather than surrender. Aside from the Mimban campaign, Grand Moff Tarkin effectively razed Salient, destroying whole cities because the occupants there had attempted to rebel against the imminent control of the Empire. The Empire's occupation of Ralltiir—which had previously been a major financial hub—in 1 BBY, became so drawn out that attacks on civilian infrastructure were increasingly common. At least one populated town was attacked by Imperial forces who were informed it was a secret rebel base.[10] In order to train and contain the situation, Imperial forces instituted a blockade that effectively isolated the planet from the nearby Perlemian Trade Route.

The examples detailed above are representative of many more such massacres on dozens or hundreds of other planets. They also do not take into account the accidental killings of civilians through negligence, such as in the release of a deadly chemical on Falleen or the instances when civilians were casually murdered simply as part of wider construction efforts or industrial processes such as on Sullust. They also do not include examples of extinction by apathy, such as the B'ankora, who had inhabited a designated refuge on Coruscant for generations before they were forcibly evicted in 19 BBY by Imperial edict for the land to be given over to weapons research teams.[11] The B'ankora were relocated to the

[10] Imperial Archives, Section: Ralltiir Occupation, File: Communication Order 83324
[11] Imperial Archives, Section: Imperial Military Department of Advanced Weapons Research, File: B'ankora Refuge

dying world of Parau VI which had, in passable terms, similarities with their lost homeworld. However, this deportation had grave consequences for the species who slipped into extinction within just a few decades.

The planet Wobani had been effectively devastated by its failure to meet—seemingly impossible—agriculture quotas set by the Empire. A mix of ever-increasing fines and systemic over farming by Imperial officials who had no interest in the planet's population effectively led to the collapse of all infrastructure on the planet. By 3 BBY the population had begun to starve in huge numbers while the Empire cut non-essential travel to the world in order to both prevent undue word from spreading and to trap the occupants there. Like Wobani, the planet Chasmeene had also failed to meet their quotas and a mix of famines and punitive Imperial bombardments left the world a ruin. While incidents like these resulted in significant numbers of deaths, they were often under-reported and acknowledged, being viewed simply as localized "wastage"—a necessary outcome of required Imperial activity.

The idea of violence being a necessity for the Empire either to send a message or because of a distinct lack of imagination from Imperial officials is an important one. The Empire routinely used violence to solve its problems, whether that was a stormtrooper shooting into a crowd to stop a thief or an orbital bombardment being used to subdue a whole world. This regular application of violence to achieve its ends was, as previously mentioned, often designed to both achieve a localized objective and, where publicly known, make an example. But violence desensitizes people over time. The Empire recognized this and found inventive ways to manifest fresh horrors.

In the Outer Rim, people already lived their day-to-day lives alongside the symbols and consequences of Imperial occupation. When an attack by early aspects of the Rebel Alliance was traced back to the world of Christophsis, the planet was "pacified" in retribution. The language of this act belies the reality of three Imperial Star Destroyers entering orbit above the capital city and opening fire. The purpose of this attack was to create such a fear in the population, and by proxy in the Senate when it was reported by Grand Moff Tarkin, as to render future resistance inconceivable.[12] It was for this reason that the Star Destroyers began by demolishing the city's hospitals.

Closer to the Core, examples and understandings of Imperial violence were very different, and one of the most shocking episodes of Imperial brutality played out on Ghorman in 2 BBY, with the deaths of hundreds if not thousands of civilians protesting against the Empire.[13] This attempt to crush dissent may have been a serious miscalculation by the Imperial officials who orchestrated it. Rather than terrify the wider civilian population into accepting Imperial rule, it showed many with rebel leanings that if even peaceful protest would be greeted with death, then there could be no political solution or compromise. If people were going to die regardless of how they resisted, then it may as well become an armed resistance. This would have—as will be discussed in a forthcoming chapter—dramatic and long-reaching consequences during the Galactic Civil War.

Unfortunately, while the events outlined above were shocking and resulted in the deaths of huge numbers of civilians, they were not even the most extreme examples of how the Empire would treat those it deemed to be problematic or adversarial. Given that violence was often the tool that Empire reached for to solve its issues, genocide was the escalation beyond it.

Genocide and Exterminations

Horrifyingly it is not possible in the space allotted to us here to provide a full account of all the genocidal activity undertaken by the Galactic Empire. It is entirely possible that some events were so catastrophically

[12] Imperial Senate Proceedings, File: 7661.6
[13] Imperial Archives, Section: Ghorman, File: Reprisal Activities

destructive that we do not even know they occurred. However, through a few selected case studies we can begin to piece together the common themes of Imperial genocide.

The Galactic Empire effectively carried out its first genocide before it had even been formally declared. The extermination of the Jedi during Order 66 was Palpatine's first overt move to annihilate groups that could oppose his planned Empire. The use of clone troopers to kill Jedi in the field and simultaneously at the Temple on Coruscant remain key parts of what can be understood as the Great Jedi Purge, but they were not all its aspects. Palpatine did not want to just kill the Jedi, he wanted to ensure that any survivors would be too scared of the rest of the population to ever show their faces again. Every part of the purge was designed to annihilate the Order and make it too dangerous for those that remained to act against the Empire. Some of the Jedi hunted down by the Inquisitors had their bodies displayed in public as a warning and a message. As previously discussed, Imperial propaganda hammered home the ways that the Jedi had apparently betrayed the Republic, manipulated the war, and attempted to take over the galaxy.[14] Within just a few short years the overwhelming majority of Jedi had been exterminated by Imperial forces with the few survivors driven underground and presumably terrified by how quickly the galaxy had turned against them. So successful was the Imperial action against them that even now, decades later, there are groups around the galaxy who still act with fearful suspicion at the mention of the Jedi.

As with the Jedi, the Empire was all too willing to effectively eradicate those species—and non-humans were often the targets—that posed military or political threats. The Lasat had largely avoided involvement in the Clone Wars but that did not prevent the Empire from noting their warrior traditions and perceiving them as a threat. Details regarding the events that led to the Siege of Lasan in 7 BBY remain sketchy. Many of

[14] Imperial Archives, Section: Propaganda Materials, File: The Jedi Threat

the Imperial records appear to have been purged. What appears clear from testimony from survivors like Garazeb Orrelios is that a demonstration on the planet was viewed as the perfect excuse by Imperial officials to act. By deploying T-7 ion disruptor rifles—weapons that caused horrendous damage to organic neural pathways—against the population alongside attacks by TIE bombers, the Lasat people were almost completely eradicated. The entirety of the royal family was killed as were most of their honor guard. Bombing runs on the major population centers immolated countless civilians, many of them left cowering with their loved ones as their homes exploded around them.[15] The species' population was reduced to a mere handful and would have likely become extinct if their original homeworld had not later been rediscovered. The consequences for the Empire in destroying Lasan were relatively small. In response the Senate banned the production and use of T-7 disruptors, but Imperial officials had already been delighted at the outcome of their field test and incorporated the findings into future weapons.[16]

Furthermore, the success of the attacks on Lasan provided a blueprint for other Imperial officers. Moff Gideon's forces incorporated them into their attacks on Mandalore during "The Night of a Thousand Tears." As with Lasan, TIE bombers dropped huge quantities of explosives (in Mandalore's case, fusion bombs) while ground troops and Imperial droids massacred active combatants. So heavy was the bombardment that parts of the planet's surface were effectively compounded into glass. In an attempt to halt the attack, Mandalorian ruler Bo-Katan Kryze surrendered the planet and her forces to the Empire. Once these Mandalorians had been disarmed, Moff Gideon reneged on the agreement and slaughtered the remaining survivors. Mandalore came to serve as a cautionary tale to other Imperial enemies as the Galactic Civil

[15] Rebel Alliance Archives, Section: Defections & Debriefings, File: Alexsandr Kallus
[16] Imperial Senate Proceedings, File TR4713.5

War drew to a close.[17] Stories persisted for years that the world had been so badly destroyed that the atmosphere itself was poisonous and even that the planetary crust had been cracked. It was only a few years after the fall of the Empire that the remaining scattered Mandalorian survivors were able to return to their world, though—given their secrecy—the current status of the planet remains unclear.

While with worlds like Lasan and Mandalore it is possible to see and record the methods the Imperial genocide took, not all worlds have been so fortunate. It remains unclear what happened to the population of Geonosis. The world and its population had firmly sided with the Separatists during the Clone Wars and, as a result, there was little warm feeling toward them as a defeated enemy. However, the extent to which the Geonosians have been eradicated is truly shocking. The world now is little more than a barren husk, utterly empty of life. Imperial records speaking only of a "cleansing" protocol instituted upon it. Whether traditional or more experimental chemical weapons were used is unknown, though given the burrows and tunnels that lay beneath its surface, I fear the latter is more likely.[18] Regardless of the method, the outcome was the same. The Geonosians are effectively extinct. Murdered in such huge numbers that there remain no survivors who can pass on accounts of the events. They died, together, out of sight of a galaxy that had already judged them as enemies.

There is a tendency to consider the genocidal activities and approaches of the Empire as somehow being a sign of its technological proficiency. That the weapons and strategies it used to commit genocide were so advanced that the Imperial military was almost evolutionarily destined— and therefore somehow justified—in its actions. It is a viewpoint that I find deeply troubling. Yes, the Empire had far greater firepower than its

---

[17] Imperial Archives, Section: Mandalore, File: Subjugation
[18] There is a report within the archives of the Rebel Alliance stating that agents of the Spectre Cell had found empty gas cannisters on the world but had been unable to retrieve them as conclusive proof.

opponents, but there is nothing advanced in razing entire worlds. On Lasan they may have used T-7 rifles but in 18 BBY, on Yar Togna Imperial forces used clubs and rifle butts to attack civilians and destroy their property, because of a peculiar reaction within the atmosphere to the ionized disruption of the initial orbital bombardments. So ferocious were the attacks on Yar Togna, that the population began a mass migration from the now ruined planet. Such an act of cultural genocide has no sophistication to it. On Mandalore the Empire used bombs while on Wobani they used hunger. Chemical weapons may have killed many Geonosians but Darth Vader's lightsaber proved just as effective on Dhen-Moh. The motivation behind all these appalling events was the Imperial principle that mass violence was the simplest solution to almost any problem. Not all the genocides carried out by the Empire were politically motivated. Some were seen as necessary to remove a stubborn opponent while others had potential as object lessons to other groups around the galaxy. Together they all show the overwhelming willingness of the Empire to simply eradicate entire planets and populations in order to achieve its aims and objectives. Against a regime willing to stoop to such levels, armed resistance was necessary.

Which brings us to Alderaan.

There can be few who were alive at the time who do not remember where they were when Alderaan was destroyed. Though I was only a very young child, the shock expressed by my family members is seared into my own memory. The Death Star will be more fully discussed in a forthcoming chapter, but it is important to note that it was not an overnight invention. Palpatine, Tarkin, and other key Imperial figures must have recognized that a day would come when the population of the galaxy would begin to strain under the weight of Imperial oppression. The Death Star was their solution. Whereas Kashyyyk, Mimban, Mandalore, Caamas, and many other worlds had taken time and effort to conquer or purge, now the Empire could commit genocide with the push of a button. The destruction of Alderaan highlighted for many exactly what Palpatine intended for the galaxy. The ability to commit murder on such a scale remains almost unfathomable, even in the shadow of the more recent Hosnian Cataclysm and obliteration of Kijimi.

Many Alderaanians did not even realize their lives were in danger before the moment their planet was eradicated. Alderaan was supposedly selected as the Death Star's first full-scale target to compel Princess Leia into revealing the location of the main rebel base. But this is only a partial explanation. The Death Star ceased to be a secret weapon as soon as it entered Alderaanian orbit. It was never going to leave the planet intact. It is therefore highly likely that Tarkin and the Emperor had pre-selected Alderaan because of, rather than in spite of, its inhabitants' pacifism and the way their morality had caused the Empire numerous political problems in the Imperial Senate. They intended to send a message about where all forms of resistance to Imperial rule— even non-violent resistance—would now lead, something Palpatine made even more clear when he simultaneously disbanded the Senate. The fact he also authorized the construction of a second battle station tells us all we need to know about his intentions.

The Empire killed far more easily than it ever gave life. Death was almost the mortar that held the Empire together. The outcome of this poses serious issues for historians.

Lost Voices

As has been mentioned before, Imperial records relating to many of its activities are fractured and incomplete. We should all be eternally grateful to the dedicated work undertaken by the likes of J0-8O, the archival droid at the Galactic Museum and Archives on Chandrila, where many of the rarest testimonies and records have been kept and made accessible. Furthermore, survivors and scholars from those species who bore the brunt of Imperial genocides and kept the stories and facts alive have made a tremendous service to the galaxy. The victims remain the best people to transmit and translate their own experiences, and I urge readers to look for the works of figures like Pri'am Q'asl, Xugg Twam, and Froh Loeaw for invaluable insight as to how Twi'leks, Sullustans, Bothans, and other cultures have recorded the history of their own experiences. Even here there can be difficulty. The planet Bosph was subjected to repeated large-scale orbital bombardments from the Imperial fleet in 3 BBY. The damage to their world is effectively irreparable and the survivors were kept under a form of ongoing quarantine. In response these survivors have "dis-remembered" the Galactic Empire— a grave insult in their society. They refuse to acknowledge the Imperial state ever even existed. These are a species who have purposefully turned their backs on the perpetrators of attempted genocide, and their silence should be respected.

What the surviving Imperial archives tell us, however, is truly horrifying in its own way. The Empire apparently kept extensive details and reports of every crime undertaken by those in its service. Every stormtrooper shakedown, every corrupt bribe, every war crime, and every genocide. Culpability and the ways in which its orders were carried out greatly interested the Empire, for reasons that we shall discuss in a future chapter.

What the Empire did not keep records of were its victims.

There are huge empty strings of chain codes within Imperial administration files. The only information attached to these files explains that the chain codes were initially attached to an individual, and then were later rendered obsolete with the tag "subject purged, code redundant."[19] No records of species, age, gender, or anything remotely personal exists. At various points in their lives the Empire recorded these individuals, tagged them, killed them, and then deleted their data.

This is the true face and reality of Imperial genocide. The further into the archives you dig the more pronounced the sheer absence is.

[19] Imperial Archives, Section: Redundant Chain Codes

Absence of life, of names, and of voices. Soldiers, civilians, adults, and children. All of them were victims of a government that believed their deaths were more useful than their lives. All of them gone.

The billions of beings who vanished under Palpatine's rule were not just killed by the Empire—they were exterminated by a regime that could not even summon up the interest to record the names of its victims. They were murdered once by brutality and again by apathy. When now we visit the Memorial to the Missing of Ghorman, the Graveyard at Alderaan, the Wroshyr Mural on Kashyyyk, or the Hall of the Unknown on Chandrila, among others, we must reflect upon the fact that so vast was the system of Imperial genocide that we may never know anything about the majority of those we lost except for the fact that they died. There have been concerted moves in some cultures to build artistic or personal monuments to the absence created by those who vanished under Imperial rule, and many of them are deeply moving.[20]

There are some who have attempted to sow doubt on the Empire's crimes by suggesting that a lack of victims should suggest a lack of evidence. Given the resurgence of Imperial ideology through the First Order, it should sadly not surprise us that there were still plenty in the galaxy happy to lie or divert about what such ideology inevitably leads to. It is here I fear that we—and as a historian, I include myself in this—did not do enough in the post-war years. We believed that the horrors of Imperial genocide spoke for themselves. We should have done more to counter the lies of Imperial apologists and deniers. Perhaps in not being more vigorous and determined to speak up for those whose voices had been lost, we ourselves silenced them again. In doing so we might have opened the route to Hosnian Prime, Kijimi, and other newly devastated worlds.

We should have done more. I should have done more. Never again. These events should haunt and motivate us forever.

[20] I particularly recommend those included in Yim Relot's collaborative project *Filling the Vacuum: Artistic Responses to the Missing.*

Part Three

THE GALACTIC
CIVIL WAR

Chapter 14

Opening Skirmishes

One of the long-standing debates within our contemporary history has centered around trying to decide exactly when the Galactic Civil War began. As mentioned in this study's introduction, I believe that a number of my colleagues are undertaking a compiled military history of the galaxy's major recent wars and battles, and they have placed the starting point as the rebel raid on Scarif. This seems to be an entirely understandable selection from the Rebel Alliance's point of view, given that it was the first full-scale engagement for their fleet. However, a curiosity that becomes apparent from an examination of the Imperial records is that the Galactic Empire had effectively been "at war" for years before Scarif. With every expansion campaign, every pacification of an unruly world, and every genocide, the Imperial military had descended further and further into a wartime mentality. So consuming was this effect that I think many Imperial officers—judging from reports compiled by the ISB and interrogation transcripts from the New Republic—would struggle to put an actual starting point on the conflict, based upon their own experiences.[1]

---

[1] For the ISB reports, specifically see: Imperial Archives, Section: ISB, File: Morale within the Imperial Military #GY25971-DR25999* *Records captured from Yaga Minor. For New Republic records, see: New Republic Archives, Section: Imperial Prisoners, File: Interrogation reports 17, 344, 598, 778.

The fact that the Imperial military had been waging a variety of smaller wars and military actions even before Scarif provided a mix of benefits and drawbacks. Though many of the Empire's existing tactics and strategies would have to be reconsidered to deal with the Rebel Alliance, as has already been discussed and will be revisited in a forthcoming chapter, the military was relatively well-trained in the all-round basics of waging war. Many fleet captains, TIE pilots, and stormtroopers had seen some form of action across the galaxy, which would provide useful combat experience. This was not necessarily true for the soldiers of what would become the Rebel Alliance. While many had either served in the Clone Wars or taken part in insurgency campaigns, there were also those who'd joined for ideological reasons but never seen combat. These members would need to be trained and the rebels had precious little facilities—or time—in which to undertake such training. This meant that in some crucial ways the Empire was starting from a higher level of readiness than the Rebel Alliance. However, this was not without issues for the Imperials, because there is only so long that a military force can maintain its "edge" amid a state of perpetual combat readiness. The rebels had to operate in near-constant vigilance for fear of Imperial discovery, but the Empire had to continuously operate at peak military efficiency. As we will see in later chapters, as the war developed, this proved to be an ongoing problem for the Empire as fatigue, disillusionment, and low morale began to set in.

Therefore, while we can see the benefits of Imperial military domination early in the conflict and before the full outbreak of war at Scarif, such a state of being was not without a cost. As previously discussed, the underlying military training within the Empire could be fairly haphazard when actually put to the test by an insurgency that eschewed the larger pitched battles that defined the Clone Wars. Every skirmish or encounter with a "rebel" enemy that the Empire won became a justification for the continuation of the military status quo, whereas every setback, clumsy operation, or defeat that should have been a learning opportunity, instead presented a problem to a military institution that was not renowned for its flexibility or adaptability. What is also noticeable is the extent to which the Empire tended to group all its opponents together as "rebels" or "rebellious elements" and not differentiate between them. Ideologically this made sense as any who opposed Palpatine's rule were effectively an enemy. But there are some significant differences between the tactics and strategies developed by, for example, the organizers of the Ghorman demonstration and Saw Gerrera's partisans. Being able to recognize those differences and account for them on the battlefield would have made the Imperial military much more effective. But by considering them both to be the same, they made it incredibly difficult to apply relevant measures while engaged in combat. While there were some, such as Grand Admiral Thrawn, who were able to adapt their strategies based upon their opposition, there were plenty of officers who either could not or would not depart from standard doctrine.

As we proceed through the events of the Galactic Civil War, there are specific moments where it becomes clear the Empire had begun to lose the war, but it could also be argued that despite the size of their military, they may never have been able to easily wage the type of conflict they became embroiled in. That their experience of crushing small planetary demonstrations, uprisings, or defenses did not adequately transfer over to dealing with a more organized, galaxy-wide rebellion undertaken by dedicated opponents who could blend into the normal population. This is not to say that a rebel victory was inevitable—they repeatedly came incredibly close to disaster and ultimate defeat—but that their Imperial opponent did not help its own cause through the organization and operation of its military. This can be seen in a variety of examples even before the "war" officially started.

The Empire at War

Given that the Galactic Empire often saw threats everywhere they looked, they were also surprisingly bad at recognizing both the real signs of rebellion and the fact that they were stoking the flames of resistance with their every action. Some of this can be ascribed to the ISB's tendency—as noted in a previous chapter—in the earliest stages of the war, to treat the rebellion as a criminal enterprise rather than a military one. Elements of this continued right throughout the conflict and at no time did the Empire ever really view the Rebel Alliance as a legitimate opponent or consider rebel captives to be prisoners of war. This would also cause problems down the line for the Empire, as will be discussed shortly, but it also helps us to frame and understand some of their actions before the formal outbreak of war.

As might be expected from a state that, for much of its history, was concerned with constantly expanding its borders, the Empire's military tended to think in terms of planetary systems rather than a wider scale. The very concept of a galaxy-wide rebel effort was often seen as a ludicrous one. In fairness, it was not until Mon Mothma's denunciation of the Emperor and her subsequent Call to Rebellion that the most organized threads of the Alliance came together. However, in undertaking the research for this work it becomes increasingly clear that the widely accepted "official" history of the Rebel Alliance has some notable gaps in it that cannot easily be accounted for and are likely worthy of further study on their own terms. Imperial records make reference to a shadowy organizer known as "Axis" who, they eventually came to believe, was coordinating rebel activities scattered across the galaxy.[2] Despite this there is no substantive record within Rebel Alliance files as to who exactly this figure was and what role they had within the organization. It is only through pulling together material from other sources, such as an abandoned datafile recovered from a camp previously operated by Saw Gerrera, that we can suggest that the real identity of "Axis" may have been a man called "Luthen Rael," but information on him is

[2] Imperial Archives, Section: Imperial Security Bureau, File: All Stations Alert—"Axis"* *File recovered from Corellian Databanks

incredibly sparse.[3] Regardless, if, as the Empire believed, such a figure was operating within the earliest framework of the Rebel Alliance, it took them an awfully long time to realize it.

Even when considering some of the Empire's most longstanding military commitments—such as at Ryloth, Kashyyyk, or Mimban—there appears to have been a noticeable blind spot within the military as to the possibility that seemingly isolated forces might be exchanging intelligence and supplies, either directly or through third party intermediaries such as "Axis." Some of this can likely be ascribed to the tendency of some ranking Imperial officers to place their own species-based prejudices over rational military thinking. This was not helped by a doctrine that placed combat against rebel forces on a similar level to encounters with smugglers or pirates. What was considered a good tactic to use against the latter could then be misapplied to the former in ways that overlooked the different motivations between a Twi'lek defending their home and a smuggler trying to dodge an Imperial customs charge. What would cause one to try to disengage and escape would not work on the other. As the next chapter will explore, the Empire repeatedly failed to grasp this fact.

This means that even as the Empire began to recognize the reality that a network might be spreading across the galaxy, they failed to take advantage of intelligence-gathering opportunities when they arose. When the Neo-Separatist Anto Kreegyr launched an attack against the Imperial power station on Spellhaus, the Empire knew he was coming. At the very least they had captured one of Kreegyr's pilots in the lead up to the operation, and it's possible they had other intelligence information as well.[4] Within the archives of the Rebel Alliance there are references to Kreegyr and suggestions that he had, in the past, exchanged

---

[3] Museum for Galactic Conflict, Miscellaneous Objects: Saw Gerrera Datafiles #19
[4] Imperial Archives, Section: Imperial Security Bureau, File: Anto Kreegyr

information and weaponry with more reliable rebel cells.[5] If the Empire had captured Kreegyr or any of his people, they may have been able to extract worthwhile information from them that would have cast further light on the movement slowly spreading under their noses. Instead, they reacted as they traditionally had done; by utilizing violence to send a message. There is some discrepancy in the actual number of Kreegyr's associates killed at the Spellhaus raid. Rebel archives suggest it was around fifty, but Saw Gerrera's records suggest thirty.[6] Regardless, there were more than enough combatants to have given the Empire a potential intelligence coup. They squandered it.

While the armed forces struggled to tell the difference between a criminal and a partisan, the Empire also tried to maintain the careful balance of ensuring that Imperial civilians felt that their government provided order and stability, but also the right semblance of impending threat that would lead them to accept ongoing security measures. The Empire needed its population to feel safe enough not to worry if the Empire could protect them. However, Imperial officials also needed those they ruled to be concerned enough about a return to the destruction of the Clone Wars that they would turn a blind eye to military activities. This was not an easy challenge. On the Core Worlds, certainly, this could be attempted while—as outlined in previous chapters—further afield the Empire felt less concerned about public opinion. Ongoing work was undertaken by the Coalition for Progress to manage the expectations and emotions of the population. Much of this activity had an inbuilt end date with the planned unveiling of the Death Star, at which point—as we will see—the relationship between the people and the state was expected to dramatically change. However, in the earliest stages of the Galactic Civil War the Empire had to deal with a "home

---

[5] Rebel Alliance Archives, Section: Separatist Assets, File: Anto Kreegyr
[6] Compare the following records: Rebel Alliance Archives, Section: Combat Losses, File: Spellhaus Attack, and; Museum for Galactic Conflict, Miscellaneous Objects: Saw Gerrera Datafiles #23.

front" that the Rebel Alliance did not. This might lead to the expectation that as the Empire looked to manage its responsibilities and the Rebel Alliance tried to muster its strength, both sides would seek to avoid an early or unnecessary escalation. However, this assumption would be an error.

Forcing the Issue

In the Outer Rim system of Dizon, there is a moon named Dizon Fray. It was inhabited by a sentient species known as the Dizonites. Full physiological details of this species no longer appear in Imperial records, but there are references to them being a semi-amphibious species who existed in the moon's primary sea and spent most of their time in or beneath the water. Again, little is now known of their customs or their civilization except for the fact that they communicated through a form of sonar based "singing" and that these "songs" could be heard from even hundreds of kilometers away. Around eight years before the Battle of Yavin, the Empire planned to place a refueling station on the moon, possibly to assist with bringing resources from the borderlands for delivery to the Death Star's construction site. According to geological surveys undertaken by Imperial scouts, there were significant deposits of raw materials in the seabed and along the shoreline that could be converted or synthesized into fuel, making the planned station almost self-sustaining.

In preparing to build the station, the Empire apparently angered the Dizonites enough that the indigenous species began to actively sabotage Imperial construction efforts. The reason for this—beyond the obvious unwillingness to be conquered—is unclear, but there are references within Imperial records to the demolition of structures that may have been temples for the Dizonite religion. So disruptive were the resistance efforts that, eventually, by 6 BBY Imperial commanders were given permission to eliminate the species. While much about the Dizonites' lives is now lost to us, the method of their extermination was very well-documented. Utilizing a variation of an energy weapon created at the Imperial Academy on Mandalore, the Imperials lowered several pulse arc reactors from beneath *Gozanti*-class cruisers into the waters of Dizon Fray and activated them. The salted water of Dizon Fray's moon proved to be exceptionally conductive and the surge in connected currents electrocuted the majority of the Dizonite population. Over what was apparently a number of hours, the species suffered and died. As they passed, they "sang" in agony with the clearest cries seemingly emanating from the young. These calls were picked up by a variety of Imperial recording devices used to document and confirm the success of the genocide. It seems that these recordings could also prove highly traumatic to listen to and rendered several Imperial communications officers catatonic.[7] As awful as this aspect was, it seemed to pique the interest of interrogation specialists—such as one Doctor Gorst—within the ISB who used adapted versions of these sounds as torture devices on those suspected of harboring information about a wider rebellion.[8]

As previous chapters have shown, the sheer extent of the Empire's awful crimes would easily fill a work like this many times over. The point of re-telling this particular horror is that it indicates firstly both the planned and casual nature of Imperial brutality against their enemies and also the extent to which they miscalculated its effect on their opponents. The Empire wanted its opponents to know that violence, death, and torture were all that would greet them if they resisted. However, it then completely failed to understand that there might be different effects on those who took the message onboard. Imperial officials seemed to believe that, given the violence they were capable of inflicting on entire systems and species, and the suffering they could

---

[7] Imperial Archives, Section: Outer Rim Infrastructure, File: Dizon Fray*
*Recordings heavily encrypted with attached safety warnings
[8] Imperial Archives, Section: Imperial Security Bureau, File: Doctor Gorst

also then impose onto individuals through torture and interrogation, that their enemies would flee and disband in fear. Some within the rebel movement undoubtedly did exactly that. But there were plenty of others who saw this behavior from the Empire and realized that no negotiation would ever be possible, and as capture would result in—at best— horrendous torture followed by a death sentence, it was better to die fighting. Additionally, they also recognized that the Empire's barbarism would not simply plateau over time, things would only get worse, and therefore its true face had to be dragged into the light as quickly as possible for others to see.

If the Empire was allowed to fully instigate its policy of "escalating normality" then the galaxy would be lost before most of the population had noticed or could process what was happening. It has often been assumed that while the rebel movement tried to form links between the various disparate groups that would eventually form the "Alliance" it was reluctant to try and escalate the conflict. This certainly seems true for some of its leadership—we know the extent to which Mon Mothma tried to find a political solution. But it does also appear that there were others within the cause who believed that the Rebellion required further instances of Imperial violence and oppression through which to invigorate resistance. Upon reaching this conclusion, they then sought to provoke exactly that Imperial response. Intriguingly there appear to have been those within the Empire who wanted the exact same thing.

It is difficult now to look back on hundreds of incidents including those on worlds like Kashyyyk, Mimban, and Ryloth as well as the raids on Spellhaus and Aldhani and easily distinguish the coordinated from the spontaneous.[9] Different groups fought in different ways and, by the very nature of a cell system, would have very limited ways of

---

[9] The archives of the Rebel Alliance have significant gaps in them regarding operations in the early years. This may well be explained by the deaths of those who coordinated the different rebel cells at the time, but we should also consider the possibility that existing records were removed or erased.

communicating outside of their own areas. Between the different groups and cells lurked coordinating agents like "Axis" who facilitated and planned forthcoming operations and likely also provided supplies and intelligence. Capturing these figures became an ongoing obsession for some within the ISB, but the increase in rebel activity also provided an opportunity that others welcomed. While the endgame of the Imperial plan for domination was the ongoing construction of the Death Star, that project was beset by delays and shortages. Perhaps Palpatine himself began to tire of waiting for the full subjugation of those who opposed him, or alternatively others such as Tarkin decided to push forward. Regardless, impatience began to spread through the Imperial machine. With every rebel strike, every raid, every riot, and every skirmish came a chance to accelerate their plans. Rebel activity justified additional military spending, it allowed for more aggressive stormtrooper deployments, and increased punitive taxation. Long term, neither the Rebel Alliance nor the Galactic Empire could coexist alongside the other. It was to be a true war of annihilation where only oppression or liberation could triumph. But here, in the earliest years of the Rebellion, it appears that both the rebels and the Empire actually needed the other to be the most radical or aggressive versions of themselves. One would provoke the other into action that would lead to violent repercussions which in turn would produce new recruits. It was a strange symbiotic relationship that marched both down the path to war.

Before the Storm

By about five years before the Battle of Yavin it becomes clear that even if outright war did not exist between the Galactic Empire and the forces of the Rebel Alliance, they were coming into increasing levels of conflict with each other. As previously mentioned, the tendency by Imperial officials to link acts of rebellion with other crimes makes it difficult to fully assess how many incidents were perpetrated by rebel agents and which were ordinary acts of resistance or criminality. Rebel archives are similarly lacking in clear information. What is noticeable is that across hundreds of worlds acts of sabotage began to increase. Riots were organized, bombs planted, and officials assassinated. The Rebel Alliance has long tried to maintain an image that suggested they waged wars in the "right way," but not all of these acts can be attributed to extremist factions like Saw Gerrera's. My own recent military service has shown me that there is no clinical way to wage an insurgency against a stronger opponent. Some of these activities must have been approved and sanctioned by Rebel High Command, even if there were dissenting voices or reluctant figures among them. These attacks on the Empire were never intended to fully cripple the state. Imperial operations were far too large for any single incident to prove more than a short-term disruption or annoyance. Instead, the strategy appears to have been to make the Empire feel as if it was slowly being assailed on all sides, making it impossible to get an accurate assessment of how many groups were actively engaged against it. It was not immediate victory that motivated rebel operations in this period, but instead the fostering of localized chaos, compelling Imperial officials to react without proper intelligence and—often—without relevant training.

In space, Imperial forces began to encounter smaller fighters and larger transports that did not engage them in the ways traditionally associated with pirates or smugglers. They tried to breach Imperial blockades to deliver food or supplies to designated warzones rather than dropping their cargo and escaping. They did not actively prey on civilian traffic, instead aiming to attack and neutralize small Imperial patrols. If confronted with sudden Imperial reinforcements, larger ships would attempt to flee while fighters would distract any TIE pursuit. Having enemies flee before them greatly pleased many Imperial naval officers. They had been trained to expect their adversaries to run in fear, so having it happen validated their own beliefs. But there were others who saw the rebel tendency to escape as a significant problem. How could you actively defeat an enemy who refused to stand and fight?[10] Victory postponed was no victory at all, especially when those escaping were also linked to ongoing sabotage and other attacks against the Imperial state. Frustration began to grow within the navy and, as a result, so too did the tendency for more violent reprisals.

Following repeated acts of vandalism and graffiti on Imperial propaganda and recruitment posters on the small world of Ivera X, the major city was strafed by TIE fighters and bombers until seventy-three percent of its original buildings had been destroyed.[11] The surviving civilians were forced to erect new monuments to the Empire from the rubble before being permitted to rebuild their homes. On Arieli the refueling equipment for an *Arquitens*-class light cruiser was sabotaged by a local insurgency group, meaning the vessel could not leave the planet's atmosphere. While awaiting new equipment, the captain ordered his gunners to begin targeting municipal buildings such as schools, libraries, and hospitals. When reinforcements arrived, they joined in.[12] Dinwa Prime perhaps suffered worse than many others. Six years before the Battle of Yavin, the local planetary governor was killed by what Imperial officials described as a "rebel terrorist and traitor sponsored by the local community," though they presented no evidence to back up this assertion. Regardless, it was decided that a collective ongoing punishment was appropriate. Dinwa Prime lay within reach of the Hydian Way hyperspace route through the Inner Rim territories. Imperial naval ships that passed along the route would often stop at the planet to test and synchronize their weapons from orbit or allow TIE pilots to practice bombing runs.[13] Over time it was left in ruins.

[10] Imperial Archives, Section: Joint Chiefs of the Imperial Military, File: Memo # JQ3719—Issues Forcing Engagements
[11] Rebel Alliance Archives, Section: Defections & Debriefings, File: Thane Kyrell #17
[12] Imperial Archives, Section: Imperial Navy, File: *Peacemaker* After Action Report #611.3
[13] Imperial Archives, Section: Reprisal Activities, File: Dinwa Prime Firing-Range Directive

When faced with an enemy that constantly eluded them, the Empire chose to mercilessly attack the ones they could reach. While this likely helped salve some egos, almost certainly including Palpatine's, it was not a cohesive way to win an unfolding war. Every atrocity caused fear, yes, but also drove new recruits into the rebel ranks. As the various cells skirted on the edge of discovery, they began to expand their numbers and their ambitions. While the Spectre cell on Lothal had initial contact with the wider Rebellion through Hera Syndulla and one of its Fulcrum agents, their initial purview of resisting the Empire on just a single system proved unsustainable. As further Imperial forces were committed to combating them, they were inexorably dragged into the wider conflict and their sphere of influence and responsibility began to grow. Other cells likely went through a similar pathway where the encroachment of the Empire resulted in them forming stronger bonds with the centralized Rebellion.

While the Rebel Alliance tried to rally its strength, they were largely unaware that time was not on their side. The escalation that some had wanted was underway, but while they sought to distract and damage the Imperial state, out of their sight, construction on the Death Star continued. When completed and unleashed it would dramatically change the strategic picture. But, as we will see, work on the battle station was not running smoothly, and there were competing voices and visions within the joint chiefs of how best to utilize it. While Director Krennic forged ahead with his project, other Imperial officers—particularly in the navy—would have to begin reconsidering how best to use the tools at hand.

Chapter 15

Fleet and Starfighter Tactics

While we will deal with the Death Star in much greater detail in the next chapter, the very desire to construct it in the first place raises some interesting and important questions about the rest of the Imperial military, primarily: What was the Death Star designed to do that the vast Imperial fleet could not already accomplish? The Empire had spent years churning out Star Destroyers in huge numbers—and at great expense—alongside TIE fighters in almost untold quantities. Was all this firepower really not enough? Yes, the Death Star could destroy a planet with a single blast but, as we have already seen, bombardment from orbit was more than capable of devastating cities and populations. The residents of Caamas and Dinwa Prime were just as dead as those on Alderaan would soon be. What did it matter how it was achieved? Obviously, there was a degree of theatricality to the Death Star's abilities and the sheer size of it that was designed to quell all resistance. But there might also have been an underlying concern within the Imperial military, a body that often split into rival factions, about whether or not the fleet was actually being used properly, or fit for purpose.

Having emerged as the primary galactic power from the Clone Wars and undertaken an ambitious expansion of its armed forces, the Empire had both secured the power of the Imperial Navy and also, in a strange twist, almost driven it to the point of obsolescence. So thoroughly was the Separatist cause dismantled that, in many ways, the masses of Star

Destroyers that rolled out of the shipyards at Kuat, Corellia, Fondor and dozens of other installations had no obvious peer enemy to combat. While they could be—and regularly were—used to subjugate worlds or undertake orbital bombardments, they existed as a weapons platform designed to solve a problem that did not exist. Stripped of the requirement to enter dedicated ship-to-ship combat, at least until later in the Galactic Civil War, the Imperial Star Destroyer's sole purpose appears to have become just to *exist* in a menacing way. While they could deliver troops or fighters to different worlds around the Empire, so too could a variety of smaller and less expensive vessels. For something that was so crew intensive and required regular re-supply, it is not always clear exactly what the navy's Star Destroyers were supposed to be doing on a day-to-day basis.

Other vessels and weaponry within the Imperial arsenal such as the various TIE starfighters could serve different roles, from planetary defense and garrisoning to anti-pirate operations, and, as a result, were far more flexible. However, given the vast number of TIE variants that were designed, let alone those put into production, there were clearly concerns within that branch of the military that there were things the standard TIE fighter could not do. Some of them were due to issues with the design itself, but there were also probably doctrinal problems that lurked beneath the surface. As previously discussed, Imperial training could vary in quality depending on where the cadet was based. This could produce a disparate class of new recruits, but cause far greater issues within the officer corps. The ability to adequately do your job within the military was quite often viewed as less important than demonstrable loyalty, the ability to unquestioningly follow orders, or political connections. It did not matter how cutting edge the weapons assigned to the military were if those commanding them did not know how best to use them.

By examining a wealth of military records that have survived from the fall of the Empire—including briefing, debriefing, and after-action reports—alongside rebel analysis of the Imperial military and a mix of interrogation reports and post-war memoirs, it becomes possible to shine a light on the vaunted Imperial fleet in a way that was not possible before. While it may have appeared to be a smoothly ordered and orchestrated military machine on the surface, it seems that the armed forces of the Galactic Empire were far more dysfunctional than possibly even the rebels ever realized. Hobbled by a mix of outdated or unimaginative military doctrines that blunted the ability of the fleet to engage enemies in a more cohesive way, the navy in particular was split into opposing factions. In their simplest forms—and these factions were far more complicated than this overview suggests—they differed over the best way to utilize their firepower: either through massed fleet formations and damage output, or the more targeted use of smaller forces. The successes and failures through debate and promotion of these two wings of the Imperial military would have a profound impact on the war as a whole and provide many of the answers to the question, why didn't the navy just win the conflict by itself?

Diagnosing the Problem

The Battle of Scarif provides an interesting case study regarding some of the deficiencies within the Imperial approach to fighting the Rebel Alliance, and how the various factions within the navy interpreted both its causes and solutions. Although the rebel fleet under Admiral Raddus had the benefit of surprise, and Raddus was a far better military commander than his adversary Admiral Gorin, an examination of the opposing forces suggests that the two Imperial Star Destroyers guarding the planet—the *Intimidator* and the *Persecutor*—should not have been fought to a standstill and then subsequently destroyed along with the shield gate.[1] The Imperial capital ships heavily outgunned the

---

[1] For full details of the battle examine both; Imperial Archives, Section: Imperial Navy Operations, File: Battle of Scarif Analysis, and; Rebel Alliance Archives, File: Military Operations, File: Scarif Debriefing #12.

rebel opposition and could field far more TIE fighters than their rebel equivalents, and yet the battle was a tactical disaster. The local situation was salvaged by the arrival of the Death Star and Darth Vader onboard the *Devastator*, but the losses of Imperial personnel were unprecedented, and strategically the consequences were far-reaching. Was it just command ineptitude that explained the Imperial defeat or was there more to it? That question became a highly contentious topic within the Imperial military in the days and weeks afterward and was seized upon by the different schools of thought who argued that either Gorin had failed to use his forces effectively or, more concerningly from an Imperial point of view, had never possessed the necessary forces to begin with.

There were plenty within the Imperial Navy who believed that greater firepower was the solution to any military situation the Empire was likely to face. Certainly, the standard Imperial Star Destroyer possessed more than enough turbolasers to theoretically deal with most enemies, particularly given that the early Rebel Alliance was not believed to possess any rival capital ships. Similarly, when the basic TIE fighter was deployed in swarms, they would overwhelm most enemy snub fighters and were highly effective at disabling larger ships or destroying pirate vessels. In the face of the Scarif debacle some argued—as they had done in hypothetical discussions before the battle—that Gorin had not been nearly aggressive enough in utilizing his weaponry. To support this argument, supporters of the "firepower" lobby highlighted how Vader's ship had no issues with disabling Raddus' flagship upon arriving at the battle, and ascribed much of this to both Vader's natural aggression and also Captain Shaef Corssin's greater military skill. There is some truth to this argument. Gorin had allowed his attacks to be spread across the rebel fleet without ever really concentrating his weaponry. The answer, therefore, to the Scarif scenario was supposedly for Imperial commanders to seize the initiative, and for heavier, more concentrated firepower to be considered in future—as the new *Imperial II*-class and Super Star Destroyers being designed by KDY would showcase.

But this was not a viewpoint entirely shared within the fleet. Others, particularly those who had served within the—recently lost—7th Fleet under Grand Admiral Thrawn, maintained that "be more aggressive" was not an actual strategy. They feared that by embarking down some form of turbolaser-based arms race the Imperial Navy ran the risk of exacerbating existing problems. While the guns of Gorin's *Intimidator* should have been powerful enough to breach the *Profundity*'s shields—as Vader's *Devastator* did—they repeatedly proved incapable of adequately combating the rebel starfighter force. The cannons were far too slow in tracking the faster moving targets; and while they did succeed in destroying some, it appears to have been based more on luck than any technical proficiency.[2] Admittedly, dealing with enemy fighters was supposed to be the job of the Imperial TIEs –so why did they also fail? At Scarif, Gorin seemed incredibly slow to deploy extra fighters from the shield gate and, as a result, several X-wings made it through the junction to the planet below. Across the rest of the battle, TIEs struggled to fully overwhelm the rebel ships despite their far greater numbers.

Critics argued that there were serious issues both with the TIE fighter design and the ways in which they were used that hindered the Imperial war effort.[3] The standard TIE was designed to be fast, maneuverable, and with an impressive rate of fire. However, it was also designed to be cheaply mass-produced. The interior of most TIEs was often depressurized during battle—pilots were forced to wear fully enclosed flight suits—and the ships possessed no shielding. This rather reflects the tension in the Empire's military between cost effectiveness

[2] Imperial Archives, Section: Military Analysis, File: Scarif Starfighter Operations
[3] Imperial Archives, Section: Military Memos, File: TIE fighters in a cluttered battlefield* *Authorship of this memo is attributed to the "Tactics and Strategy Subcommittee," which had a revolving membership.

and capability. While the standard TIE fighter maintained the same rough specifications throughout its lifespan, the Empire did explore different variants. The TIE interceptor was notably faster and better armed than its predecessor and was developed to try and combat the faster ships of the nascent Rebel Alliance. Similarly, the TIE bomber traded speed for payload capacity and stronger hull armor. However, none of these new vessels succeeded in solving the most serious problem in the TIE line; pilot survivability. When combining available information for pilots who graduated in the top five percent of their classes at Carida, Skystrike Academy, and the Royal Imperial Academy during the first year of the Galactic Civil War the results were stark.[4] Just under seventy-two percent of those pilots were killed in action within two years of graduating. Even these estimates are slightly skewed by the pilots' varying number of missions and dangers inherent with being assigned to tours with Titan or Scythe Squadrons. Even the elite 181st fighter wing had mixed results for new recruits. The lack of shields on TIE fighters did not allow pilots—regardless of their skill level—to easily survive mistakes. While rebel pilots still needed a degree of luck to survive engagements, deflector shields were often the difference between life and death. The more pilots flew, the better they became. If the Empire's best and brightest were being killed off in high numbers early in their careers, the abilities of its pilots would always lag behind those of the Rebel Alliance.

This, therefore, prompted Grand Admiral Thrawn's attempt to develop the TIE defender as an alternative advanced starfighter. It possessed a hyperdrive, missile capabilities, and an array of laser cannons. But most importantly, it had shields. All these features together would allow the ships to operate far more independently than existing

---

[4] These records are spread across Imperial Archives as: Carida Military Academy Graduation Records #887996, Skystrike Academy Roll of Honor #BQ114, and the Royal Imperial Academy Declaration of Merit #766ADQ.12.

designs.[5] They could travel through hyperspace without requiring a carrier vessel and, crucially, would allow pilots to survive through combat and learn any lessons afterward. Thrawn's plan for the TIE defender was presumably to try and remake the Imperial Navy into something far more flexible and capable of precision operations. The loss of funding for his project, and then the destruction of the factory on Lothal, probably robbed the Empire of a fighter that was many orders better than those flying for the Rebel Alliance. It may not have been a war-winning weapon in itself, but it would have dramatically improved the options available to even the most unimaginative of military commanders.

Given that the competing viewpoints within the Imperial Navy could not agree on a clear strategy in the period before or immediately after Yavin, it now becomes instructive to examine how different military commanders made use of the forces at their disposal, or created new tactics, as well as the ways their decisions impacted the ongoing battle for control of Imperial fleet doctrine.

The Imperial Way of Warfare

As previously noted, the Galactic Empire tended to treat variations from established doctrines or unexpected imagination with a deal of suspicion. This reluctance to embrace tactical innovation, plus emerging resistance among some officers to the Empire's harsh methods, cost the Imperial military a variety of skilled analysts and tacticians, most notably Adar Tallon who defected to the Rebel Alliance having served with distinction in the Republic's military.[6]

Despite this there were those within the military who would take different approaches to combat situations or attempt to vary their tactics

---

[5] Rebel Alliance Archives, Section: Imperial Equipment Analysis, File: TIE defender flight computer* *Report filed at Yavin following material captured from Lothal.

[6] Rebel Alliance Archives, Section: Defections & Debriefings, File: Adar Tallon

and strategies in ways that might have produced new working models. Similarly, there were also those who looked to take existing approaches forward and test exactly how aggressive they could be in battle scenarios. The nature of the ideological splits within the military meant that, at best, around half of the officers invested in the dispute would either welcome or decry the outcome of each new evolution of Imperial strategy, so results would have to be hugely conclusive to stand a chance at winning over a majority of invested personnel. For those who favored the more flexible or precise approach to waging war, Grand Admiral Thrawn was seen as the clearest example of what could be achieved. However, a study of Thrawn's approach perhaps requires a bit more nuance and analysis than was certainly the case within the Imperial Navy and in many studies since.

While many have tried, and failed, to replicate Thrawn's ability to critically deconstruct his opponent's psyche and likely methods through their artistic preferences, there were more easily discernable tactics that the Empire could look to replicate if it had desired to do so. Alongside his plans for the TIE defender, Thrawn also had his starfighter commanders approach combat in a more structured manner. While many Imperial engagements would see TIEs deployed in various mass formations to create a swarm, Thrawn seemed to prefer his fighters to approach the enemy in smaller groups of three or four in order to quickly overwhelm rebel wingpairs without also cluttering the battlefield and making it impossible for any of his light cruisers to engage.[7] When he did allow TIEs to attack en masse, such as in the second phase of the defense of Lothal, the decision was made as much on the basis of the damage it would do to rebel morale as for military necessity. Thrawn also recognized, notably earlier than many of his peers, that the Empire was unlikely to find long-term success on the

---

[7] Imperial Archives, Section: 7th Fleet Standing Orders, File: Fighter Command—Formations and Tactics #WB375* *Information recovered from wreckage at Lothal

battlefield if they could not force the rebels to fight on it. His use of Interdictor cruisers to trap the rebel fleet at Atollon was a perfect demonstration of his ability to predict his enemies' decisions and counter them in advance.[8] However, both at that battle and later at Lothal, Thrawn showed his approach to precision warfare was not necessarily born out of any absolute aversion to utilizing significant firepower, but rather because he felt it was simply a more effective way to win battles.

At Atollon, Thrawn ordered an orbital bombardment of the rebel base. This was, ostensibly at least, to test their shield generator and also destroy their morale. But if the shield had collapsed then the base would likely have been obliterated along with the various rebels he aimed to capture. That outcome would not have been much of a testament to finesse and precision. Similarly, he also bombarded civilian quarters on Lothal in an attempt to blackmail rebels in control of the Imperial command building to lower their shields and surrender. Thrawn was not unwilling to revert to brute force if he judged the situation to warrant it, he simply saw more value in other approaches. Thrawn was also not, for all the reputational gloss he has apparently gained since the Galactic Civil War and the events that followed, immune from making bad decisions. At Atollon the failure to capture the rebel leaders can largely be traced back to several errors of Thrawn's judgment. While information about an intervention staged by a creature known only as "the Bendu" is scarce and—even given my own research into the realities of the Force— seems highly improbable, whatever role it actually played in the battle does not overcome the poor staffing choices Thrawn himself made.

Given the importance placed on the two Interdictor cruisers pre- venting a rebel escape, it seems ludicrous now to have placed Admiral Kassius Konstantine in command of one. Konstantine was a man who

---

[8] Imperial Archives, Section: 7th Fleet, File: Battle of Atollon—Fleet Composition and Formation

owed most of his promotions to his political connections and had a litany of battlefield failures in his own history.[9] Even allowing for Thrawn's supposed lack of political skills, his own military instincts should have told him this was an unwise decision before it cost him one of his most important vessels. Similarly, the initial attack on Atollon had been led by the tactically astute Captain Corf Ferno aboard the *Dark Omen*. When Thrawn decided—unwisely—to lead the ground offensive, he could have returned command of the space battle to that ship. Instead, he left Lothal's Governor Pryce in charge, who appears not to have possessed any military abilities.[10] She subsequently lost control of the situation and allowed the rebels to escape. Thrawn's failure to destroy what was perceived—wrongly, as it turned out—to be the majority of the rebel fleet was a boon to those who opposed either his non-human heritage or his vision of warfare. It also placed significant shadows over several of his officers following the Battle of Lothal and Thrawn's disappearance.[11] While Captain Ferno would eventually be promoted through the ranks and escaped relatively unscathed, since his ship was not present at Lothal due to ongoing repairs, Captain Gilad Pellaeon—who survived the disastrous Lothal engagement—does not appear to have been immediately promoted in the same way, despite his obvious talents. Much of this can perhaps be attributed to decisions taken by those who were keen for Thrawn's legacy to be one of failure.

By contrast, officers like Admirals Conan Motti and Kendal Ozzel, both of whom would eventually experience their own failures, saw the Imperial military as a weapon of destruction to be used vigorously against the enemy. Both believed that the Rebel Alliance could be

[9] Rebel Alliance Archives, Section: Imperial Analysis, File: Admiral Konstantine—Shortcomings
[10] Imperial Archives, Section: 7th Fleet Standing Orders, File: Battle of Atollon—Order #YA715—Temporary Change of Command
[11] See: New Republic Archives, Section: Imperial Prisoners, File: Interrogations 142 & 212

defeated either by overwhelming firepower, such as the Death Star, or by inflicting a sense of fear and dread through the appearance of the Imperial fleet, as Ozzel attempted at Hoth (and as will be discussed in greater detail later). This—often unshakeable—belief that technological solutions should focus around enhancing the damage output of the Imperial Navy also found receptive supporters in other branches of the military. Both General Octavion Sorin and General Vitsun Weiss of the Imperial Army looked to incorporate additional firepower into their armaments and strategies. Sorin was a strong proponent of upscaled AT-ST walkers that featured enhanced weaponry, seeking to make up in damage output what they lacked in accuracy.[12] Similarly, General Weiss pioneered a form of combined-arms combat that utilized repulsortanks, orbital bombardments, and TIE fighter support.[13] Though both would ultimately meet defeats against the Rebel Alliance, their desire and lobbying for increased weaponry found support within the navy and, perhaps just as importantly, those Imperial officials with connections to KDY who would potentially benefit from increased armament contracts. In many ways these two spheres often worked hand in hand. Because if the Empire could not think their way to a war-winning solution, there were plenty who thought they might be able to build their way to it.

Alternative Solutions

While the construction of the Death Star was an ongoing concern and essentially intended to be the final word of both Imperial industrial output and military doctrine, it was not the only attempt the Empire made to come up with adaptable solutions that would serve their

[12] Imperial Archives, Section: Imperial Army, File General Sorin—AT-ST Design Schematics #JQ716

[13] Imperial Archives, Section: Imperial Army Doctrine, File: General Weiss' Combined-Arms Formation

purposes. As previously mentioned, Grand Admiral Thrawn's TIE defender program could, if it had been allowed to succeed, have produced a formidable weapon. While acknowledging that there were plenty within the military happy to see it—and Thrawn—fail, the very fact it was under production at all is a sign that the Empire was not close-minded to new weaponry. It does, however, raise questions about why the Empire designated funding in the directions that it did.

The artificial gravity-well technology that allowed Interdictor cruisers to prevent ships escaping into hyperspace was both incredibly complicated and expensive. It took the Rebel Alliance years to gather up enough different parts to even begin the reverse engineering process. However, despite the cost, surely a ship that prevented the rebels from escaping was worth greater investment. Interestingly, there are record fragments within the Imperial archives that suggest the navy undertook repeated tests—involving a series of highly expensive tracking beacons—to detect ships moving into and out of hyperspace.[14] This would presumably have been of interest to those designing the Interdictor's sensor arrays, but there is no record within that project of the outcome of these hyperspace tracking tests being incorporated at all. As a result, it is unclear exactly what the purpose of them was. Regardless, by the end of the war the Empire had—according to admittedly incomplete records—constructed maybe only a few dozen Interdictors.[15] This was despite the fact they offered the best chance to overcome one of the most pressing obstacles to the Imperial fleet. Meanwhile, it seems like huge amounts of credits were poured into the creation of the *Onager*-class Star Destroyer. This was a ship that was seemingly under design at the end of the Clone Wars and the Empire persevered with it. Design schematics show that a huge cannon was designed to fire directly down the

[14] Imperial Archives, Section: Research and Development, File: Hyperspace Beacons* *These files appear to have been heavily censored or deleted.
[15] Kuat Archives, Section: Imperial Contracts, File: Interdictor Cruiser

length of the vessel in order to destroy enemy blockades and key command ships.[16] Rebel Alliance records suggest that few of them ever saw service in the war, though it's possible that their technological developments were later incorporated into the fleets of the First and Final Orders. Regardless of the ship's negligible impact, it seems that the Empire spent more money and resources on developing the Onager than they ever spent on producing further Interdictors.[17] The belief that extreme firepower could solve all problems repeatedly hobbled alternative Imperial production efforts, as a newer and bigger gun was always just around the corner.

As a result, the Imperial military—and specifically the fleet—was perpetually caught between competing ideological factions within itself, while also being driven in directions that were not necessarily advantageous by those who would profit from their KDY affiliations. For many frustrated Imperial commanders, the only silver lining to this situation was the fact that, soon enough, it would be rendered a moot point. For those who backed increased firepower, the Death Star was seen as the tool that would not simply solve the war but also guarantee rule over the galaxy. For those who wished the Empire to spend its resources more carefully, it was seen as an inevitability that would have to be lived with. While Tarkin was clearly invested in the project he would soon take control of, it is more accurate to say that he believed the threat of firepower and destruction was far more advantageous than the ongoing use of it. As it turned out, the reality of the Death Star was to have far-reaching implications on the entire Imperial war effort.

[16] Kuat Archives, Section: Imperial Contracts, File: *Onager*-class Star Destroyer
[17] Kuat Archives, Section: Finances, File: Incoming Investments #KV2001 & #LQ3817

Chapter 16

The Tarkin Doctrine and the Death Star

The Death Star project casts its shadow over the early years of the Empire, the course of the Galactic Civil War and, indeed, this study so far. In many ways the declaration of the Death Star reaching full operational status, its use on Alderaan, and then destruction at Yavin split the timeline of the Empire in two. Before this point all the efforts, resources, and energies of the state were deployed in making the battle station a reality. Afterward, the Empire was left to try and construct a new short-term strategy to combat the Rebel Alliance while Palpatine insisted on a new and improved design, to be constructed at Endor. Virtually all who played a major role with the first Death Star were either killed or changed by the experience. While Darth Vader and General Tagge survived—for a while at least—the disaster, the likes of Admiral Motti, Director Orson Krennic and, most crucially, Grand Moff Tarkin perished. The vacuum left by those figures—Tarkin especially—and the destroyed Death Star warped almost every aspect of the Imperial military and significant parts of the Imperial state infrastructure. Never had the Empire suffered such a grievous defeat, nor had the shortcomings of its military and propaganda wings been left so exposed. The destruction of the Death Star was, in many ways, the first sign of the Empire's eventual collapse.

However, to truly understand why this was the case, it is necessary to explore, analyze, and reconsider much that we previously "knew" about the Death Star project. It has become apparent just through the material explored so far, that the Imperial military was nowhere near as unified behind the project as those within the Rebel Alliance may have believed. Similarly, the power struggle between Krennic and Tarkin took place largely out of sight of the rebels, with much of the maneuvering happening in the upper echelons of the Imperial hierarchy. While the Death Star has become indelibly linked to Tarkin, it certainly appears that ownership of the project was a more contested issue than was once appreciated. Furthermore, the dissolution of the Senate occurring just as the Death Star was brought online no longer looks to be quite the coincidence that it may have appeared at the time. It seems apparent that Palpatine himself had placed a great deal of importance on the weapon's construction, and it formed the cornerstone of his long-term plans for galactic domination. What did those plans actually look like and how well did the Empire—and the Emperor—react to losing what was to be the central pillar of their military power?

On the surface, the point of the Death Star seems entirely obvious—to destroy planets and eliminate their populations. But while the Empire had no compunctions about committing genocide or causing widespread destruction, the Death Star was not envisioned to be a casual weapon. It had a greater purpose than that. Dead civilians did not, in the long-term, produce much benefit for the Empire in isolation. But the fear their deaths created was a much more useful and sustainable resource. In this sense we should not simply look at the Death Star as a genocidal weapon, but as a terror one instead. Its construction and use were the final step in a political strategy shared by both Emperor Palpatine and Grand Moff Tarkin—and in fact pioneered by the latter. This strategy had informed virtually every major decision and project undertaken by the Empire in the first 19 years of its existence. It was collectively known as the Tarkin Doctrine, and while it resulted in untold death and suffering across the galaxy even before Alderaan, it may also have cost the Empire the war.

Through Fear of Force

While Grand Moff Wilhuff Tarkin was the primary driving force behind the strategic doctrine that would bear his name, he was not its sole creator. In many ways the entire history of the Galactic Empire had led up to this point. While, as we have seen, there is ample evidence to show just how comfortable the Empire in general—and Tarkin in particular—was with killing large numbers of civilians if the need arose, there is also something else lurking in the evidence that we have examined so far. Almost all aspects of the Imperial infrastructure, every unspoken "rule" that civilians acquiesced to, every initiative brought about by concerned parents, every understanding of the law, every blind eye that was turned, helped confirm a single truism that the Empire was slowly coming to recognize. While ruling the galaxy would require an ongoing military presence and the application of force, it was many times easier if those who were to be ruled acquiesced on their own account. If the population of the galaxy could be brought to accept and conform to what the Empire wanted without Imperial authorities having to actually impose it upon them, then a great deal of effort, expense, and risk could be removed from proceedings.

It was this acknowledgment that laid the foundations for what would become known as the Tarkin Doctrine. Yes, the Emperor wanted to rule the galaxy and, presumably, to do so in as cruel and oppressive a manner as possible. But Tarkin realized that there were multiple routes to achieving that objective. Tarkin argued, seemingly directly to the Emperor, that while force was a necessary motivator for the civilian population and often a solution to some of the problems that the Empire would face, it was not a universal option.[1] This may have itself been a

[1] There are various fragments of the initial memo from Tarkin to the Emperor within the files recovered from the Empire. The most complete versions of these can be found in; Imperial Archives, Section: Grand Moff Wilhuff Tarkin, Communications with Coruscant, Dispatch PA0819 and; Imperial Archives, Section: Grand Moff Wilhuff Tarkin, File: Communications with COMPNOR #4336.

reflection of Tarkin holding concerns about the ability of the Imperial fleet to fully exercise what was required of it, without exacerbating problems by either bungling operations or provoking stiffer resistance than expected. When relying upon force itself there was always the risk that it would instill rebellion rather than compliance, or backfire because of the decisions of those in command. The fear of that force, however, was a much more powerful motivator. In the minds of those who the Empire wished to rule, the death that could rain down on them in a worst-case scenario was always total, the orders flawlessly executed by those who were both ruthless and competent. By weaponizing peoples' fears, the Empire never ran the risk of coming up short in practice.

This is not to say that, to quote Tarkin, "ruling through fear of force rather than force itself" was a flawless method. The very existence of an emerging Rebel Alliance indicated that the threat of Imperial retribution was not enough to make all forms of opposition dissipate, regardless of what the Emperor or other senior Imperial figures may have desired. If the spirit of defiance within those groups was to be truly crushed it would require more than just a few extra Star Destroyers or a larger Imperial garrison on each planet. Ordinary forces were seemingly enough to maintain control on many worlds, but there were those who despised Imperial rule enough that they had potentially become desensitized to the existing symbols of military might. It would require something different, something exceptional, to break their spirit. To achieve this the Empire required a tool that was so transformative, so terrifying, that it would even render the Imperial Senate obsolete and force the galaxy under Palpatine's rule forever.

The Ultimate Weapon

The actual origins of the weapon that would become the Death Star are complex. Surviving records from the Republic Special Weapons Group—which would eventually become the Imperial Military

Department of Advanced Weapons Research—suggest that the initial concepts for the battle station were created by the Geonosians during the Clone Wars at the behest of Count Dooku.[2] Given that Palpatine was orchestrating this effort from behind the scenes, it seems likely that he was utilizing the Geonosians' formidable weapon-design capabilities as a starting point. Where and when the Republic came across these plans is unclear, but it prompted a move within the—soon to be fallen— state to begin the creation, in secret, of their own weapon to combat what they believed to be a Separatist plot. While the Republic itself did not survive the end of the war, the work it began on building what would become the Death Star continued unbroken.

What is particularly interesting about the early stages of the Death Star's development is the complicated nature of the project's ownership. Certainly, when examining administrative documents, it would seem that Director Orson Krennic, who had previously served within the Republic's Special Weapons Group, was charged with the development of the superlaser armament and the overall construction of the weapon.[3] Many of the orders and requisition forms for the project required Krennic's ultimate approval, further suggesting that he was at the top of the bureaucratic tree. However, it is equally clear that he was not alone in having a great deal of interest and influence on the project—Grand Moff Tarkin cast a long shadow over the proceedings. Indeed, the very organization within the Imperial Military Department of Advanced Weapons Research charged with the development of the Death Stars was known as the Tarkin Initiative. Stories were rife within the Imperial court as to the ongoing animosity between Krennic and Tarkin, with many attributing it to the former's sense of inferiority given Tarkin's elevated social class and importance to the Empire.

---

[2] Imperial Archives, Section: Republic Special Weapons Group, File: Superweapon Development* *Record marked as "Restricted from the Jedi Council"
[3] Imperial Archives, Section: Project Stardust, File: Command Hierarchy

Examining the balance of power between the pair now, at some distance, it does appear that Tarkin was reasonably content to allow Krennic to maintain administrative and day-to-day control of the Death Star's development—and all the inherent risks associated with it—while ensuring that he himself had control over the infrastructure involved in its production. Even the weapon facility on Eadu, where much of the work to design the superlaser itself was undertaken, was leased to the Empire—and therefore Krennic—from the Tarkin family.[4] Through measures such as this, Tarkin was able to exert a degree of control over Krennic's activities and also interpose himself as a buffer between Krennic and other Imperial leaders such as Darth Vader or the Emperor himself. To get the audiences and information he required, Krennic would often have to go through Tarkin first.

The actual production of the Death Star was often a fraught and costly affair. Nothing so large or powerful had ever been constructed and many of the technologies required to power the station and the main superlaser needed to be invented almost from scratch. To achieve this the Empire, through Krennic, harvested many of the brightest scientific minds that were available throughout the galaxy. Foremost among these was Galen Erso, a long-time friend and compatriot of Krennic. Erso's apparent lack of social skills belied his dazzling intellect. Having previously been rescued from Separatist imprisonment during the Clone Wars, it appears that Erso was slowly drawn into the Death Star project through a variety of subterfuges that hid the real nature of the weapon.[5] Erso was a renowned scientist, particularly in the field of kyber-crystal research and power generation. The peaceful implications of this research could have been enormous, but Krennic cared only for its destructive potential. In time, Erso apparently came to realize what he was really working on as part of "Operation Celestial Power," and

[4] Imperial Archives, Section: Project Stardust, File: Eadu
[5] Imperial Archives, Section: Galactic Republic, File: Vallt Rescue Operation

was spirited away from Coruscant by Saw Gerrera in a bid to rob the Empire of his abilities.[6] In Erso's absence Krennic was forced to try and persevere with his other captive scientists, none of whom possessed the raw intellect of the man he had lost. By the time Galen was eventually recaptured, the Death Star was years behind schedule and still no closer to fully unlocking the required technology to operate a laser capable of destroying entire worlds.

It was here that Krennic made what may have been the most serious miscalculation imaginable. While Galen Erso had been recaptured, his wife was murdered in the process and his daughter had disappeared and was presumed dead. Galen now appeared to be a broken and pliable man. Like many other Imperial officials, Krennic had a tendency to judge reality based upon what he expected or desired to see. He had reclaimed his most prized asset and Erso was now willing to cooperate. Desperate to get the project back on schedule, and fend off the circling presence of Tarkin, Krennic never took the time to ponder why Erso now seemed willing to build such a horrifying weapon. Evidently, Erso had realized the Empire would get its weapon eventually, with or without him, and so while the focus was on completing the station, Erso ensured that weaknesses were carefully slipped into vital systems.[7] For an Empire so obsessed with stamping out rebellion, it often seemed incapable of recognizing when it might be festering directly in front of its face.

Unaware of what Erso was planning, Krennic pushed forward with construction. Shortages of valuable resources and minerals led to the Empire pillaging worlds with greater haste and ferocity. Entire systems were strip-mined to provide the raw materials required to make the concept a reality. It may take generations to fully catalogue and

[6] Rebel Alliance Archives, Section: Erso Family, File: Association with Saw Gerrera* *Document prepared on Yavin IV ahead of initial briefing with Jyn Erso
[7] Rebel Alliance Archives, Section: The Death Star, File: Jyn Erso testimony to Alliance High Command at Yavin

understand the consequences of the Imperial excavation projects that were required to construct the Death Star. The damage to so many worlds was so vast that it almost defies belief, and yet even this was scarcely enough. Five years before the weapon was finally activated it appeared that production was in danger of stalling completely before— according to heavily redacted records in the Imperial archives—a significant breakthrough was achieved that freed up vast quantities of material to help finish the project.[8] It was not just raw materials required either. The amount of food needed to sustain the crew operating the station was gargantuan. Stormtroopers required weaponry and armor, TIE pilots replacement flight suits, and—according to requisition forms—once Tarkin assumed control of the project, requests for uniforms, especially boots, grew exponentially.[9] So voracious was the Death Star's construction that the project began to siphon resources away from other operations in such quantities that some Imperial officers, such as Grand Admiral Savit, were motivated to treasonous activity in an attempt to prevent "Project Stardust" from consuming the entirety of the Empire's materiel.

Savit's actions—which eventually saw him arrested and executed— give an indication of the fact that the Imperial military was not united in supporting the battle station that was under construction. Whether this was because of the knock-on impact it had to their own budgets or career prospects, or because of the aforementioned splits in military ideology, it can be confidently stated now that the navy in particular was not convinced that the Death Star was worth the trouble or expense. Though Director Krennic had a degree of control over the

[8] Imperial Archives, Section: Project Stardust, File: Resource Acquisition #HA5779* *These records do not contain firm details as to what this breakthrough consisted of, but it was crucial enough to be highlighted to Krennic, Tarkin, and potentially the Emperor himself.
[9] The collection of supply requests for the operation of the Death Star is enormous and only a fraction have been catalogued so far: Imperial Archives, Section: Project Stardust, Collection: Requisition Forms.

project, many in the upper echelons of the Imperial military had no qualms about telling him exactly what they thought about both his management style and his creation.[10] Krennic could be a spiteful man but he did not exude authority in a way that threatened the various admirals and leaders of the Imperial fleet and, as a result, few mourned his death at Scarif. However, what could be said directly to Krennic could never be said to Tarkin. The Death Star was to be a terrifying weapon, but military leaders—especially those who had seen combat—confronted weapons all the time. What made the Death Star truly dangerous was not just its destructive power, but the man who would command it.

Tarkin's Folly?

Having eventually maneuvered Krennic out of the way, Tarkin assumed full control of the weapon before subsequently unleashing it on the Scarif Citadel, killing his erstwhile rival. Upon his declaration that the weapon was fully functional, a long-planned-for new era of the Empire was triggered. Palpatine had endured the Imperial Senate and its ability to place obstacles—regardless of how minor—in his path purely for this moment. With the completion of the Death Star, the weapon he had long dreamed of, he finally dispensed with any semblance of democracy within his Empire. The Senate was immediately dissolved, and power transferred to the various regional governors and Moffs. This decentralized system of government had been designed and implemented by Tarkin in consultation with the Emperor. Together they had reached the point where the Galactic Empire no longer needed to concern itself with the competing

---

[10] Imperial Archives, Section: Director Orson Krennic, File: Insults and Recriminations* *This record appears to be from Krennic's own files and outlines the various slights directed at him by officers in the Imperial Navy.

demands of different star systems. Ruthless Imperial leaders would deal with such issues themselves and, if they were unable to do so, then the Death Star would do it for them. Tarkin's use of the weapon on Alderaan was designed to be a highly effective demonstration of exactly how powerful the station was and a thorough explanation of exactly what the Empire could do to those who stepped out of line.

There are, therefore, multiple aspects of the new reality created by Palpatine and Tarkin that must be explored and understood. As is apparent from the chapters of this study leading to this point, it is highly likely that Grand Moff Tarkin was the most important person within the Empire outside of Palpatine. He was certainly far more involved and active in the running and administering of the Empire than the Emperor was. While Palpatine possessed a great deal of political skill, it seems likely that Tarkin was the man with both the vision and the drive to make Palpatine's desires plausible. If this was indeed the case, it must also be acknowledged that placing a weapon that could destroy whole planets into the hands of another was a tremendous risk for the Emperor, and that he must have had an incredible degree of trust in Tarkin's loyalty to do so. It is notable that Darth Vader was not given command of the operation. This may well have been reflective of Tarkin's specific skillset, but given the fear of betrayal that permeates the Sith ideology, Palpatine may have had justifiable concerns about what Vader would do with a weapon like the Death Star.[11] If this was indeed part of the rationale behind allowing Tarkin overall command, then it once again reflects the high degree of trust that Palpatine placed upon him. Was this trust justified?

While no records exist that outline the content of private conversations between Tarkin and the Emperor, there is ample evidence to show

[11] Further details of historic betrayals between Sith masters and apprentices have recently been excavated and translated on Exegol and are catalogued at: Exegol Excavation Project, Section: Sith Hierarchy, Files: Betrayals* *Histories recovered from the Hall of Statues

how regularly the pair met whenever Tarkin was on Coruscant.[12] To become a Sith Lord is to gain a degree of paranoia and, if suggestions of Palpatine's abilities with the Force are correct, he presumably was able to get a fairly good reading on Tarkin's loyalties over the years. But the Emperor was not infallible, as proven by his death at the hands of Darth Vader. Tarkin must have given the Emperor various assurances that he would not turn the Death Star against him, and there is certainly a judgment that can be made that Tarkin was reasonably content with his position and influence. But he was also not the only person on board. Interestingly, buried within some of the few surviving records from COMPNOR are files relating to Admiral Motti that pose some intriguing questions regarding his own loyalty to the Emperor.[13] Motti was incredibly well-connected within the Imperial court, which probably insulated him in ways that other officers would not have been. Whether COMPNOR reached any conclusions about what Motti might wish to do with the Death Star is not clear, and his death at Yavin ended the investigation. However, the fact that suspicions existed about Motti is indicative of the wider threat that the Death Star may have represented to the Empire if it fell into the wrong hands.

Perhaps there were also those in the Empire who did not fully understand or accept what the Death Star was capable of. Alderaan changed that. Tarkin used Princess Leia Organa's own homeworld against her—something that haunted her for years—but I believe it is fair to suggest that Alderaan would have been at the top of the list for destruction regardless. Palpatine and Tarkin may not have had any direct evidence that the Organas were fomenting a rebellion, but they were not stupid.

[12] Imperial Archives, Section: Royal Palace Security Records, File: Grand Moff Tarkin* *These records give details of all the trips Tarkin made to the Royal Palace and the times he was admitted into the Emperor's throne room or private quarters.
[13] Imperial Archives, Section: COMPNOR Investigations, File: Admiral Conan Antonio Motti* *These are partial records which makes the size of the actual investigation difficult to assess.

Alderaan's pacifism and its morality were enough to threaten what the Empire had planned, even if the world's leaders were not also up to their necks in what would be termed treasonous activity. By destroying Alderaan, Tarkin hoped to similarly destroy the galaxy's soul. As will be discussed in more detail in the next chapter, this was the first of several terrible miscalculations by Tarkin at the end of his life. While he succeeded in spreading fear and terror throughout the population, it proved to be a motivating factor rather than an oppressive one.

Imperial propaganda immediately moved to explain that Alderaan's destruction was the punishment for its extreme disloyalty. While horror and outrage rippled around the galaxy, Tarkin pushed forward toward the newly discovered rebel base at Yavin. He reasoned that if he was able to destroy it, and kill the leadership stationed there, then the Rebellion would effectively be defeated. How true this actually was is debatable. The destruction of the rebel base would have caused the Alliance a great deal of trouble in coordinating its cells across the galaxy. But, at the same time, much of the rebel fleet that had escaped from Scarif had not yet returned to Yavin, and Mon Mothma was not present at the time of the battle either. Regardless, there was a certain military sense in decapitating the insurgency. This then makes Tarkin's actions at Yavin all the more perplexing. Why did the Death Star travel to the planet alone and unaccompanied by any escorting Star Destroyers? Why did Tarkin hold back the vast majority of his TIE fighters when the rebel starfighters attacked? If the rebels had attempted a mass evacuation, how did Tarkin intend to prevent them escaping? Tarkin, as with many senior Imperial leaders, was not short of confidence or arrogance. Perhaps this blinded him to the threat to the reactor placed within the Death Star's system by Galen Erso and uncovered by the Rebel Alliance. But it does seem peculiar that, with apparent absolute victory within reach, Tarkin held back. Imperial analysts after the battle appear to have sifted through recordings to try and determine the causes of the calamity and much of the blame was placed on the fighter screen.[14] But the failure of individual fighter pilots does not explain the wider blunders made by those in command of the battle.

When news of the Death Star's destruction reached the rest of the Empire, a form of panicked chaos began to set in. The Empire had gambled nearly two decades on the Death Star and the way it was intended to maintain peace and order. Within days of its activation the entire battle station had been lost, and many of the top military leaders of the Empire had been killed, including Tarkin (who was the most important of them all). Most significantly, instead of eradicating the Rebellion the Empire had succeeded only in invigorating their cause and handing them a tremendous victory. It did not take long for blame to be apportioned and many within the Imperial Navy sought to place it squarely on Tarkin. Presumably the fact he had died emboldened them to measures they would not have dared taken while he was alive. Blame, however, did not conceal the harsh reality of the situation. The Empire was now fully at war and had lost the first two major engagements of the conflict. More critically, the strategy that had guided military decisions for years had collapsed. Significant vacuums had opened within the Imperial command infrastructure and the military had no overarching plan for fighting the war they were now locked in. What could the Empire do to strike back?

[14] Imperial Archives, Section: Imperial Navy Operations, File: Battle of Yavin Analysis

Chapter 17

Imperial Military Operations post the Battle of Yavin

While the Galactic Empire would suffer far more devastating military defeats in the years to come, the disaster at Yavin threw much of the Imperial military into a state of almost panicked chaos. While—as previously established—there was a sizeable contingent within the Imperial fleet who were very happy to see the Death Star fail so spectacularly, its destruction and the deaths of many senior leaders only exacerbated the existing problems within the armed forces. The entirety of Imperial military strategy had been built around the planned implementation of the Death Star, with the likes of Grand Moff Tarkin leading the way. Stripped of both the battle station and the man who was effectively leading the military response to the Rebel Alliance, how was the Empire supposed to react? Furthermore, the problems were not simply restricted to Yavin. The defeat of Grand Admiral Thrawn at Lothal, and the destruction of much of the 7th Fleet, had robbed the Empire of another senior military strategist.

While, as we will see, the post-Yavin period saw the Empire embarking on an aggressive series of operations to try and hunt down various rebel headquarters, I believe there are questions regarding how much this represented a coherent strategy, as opposed to a response born out of the reflexive desire to try and do *something* to force a speedy resolution to the conflict. The pressures of this were notable throughout the Imperial military hierarchy. Grand General Tagge—largely by virtue of having left the Death Star before the Battle of Yavin—was initially tasked with leading the response, but there appear to have been significant conflicts between him and Darth Vader. That Vader was not immediately given control of anti-rebel operations perhaps indicates that the Emperor held his apprentice personally responsible for the Death Star's destruction. If this was the case, then placing him under the command of a man like Tagge was probably an intentional insult. Despite this, Vader's own star appeared to rise in the months that followed until he effectively became the face of the Imperial effort to find and destroy the Rebel Alliance—and, as a result, became a much more publicly recognized figure. Interestingly the Emperor himself seems to have become even more reclusive after Yavin. His trips away from Coruscant had become increasingly rare even before the Galactic Civil War had gotten fully underway, but now following the destruction of his long-prized weapon and the death of Tarkin, he seems to have withdrawn into his palace on Coruscant to an even greater extent.[1] Whether this was because of an increased paranoia about his own safety, or some other reason is uncertain.

What is clear though, is that the war would now have to be waged by the Imperial fleet, despite the ongoing splits over strategy within its surviving leadership, and significant concerns about the effectiveness of many officers who held their posts for political reasons. The navy was able to greatly expand its own sense of control over the war effort, including taking control of intelligence operations as the ISB and other—more political—organizations suffered a loss of esteem and influence following their perceived failures. However, serious questions remained regarding whether the fleet was really a weapon that could adequately combat a rebellion that was buoyed by a series of unexpected victories. To deepen the issues facing the Empire, the nature of the

---

[1] Imperial security records show a notable drop off of individuals being permitted access to Palpatine's chambers after Tarkin's death.

rebel victory at Yavin and the fallout of the destruction of Alderaan were causing serious ripples across the galaxy. With the battle lines being drawn it became apparent that what had once been a steady trickle of recruits joining the Alliance was suddenly becoming a veritable flood, as "Remember Alderaan!" became a rallying cry on countless worlds. Worse still, a number of these recruits were defecting from the Galactic Empire.

Resurgent Rebellion

One of the most difficult lessons the Empire had to learn in the immediate aftermath of the battles at Scarif and Yavin was the extent to which virtually everything they had previously believed about the Rebel Alliance was wrong. While some officers and military leaders had recognized the growing threat of the Rebellion, it was widely accepted that this enemy lacked the substantial capital ships and firepower to adequately threaten the Empire in a pitched battle. The size of the rebel fleet at Scarif had caught Admiral Gorin almost completely by surprise. Furthermore, the rebels appeared to be gathering starfighter assets quicker than had been thought possible. Although some of these ships— like the Y-wing—were thought to be obsolete since the Clone Wars, the rebels were finding ways of making them a viable resource in battle. The number of X-wings that were deployed at Lothal, Scarif, and then Yavin also suggested that the Rebel Alliance had its own infrastructure that allowed for the production of these fighters and enough spare parts to keep them operational. While the production capacity of Kuat alone absolutely dwarfed what the rebels could undertake, the Alliance clearly had access to factories, shipyards, and resources that the Empire had failed to identify.[2] The rebels' ability to wage war would only be enhanced in the months after Yavin when a sizeable mutiny at Mon Cala led to the

---

[2] Rebel Alliance Archives, Section: Military Resources, File: Starfighter Production

Alliance gaining control of a number of significant capital ships.[3] These vessels would form the backbone of the expanded rebel fleet for the duration of the war.

However, while weapons and other military materiel would be crucial for the Alliance going forward, it was not their most important resource. X-wings and Mon Calamari cruisers were effectively useless without individuals to pilot and crew them. Before Yavin, the Rebel Alliance had been the recipients of various types of volunteers. Some had seen military service in the Clone Wars or fought the Empire in small-scale insurgencies on any of hundreds of worlds. Others were more idealistic and brought a philosophical or ideological weight to the Rebellion's revolutionary ideas. These groups were enough to keep the Rebel Alliance in action but they would need reinforcements when the war began. It is unlikely that even in the wildest dreams of Mon Mothma or other leaders that their ranks would be so suddenly swelled. For some time, there had been a steady stream of defectors from the Galactic Empire joining the Rebellion. A number of the pilots who flew at Yavin had been trained in various Imperial academies before jumping ship as soon as the opportunity appeared.[4] The rebels were more than happy to take these individuals in and several of their own leaders, such as Jan Dodonna and Crix Madine, had experience of serving in the militaries of the Republic and then the Empire.[5] These defectors brought a level of training with them that the Alliance could not immediately replicate, as well as a degree of insight into the state of the Imperial military. However, following the destruction of Alderaan, defections rose enormously.

While Alderaan as a world was noted for its pacifism, there were any number of Alderaanians serving within the Imperial military. As

---

[3] Rebel Alliance Archives, Section: Military Operations, File: Mutiny at Mon Cala
[4] Specifically see the military records for Biggs Darklighter and Wedge Antilles, as well as pilots who did not participate in the battle like Derek Klivian.
[5] Rebel Alliance Archives, Section: Military Personnel, File: General Jan Dodonna

previously noted, in many sectors it was difficult to advance without some form of Imperial service. Additionally, some Alderaanians likely believed that maintaining peace and order in the galaxy through military service was in keeping with their world's wider pacifist ideals. Once the truth emerged about the Death Star's destruction of Alderaan, many of those serving abandoned their posts. Some simply slipped away into the wider galactic population and became part of the transitory groups of Alderaanians who were now refugees. But others made their way into the ranks of the Rebel Alliance, determined to fight to liberate the galaxy from Imperial tyranny. Rather than quelling the population of the galaxy, the use of the Death Star had greatly increased the number of enemies to Imperial rule. With their forces now in disarray, Imperial strategy hinged upon whoever could take control of the situation.

Competing Commanders

It is entirely possible that the primary beneficiary of the Death Star's destruction—at least outside of the Rebel Alliance—was General Cassio Tagge. Given that many of his peers perished at Yavin, this should perhaps not be too surprising. But Tagge's elevation to grand general and effective supreme commander of Imperial forces was not simply due to being the last one standing. Before Yavin he had voiced concerns about both the organization and abilities of the Rebel Alliance and significant doubts about the viability of the Death Star. Having been proven right on both counts, it seems the Emperor had a newfound respect for both his insights and his abilities. Furthermore, it's possible that Tagge represented something of a unifying figure between the two major factions within the Imperial military. Those who wanted the Empire to diverge away from superweapons like the Death Star were able to find a supporter within Tagge, while he also pushed forward with the construction of several Super Star Destroyers which appealed to the "firepower" lobby. By straddling both camps—but without ever fully vindicating either—Tagge was, initially at least, able to pull the leaders of the military in the same direction. Simply ensuring that the Imperial fleet was prepared to act in a vaguely unified manner was a notable achievement by itself.

Despite this, there were some notable issues and individuals that Tagge had to navigate. In the years before his death at Yavin, Grand Moff Tarkin had been mentoring a young Imperial officer named Ellian Zahra. Commander Zahra was, according to reports at the time, effectively being groomed by Tarkin as some sort of protégé.[6] However, Tarkin seems to have cut Zahra loose following her failure on a mission to destroy some self-styled Nihil holdouts on Ikkrukk.[7] Tarkin was killed before Zahra could reclaim his favor and one of his final orders was to have her reassigned to command a mining facility on Kessel.[8] Contemporary reports suggested that Zahra lobbied others in the Imperial military to try and reclaim her stalled career.[9] There were those who had been close allies to Tarkin who were minded to grant her request while others, who wanted to distance themselves from Tarkin's perceived failures, had no interest in elevating an heir to his power. Tagge seemed determined to keep Zahra at arm's length if for no other reason than she threatened the tentative balance he'd manage to achieve within the armed forces.

A different problem was posed by those survivors of Grand Admiral Thrawn's 7th Fleet. Thrawn had few friends within the upper echelons of a military that balked firstly at his non-human heritage and then again at his almost mystical abilities. Despite this there were those who, to varying levels of enthusiasm, had supported his more nuanced and

[6] Imperial Archives, Section: Grand Moff Wilhuff Tarkin, File: Commander Ellian Zahra Progress Reports
[7] Imperial Archives, Section: Military Operations, File: Mission to Ikkrukk
[8] Imperial Archives, Section: Grand Moff Wilhuff Tarkin, File: Personnel Assignment Order #9337118q
[9] Imperial Archives, Section: Kessel Communications, File: Commander Ellian Zahra #7132-7281

precise approach to warfare. While Thrawn had vanished following the defeat at Lothal, there were questions regarding what to do with those surviving officers and ships who had served under him and still had a great deal of loyalty to their missing commander. Tagge's solution to this problem was reasonably inventive. The destruction of the Death Star hadn't simply wiped out the upper echelon of the Imperial military, it had claimed significant numbers of officers at various levels of the hierarchy. This vacuum would have to be filled and Tagge seemed keen to elevate those who had actually fought the rebels so far. As a result, Tagge elevated Captain Corf Ferno to the rank of vice admiral, put the last remnants of the 7th Fleet—which only comprised a few capital ships and support vessels that had not been present at Lothal—under his command and then immediately sent them to patrol parts of the Outer Rim.[10] This helped keep all the supposed Thrawn loyalists together in one place where they wouldn't cause any problems for those within the Imperial fleet who believed they had been compromised by close association with the missing grand admiral. While Tagge also made moves to begin to rebuild the joint chiefs after the deaths of most of its more recent members, he was also content to assume the powers granted to him as supreme commander and wield them as he saw fit.

For all his skillful moves in dealing with the different factions and egos within the Imperial military it appears that he made one significant misjudgment that probably cost him both his command and his life. Because while he could treat capital ships and their commanders as resources and tools to be deployed—that was what they'd been built and trained for—doing the same with Darth Vader was a different matter entirely. As previously mentioned, it is entirely possible that the Emperor held Vader responsible for the Death Star's destruction and overlooked him for command of the Imperial fleet as a punishment. If Tagge,

---

[10] Imperial Archives, Section: Fleet Compositions, File: 7th Fleet Reorganization*
*Records taken from the Imperial Star Destroyer *Dark Omen*

however, thought that his control over Darth Vader was a permanent affair, or in any way comparable to the type of relationship Vader and Tarkin had, then he was gravely mistaken. It is entirely possible that Tagge did not really understand the nature or realities of Sith teachings, given the extent to which Palpatine and Vader kept them secret, but there is a long history of Sith masters testing their apprentices in such a manner to see if they are worthy of regaining power. Though there are some records of Tagge supposedly viewing Darth Vader as one of the Empire's most formidable weapons, he also made a serious error of judgment if he believed that the "Sith Lord"—a title that appears to have been attached to Vader by some within the military, and one that Tagge would have been aware of—would allow anyone other than the Emperor to wield him for long.[11]

Striking Back

General Tagge took a far more data driven approach to warfare than the likes of Tarkin or other peers. He was not necessarily a strategic genius in the way that either Thrawn or Gial Ackbar were, but his ability to analyze large quantities of data to discover useful patterns and sculpt his tactics around them had notable military benefits. This was particularly important as the defeat at Yavin had made the Empire look weak and vulnerable for possibly the first time since its formation. As a result, enemies began to circle and test Imperial strength. From the bridge of his command ship, the Super Star Destroyer *Annihilator*, Tagge studied information relating to ongoing pirate raids on Imperial shipping that had increased following the defeat at Yavin. While there were no explicit links between the Rebel Alliance and these pirate organizations, Imperial rule could be undermined from multiple directions if they

[11] Imperial Archives, Section: Grand General Cassio Tagge, File: Personal Diaries #411

were permitted to continue, and he tasked Vader with dealing with these groups.[12]

While Tagge and Vader focused their main attentions on an enemy they could find, the rest of the fleet was ordered to begin more aggressive operations in an attempt to try and locate the rebel headquarters after the Alliance fled Yavin. The destruction of the Death Star was a decisive defeat for the Empire, but it did result in a huge amount of resources being freed up that would have otherwise been spent on maintaining the battle station. Tagge intended for these to be distributed on expanding and enhancing the fleet and was already determined to push forward with the construction of further Super Star Destroyers at Kuat. The rebels recognized that the Empire still held a vast industrial advantage over them and sought to disrupt it with attacks on weapons factories, such as a raid on the production facility on Cymoon 1 shortly after Yavin.[13] Despite their recent victories, the rebels were not in a position to fully challenge the Empire in ongoing pitched battles, especially not while still searching for a new base of operations, so they aimed to restrict many of their military actions to hit-and-fade operations that disrupted Imperial logistics and infrastructure.

While the Empire regathered its strength and attempted to chase down both the pirates and the rebels now harrying its forces, the decision was also taken to begin making greater use of alternative weapons within the Imperial arsenal. While Star Destroyers and TIE fighters would play their part in the upcoming battles, there were those within the Imperial military who still favored a different approach. Within the special-forces branch of the Imperial Navy, Admiral Garrick Versio pioneered the creation of an elite group of four agents, including his daughter Iden, that was christened Inferno Squad.[14] There also appear to

[12] Imperial Archives, Section: Military Operations, File: Anti-Piracy Actions #187
[13] Rebel Alliance Archives, Section: Military Operations, File: Raid on Cymoon 1
[14] Imperial Archives, Section: Imperial Navy, File: Special Operations—Inferno Squad

be several similar units operating under Imperial control, with—heavily redacted and censored—records indicating the existence of Task Force 99 and SCAR Squadron as notable examples. Much of the information we have about Inferno Squad was provided to the Rebel Alliance following Iden Versio's eventual defection. But the existence of Inferno Squad, and others like it, does give an indication that there were those within the Imperial fleet, if only the special forces aspect, that favored a more targeted approach to dealing with the Empire's enemies. Inferno's first substantive assignment was to infiltrate the last vestiges of Saw Gerrera's partisans, who had now rebranded themselves as the "Dreamers." Gerrera himself had died when the Death Star destroyed Jedha City, but both he and his followers had been an ongoing menace to Imperial operations. Though they had been effectively excommunicated by the rest of the Rebel Alliance, if left to their own devices they could cause a great many problems while the Empire attempted to regroup after Yavin. Inferno Squad rapidly discovered that the Dreamers had ongoing plans to launch a series of attacks against Imperial military and civilian targets to sow further destruction and confusion.[15] Though it would eventually cost them one of their members, Inferno Squad were successful in effectively dismantling the Dreamers and killing many of Gerrera's surviving followers.[16]

The need to tackle both the Rebel Alliance and other threats such as increased piracy posed a problem for the Empire. In theory they had the resources to tackle both, but with the Death Star no longer providing the "threat of force" needed to keep systems in line, much of the shortfall was being picked up by Star Destroyers that could otherwise have been guarding shipping lanes or hunting for the rebel base. Specialist operatives like Inferno Squad were able to undertake different sorts of missions

[15] Rebel Alliance Archives, Section: The Dreamers, File: Iden Versio's account of operations
[16] Imperial Archives, Section: Imperial Navy, File Special Operations—Inferno Squad: The Dreamers Infiltration

and win successes for the Empire but they were not enough to fully plug the gap. Despite piracy being an ongoing problem, it would seem logical to think that the Rebel Alliance needed to be the primary target. To a point, Tagge recognized the situation and did increase leeway for fleet commanders to chase down leads and crack down on rebellious activity. But he failed to realize that he was misusing possibly his greatest tool.

Darth Vader may have been many things, but a patient man was clearly not one of them. While, for whatever reason, he was initially content to chase down pirates for Tagge, this was not a relationship that could have longevity. Vader must have chafed under both Tagge's command and, presumably, his master's disappointment. But there may have been another aspect that was motivating the Dark Lord. Vader was already nurturing an interest in the young rebel pilot who had destroyed the Death Star. Vader had flown against him in combat, and it is entirely possible the pair had shared some form of Force connection. It is unclear at exactly what point Vader discovered the pilot's identity as Luke Skywalker and made the connection that he was his son.[17] The anger this revelation likely produced must have been immense. If, as later events suggest, Vader's initial instincts were now to hunt down and recruit his son to the dark side, then Tagge's orders and errands must have grated even more ferociously than before. Vader could not achieve his goals without the freedom provided by his master's approval, or while trapped under Tagge's diktats.

It is similarly unclear exactly what Vader did to achieve his resurgence within the Imperial hierarchy, but there are hints within the Empire's records of an attempted coup by an Imperial cybernetic expert named Cylo.[18] How real this attempt actually was is uncertain but in

---

[17] The biographer Kitrin Braves has informed me that any traces of information relating to this matter appear to have been purged from all Imperial archives and databases.

[18] Imperial Archives, Section: Notable Personnel. File: Cylo* *This document has been heavily redacted.

foiling it Vader achieved two victories. Firstly, in demonstrating his continued worth to the Emperor, and secondly, in undermining Tagge's command of the Imperial military and security forces. The reward for these efforts was for Palpatine to elevate Vader to the position of supreme commander of the Imperial fleet. This included personal control of the Super Star Destroyer *Executor* and the vaunted Death Squadron task force. Vader's first action in his new role was to use the Force to choke Tagge to death.

Vader's control of the Imperial military would cause some significant problems, but his new position did solve some as well. One significant benefit for overall military strategy was that Vader was utterly focused on finding the rebel base, though for very different reasons than the rest of the fleet. As a result, the need to chase down pirate threats became a much less pressing concern. Vader also had his own relationships with the various crime bosses and underworld kingpins who operated around the Empire and presumably made explicitly clear to them what the price for preying on Imperial shipping would mean. While other Imperial leaders may have been susceptible to bribes or blackmail, Darth Vader was clearly not among them, and fear of summary execution at his hands could be a powerful motivator. Furthermore, while many in the fleet retained a suspicion of Grand Admiral Thrawn and those who had worked under him, Vader seemed to have had a far more productive working relationship with Thrawn and he had no qualms in bringing some of the previously exiled ships and officers back into the fold.[19]

There were, however, notable strategic shortcomings from placing overall control into Darth Vader's hands. Given that Vader took little interest in orders passed down from anyone but the Emperor, his

---

[19] Imperial Archives, Section: 7th Fleet Operations, File: *Chimaera*—Mission to Batuu* *This record lists Darth Vader as having spent time on a separate mission with Grand Admiral Thrawn, though the circumstances of it are not disclosed.

interactions with the joint chiefs were limited and he seemed content to let them organize things from behind the scenes as long as they did not encroach on his own plans. Vader cared little for administrative matters or, it seems, wider-scale strategy. The result was that Vader demanded operations to locate the rebel base be exponentially increased, but then passed the task of making his orders feasible to the joint chiefs and others in the upper echelons of command—with the implicit threat of what failure would mean. Because of this, while Vader pushed forward with a single-mindedness that bordered on the obsessive in his hunt for the Rebellion, the rest of the fleet found itself dragged along for the ride, forced to constantly react to whatever Vader was doing or commanding in any given situation. As probe droids scoured the Outer Rim for signs of the rebel base, Vader's impatience and anger only grew. In time it would result in the Empire suffering perhaps its worst "victory" of the entire Galactic Civil War.

Chapter 18

The Battle of Hoth and Imperial Morale

The Imperial assault on the rebel base on Hoth has long been considered one of the darkest days for the Rebel Alliance, and with good cause. Following their victory at Yavin and the relocation of their headquarters, the Rebel Alliance had been trying to solidify its own war effort and structure while dodging the increased activity of the Imperial fleet. Even in the prelude to Hoth the Empire had managed to inflict some notable defeats on the rebels that cost them supplies and firepower. The subsequent attack on Hoth was effectively a disaster for the Alliance. The Imperial ground offensive on the snow-covered planet and the blockade above its surface cost the rebels significant casualties and forced them to scatter across the stars before being able to regroup. In many ways, Hoth was the worst day the Rebel Alliance suffered in the entire war. It was the day when their base and significant members of their leadership were destroyed, captured, or killed.

But that isn't entirely what happened. The above version of events has been widely accepted—by myself included—as the clearest understanding of the Battle of Hoth from the Rebel Alliance's point of view. There have been some excellent works already created that focus on the Rebel Alliance at Hoth.[1] The strength of the base's shield generator and

---

[1] I particularly recommend *Left Beneath the Snow: Rebel Grief on Hoth* by Asht Skil.

ion cannon barrage managed to turn a catastrophic, potentially war-ending, defeat into just a disastrous rout. However, the Rebel Alliance were not the only participants in that battle. The Empire was there too. To date, far less examination has been given to the Imperial experience of that battle or the impact it had on the Empire's wider war effort. This is something that I feel needs to be corrected because when taking in some seemingly disparate aspects of evidence from within Imperial records, testimonies from soldiers and officers who were there, and also the wider reaction to Hoth beyond Death Squadron, some very interesting interpretations can begin to appear.

The assumption has always been that the Empire, having achieved a decisive military success at Hoth, would have been pleased with the battle's outcome and its impact on disrupting the Rebel Alliance. But I am unsure if that was really the case. The evidence I will present in this chapter—and I acknowledge that this may be critiqued by my peers—suggests something very different. For I believe that the Battle of Hoth can actually be viewed as a defeat for the Galactic Empire, and one that took a heavy toll on Imperial morale across the galaxy. Rather than being the moment the Rebel Alliance nearly met its final defeat, it could—and perhaps should—also now be viewed as the point when many Imperials began to wonder not just if they could even win the war, but if they might well be in danger of losing it.

Cutting the Strings

While Darth Vader was almost solely committed to uncovering the rebel base, the rest of the Imperial fleet, as organized by the joint chiefs, was given a degree of freedom to deal with the rest of the war effort. As long as they did not undertake actions that undermined Vader's quest or in any way challenge his authority, it appears that their new commander was content to leave them to their own devices. Unexpectedly, this freedom to operate (which had not been granted to them by Tagge or Tarkin before him) gave the Imperial fleet an early advantage. With full control of the search for the rebel base assumed by Vader, the rest of the fleet could concentrate their efforts elsewhere. In the lead up to Hoth, the focus of the joint chiefs fell on the rebels' ability to supply and sustain their own military efforts. If these could be disrupted, then the Rebellion might be defeated by weapon shortages and hunger. It was not the sort of destructive defining victory envisioned by Tarkin, but would leave the rebellion just as dead. Significant resources were therefore committed to discovering rebel shipyards and supply bases and denying them to the enemy.

While the rebels had successfully stolen several Mon Calamari cruisers during the mutiny on Mon Cala, these alone would not be enough to directly engage the forces of the Galactic Empire. The rebels needed to modify them for combat, build more capital ships and fighters, and produce enough replacements and spare parts for the ones already in operation. That level of industrial output required rebel-controlled shipyards. So far, the Empire had not been able to locate them, but that was about to change.

The defeat of the Death Star at Yavin had sparked various uprisings against Imperial rule. One of these had occurred on the mining world of Shu-Torun and the ensuing civil conflict there had been won by the planet's ruler, Queen Trios. However, unbeknownst to the Rebel Alliance—with whom Queen Trios cultivated connections—the Empire had supported her claims to the throne and held her true allegiance.[2] As Imperial activity increased across the Outer Rim in an attempt to find the rebels' manufacturing center, Trios transmitted information regarding the rebel shipyard at Mako-Ta to Darth Vader. Breaking off his hunt for the rebel base, Vader brough Death Squadron—including the Super Star Destroyer *Executor*—to the system and devastated the Alliance forces there. Half of the rebel cruisers present were destroyed

[2] Imperial Archives, Section: Shu-Torun Conflict, File: Queen Trios

and around ninety percent of the fighters as well.[3] Senior rebel commander Vanden Huyck Willard was killed in the initial assault and Leia Organa and Mon Mothma only escaped after General Jan Dodonna sacrificed his life and flagship to ensure their survival.[4] With rebel production curtailed and a significant dent put into the rebel fleet, focus shifted to their supply lines.

For some time, the rebels had been moving supplies through the Derra system on the Outer Rim. These convoys contained a variety of weapons, equipment, food, and medicines that were required for various rebel cells across the galaxy. More importantly, over eighty percent of the stockpiles were allocated to equipping the hidden rebel base. While the location itself remained a mystery, cutting off the Alliance's line of supply would significantly increase the Empire's chances of a wider strategic victory. Ironically the action that destroyed a significant convoy near Derra IV and ambushed the vaunted Renegade Squadron of the Rebel Alliance was carried out by officers and forces who had been partially exiled from mainstream Imperial operations. It was Vice Admiral Rae Sloane—a figure of huge importance in the Empire's future—onboard the Star Destroyer *Vigilance,* in cooperation with remnants of the 7th Fleet, who were able to establish the likeliest candidates for rebel shipping routes in the Expansion Region and narrow the list down to Derra.[5] Though the Rebel Alliance were not able to ascertain exactly what happened at Derra IV, we know now that the *Vigilance* took the lead—given it was Sloane's plan—but was ably supported by the *Dark Omen* and, most importantly, the Interdictor cruiser *Retention* that helped isolate the convoy and enabled its destruction.[6] As far as the Imperial fleet were concerned, it was a near perfect victory,

---

[3] Imperial Archives, Section: Military Operations, File: Assault on Mako-Ta
[4] Rebel Alliance Archives, Section: Mako-Ta Shipyards, File: Losses and Debriefing
[5] Imperial Archives, Section: Military Operations, File: Derra IV* *Information recovered from the damaged computer core of the *Vigilance*
[6] New Republic Archives, Section: Imperial Prisoners, File: Interrogations 143

and one achieved entirely from their own merits. Sloane had previously been demoted to commodore before Yavin and was still working her way back up the rank hierarchy. This victory granted her a promotion to full admiral and saw her and other Imperial leaders reincorporated back into the main fold of operations. It also granted her a place on the joint chiefs.[7]

Stripped of their manufacturing abilities and with their major supply line cut, the Rebel Alliance was already facing a disaster. It had been three years since Yavin and they had not been able to significantly progress the war in their favor. With Vader hunting down their base, a point of reckoning was approaching.

Assault on Hoth

The rebels' account of events at Hoth—their discovery of an Imperial probe droid moments before Vader's fleet arrived—is relatively well established. Safe from an orbital bombardment beneath their shield generator, the rebels fought a holding action on the planet's icy surface while evacuation transports attempted to break through the Imperial blockade, supported by ion cannon fire designed to disable the Star Destroyers above. Despite the best efforts of rebel pilots and soldiers only 13 of the 30 transports launched from the surface survived to escape into hyperspace, and many hundreds of personnel were either killed on the surface, shot down, or captured. This overview gives a reasonably adequate account of the rebel experience of the Battle at Hoth.

But it is also instructive to now examine what we know of the Imperial plans for the battle and to begin to assess the potential flaws or errors that manifested themselves. Darth Vader had control of Death Squadron, but it was Admiral Kendal Ozzel who undertook most of the

---

[7] Imperial Archives, Section: Military Personnel, File: Rae Sloane—Promotion to Admiral

actual command duties from onboard the *Executor*. Ozzel has been judged as a—at best—limited military officer in the years since his death and he certainly wasn't blessed with any great strategic abilities. But he also was not stupid, either in military matters or in recognizing the precarity of his position as Darth Vader's chief underling. Ozzel appears to have been present on the bridge of the *Executor* when Darth Vader executed Grand General Tagge.[8] He therefore knew what working under Vader could mean. While he failed at Hoth, Ozzel must have possessed some skills that made him useful enough to be kept alive until that point and to have reached the rank of Admiral on a vessel as important as the *Executor*.

Ozzel's mistake at Hoth appears to have been one that was endemic within the Imperial fleet, particularly among those who placed great value in the firepower of their ships. He believed that by dropping out of hyperspace directly into Hoth's orbit that the rebels would be too surprised to adequately react. Having not foreseen that the rebels may have a ground-based shield generator (which also suggests he had not read Thrawn's debriefing from the Battle of Atollon), Ozzel's overconfidence removed the opportunity for the fleet to influence a battle that would now have to be fought on the ground. This error cost him his life.[9]

With the need to destroy the shield generator now of paramount importance, General Maximilian Veers was forced to land AT-AT walkers a safe distance away and then march them at speed across the ice. Veers was probably the Empire's preeminent army commander and had effectively created an entire ground doctrine and tactical formations for the use of walkers in combat.[10] However, the need for haste meant Veers had to push his forces forward far quicker than was reasonably safe and several of his AT-ATs were left behind in crevasses. Despite

---

[8] Imperial Archives, Section: Admiral Kendal Ozzel, File: *Executor* bridge log YQ1872* *This record states that Ozzel was present at Tagge's death.
[9] Imperial Archives, Section: Admiral Kendal Ozzel File: Unedited obituary
[10] Imperial Archives, Section: Army Command Doctrine, File: Veers Formation

this, the Imperial ground forces were able to overwhelm the rebel defenses and the AT-AT personally commanded by Veers destroyed the shield generator with concentrated fire. With it eliminated, Vader was able to land his assault force directly on top of Echo Base and enter the rebel facility. The last evacuation transports no longer took off under the safety of the energy shield and were much more vulnerable to attack from both above and below. With the rebel base completely breached, the last stragglers either safely made it offworld or were swiftly captured.[11] When considered along these lines Hoth appears to be an Imperial victory won under difficult circumstances. But even this may not produce a full accounting of the Imperial efforts there.

As with Palpatine during the Clone Wars, the assumption that Darth Vader was fighting the same Galactic Civil War as the rest of the Imperial forces appears to have been mistaken. Vader may have been spearheading the hunt for the rebel base, but this was not out of any interest in destroying it or capturing the rest of the rebel leadership. Instead, he was absolutely focused on capturing Luke Skywalker. This single-mindedness had huge implications for the Imperial battleplan. It's possible that Ozzel's decision to emerge directly on top of Hoth was motivated by a desire to appease Vader's demands for progress at great haste. This decision also had a noticeable impact on the ground assault. General Veers suffered serious wounds when his AT-AT was struck by a rebel snowspeeder while undertaking a ground offensive that would not have been necessary if the battle had been better controlled. While rebel evacuation transports escaped at the collapse of the energy shield, Vader was also content to ignore them in favor of chasing the *Millennium Falcon* in the erroneous belief that Skywalker was onboard. This determination led to three of the blockading Star Destroyers being ordered out of their positions to try and chase the ship as it ran for a nearby asteroid field, allowing several rebel transports to escape through the

[11] Imperial Archives, Section: Military Operations, File: Ground Assault on Hoth

newly opened gap. Ordinarily the Empire would have ceased pursuit at the edges of the asteroid field, but Vader ordered his ships to continue the chase, resulting in two of the Star Destroyers—the *Ultimatum* and the *Conquest*—being pulverized with the loss of all hands.[12] No sooner had those lives been lost in the fruitless quest, than Vader personally executed Captain Needa of the *Avenger* for allowing the rebel ship to escape for a second time. Vader subsequently ordered Admiral Firmus Piett—newly promoted to replace Ozzel—to scatter the rest of the Imperial fleet in an ongoing hunt for a single vessel that seemed to be long gone.

What should have been an overwhelmingly decisive Imperial victory had collapsed through a mixture of bad initial planning and Vader's determination to place his hunt for Luke Skywalker over the primary strategic objective. It seems scarcely believable, but because of the two lost Star Destroyers the Empire actually suffered personnel losses many times greater than those of the Rebel Alliance.[13] Added to this were several leading officers dying at the hands of Vader himself, and Veers being so gravely injured as to almost vanish from Imperial records after the battle.[14] Hoth should have been a decisive moment for the Empire in the Galactic Civil War. Instead the repercussions reverberated through the Imperial military at all levels.

After the Victory

To understand what appears to have been the underlying reaction within the Imperial military—particularly the fleet—in the aftermath of Hoth it is necessary to begin by remembering the history that led up

[12] Imperial Archives, Section: Military Operations, File: Battle of Hoth—Naval Losses

[13] Imperial Archives, Section: Military Operations, Battle of Hoth—Losses

[14] Imperial Archives, Section: General Maximilian Veers: File Emergency medical evacuation* *This record shows him being evacuated to Imperial medical facilities near Carida but after this it becomes impossible to track down his status.

to this moment. As mentioned in a previous chapter, many within the Imperial fleet would not necessarily be able to say when the Galactic Civil War began. The primary reason for this was because the Empire had essentially been at war since its inception. Though battles designed to conquer worlds or subjugate small uprisings did not really compare with the larger engagements that were to come, they were still combat operations for a military stuck on a perpetual wartime footing. All those months and years expanding the Empire's borders or crushing its enemies would add up over time. There is only so long that a military can keep operating at the same tempo without beginning to lose its edge as fatigue sets in.

In the period before Hoth there are intriguing signs within surviving Imperial records that suggest things may not have been well within the military. Requests for additional morale officers or recreation materials had already doubled within the fleet in the two years after Yavin, only to double again in the months leading to Hoth.[15] Instances of both army and navy personnel requesting "shore leave" also increased exponentially as the war dragged, which came to the attention of COMPNOR, who seemed to believe it was the result of a bug in the request system.[16] Additionally, ISB loyalty officers—who were not well-loved to begin with—had begun carrying out intensive sweeps of military staff seemingly in response to the defections after Alderaan.[17] The ongoing air of suspicion that these investigations caused appears to have grated on soldiers already under significant combat stress.[18]

[15] Imperial Archives, Section: Imperial Navy, File: Special Requisition Orders*
*Specifically see charts 1665f, 3721b, and 4511u
[16] Imperial Archives, Section: COMPNOR, File: Investigation into extraneous leave requests
[17] Imperial Archives, Section: Imperial Security Bureau, File: Increased Loyalty Officer Operations #GT81625—Authorization
[18] Rebel Alliance Archives, Section: Intelligence Gathering, File: Seized Imperial Communications #3001881* *These communications were captured in their unedited form during a data raid on Sullust.

Individually all of these items may not add up to much, but together they begin to paint an picture of an Imperial military that was starting to fray at the edges before the Battle of Hoth. We know a great deal about the pressures placed on the soldiers of the Rebel Alliance during this period, but what about those of the Empire?

The obvious assumption, and the one that has lasted until now, is that given Hoth's status as an Imperial victory, the soldiers who fought there would have been elated at their success. They had, after all, chased the rebels from their secret base and inflicted serious casualties upon them. But I do not believe this was the widespread reaction to Hoth, either from those on the ground or those elsewhere. Interrogations of Imperial forces after the war back this belief up to an extent.[19] Because—to many Imperials—I believe Hoth represented a huge and demoralizing missed opportunity. Some of this critique came from the fleet in examinations of the battle that, while carefully avoiding overtly blaming Darth Vader, questioned various aspects of the battle plan. The "surprise" emergence out of hyperspace could have been mitigated if Death Squadron had brought Interdictor cruisers with it.[20] Vader and Ozzel were surely able to request whatever forces they desired, and gravity-well technology had been incredibly useful at Atollon in preventing the rebels there escaping a planetary blockade. Similarly, the decision to scatter the fleet in a futile hunt for Luke Skywalker had resulted in huge casualties, many of whom were not just names on internal logs but known colleagues and friends. There must have been many within the military who were wondering whether they too would be sacrificed pursuing a single rebel operative in missions they did not understand.

Perhaps the biggest outcome of Hoth, however, was the feeling within the Imperial military that a narrative was beginning to develop

[19] See: New Republic Archives, Section: Imperial Prisoners, File: Interrogations 145, 231, 459
[20] Imperial Archives, Section: Joint Chiefs of the Imperial Military, File: Battle of Hoth Analysis

Chapter 14: Opening Skirmishes

ISB Surveillance image of an individual tentatively identified as "Axis."

Stormtrooper helmet cam recording of fighting on Jedha.

Saw Gerrera. Image taken from Rebel Alliance archives.

Only known image of early rebel political theorist Karis Nemik. Rebel Alliance archives.

Unidentified rebel pilots arrested for "treasonous activity."

Rebel Alliance Conference on Yavin 4. Image recorded by internal security.

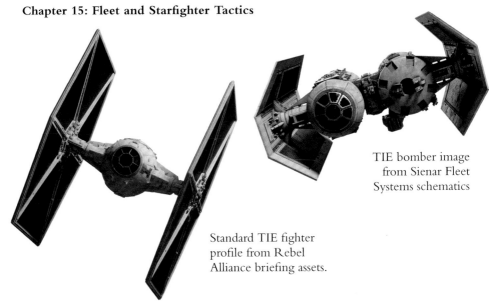

TIE bomber image
from Sienar Fleet
Systems schematics

Standard TIE fighter
profile from Rebel
Alliance briefing assets.

Grand Admiral
Thrawn. Image
recovered from the
ISD *Dark Omen*.

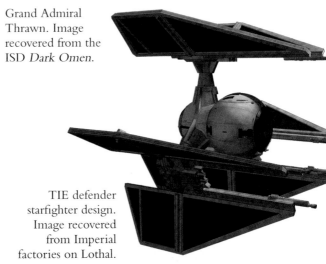

TIE defender
starfighter design.
Image recovered
from Imperial
factories on Lothal.

The ISDs *Persecutor* and *Intimidator* collide above Scarif.
Image taken from Y-wing gun camera.

Chapter 16: the Tarkin Doctrine and Death Star

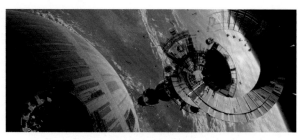

Construction of the Death Star superlaser above Scarif.

Director Orson Krennic.
Imperial Security Image.

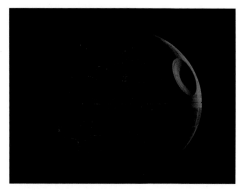

The Death Star. Image taken from
ISD *Devastator*.

Galen Erso. This image was captured at long
range by a rebel operative during the attack
on the facility at Eadu.

Chapter 17: Imperial Military Operations post-Yavin

Death Squadron on deployment prior to the
Battle of Hoth. Image taken from ISD *Avenger*.

General Cassio Tagge. One of only
two surviving images claiming to
show the pre-Yavin summit aboard
the Death Star.

Chapter 18: The Battle of Hoth and Imperial Morale

Destruction of shield generator. Image taken from Imperial AT-AT Blizzard 1.

Imperial security record of Admiral Ozzel's execution.

Rebel evacuation of Hoth in the battle's latter stages. Image taken by Corwi Selgrothe.

General Maximilian Veers. Image from pre-battle briefing aboard the SSD *Executor*.

Chapter 19: Crimson Dawn

Lady Qi'ra of Crimson Dawn. Surveillance image from Kessel security records.

Crimson Dawn signet ring

Chapter 20: The Battle of Endor

Opening TIE attack wave. Image taken from gun camera of TIE interceptor piloted by Lieutenant Carrix Felth.

Destruction of the ISD *Devastator* following attack by Blade Squadron.

Moff Tiaan Jerjerrod, who perished aboard the second Death Star.

Admiral Firmus Piett. Image transmitted to Coruscant attached to Piett's (now disputed) briefing report.

Chapter 21: Fracture and Cinder

"Endor is a Lie" propaganda poster created by Governor Ecressys

Operation: Cinder attack on Vardos. Image taken by ISD *Eviscerator* bridge deck camera.

Chapter 22: The Road to Jakku

Prototype Starhawk under construction at the Nadiri Dockyards.

Battle of Jakku. Commemorative artwork produced for the ceremony marking the battle's 10th anniversary.

Crashed Star Destroyer on Jakku. Image taken by New Republic Survey Corps.

Chapter 23: Truth and Reconciliation

Former Imperials put to work in the Karthon Chop Fields. Image taken by security droid.

New Republic Amnesty Housing on Coruscant.

Dr. Penn Pershing at the Galaxies Opera House. Image from *Coruscanti Society* #4125

Standard New Republic Parole Droid attached to the Amnesty Program.

Chapter 24: Complacency and Appeasement

Public relations image of New Republic Senator Hamato Xiono, who spoke out against former members of the Rebel Alliance.

Chapter 25: The First and Final Orders

Allegiant General Enric Pryde. Image recovered from First Order security archives.

General Armitage Hux's infamous "Address at Starkiller Base."

The Hosnian Cataclysm. Image recovered from New Republic defence satellite 819D.

First Order Operation Command (note the youth of the personnel shown).

First Order occupation force on Kijimi. Image secretly captured by smuggler who left Kijimi prior to its destruction.

Opening Resistance attack on Exegol. Image from Nimi Chireen's X-wing gun camera.

that was not in their favor. While there would have been precious few serving in the Empire's armed forces that believed in the Force—or would ever say so out loud—soldiers can be superstitious. Morale in military environments is a peculiar thing. It is based almost entirely on personal and shared feelings. My own service with the Resistance has given me experience of the ways morale can ebb and flow. If soldiers believe they are winning, their chances of doing so increase exponentially. They become willing to fight harder, suffer longer, even sustain personal wounds and losses, simply because it *feels* like victory is in reach and the casualties become worth it. The reverse of this can begin to happen when soldiers believe they are losing. And the narrative emerging within some sections of the military pointed to the fact that every time the Empire had a chance of winning the war and defeating the opposition—their enemy escaped. It happened at Atollon. It happened at Yavin. It happened at Mako-Ta. And now it had happened again at Hoth. And with every subsequent escape, every Imperial "victory" that did not bring the conclusion of the war closer despite their own forces sustaining heavy losses, Imperial morale eroded away.[21]

By the Battle of Hoth most soldiers serving the Empire who were going to defect and join the Rebel Alliance had already done so. There were still those waiting for the right opportunity, but years had passed since the Empire's worst crime and then greatest humbling. Defection was, regardless of what the ISB loyalty officers seemed to believe, no longer an ongoing concern. The same cannot be said of desertions. These records are buried very deep within remaining Imperial holdings, and they are still heavily redacted to this day, but there appears to have been a noticeable spike of desertions from the army and navy in the

---

[21] There are further suggestions of this within memoirs published by Imperial soldiers after the war, which will be discussed in greater detail in due course.

immediate aftermath of Hoth.[22] It is possible that these soldiers were either so fatigued or demoralized by the ongoing nature of the war that they just disappeared. Or they simply abandoned their positions and slipped away into the civilian population. The Empire could not spare the resources to track them all down. Not during an ongoing war.

The impact of Hoth on a military that was already becoming tired and ground down by the nature of the conflict they were engaged in, does not appear to have been any form of joy. At best a weary resignation that the struggle would have to be maintained set in. But even this was undermined by a nagging, but growing, fear that whatever war they were fighting was not one shared by their commander, Darth Vader. And if it was not shared by him, then was it not shared by the Emperor either? How was it going to be possible to win the war if their leaders ignored the obvious objectives directly in front of them in favor of their own agendas? How many times would victory be allowed to slip away for reasons the rank and file did not understand?

As the Alliance scrambled to escape Hoth, some rebel units aimed to create as much havoc and chaos as possible in order to alleviate the pressure on their fellows. From this idea came the abortive Operation Ringbreaker undertaken by the rebels' 61st Infantry Company, who sought to fight their way across Imperial space in an attempt to take the shipyard at Kuat.[23] While this push ended prematurely at Sullust, it may have been far more successful in exacerbating the damage to Imperial morale than the soldiers of Twilight Company could have ever expected. Imperial soldiers across the galaxy had gone from waiting with anticipation for news of an Imperial victory that ended the war, to suddenly having to deal with unfolding hit-and-fade operations in previously

---

[22] To unpack these records it is necessary to compare urgent requests to the ISB for investigations alongside emergency replacement orders for soldiers and crew who do not appear within any casualty logs.

[23] Rebel Alliance Archives, Section: Military Operations, File: Operation Ringbreaker

secure strongholds. The damage to infrastructure was notable but the damage to the psyche of Imperial soldiers may have been more severe.

As the war dragged on, I believe that faith in an Imperial victory was beginning to ebb away within the military. Sapped by fatigue and fear of what was to come, the Imperial Navy was losing both its edge and its control over military operations that clashed with Darth Vader's own desires. The Empire could not easily survive many more victories such as the one achieved at Hoth. This would lead to a serious reconsideration of strategic options in the lead up to Endor, but it also made many within the military vulnerable to the approaches of an organization that was separate from the Rebel Alliance, but which had also identified the main problem in the galaxy as being the rule of Darth Vader and his Emperor.

Chapter 19

Crimson Dawn

With the Galactic Civil War ongoing and no immediate end in sight, the Empire was concentrating the vast majority of their forces on maintaining control of the galaxy and attempting to defeat the Rebel Alliance. The inability, largely as a result of the Death Star's destruction at Yavin, of the Empire to win the war swiftly had produced a deepening crisis across Imperial territory. The longer the conflict dragged on and the greater the perceived difficulties of the Empire in defeating the Rebellion, the more populations began to wonder—some openly—whether Imperial control was sustainable in the long run. The survival of the Rebel Alliance was producing circumstances that would soon beget more rebellions. As a result, the Empire was caught in a trap largely of their own making. They had trained—through tyranny—a population that would not question their brutal methods because the Empire was strong enough to deal out summary violent retribution. But that strength ebbed away every day that the rebels eluded the Imperial military. To compensate, Imperial forces and garrisons were increased on particularly rebellious or unstable worlds to try and maintain order, but at the cost of weakening the forces that might catch and destroy the Alliance.

However, in focusing so much on the immediacy of the rebel threat, the Empire had allowed itself to be distracted from a very different enemy that was lurking beneath the surface. Imperial forces, including Darth

Vader, had always had an unusual relationship with the galaxy's major criminal enterprises. While there were plenty of Imperial soldiers and officers who were also on the payrolls of groups like the Hutt Cartel or Pyke Syndicate, there was also a generally understood arrangement that direct encroachment or obstruction of Imperial business, particularly the war effort, would be met with harsh reprisals. The likes of Black Sun may have been strong, but they were in no position to slug it out with the Imperial fleet. As the Empire shifted increasing forces away from maintaining the infrastructure of the state—particularly trade and industry—they abandoned many previously controlled aspects of civilian life, especially the supply of various goods and services (particularly food). Into this vacuum stepped the various gangs of the criminal underworld who began to reap the profits of black markets. The Empire was largely willing to turn a blind eye to these operations as long as the various factions and cartels reserved their activities for everyday items and avoided weaponry or anything that might overtly benefit the rebellion.

However, within the criminal underworld there was another enterprise that was reasonably well known but, as it transpires, not remotely understood. They had existed for almost the entirety of the Empire. For years their public face was the gangster Dryden Vos before his death around a decade before Yavin.[1] But he was not the true power or driving force of Crimson Dawn. Originally it had been the fallen Sith Lord Maul.[2] As he had done during the Clone Wars with the Death Watch Mandalorians, Maul used the criminal groups governed by Crimson Dawn as a way to build his own powerbase, while he controlled the direction of the group through Vos, but more specifically through his protégé; a young Corellian woman called Qi'ra. If Maul had been the origin of Crimson Dawn, his disappearance left Qi'ra as the inheritor of

[1] Rebel Alliance Archives, Section: Crimson Dawn, File: Han Solo Testimony
[2] Exegol Excavation Project, Section: Sith Lords, Files: Darth Maul—Criminal Activities* *Information retrieved from the Sheltered Keep

it. She had apparently learned a great deal from Maul and was, under the cover of the Galactic Civil War, preparing her own conflict.

But hers was not one aimed simply at the Empire, broadly defined. Instead, she had a very specific target in mind, one that she had identified through Maul's teachings and her own work in gathering information and secrets across the galaxy. For while the rebels sought to confront the Empire in all its guises, Qi'ra and Crimson Dawn were about to declare war on the Sith.

The Specter of Crimson Dawn

There are a great many questions about the operations and activities of Crimson Dawn during the period between the battles of Hoth and Endor. A little frustratingly there are also precious few official answers to those questions. This means it becomes necessary to evaluate the evidence that is available to us, including material that might seem tangential to the topic, while also evaluating the various aspects of Crimson Dawn's mythos. In the simplest terms there is a single unifying aspect to the story of Crimson Dawn's assault on Emperor Palpatine and Darth Vader. Essentially, through a mixture of bribery and financial incentives and through playing on the sentiments of both criminal operatives and Imperial personnel, Crimson Dawn—under the command of Qi'ra—allegedly infiltrated almost every level of the Empire's hierarchy and used this power to try and destroy the Sith.

It was this version of events that was reported by Luke Skywalker and Leia Organa, having been recounted to them through a holocron—a Jedi tool used for recording history—by someone calling herself "the Archivist." Descriptions of her suggest she may once have been a scholar at the University of Bar'leth.[3] While there is no specific reason to doubt

[3] New Republic Archives, Section: Crimson Dawn—The Archivist's Holocron, File: Overview by Leia Organa

this version, and elements of it will be included here, there are significant issues in corroborating it. Much of this is understandable. For example, there are precious few surviving references to Crimson Dawn within Imperial archives or records. However, I would expect this to be the case whether the stories were true or not. If the Archivist was mistaken—or lying—then there would be no supporting evidence to exist in the first place. Similarly, if Crimson Dawn had so thoroughly infiltrated the Empire as claimed, then that feels like exactly the sort of situation where Imperial authorities would purge all records of the events in question. Therefore, regardless of whether the Archivist was correct, the absence of evidence in the Imperial records remains the same. Fortunately, we are not restricted to just the "official" version of events that the Empire has left us with. There are other ways of examining this moment.

While the Imperial archives do not contain much information that is of use to us, there are other ways of gathering information regarding this period in the Empire. Numerous captured Imperial soldiers and officers spoke about Crimson Dawn when interrogated by the New Republic after the war. Several more mention it briefly in their post-war memoirs. What is interesting from these recollections is the extent to which Crimson Dawn almost came to resemble a strangely intangible ongoing fear within the Empire. If something bad happened, something broke, or a comrade went missing—who quite possibly could have deserted—it seems to have become the norm to wonder if Crimson Dawn were behind it. As a result, some of the stories Imperials seem to have told each other about the actions of Crimson Dawn and Lady Qi'ra are even more outlandish than the version the Archivist presented to Luke and Leia. This in fact may have been a significant aspect of the Crimson Dawn operation in effect. They did not have to even attempt a fraction of the things that were later attributed to them. If enough Imperials believed they were behind anything and everything that was happening during this period—a period that, as has already been mentioned, saw Imperial morale already dropping significantly—then their reputation was enhanced regardless. The mystique of Crimson Dawn grew simply by people believing and sharing stories about their alleged activities. In this sense Crimson Dawn's reputation worked in a strangely similar way to how the Death Star had been intended to operate under the Tarkin Doctrine: the fear of their involvement was more powerful than their actual actions.

Additionally, the Galactic Empire was not the only organization interacting with Crimson Dawn. The Rebel Alliance had their own dealings with Qi'ra's group and made their own evaluations as a result. While it does not appear that Crimson Dawn actively courted the Rebel Alliance as a full ally, perhaps instead preferring to use them as a distraction for the Empire, there were apparently some meetings between the likes of Qi'ra and Leia Organa, ostensibly about Han Solo who was sealed in carbonite at the time.[4] The rebels were able to view aspects of unfolding events from the sidelines and there were certainly some within rebel High Command who believed that Crimson Dawn was attempting some form of attack on the Empire.[5] Alongside this, parts of the galaxy's criminal underworld were also caught up in what appears to have been an internecine conflict for the Emperor's favor, which may have also been prompted by Crimson Dawn, and this at least does appear in Imperial records.[6]

Trying to gauge the actual membership of Crimson Dawn is difficult. At various points in its lifespan it was either advantageous or dangerous to claim allegiance to the group. For some, suggesting they were a member could grant them extra clout within the underworld or—if an Imperial soldier—the possibility of being spared when captured by the Rebel Alliance. Similarly, disavowing any connection to

[4] Rebel Alliance Archives, Section: Crimson Dawn, File: Lady Qi'ra—Meeting on the *Millennium Falcon*
[5] Rebel Alliance Archives, Section: Crimson Dawn, File: Ongoing analysis #25
[6] Imperial Archives, Section: Underworld Activities, File: Syndicate War

Qi'ra after Crimson Dawn's fall, or when placed at the mercy of an Imperial interrogation droid, might be enough to avoid death. Many who said they were part of Crimson Dawn probably were not. Some who denied it certainly were. It is increasingly difficult following the passage of time to discern the fact from the fiction. But despite this, we can begin to draw some conclusions.

War on the Sith

While Darth Vader was sometimes referred to within the Imperial hierarchy as a "Sith Lord"—whether Imperial officers really understood what that meant or not—Palpatine continued to keep his own true powers and loyalties highly secret. As a result, the list of people who would have known about them—and been willing to risk speaking about them—is exceptionally short and has to include Maul. There is enough material already gathered from the excavation here on Exegol to show that Palpatine took an ongoing interest in the activities of his former apprentice, with a significant increase in notations and records relating to his relationship with Crimson Dawn. It is therefore not a huge leap to suggest that Palpatine at least believed that Maul may have been the one to provide details of his true identity to Qi'ra. Why exactly Qi'ra saw fit to proceed with an attack against Palpatine and Vader is unclear. The Archivist alleged that it was born out of an anger and frustration at how the Sith manipulated the rest of the galaxy to live in varying degrees of misery.[7] Given what we know of Qi'ra's early life growing up in the slums of Corellia—where she also spent time enslaved—her anger at the rulers of the galaxy is not that different to the sort that motivated many others to join the Rebel Alliance.[8]

[7] New Republic Archives, Section: Crimson Dawn—The Archivist's Holocron, File: Qi'ra's motivations
[8] Rebel Alliance Archives, Section: Crimson Dawn, File: Qi'ra's Background*
*Contains details provided by Chewbacca and Han Solo

What is interesting about the actions that Crimson Dawn aimed to take against the Sith is how surprisingly unprepared the Emperor and Darth Vader were for them. The Galactic Civil War was likely an ongoing distraction, particularly given the emergence of Luke Skywalker. Similarly, there was no shortage of people who wanted Palpatine or Vader dead. Perhaps the almost universal defeat of the Jedi Order had left the two Sith Lords a little complacent regarding their own position and identities—this would not be the last time that Palpatine in particular would misread a danger to himself—and they assumed that direct attacks on them were likely to come via the Rebel Alliance as part of its war on the Empire. However, as this work has aimed to highlight, the Sith and the Empire are not entirely synonymous. While this has relevance for the way in which the rebels fought their war, it also relates to how Qi'ra had less interest in fighting Imperial forces than she did on gunning for the two stood at the top of the hierarchy.

The opening moves of this attack appear to have been carried out while many in both the Empire and the criminal underworld were trying to take ownership of Han Solo's carbonite-encased body. Following some sort of controversy between Darth Vader and the Hutt lord Bokku over an auction for Solo, Bokku launched an attack on the Super Star Destroyer *Executor* to try and reclaim his prize. While this attack failed and led to the death of Bokku and the rest of the Hutt council, Boba Fett was able to take possession of Han Solo and deliver him to Jabba the Hutt, whose position was now greatly strengthened.[9] However, a rumor began to spread that, because of the Hutts' treachery, the Empire was now willing to dissolve their previous preferential relationship and replace them with a new syndicate. So convincing was this rumor that it even reached Director Barsha—of whom very little is

[9] Rebel Alliance Archives, Section: Hutt Cartel, File: Attack on the *Executor*—Leia Organa's eyewitness report

known—of the ISB.[10] The result of this rumor, which was almost certainly started by Crimson Dawn, was an outbreak of inter-rival warfare between the various crime lords of the galaxy and their related organizations. To try and put down this conflict the Empire was forced to pull ships from actions against the rebels, therefore weakening its efforts in the Galactic Civil War and providing an ongoing distraction.[11] It was apparently this distraction that Qi'ra desired in order to stage an escalation of her plans.

Events from this point onward become a mix of convoluted and potentially implausible. According to the Archivist, Crimson Dawn fashioned a loose alliance of assorted criminals and Imperial personnel who had been acting as sleeper agents to wage war on multiple fronts.[12] At least part of this plan involved overt moves against both Darth Vader and the Emperor. The Archivist suggests that one aspect of this was a mass assassination by poison of the Imperial Royal Guard serving at the Imperial Palace on Coruscant. How this would have been possible is hard to imagine, as these individuals must have been some of the most carefully isolated and vetted people in the galaxy. However, there is also a record in Imperial databases requesting additional personnel be transferred to Coruscant from Yinchorr—one of the training hubs for the Royal Guard—so while implausible it is possible there is some underlying truth to the claim.[13] Events like these may also be examples from within the Imperial military of the impact the threat of Crimson Dawn was having. Even if something did happen to those Royal Guard it is not necessarily the case that Crimson Dawn were behind it, but the belief

[10] Imperial Archives, Section: Imperial Security Bureau, File: Syndicate War—Query memo from Director Barsha
[11] Imperial Archives, Section: Imperial Navy, File: Highest Priority Redeployment Order #51192—Emperor Palpatine's Clearance Code
[12] New Republic Archives, Section: Crimson Dawn—The Archivist's Holocron, File: Crimson Reign
[13] Imperial Archives, Section: Yinchorr Training Facility, File: Urgent transfer order #XJ8177

that they could be—and could in fact strike anywhere, even more so than the rebels—stoked a particular form of paranoia which was undoubtedly beneficial to Qi'ra.

There are certainly signs that this paranoia had begun to reach into the upper echelons as well. There appears to have been a significant purge of Imperial military personnel and advisors who were suspected of having been affiliated with Crimson Dawn.[14] Again, the Archivist suggests that this purge was based upon false information provided to the Empire and that around fifty percent of those on the list were Imperial loyalists.[15] This is incredibly difficult to verify. Regardless, while the Emperor and Vader perhaps believed this was the surest and safest way of rooting out the Crimson Dawn agents within the Empire, we can only wonder how badly it impacted wider Imperial morale at a time when it was already dangerously eroding.

The culmination of Qi'ra's plans appears to have been executed at Amaxine Station. It was there that she gathered the majority of Crimson Dawn's military forces in preparation for a battle against the *Executor* and, on the station itself, against the two Dark Lords of the Sith. The focal point of this battle is especially difficult to unpack. The Archivist mentions a form of Force weapon known as the Fermata Cage, and there have been references to it uncovered on Exegol.[16] Exactly how this weapon worked, or what Qi'ra intended to do with it isn't clear. But it was clearly concerning enough to lure Palpatine from Coruscant— something that was practically unheard of by this point in the Empire's history. We may never know exactly what happened on the station itself, but there is evidence that the battle caused some sort of disturbance in

---

[14] Imperial Archives, Section: Crimson Dawn Purge, File: Execution Orders* *This list is lengthy and many of the names on it had been removed.

[15] New Republic Archives, Section: Crimson Dawn—The Archivist's Holocron, File: False collaborators list

[16] Exegol Excavation Project, Section: Force Artifacts, Files: Fermata Cage* *Information retrieved from the Arcane Library

the Force. For some time afterward Luke Skywalker noted that his ability to use the Force was greatly hampered and that the energy field itself seemed to be in some sort of flux.[17] Whatever happened on Amaxine Station, both Palpatine and Vader survived it seemingly unscathed. In orbit the forces of Crimson Dawn were demolished by the *Executor* and Admiral Piett gave orders that no prisoners were to be taken and no lives spared.[18] At the conclusion of the battle Crimson Dawn was effectively destroyed and Lady Qi'ra had vanished. Whatever the intended outcome of her long-running plan, Qi'ra had clearly failed. The Archivist mentioned that she never heard from the leader of Crimson Dawn ever again.

After the Dawn

In some ways this might be thought of as the end of Crimson Dawn and their influence on the galaxy. Certainly, they do not appear to have been major players for the rest of the Galactic Civil War, though various off-shoot organizations rebranded themselves as the inheritors of Qi'ra's power and legacy. The failure of Crimson Dawn ostensibly left the Empire—and particularly Palpatine and Vader—free to focus on the threat of the Rebel Alliance. However, events rarely end so swiftly and without ongoing consequences. Though they had won their battle against Crimson Dawn, the Empire was notably weakened by it, and this would have repercussions.

In military terms, Palpatine and Vader had pulled numerous ships of the line out of the war against the rebels and redeployed them to crush Crimson Dawn. While this had obvious benefits in wiping out an additional enemy and maintaining order in the galaxy, it also provided yet

[17] Rebel Alliance Archives, Section: Luke Skywalker, File: Force Wave
[18] Imperial Archives, Section: Military Operations, File: Battle at Amaxine Station—Admiral Piett's rules of engagement

another example of the Emperor and Darth Vader paying scant regard to the requirements of the people who were actually running the war effort. From the joint chiefs down to individual commanders, the military found themselves creating plans for various potential military engagements using forces that were then relocated at the last moment and not replaced. During this period the Rebel Alliance had—having been burned by their flight from Hoth—largely eschewed planetary bases of operations and were running the war effort out of the rebel fleet itself. This presented some obvious dangers, should the ships be ambushed or trapped by Interdictor cruisers, but did give them more flexibility when it came to making their escape. It was also not a long-term solution—it was expensive for the rebellion to keep its fleet constantly on the move and its vessels required ongoing supply.[19] While it is difficult to know whether or not the extra ships that were diverted away from the front lines to fight Crimson Dawn would have made a difference in tracking down the rebel military, their absence certainly did not help.

Furthermore, many Imperial officers and soldiers had witnessed friends and comrades be summarily executed for alleged links to Crimson Dawn. Whether those links existed or not is almost immaterial—particularly as those giving the execution orders had no interest in showing their evidence to bystanders—but the impact was noticeable. Numerous Imperial prisoners after the war have expressed how a mixture of fear and horror had spread through the fleet as yet another purge was carried out, this one in in the middle of a significant ongoing conflict.[20] Imperial morale may already have been in a downward spiral and having significant numbers of experienced soldiers killed for treason which may not have existed, only exacerbated the situation. There were also additional military implications. Seasoned captains and commanders,

[19] Rebel Alliance Archives, Section: Fleet Operations, File: Supply Convoy Activities #DT7425
[20] See: New Republic Archives, Section: Imperial Prisoners, File: Interrogations 147, 351, 419, and 834 for examples

experienced pilots, battle-hardened soldiers were among those to die. These were incredibly valuable for a state at war. While new reinforcements could take their place, the experience and military know-how they possessed was lost. Palpatine and Vader were primarily focused on the importance of loyalty, but this came at the expense of weakening their own military as the war was reaching its endgame.

Because, in and among all the other activities of Crimson Dawn, was one which would have enormous repercussions on the outcome of the Galactic Civil War. In many respects Lieutenant Jon Melton and his wife Bevelyn—a cargo worker—were unremarkable Imperial personnel among millions of others. However, because of Lt. Melton's job as an aide to Moff Tiaan Jerjerrod, he was privy to one of the greatest secrets currently held by the Empire: *the existence* of the second Death Star currently under construction. They were also sleeper agents for Crimson Dawn. The pair were subsequently activated and instructed, along with many others, to assist in causing chaos within the Empire. In response Jon Melton and Bevelyn took their children, stole an Imperial shuttle, and subsequently defected to the Rebel Alliance, bringing their information with them.[21]

The news they brought sent ripples of shock through the rebel High Command, but also exposed the determination with which Palpatine still clung on to his vision of a galaxy ruled by the fear of a Death Star. This revelation dramatically changed the long-term objectives of the Rebel Alliance at exactly the point when the Imperial Navy was being forced to reconsider its own approach to the Galactic Civil War. While Lady Qi'ra of Crimson Dawn may have failed in her own quest to destroy the Sith and liberate the galaxy, she had—perhaps unwittingly—put the Empire and the Rebel Alliance on a collision course for a grand battle that would decide the outcome of the war. Maybe she had won after all.

[21] Rebel Alliance Archives, Section: Second Death Star, File: Jon Melton and Bevelyn Debriefing

Chapter 20

The Battle of Endor

I t is hard to imagine a more seismic moment—even given recent events—in contemporary galactic history than that which transpired at Endor more than 30 years ago. Even regardless of the battle's eventual outcome, the rationale for fighting it in the first place was the end point of years of accumulating decisions, political circumstances, and military concerns. I know that Rey, Leia Organa, and Luke Skywalker believed—as did Emperor Palpatine and Darth Vader—that the Force could influence events to almost make them seem pre-destined. Given everything that has been outlined in this study so far, it is perhaps true that the Battle of Endor was the natural conclusion not just of Palpatine's Empire but the decisions he and others had made while ruling it. If Endor was to prove the death of the Empire, it was one of Palpatine's own making.

As with other battles that have been mentioned in this work, the intention here is not to go over old ground regarding exact troop movements and the like. Particularly not as an updated version of that analysis is underway from several of my colleagues. However, there are things that I believe need to be either re-evaluated or, alternatively, examined for the first time regarding the Battle of Endor. Some of this material—as with my new conclusions relating to the Battle of Hoth and other crucial moments in the Empire's history—is contested, for reasons that are understandable and will be covered in greater detail below. But while the Imperial tactics at Endor have been the subject of ongoing consideration by both military historians and practitioners, I still believe there to be significant question marks regarding why the Empire chose to fight at Endor at all and the background to their battle plans. It is only through the wider considerations that I have attempted to highlight throughout this study that answers to some of those questions are now beginning to appear.

This is because the events of Endor did not take place isolated from all that had come before. While Emperor Palpatine and Darth Vader were both present at Endor, their focus on Luke Skywalker essentially meant that the battle outside was left to the servicepeople of the Imperial fleet. In theory the greatest collection of ships that the Galactic Empire had ever committed to battle should have been ample to destroy a rebel fleet that had been caught completely by surprise. Similarly, the Imperial forces on the surface of Endor should not have been outmaneuvered and defeated by a mixture of rebel commandos and indigenous Ewoks. And yet both defeats happened. The reasons why likely rest on everything that had happened, and would happen, in the prelude to the rebel fleet emerging from hyperspace.

Strategic Crises

In the lead up to the Battle of Endor both the Galactic Empire and the Rebel Alliance were effectively grappling with the same strategic problem: neither of them was actually getting any closer to winning the war. While there had been various notable victories and defeats along the way, the overall balance of power in the galaxy was much the same as it had been for most of the war. The rebels were continuing to grow in number and power but not so much as to threaten the type of sudden surge or revolution that might sweep them to victory. Similarly, the Galactic Empire's forces faced much the same challenge as they had since Yavin—they were struggling to locate rebel bases or force the rebel fleet into a decisive engagement. Recent events had not improved matters noticeably on either side.

The issues the Empire had recently faced in dealing with Crimson Dawn had ongoing repercussions. Some form of droid infection aboard the *Executor* had resulted in several Star Destroyers being forced to try and destroy the vessel to prevent it from spreading. While the Super Star Destroyer had eventually been purged, it had come at the expense of at least one of the attacking Star Destroyers and the death of Admiral Corleque.[1] The need to retain the *Executor,* given its vast expense and firepower, but also because many of the best officers in the fleet were onboard, was obvious. But the death of Corleque and the destruction of his flagship the *Unbreakable* once again robbed the Empire of an officer, crew, and vessel who were desperately needed. Similarly, the ships that had been pulled from service to deal with Crimson Dawn had left gaps in the Imperial fleet deployments that had still not been rebalanced. At the Battle of Ponolapo a small rebel fleet had ambushed an Imperial convoy. Ordinarily the escorting Star Destroyer *Steadfast* would have been accompanied by several Gozanti or Arquitens light cruisers but, in this case, it was alone. As a result, the rebels were able to destroy most of the Imperial shipping and damage the *Steadfast*—even managing to kill Commodore Freylon—on the way out.[2]

Across the galaxy the rebels and the Empire were engaging in small skirmishes that resulted in ships and lives being traded on both sides, but never in great enough numbers to shift the wider dynamic of the conflict. The rebels were just as wary as ever of committing to a battle that, if lost, would cost them the war. The Empire continued trying to marshal their forces while balancing their strategic focus between the likes of the Rebellion or Crimson Dawn. However, there was also

[1] Imperial Archives, Military Operations, File: Attack on the *Executor** *This record and others like it have been censored heavily.
[2] See; Rebel Alliance Archives, Military Operations, File: Battle of Ponolapo, and; Imperial Archives, Section: Imperial Navy, File: Commodore Freylon Obituary

another major construction project underway that would change the thinking of both sides of the Galactic Civil War. The ongoing development of the second Death Star showed in the clearest of terms that Palpatine had not changed his aims since Yavin. He wanted the ability to destroy entire planets and the fear that such a battle station would provide. The intervening years had not dimmed this desire and he had once again resolved to dedicate as many resources as were necessary to achieve it. Perhaps the most noticeable change with this new project was the decision as to who was placed in charge. As previously noted, the original Death Star had become a battlefield upon which Wilhuff Tarkin and Orson Krennic played out their ambitions. Though Tarkin had won that struggle, his victory had been brief. His death at Yavin had been a tremendous blow to the Empire. The person chosen to replace him on the new construction project—Moff Tiaan Jerjerrod—was not another Tarkin.[3] But perhaps that was the point. While Jerjerrod lacked Tarkin's vision and ability to project power, he also appears to have been much less ambitious. Jerjerrod had served stints on the joint chiefs in the years since Yavin and was not viewed as a burgeoning "power behind the throne" figure in the ways that Tarkin had sometimes been. Jerjerrod was a more limited man but was also all the more controllable as a result. Put simply, someone like Vader could threaten and scare him in a way that he could not do with Tarkin.

While the new Death Star had been under construction for some time, the Rebel Alliance had learned of its existence probably sooner than the Empire would have liked. The site at Endor was well-defended both by assets from the Imperial fleet and by a shield generator on the Forest Moon's surface. But ongoing delays had slowed progress and there were still questions over when the main infrastructure and firepower of the station would be completed. However, the Death Star also

[3] Imperial Archives, Section: Second Death Star Construction, File: Moff Tiaan Jerjerrod

accelerated wider strategic conversations within both the Empire and the Rebel Alliance regarding how best to bring the war to a conclusion. Interestingly it seems that the conclusion taken on both sides resembled an exchange of military stances. The problem facing the Galactic Empire had long been that they could not force the Rebel Alliance into a confrontation that might result in a decisive victory. There had been numerous attempts over the years—not least at Atollon, Yavin, Mako-Ta, and Hoth—but they had been squandered. As time had gone on the rebels had become even more reluctant to stand and fight on a battleground they themselves had not chosen. When faced with the choice between victory or survival, the rebels often chose survival and escaped. The Empire could chase the rebels around the galaxy for years to come and still get no closer to winning the war. They needed to find some way of making the rebels come to them.[4]

At the same time, the Alliance military was also grappling with the problem that while survival was necessary to ensure the Rebellion's ongoing chances, simply existing was not the same as winning. The rebels, understandably, were highly reluctant to risk their combined military forces in any battles that would not dramatically benefit their overall chances of victory. But, as a result, their reticence to fight meant that the Empire remained in control of the galaxy and billions continued to struggle under its oppressive conditions. The rebels were not willing to just throw their fleet into any battles that appeared, but the longer liberation of the galaxy was delayed, the greater the chances that people would begin to lose hope it was ever coming. If the steady stream of recruits and resources from across the galaxy was to dwindle, then the Alliance could founder. Leading rebel military figures were already evaluating possible targets for a concerted attack that would provide both a needed morale boost and

[4] Imperial Archives, Section: Joint Chiefs of the Imperial Military, File: Military Strategy Conference #JT2198

potentially tip the balance of power in their favor. Then news of the new Death Star arrived.

There was an understandable amount of doubt and suspicion about the news, and rebel spies were deployed across the galaxy to try and confirm it.[5] The Alliance particularly drew upon the efforts of Bothan spies in order to gather information.[6] Not only did these attempts produce information regarding the Death Star's location, defenses, and general state of completion, it also provided news that nobody in the Rebellion could have foreseen: Emperor Palpatine himself was due to visit the battle station to inspect its construction. Even before the Battle of Yavin, Palpatine had effectively become a recluse on Coruscant. In the years since, the very notion of him publicly traveling beyond the Imperial capital was almost unheard of. If Palpatine was going to be away from the safety of Coruscant aboard a target the rebels were already planning to attack, then suddenly the war-winning opportunity they had long been searching for had arrived.[7]

We now know that Palpatine's presence at Endor was not the coincidence the rebels believed it to be. Great efforts were made to ensure that the rebels knew exactly when Palpatine would be on board the battle station.[8] The Empire's need to drag the rebels out of hiding was just as strong as the rebels' need to secure a military victory. The outcome was to heavily bait the trap at Endor by seemingly providing the rebels with all the motivation they required to finally come out and fight. In a peculiar way Endor was almost designed as a reversal of the Battle of Yavin,

[5] Rebel Alliance Archives, Section: Intelligence Operations, File: Second Death Star
[6] Bothawui Archives, Section: Espionage Network, File: Rebel Alliance Operation #RM612* *This record is almost entirely redacted.
[7] Rebel Alliance Archives, Section: Military Operations, File: Battle of Endor Briefing* *This record was created and filed by Dora Mar in her role as a Chronicler on *Home One*.
[8] Rebel Alliance Archives, Section: Military Operations, File: Battle of Endor Preparation—Ciena Ree Debriefing

with the rebels looking to launch a destructive assault, while the Empire aimed to draw them into a trap. As a result, it seems like the Empire had all the advantages it could possibly require. What happened next remains highly contested.

Breaking Point

There are points during the work of a historian when you discover accounts of a single event that are so contradictory as to cause serious problems in attempting to understand what actually happened. How could eyewitnesses and participants of something produce such wildly differing accounts of an event they all supposedly experienced? How do we begin to discern which version is the most likely? These are questions that are highly relevant when it comes to an examination of Admiral Piett's briefing on board the *Executor* before the Battle of Endor.

Before digging into the conflicting accounts of this meeting, it is perhaps best to begin by confirming what is already established in various records and considering the arguments this study has made regarding the overall position of the Imperial Navy at this point in the war. The details of the exact vessels that the Empire fielded at Endor are already well known, but it is worth acknowledging that whether it was Piett himself or the joint chiefs who made the decision regarding the fleet's composition, a number of the most experienced commanders and ships were present. Admiral Sloane and the *Vigilance* were present, as were Admiral Versio's *Eviscerator*, Vice Admiral Ferno's *Dark Omen*, and Admiral Montferrat with the *Devastator*.[9] These ships and their commanders had seen extensive action against the Rebel Alliance across the entirety of the war. While there were those like Commodore Scaanos aboard the *Steadfast* or Captain Inalis

[9] Imperial Archives, Section: Military Operations, File: Endor Fleet Composition

of the *Interrogator* who did not have quite as extensive military careers, by and large the Imperial fleet at Endor was an incredibly capable one, with Moff Jerjerrod himself joining the briefing remotely. However, when considering the senior officers present it is also important to note that they were spread across the ideological and doctrinal split within the military and also, because of the nature of their service to date, were perhaps some of the longest-serving. This becomes relevant in due course.

What is also established is that at the opening of the meeting, Admiral Piett gave a shorter briefing regarding the expected nature of the ground battle to General Falk who commanded the army forces and Major Hewex who led the naval contingent on the moon's surface. Communication records captured after the battle indicate that the briefing communication sent from orbit was not a lengthy one.[10] Similarly, orders were also given to the assorted starfighter commanders regarding general battle formations and the initial wave that was designed to disrupt rebel fleet formations and pin them in place. All of these aspects are either corroborated within the records of various Star Destroyers after the briefing concluded or, in the case of the *Executor*, transmitted back to Coruscant.[11] Admiral Piett's transmission also effectively contains what has become the official version of the senior officers' briefing which was also, apparently, reasonably short. In it he outlined that the assembled fleet would hold their position between the rebels and their escape route, while Interdictor cruisers would ensure there was no chance of their enemy fleeing into hyperspace. While details were not given about the "special" plans of Emperor Palpatine, it was made clear that the assorted Star Destroyers were not expected to take an active

[10] Rebel Alliance Archives, Section: Endor, File: Captured Imperial communication logs #YN309
[11] For evidence of this see the records recovered from the *Dark Omen* and the wreckage of the *Steadfast* and *Devastator*.

part in the battle.[12] Versions of this account are also found within the records of the *Steadfast* and the *Interrogator*.

However, this is not the only account of this meeting and the alternative one, while seeming in some ways highly implausible, does have some very compelling and interesting aspects. Because this version suggests that rather than a relatively simple pre-battle briefing, what actually occurred was—upon hearing of the Emperor's orders—an outpouring of all the built up tension, stress, and fatigue of years of warfare from the assembled officers in the form of a blazing argument. Several of those who either recorded elements of this event, or recalled it after the fact, have made a tendency to anonymize those speaking, but some efforts can be made to identify specific individuals. It appears that at least some of those present were incensed by the idea of luring the Rebel Alliance into a trap and then not finishing them off as quickly as possible. One officer is quoted as shouting, "Can we just once, for kriff's sake, win the war?! How many times do we have to let Vader or His Majesty mess things up when victory is right here? It's right here! Just win the war!" This outburst provoked accusations of high treason from an unnamed source, who was probably either Admiral Montferrat—given his close affiliation to Darth Vader—or Admiral Versio, who was a diehard loyalist.[13] A side argument also appears to have emerged regarding the plan of sending in the starfighters first, but without backing them up or holding enough reserves in place to defend the fleet. This part laid bare the ongoing factions and differences in opinion regarding the way the Imperial Navy should have been waging the war. One officer, presumably Vice Admiral Ferno, began an explanation of how Grand Admiral Thrawn had coordinated the fighters and fleet at Atollon before another figure reportedly shouted him down with a cry of, "If I have to

---

[12] Imperial Archives, Section: Military Operations, File: Battle of Endor—Admiral Piett's Briefing Summary Transmitted from the *Executor*

[13] New Republic Archives, Section: Imperial Prisoners, File: Interrogations 149

listen to one more lecture about what that ludicrous alien would have done, I am going to allow my ship to indulge in friendly fire!"[14]

Before beginning to ascertain the evidence that either supports or undermines this version of events, it is important to begin by considering why it may have happened at all. For Imperial officers, particularly those of a higher rank, to dislike each other is not particularly surprising. Senior figures throughout the Empire tended to treat their fellows with a degree of suspicion. The system practically encouraged it. Furthermore, we also know that the Imperial military, and the fleet especially, had long been riven with factions and splits regarding overall strategy and doctrine. This had simmered under the surface for a prolonged period with occasional outbreaks of infighting at moments when the war was going badly. I have also argued that, following the Imperial "victory" at Hoth, a lot of military personnel had begun to feel the strain of waging the Galactic Civil War and morale had begun to degrade as opportunities for victory slipped through their fingers. Is it possible that the stress of these circumstances had finally pushed some of the gathered officers over the edge? That the notion of the rebel fleet landing directly into a well-laid trap only for the whole victory to be jeopardized because "the Emperor had something special planned" was so infuriating to senior fleet personnel that they would actually criticize both Vader and Palpatine in such an overt way? It does not seem to be so unrealistic as to be impossible.

So how do we assess the evidence? Well, the records of those who say this argument did not happen are fairly clear. While several of these sources are junior commanders—at least in comparison to some of the others assembled—Admiral Piett is a pretty strong source and his broadcast to Coruscant is straightforward in its appraisal of events.

---

[14] Found in an unpublished memoir entitled *Hero of the Empire* written by an anonymous Imperial commander that was located within the records captured at Yaga Minor.

According to both Piett's transmission and those junior officers, this argument simply did not occur. However, there is room for contemplation regarding these sources. For example, Commodore Scaanos returned to the *Steadfast* a full standard hour and a half before Admiral Rae Sloane returned to the *Vigilance*. Is it possible that the more fiery events actually took place in a closed briefing for the senior officers to air their grievances and that Commodore Scaanos did not report the arguments simply because he was not there to witness them? This may have been a way for Piett to consult with the highest-ranking commanders—many of whom had served together on the joint chiefs— in a way that allowed him to keep the dispute "in fleet" without causing him an issue with his own reports. This seems like a possible explanation, but we must also be critical with the accounts of those who claim the dispute took place. Several of those who have provided information on the argument did so while under interrogation by the New Republic at the end of the war. In those circumstances, presenting a version of events which distanced them from the Emperor and Darth Vader and allowed them to appear as professionals just trying to do their job, had obvious benefits. Additionally, an unpublished anonymous memoir, while interesting, presents any number of problems when it comes to evaluating its veracity.

There is one curious outcome of the meeting though that may provide us with an opportunity to decide on its likelihood one way or another. As has been mentioned before, the ISB's loyalty officers were not beloved individuals across the Imperial military. They were often viewed as unwelcome additions onboard a ship at best and, at worst, spies who fomented more trouble and suspicion than was ever in existence in the first place. I have previously argued that the activities of ISB loyalty officers around the Battle of Hoth and then the activities of Crimson Dawn probably caused a great deal of damage to the morale of Imperial soldiers. Shortly after the briefing on board the *Executor* took place, it appears that contingents of loyalty officers were redeployed from the Death Star onto the various Star Destroyers gathered at Endor.[15] Why exactly this was done and who gave the order for it are unknown. But it certainly strikes me as highly interesting timing that, so soon after a supposed outbreak of almost treasonous or mutinous anger within the fleet, loyalty officers would be placed upon the bridges of those vessels.

We may never know for certain what, if anything, happened in the command chamber of the *Executor* that day. Many of those present were either killed in the battle or in those to come. However, I do not believe it is implausible to say that there were some among the gathered officers who feared an imminent disaster. They were correct.

Cataclysm

As previously noted, there has been—and will continue to be—much in-depth analysis as to exactly how the Empire managed to construct an absolutely crushing defeat from a situation that greatly favored their victory and I have no wish to refight the battle here. However, there is some value in trying to explain exactly why the Imperial fleet ended up functioning so far below its expected combat abilities. Obviously, it is important to note quite how hobbled the Star Destroyers were by Emperor Palpatine's orders not to move forward to engage the rebel fleet. It cost them a great deal of their advantage, a significant portion of their TIE forces, and most of the initiative.

But these were not the only factors in play at Endor. It is entirely possible that the rebel fleet was better led than the Empire's, as Admiral Ackbar was a formidable battle commander. But combat is not simply decided by those in charge and, regardless, there was a great deal of military experience on the Imperial side. There is a benefit at this point to considering the *Executor* as a case study. It had long been believed

---

[15] Imperial Archives, Section: Imperial Security Bureau, File: Additional Deployment at Endor

that being assigned to Darth Vader's flagship was a fast track to potential promotion and command. Given Vader's moods, however, it was also possibly a death sentence. And this in itself indicates a wider problem. How many talented junior officers, or gunners, or fighter commanders died on the *Executor*—even before Endor—simply because they displeased Vader in some way? How much knowledge and ability were squandered by the Empire on the capricious whims of Palpatine's apprentice? Additionally, while the other Star Destroyers in the assembled fleet had a great deal of combat experience, was this really true of their crews? Given the way the navy had been purged of those deemed disloyal during the Crimson Dawn affair, how many newly trained officers sat in positions previously held by battle-hardened professionals? How many green pilots were flying into battle against the best the rebellion had to offer? How many capable soldiers who would have served either aboard ships or in the army at the shield generator, had deserted in the aftermath of Hoth? The Empire had been eroding its own military from the inside for years. Endor may have been the moment when those weaknesses proved fatal.

The Death Star's intervention in the battle, while dramatic, was also indicative of the embrace of firepower without giving due consideration to its targeting. Perhaps Moff Jerjerrod believed that Emperor Palpatine wanted to draw out the destruction, which is why he—having been ordered by Palpatine to fire at will—instructed the superlaser to target ships other than *Home One*.[16] Regardless of its rationale it made very little military sense. Destroying the rebel flagship would have crippled the enemy's ability to coordinate their forces. Leaving it alone only highlighted the extent to which some in the Imperial military—presumably including the Emperor himself—believed that

---

[16] This order from the Emperor to Jerjerrod was recalled after the battle by Luke Skywalker; Rebel Alliance Archives, Section: Luke Skywalker, File: Debriefing after the Battle of Endor.

raw destruction would be enough to quell their opponents without anticipating how the rebels may react to it.

Down on the Forest Moon itself, the gathered stormtroopers and army personnel were all notionally combat veterans who had served for at least three or four years.[17] But together they had all missed the dangers posed by the indigenous Ewoks. Why? Could it be that an Empire—which had drilled into its armed forces and citizens that "aliens" were inferior and that, in most combat situations, enemies should be expected to fear them and flee—had stopped learning from the war they were embroiled in? That it was now almost ideologically incapable of understanding its own blind spots? Much time has been spent on wondering why the Empire failed at Endor when the truth may be that this outcome was the almost natural conclusion to the path the Imperial military had been set upon. That Imperial society had sucked the ingenuity and imagination from its own personnel to the extent that they were no longer intellectually capable of dealing with an enemy like the Rebel Alliance.

There were at least some within the gathered leaders who could recognize what was happening at Endor as events began to unravel. Battle recordings show that Admiral Sloane realized how vulnerable the *Executor* had suddenly become and was in the process of moving her *Vigilance* into a supporting position when the Super Star Destroyer's bridge was struck by an A-wing and the enormous vessel sank into the Death Star's gravity well.[18] As the ship exploded onto the battle station's surface, taking many of those best young officers with it, Sloane took command of the fleet and prepared for the retreat.[19] She at least had

[17] Imperial Archives, Section: Military Operations, File: Battle of Endor—Ground forces composition
[18] Imperial Archives, Section: Military Operations, File: Battle of Endor—*Vigilance* movements
[19] Imperial Archives, Section: Military Operations, File: Battle of Endor—Retreat order

understood that not only was the battle about to be lost but that the entire framework of the Empire was about to utterly change. Because within the battle station Emperor Palpatine, in his arrogance, had set in motion a series of events that would spell his own death. So fixated had he been on his attempts to lure Luke Skywalker to the dark side he had hamstrung his own military forces and turned his own apprentice against him.[20]

As the Death Star exploded into fragments, the Imperial fleet made a desperate escape into hyperspace. Behind them they left a jubilant and disbelieving Rebel Alliance. Throughout the night on Endor a myriad of species and soldiers wildly celebrated the death of the Emperor and the final destruction of the Galactic Empire.

As it would transpire, they were wrong on both counts.

[20] Rebel Alliance Archives, Section: Luke Skywalker, File: Debriefing after the Battle of Endor

Part Four

FALL AND CONTINUATION

Chapter 21

Fracture and Cinder

Despite all the horrors that had preceded it, in many ways, the final year of the Galactic Civil War was one of the worst. Elated soldiers of the Rebel Alliance went to sleep in the aftermath of celebrations on Endor expecting to wake up to news of the Empire's collapse or surrender, only to find that—for various reasons that will be discussed below—the Imperial military had generally resolved to continue the struggle. Having assumed victory was all but achieved, these soldiers had to remobilize themselves to continue a war that, rather than having been won, was on the verge of becoming a destructive and attritional grind. The impact this had on the psyche of many rebel soldiers was severe, and after the Rebel Alliance evolved into the New Republic, it became apparent that a great many of those treated for various forms of mental and emotional breakdown had been tipped over the edge by the war's last months.[1]

Within the Empire the catastrophic events of Endor had repercussions right through the Imperial system. Imperial soldiers and military personnel had been instructed about the importance of loyalty for years, in some instances since birth. What was to become of an Empire stripped of its Emperor? If personnel were expected to be loyal, loyal to

[1] New Republic Archives, Section: Veteran Support, File: Post-Combat Breakdown Register of Patients from 4-5 ABY

what . . . or whom? It was not immediately clear who was now giving the orders within the Galactic Empire, a situation only exacerbated by those who saw Palpatine's death as an opportunity to seize power for themselves. Meanwhile, as the reality of Endor set in, many Imperials also seemed to be pushed beyond breaking point. For every desertion or defection, it seems another soldier elected to choose a violent response. Spontaneous executions and massacres of civilians—not all of whom were celebrating Palpatine's death—rocketed in the immediate aftermath of the destruction of the second Death Star.[2]

Horrifyingly, even these seemingly isolated attacks on the civilian population would soon pale against the devastation that would shortly be unleashed. Because, as has been made clear by far more recent events, killing the Emperor was not enough to undo all of his plans and his hatred. Even as the last vestiges of the Death Star continued to plummet onto the moons of Endor, Palpatine's contingency plans were beginning to activate. Soon new orders would be delivered to those selected military leaders who, it had been predicted, would choose to continue the fight.

To the Bitter End

There were many reasons why some Imperial soldiers and officials continued to wage the war even after the death of the Emperor. From the outset it is important to state that the Rebel Alliance didn't necessarily help their own cause. Recordings of the Death Star's destruction and the subsequent celebrations on Endor were sent through HoloNet News and viewed across the galaxy. While this was enough to spark uprisings on some worlds—including a short-lived one on Coruscant itself—within the Imperial military structure it provoked very different emotions. Many soldiers noted the lack of Imperial prisoners at

[2] New Republic Archives, Section: Civilian Casualty Estimates, File: Post-Endor Massacres

Endor and the use of empty armor as musical instruments by the Ewoks. Wild, but fearful, rumors began to spread about what exactly the "indigenous creatures" on the moon had done to captured Imperials.[3] Many of those within the Imperial military already had concerns about what might happen to them if captured, and these additional fears—stoked by an underlying and very Imperial species bias—only compounded the problem.

In general, however, the decisions made by various military personnel to keep fighting were complicated. Imperial propaganda had spent years hammering home the point that the Rebel Alliance—or any group that defied the Empire—were set on destroying all aspects of galactic civilization. While we know that it was in fact the Empire itself that meted out destruction across the galaxy, we should not doubt that there were plenty, both in Imperial service and living out their lives within the Core Worlds, who believed this lie to be true. As a result, they rationalized that to keep fighting was in some way protecting their homes and families against a terrible threat.[4]

In addition to this, many others resolved to stand by their posts simply because they had nowhere else to go. In a galaxy that appeared to be coming apart at the seams, many soldiers had been drafted into the military so long ago that it was now essentially the only life they knew. The soldiers who served around them were the closest thing to family many had, even accepting that such feelings would have been frowned upon by senior military figures.[5] As a result, for some soldiers the decision to keep fighting was less about devotion to the cause and more about loyalty to their friends.

[3] Imperial Archives, Section: Imperial Security Bureau, File: Inquiries into captured soldiers at Endor
[4] New Republic Archives, Section: Imperial Prisoners, File: Report on refusal to surrender in Imperial military personnel
[5] Imperial Archives, Section: Imperial Military Forces, File: Acceptable forms of comradeship* *This appears to have been some form of instructional material circulated among the Imperial armed forces.

What is interesting about all these motivations is that to varying extents, all of them feature an element of fear. While there were undoubtedly plenty of loyalist diehards who continued fighting, there is no great mystery behind their motivation. But for those who were not as ideologically committed to the cause, it does seem that fear played a significant role in their thought process. Fear of what might happen to their families if the Empire lost. Fear of what might happen to their comrades should they abandon their posts. Fear of being ritualistically devoured by feral species on far off worlds. But there was another aspect to this fear, and it was based around what might happen should they be captured and put on trial.

Regardless of all the wider justifications of order and peace, in most ways the Empire was built and predicated on cruelty and complicity. Virtually all who existed within it suffered from this cruelty. But it was not delivered remotely or just conjured into being because Palpatine wished it so. It was perpetrated by the ordinary people who facilitated the Imperial system. Every stormtrooper who used lethal force where it wasn't needed. Every administrative official who abused their power. Every fleet officer who opened fire with indiscriminate barrages. Cruelty permeated the Empire. And the Empire kept records of all of it. Deep within Coruscant lay enormous databanks which carefully logged and registered every crime, every murder, every act of wanton cruelty that servants of the Empire carried out.[6] Knowledge of these records was not widespread, but that almost didn't matter. The people who'd committed the crimes knew what they'd done. Whether they believed it to have been wrong or not, they suspected that the Rebel Alliance would take a dim view of it. As a result, they were afraid of the consequences of their own actions. Though they had not realized it at the time, service to the Empire was almost a binding pact of mutual destruction. The

[6] New Republic Archives, Section: Survey of Occupied Coruscant, File: Imperial Records Database

only way that many soldiers thought they could avoid a tribunal and—in their worst fears—a public execution, was to keep faith with a state that had allowed them to indulge the worst aspects of their own morality. Fear and cruelty had powered the Empire while Palpatine was alive. It continued to do so now he was dead.

But while many in Imperial uniforms felt this fear, others did not. They looked at the debacle at Endor and the now empty throne and decided that, finally, their time had come.

An Empire Divided

The reaction of some within the Empire to news of Palpatine's death was almost a reflex one: deny everything. Some Moffs and sector governors looked to disconnect their own territories from the holonet to try and curb the spread of what they called "rebel propaganda" while they could come up with a viable alternative message.

Governor Ecressys of the Velcar sector was one of the quickest to react to the situation. He commissioned and then spread the—now infamous—"Endor Is A Lie" image that depicted Palpatine on his throne.[7] Even before getting to the actual thought process behind the image, there are interesting things to note about its actual design. As previously mentioned, the Empire had gone to varying lengths at times to avoid depicting Palpatine's actual appearance, instead relying on older depictions of him from the Clone Wars. Ecressys completely eschewed this in his image by showing the aged and withered version of the Emperor who existed in his later years. Perhaps this was seen as an acceptable trade-off by attempting to suggest it was a more recent—and therefore "truthful"—representation. But the underlying message, that Emperor Palpatine was still alive, well, and ruling the Empire, was

[7] New Republic Archives, Section: Imperial Propaganda Collection, File: "Endor Is A Lie"

designed, firstly, to try and buy Ecressys time. He knew, as did many other Imperial officials, that the realization of quite how weak the Empire suddenly was could spark a mass uprising that would rip the galaxy from their grasp. There would, perhaps, come a time in the future when the Empire would admit the truth about Palpatine's death to the wider galaxy, but that time was not now.

Governor Ecressys also then took the step to, effectively, close the borders of the Velcar sector in the belief—or more likely the hope—that the rebels would be far too busy to bother immediately rooting him out of his capital. With the Galactic Civil War going on elsewhere, Ecressys used the Imperial forces available to both maintain his control over the sector and assist him in looting the wealth of those planets under his rule.[8] Eventually the New Republic did arrive to liberate the Velcar sector, but Governor Ecressys was long gone, together with much of his plunder.

In theory, with Emperor Palpatine and Darth Vader both presumed dead, most within the Imperial system should have turned their eyes toward Coruscant for new instructions, but that did not happen. Palpatine had taken many of his closest advisors—like Sate Pestage and Sim Aloo—with him to Endor, where they'd also perished.[9] All that was now left on Coruscant, aside from the functioning bureaucracy of the Imperial state, was Mas Amedda. The assorted Moffs, governors, and leading military officers of the Empire may have, at times, courted Mas Amedda when the Emperor was alive because of what he symbolized. As Palpatine's grand vizier he was crucial to getting the Emperor's attention. But as an actual individual many had—at best—tolerated the Chagrian, while others held him in outright contempt. Some of this was motivated by the fact he was non-human. But with the Emperor dead and the throne empty, any thoughts Mas Amedda may have had about ascending it himself were swiftly crushed by the realization that nobody

[8] Imperial Archives, Section: Velcar Sector, File: Wealth redistribution
[9] Imperial Archives, Section: Emperor Palpatine's Inner Court, File: Transfer to Endor

else in the Empire now cared what he thought. Where Coruscant had once been the center of the Galactic Empire it now became little more than a performative symbol. Amedda himself was reduced to a figure-head, simply repeating the orders of other leaders, all while wondering when the rebels would arrive to storm the capital.

What is also interesting about this time period, is the various strange ways that some Imperial officials sought to position themselves as the heir to Palpatine. Grand Moff Plorest of the Corusca sector had been, to all intents and purposes, a leader in name only. Given that the Empire's capital lay within his sector, much of the actual governing was done from Coruscant. But following Palpatine's death, and the realization that Mas Amedda was not going to work as a replacement, he contacted Imperial forces across the galaxy to declare that he was invoking Imperial Security Code 88173.1—which did not exist—to declare himself Emperor.[10] His "rule"—which was ignored by the military—lasted less than three days before he was murdered by one of his lovers. However, Plorest was not alone in making a bid for vacant power. Grand General Levinous attempted to organize his own power base on Carida and declare himself Emperor. So did Admiral Rolas of the 14th Fleet. Neither of them was able to inspire much in the way of loyalty and were swiftly deposed and arrested by the forces under their control.

However, not all attempts to seize control were as haphazard as those noted above. Indeed, the previously mentioned Governor Ecressys was not the only Imperial leader to see the potential of shutting off their sector of the galaxy while plotting their next move. Where Ecressys saw the potential for plunder while the eyes of the New Republic were elsewhere, Moff Ubrik Adelhard appears to have decided that the forces under his command gave him the chance to grab control of the Empire for his own purposes. In the immediate aftermath of the Battle of Endor, Adelhard

---

[10] Imperial Archives, Section: Corusca Sector, File: Declaration of the Transfer of Imperial Power

acted quickly to institute what became known as the "Iron Blockade" of the Anoat system in order to protect his own power base and forces.[11] With the New Republic having to deal with a suddenly disunified Imperial opponent, their forces were spread quite thinly in places, which allowed for Adelhard to achieve some notable military successes. While Adelhard's attempts to bring control of the Empire under his own banner were unsuccessful—not least because of what appear to have been issues with other Imperial rivals—it took the concerted efforts of the New Republic military and interventions by Leia Organa, Luke Skywalker, and Han Solo to defeat him in the lead up to the Battle of Jakku.[12]

Perhaps strangest of all were those who sought to circumvent the Imperial military entirely and instead claim legitimacy for the throne through blood. From my own research I have been able to find traces of at least seven humans who claimed they were Palpatine's son or daughter and therefore destined for the throne. The most famous of these was "Lady" (an honorific she gave herself) Ederlatth Nataasias Pallopides, who maintained a presence within the Coruscant elite for years after the war, despite the fact there was no evidence whatsoever linking her to Palpatine.[13] A further nine people claimed to have married Palpatine in a variety of secret ceremonies, and one nineteen-year-old ensign on Corellia claimed that Palpatine had appeared to him in a vision and ordered him to take the throne. He was executed by an ISB loyalty officer.[14]

Given the vacuum left by the apparent death of the Emperor it is not particularly surprising that many within the Imperial hierarchy saw a chance to claim the throne for themselves. But most of them made the same error. They believed that by highlighting their—often fictional—close ties to Palpatine it would give their claims legitimacy. In

[11] Imperial Archives, Section: Anoat Sector, File: "Iron Blockade" Initiation
[12] New Republic Archives, Section: Military Operations, File: Anoat Sector & Moff Adelhard
[13] She was notably featured in the "Profile" section of *Coruscanti Society* #4117
[14] Imperial Archives, Section: Treasonous Pretenders, File: Ensign Dakous

doing so, they showed how fundamentally they had failed to understand Palpatine's thought process. The Empire had been carefully constructed with him at its center. A great deal of time, effort, and violence had been spent ensuring that *nobody* but Palpatine could ever sit upon the throne. He had no intention of sharing that power in life, he had even less interest in bequeathing it to another in death. There was no heir apparent, partly because Palpatine did not intend to ever die. But, in the event that he did, he was not going to have his Empire presented to someone else.

He intended to burn it, and the rest of the galaxy, to the ground in punishment.

Operation: Cinder

The actual timeline of what became Operation: Cinder is difficult to fully unravel. In some way—and it remains unclear how—the moment of Palpatine's death set in motion a series of events that would lead to the deaths of millions. Possibly billions. During his reign, Palpatine appears to have overseen the construction of very specific and unusual droids known as "Sentinels." Luke Skywalker witnessed a construction facility for these on Vetine in the months after Endor.[15] Behind their glass faceplates, a hologram of the Emperor himself was projected. Some have argued that each droid carried some sort of essence of Palpatine himself, though that seems both disturbing and improbable.[16]

Following Palpatine's death these droids were somehow activated and began to disperse across the galaxy to locate specific Imperial units and personnel. They could only be unlocked by someone whose blood sample—extracted by the droid—matched the details within its databases. How these Sentinels selected the units and officers they did

---

[15] Rebel Alliance Archives, Section: Luke Skywalker, File: Vetine Debriefing
[16] New Republic Archives, Section: Palpatine's Sentinels, File: Partial Deconstruction

remained a source of some discussion within the headquarters of New Republic Intelligence. The most likely explanation is that the droids were cross-referencing information held within the aforementioned database of Imperial crimes on Coruscant, using it to find those individuals most willing to engage in acts of extreme violence or mass murder.[17] Once these groups or individuals were identified, the Sentinels began to issue new orders that seemingly had come directly from Emperor Palpatine.

There remains a huge amount of debate and controversy over why exactly Emperor Palpatine had developed the contingency plan known as Operation: Cinder. The selection of targets—as will be discussed below—seemed to be far too haphazard and random to reflect any kind of specific strategy that anyone has been able to discern. Already, following his apparent resurrection on Exegol, I've heard fellow academics wonder whether or not some base level of horror and death needed to be maintained in the aftermath of Palpatine's death to allow him to transfer his essence through the dark side of the Force. This could be possible, my research has shown the Sith could manipulate the darkest emotions in bizarre ways. But I do not believe this to be the answer. I believe—looking back to the very first chapter of this study—that he prepared for Operation: Cinder to be undertaken posthumously, because he was a vindictive and murderous monster. That his fragile ego could not comprehend that he might fail, and the galaxy would reject him. As a result, all—but particularly those within the Empire—had to be punished for failing him in life. It is hard to draw any other conclusion regarding Operation: Cinder than that it was motivated almost entirely by spite. The outcomes were horrifying.

There has long been an assumption that the weapons used in Operation: Cinder were entirely based around manipulation of the

[17] New Republic Archives, Section: Palpatine's Sentinels, File: Speculation on Operational Processes

weather. This is only partially true. While a great many of the atrocities did utilize some form of satellites that could exacerbate climatic conditions on different worlds, there were numerous examples where ordinary turbolaser bombardments were used. In the years after the massacres, many wondered why these weapons were used at all when the Empire clearly possessed the technology linked to the Death Star superlasers. My theory, having now encountered the smaller superlasers attached to the Star Destroyers at Exegol, is that it seems plausible that most superlaser technology within Imperial hands before Endor had either been deployed on the Death Stars themselves or funneled out to Palpatine's secret fleet. This left Imperial forces with only experimental or traditional weapons available to them.

On worlds like Naboo and Vardos, the Empire deployed specially designed satellites into orbit that, through coordination of carefully calibrated lasers, began to destabilize the weather and climate in hugely destructive ways. On Vardos the planet's main population centers were almost entirely destroyed, with only a tiny number of selected Imperial citizens being evacuated. Vardos had long been an Imperial loyalist stronghold, but it seems that this devotion to Palpatine was not enough, and the population was almost completely exterminated. Having realized what was about to happen to her homeworld, Commander Iden Versio of Inferno Squadron abandoned the Galactic Empire and would shortly afterward defect to the rebels.[18] It was her assistance on Naboo that helped Leia Organa disrupt and prevent the Imperial attempt to destroy Palpatine's own planet.[19] Many other worlds were not so fortunate.

On Nacronis, TIE bombers of the 204th Imperial Fighter Wing dropped munitions called "vortex bombs" within the upper atmosphere, above storms that already raged over the world. These explosives

[18] Rebel Alliance Archives, Section: Operation Cinder, File: Vardos—Iden Versio's Account
[19] Rebel Alliance Archives, Section: Operation Cinder, File: Naboo—Leia Organa's Account

dramatically increased the speed and power of the storms so that they began to spread destructively across the entire planet.[20] Though Rebel Alliance forces attempted to prevent the attack they were unsuccessful and suffered significant casualties. As a result, the whole population was wiped out. Burnin Konn, by way of contrast, was a planet with significant volcanic activity. The cities across its surface were almost entirely powered by geothermal reactors that helped harvest energy from the various magma shifts. To punish that world General Valin Hess deployed Imperial forces to plant plasma bombs within the generators. Once detonated they massively destabilized the plate tectonics of the world. Whole cities collapsed in on themselves as lava flooded their streets. In one major population center, Chakonnis, a series of volcanic eruptions took place almost immediately after the detonations, destroying the city and costing the lives of the Imperial division deployed there, who were cut off from their escape route and left to burn with the rest of the population.[21]

These attacks were not the only atrocities carried out in the aftermath of Endor. Others occurred that may not even have fallen under the heading or criteria of Operation: Cinder. On Coruscant wild celebrations broke out even on the upper levels of Imperial City. Statues of Palpatine were pulled down and crowds of protesters attacked Imperial stormtroopers. This unfolding revolution was soon halted by the arrival of greater Imperial forces who opened fire indiscriminately on the crowds and soon swept them back into the city's subterranean levels.[22] On Mandalore, Moff Gideon authorized the purge of the planet and the wholesale destruction of its cities and population. Everywhere you looked across what had once been the Galactic Empire, whole systems suffered and died.

[20] Rebel Alliance Archives, Section: Operation Cinder, File: Nacronis
[21] Rebel Alliance Archives, Section: Operation Cinder, File: Burnin Konn
[22] Rebel Alliance Archives, Section: Coruscant, File: Attempted Revolution—Eyewitness Reports

As further examples of death and destruction were carried out across Imperial worlds, it still remains difficult to understand what exactly Imperial forces thought they were gaining by launching these attacks. While we can ascribe Palpatine's orders to petty vengeance, why did so many Imperial forces follow them? Was it simply out of blind loyalty to a dead Emperor? The targets selected were—with some exceptions such as Mon Cala—mostly loyal Imperial worlds. What was it about these worlds that made them prime targets for Palpatine's revenge? Some of them were so obscure as to be almost unheard of even by the Rebel Alliance. It has been this aspect which has led many to wonder if the forces carrying out Operation: Cinder were essentially opportunists attacking the most convenient, and less defended, options. However, there may be more to the target selection than previously thought. When records of Imperial resource deployment are cross-referenced against Operation: Cinder targets, a remarkable correlation begins to emerge. It certainly appears as though significant funds were diverted toward various censored "black sites" on many of these planets.[23] Was this then an additional purpose of Operation: Cinder? To destroy the most sensitive records of what the Empire had actually been doing and, in addition, to murder all the witnesses? What information was eradicated during these attacks? What else was the Empire hiding?

Regardless of the underlying motivations, destroying civilian populations was not furthering the Empire's war effort or overly burdening the Rebel Alliance. The Empire was simply immolating itself. Perhaps this was also the point. Maybe those carrying out the atrocities believed that if they could just kill enough "disloyal" civilians or perhaps eradicate one more planet, that the Empire would be purged of the weaknesses that had brought it to this point. Perhaps it would, newly purified, rise up to victory against the Rebel Alliance and prove itself worthy of the

[23] Imperial Archives, Section: Covert Operations, File: Funding and Supply Accounts #IV83017

faith Palpatine had invested in his most loyal soldiers. This rationale seems to be utterly ludicrous now. It is genocide and mass murder masquerading as reason. But it does provide us with an important lesson and something we should all endeavor to remember as we reconsider the Empire and Emperor. Palpatine could issue however many murderous orders he wished, but no deaths would have occurred if others had not accepted them blindly and perpetrated the atrocities. The worst crimes of the Empire were not simply rooted in the desires of the man who sat upon the Imperial throne, but rather within the actions of those willing to discard their own morality, simply because they were ordered to do so. Those who resolved to murder their fellow Imperial citizens did so willingly. We should never forget that.

How though should we remember those who died in the storms and infernos unleashed within Operation: Cinder? As previously noted, many would easily have been described as loyal Imperials up until the moment of their deaths. Many had supported Palpatine's reign and quite possibly benefited from it. Should their ultimate betrayal absolve them of the guilt of having previously watched other worlds burn and yet stayed the course? There is always the temptation to give in to feelings of retaliatory violence when confronted with examples like this. To declare that these people accepted Imperial genocides elsewhere, so it is only fitting that they suffer in discovering the error of their ways. But I can take no solace in mass murder. Having recently witnessed worlds and populations eradicated by the First Order, death and destruction are not justice. In many ways the Empire always traded in violence. Whether it used it against its enemies or its own population, the result was always the same. So many lives were lost to the ego of a dead Emperor and the willingness of his forces to commit the worst crimes imaginable. As the galaxy Palpatine had once ruled began to burn, the war dragged on and yet more lives were lost. The end, when it came, was not soon enough.

Chapter 22

The Road to Jakku

While Operation: Cinder unfolded, the war between the Galactic Empire and the Rebel Alliance—now in the process of evolving into the New Republic—continued to rage. Previously the Empire had held many of the advantages in infrastructure, manufacturing, and military strength, but the situation was rapidly degrading for them. With the outcome of the conflict seemingly no longer in doubt, systems were flocking to join the Rebellion and providing them with increasing quantities of weapons, ships, and soldiers. Furthermore, the Rebel Alliance was learning from each engagement at a much faster rate than the Empire. Having successfully taken down numerous Star Destroyers at Endor, they were now beginning to perfect their combat tactics against them, with the benefit of the additional firepower they were accumulating. Previously secure strongholds or key strategic locations such as Kuat suddenly found themselves on the front lines. The once mighty Imperial fleet was beginning to buckle.

Of additional concern for the Imperial forces was the ongoing collapse of the chain of command. While, on the surface, Admiral Rae Sloane appeared to have maintained the loyalty of much of the Imperial military, rumors persisted of shadowy figures in the background who were really wielding power. The Empire's war efforts had often been hampered by the dysfunctional relationship between the navy and the likes of Darth Vader; but there had, at least, been no real confusion over where the orders originated or who was in charge. That clarity of command had evaporated since Endor and increasing numbers of Imperial forces were either going rogue or receiving conflicting orders from within the surviving hierarchy. This lack of transparency regarding either the loyalty of some military forces or their real mission further accelerated the collapsing cohesion.

The Empire that had originally been planned to stand for ten thousand years unraveled in just a single year following the death of the Emperor. But these final months would not be a straightforward march to victory for the emerging New Republic. The sudden apparent proximity of victory was already leading to debates within their command hierarchy of how best to finish the war, and what sort of government should be put in place at its conclusion. The rebels had never needed to spend a great deal of time governing while waging war. The New Republic did not have that luxury. The decision to pursue a peace attempt with what was left of the Empire would result in a betrayal that would cost the lives of many on Chandrila, stiffening the New Republic's resolve in forcing one final confrontation with the Galactic Empire designed to extinguish its evil forever.

Shifting Power

Having spent much of the Galactic Civil War trying to scrape forces and soldiers together while the Imperial fleet had all the advantages of major shipyards and supply lines, the likes of Admiral Gial Ackbar and General Hera Syndulla were well-positioned to seize the advantage when the momentum swung after Endor. While the New Republic military was now expanding exponentially, its leaders recognized both the deficiencies in their own armaments and the need to try and further cripple the Empire's war machine. In many ways the roles of the Galactic Civil War were now reversing, with the Imperial military avoiding conflict for fear of being ambushed, while also scrabbling to make the most of its dwindling supply of war materiel. The New Republic's plan, therefore, had two key aspects: firstly, to bulk up their fleet in order to force the Empire to fight on their terms, and secondly, restrict the Empire's ability to maintain its own forces. Having spent years running from the Imperial fleet, New Republic commanders knew how to deprive the Empire of the same opportunities they themselves had previously exploited. Most crucially, this meant disrupting the Empire's ability to replenish their dwindling resources. In the past the rebels had been forced to try and patch battered ships and starfighters together for combat. Now it would be the Empire's turn.

The Battle of Endor had left the New Republic in control of various wrecked Star Destroyers.[1] Further engagements like the Battle of Yavin Prime gave them control of still-operational vessels such as the *Victorum*.[2] There was significant debate within the New Republic's High Command regarding what to do with Star Destroyers that were still battle-worthy. There were plenty who believed that they should be sent back to the front lines with new crews to fight the Empire and, indeed, several vessels—such as the *Deliverance*—saw exactly that outcome. The rationale given was that the easiest way to end the Empire's oppression was to win the war, and the quickest way of doing that was to draw on every weapon available.[3] However, the Star Destroyer had long been a symbol of the Empire's tyranny and destructive tendencies, and the idea of reusing them with a New Republic crest on their hulls was not universally popular.[4] Fortunately, an alternative option was now available.

---

[1] New Republic Archives, Section: Captured Imperial Weaponry, File: Battle of Endor Audit
[2] New Republic Archives, Section: Military Operations, File: Battle of Yavin Prime
[3] New Republic Archives, Section: Military Planning, File: Order for requisition of captured Imperial equipment
[4] New Republic Archives, Section: Military Planning, File: Memo of complaint regarding use of Imperial weaponry* *This note was compiled by Admiral Hiram Drayson and signed by a variety of leading New Republic military personnel.

In secret, the New Republic had been constructing a new battleship at the Nadiri Dockyards, largely out of parts of repurposed Star Destroyers. They called it Project Starhawk. The prototype *Starhawk* possessed a tremendous amount of firepower and the ability to carry numerous fighter squadrons. This meant it could certainly outgun most vessels within the Imperial fleet outside of the Super Star Destroyers. But that was not its main benefit. Its designers had brought together the tractor beams from scrapped and destroyed vessels to create something ten-times stronger than normal. This tractor beam was more than capable of holding an opposing Star Destroyer in place or even dragging it around the battlefield. Where the Empire had tried to use Interdictor cruisers to prevent rebel ships from escaping (but had failed to deploy them in sufficient numbers), the *Starhawk* would use its tractor beam.

The first use of this new weapon was during an ambush of the Imperial Star Destroyer *Overseer* at the Zavian Abyss. The *Overseer*'s commander, Captain Terisa Kerrill, was outmaneuvered by her long-time opponent, Commander Lindon Javes, who lured her into a trap. The *Starhawk* then successfully froze the *Overseer* in place, preventing its immediate escape, before dragging it into the path of an asteroid.[5] Heavily damaged, the *Overseer* was forced to make a blind jump into hyperspace. The first test of the New Republic's latest weapon had been a resounding success, and it returned to the Nadiri Shipyards for fine tuning. However, the action brought Project Starhawk to the attention of Grand Admiral Rae Sloane, who launched an attack on the shipyards in an attempt to destroy both the prototype and the scientists behind its creation—therefore robbing the New Republic of both the weapon and the expertise to replace it.[6] The attack was a partial success, in that both

[5] New Republic Archives, Section: Military Operations, File: Zavian Abyss—Report from Commander Lindon Javes
[6] Imperial Archives, Section: Imperial Navy Operations, File: Order to disrupt Project Starhawk

the *Starhawk* and Commander Javes' cruiser *Temperance* were badly damaged and could only undertake a slow retreat.[7]

This attempt to flee came to an end at Galitan where a fleet of Star Destroyers aimed to block the *Starhawk*'s escape and complete the destruction of the ship. However, the battle was a disaster for the Imperial forces. The already badly damaged *Starhawk* was sabotaged by New Republic pilots to ensure that the tractor beam generator would catastrophically overload. The ship was then put on a collision course with the exposed core of the shattered moon of Galitan. While some Imperial ships attempted to flee, it seems that others disregarded orders and resolved to stand and fight their enemy.[8] When the *Starhawk* collided with Galitan the explosive shockwave destroyed at least six Star Destroyers and numerous supporting vessels.[9] While the prototype was lost, the scientists behind its creation had survived and the production of more ships in the class would continue. For the Empire, the loss of so many heavy capital ships was a disaster. Especially as replacing them would soon no longer be a viable option.

During the years between Yavin and Hoth, the Empire had spent a considerable amount of time and resources trying to locate rebel bases and industrial centers. While they had some successes during this period, particularly at Mako-Ta, the Empire had never succeeded in completely disrupting the rebels' ability to supply and replenish their forces. The New Republic now faced a similar challenge but with one significant advantage. They already knew where Kuat was. The New Republic had realized very quickly after Endor that if they could, at the very least, blockade the main Imperial shipyard—or better yet, capture it—then it would deprive the Empire of future reinforcements and

[7] New Republic Archives, Section: Military Operations, File: Nadiri Dockyards—General Hera Syndulla
[8] Imperial Archives, Section: Imperial Navy Operation, File: Battle of Galitan—Captain Kerrill's report
[9] New Republic Archives, Section: Military Operations, File: Battle of Galitan

greatly shorten the war.[10] Grand Admiral Sloane must also have recognized this fact, as shortly before the New Republic launched their attack on the shipyards she had additional forces led by Vice Admiral Ferno deployed to the system to try and bulk up the defenses.[11]

The resulting battle was a fairly strange engagement. Both sides were equally committed to trying to defeat the other but, despite this, also seem to have operated under the shared objective of not greatly damaging or destroying the shipyards themselves. It seems likely that both the New Republic and the Empire realized that if the infrastructure at Kuat was lost then it would be of no use to them in the future. Fighting and winning a battle at the cost of the facility itself served no great purpose, though it was of greater concern to the Empire. The rebels were already operating without the benefit of KDY. The Empire could not afford to lose it. Command of the Empire's forces at Kuat fell largely to Moff Pollus Maksim, though control of the fleet itself appears to have fallen to the *Dark Omen*.[12] The fighting lasted for weeks as New Republic forces tried initially to slug it out with the Imperial fleet at a distance, before gradually shifting to target key sections of KDY's infrastructure including fuel depots and supply monorails. The strategy of Admiral Ackbar and Commodore Kyrsta Agate was to force the Empire to defend as much as possible, while also weakening the shipyards to the point that the Imperial fleet could not undertake running repairs.

As a result, the fighting was often gruelingly attritional. Pilots in New Republic units such as the B-wings of Blade Squadron flew ongoing sorties against Imperial targets that caused severe damage to the enemy, but at the cost of heavy losses of their own. For the Empire, the situation

[10] New Republic Archives, Section: Military Operations, File: Kuat Offensive—Strategic Planning Committee Report
[11] Imperial Archives Section: Imperial Navy Operations. File: Emergency Deployment to Kuat
[12] Imperial Archives Section: Imperial Navy Operations. File: Defense of Kuat—Command Hierarchy* *Record retrieved from the *Dark Omen*

grew increasingly dire. Reports from captured vessels at Kuat show that some of the Star Destroyers defending the shipyards were either being actively cannibalized to provide weapons to more intact ships or had sustained such significant personnel losses as to be operating below the threshold of a skeleton crew.[13] There appear to have been numerous discussions between Moff Maksim and the local fleet commanders as to whether it was best to defend the shipyards or to attempt to break out through the blockade and escape.[14] Eventually the latter option was chosen, with the surviving vessels attempting an escape while Moff Maksim would remain behind, unwilling to risk his life aboard one of the Star Destroyers. The attempt to break through was a desperate one. The remnants of the Imperial fleet at Kuat moved into battle formation and sallied forth to face the New Republic. However, it rapidly became apparent that the Empire's forces were no longer operating even close to full fighting capacity. Their attempt was further complicated by the presence of the Concord—a newly produced Mk.1 Starhawk that could use its tractor beam to prevent any of the Star Destroyers breaching gaps in the New Republic formation. As it became apparent that the breakout was doomed, communications intensified between the Dark Omen and Moff Maksim and resulted in the surrender being issued.[15] When the shipyards fell, the New Republic took command of the remnants of 17 Star Destroyers and assorted support vessels.

The defeat at Kuat was a hammer blow to the Imperial war effort. Being stripped of their most important industrial center was an unmitigated disaster for a fleet that was already staring defeat in the face. Morale began to collapse across the Empire's forces. It was at this point

[13] Imperial Archives Section: Imperial Navy Operations. File: Defense of Kuat—Force Evaluation Report #319* *Record retrieved from the Dark Omen
[14] Kuat Archives, Section: Defense of the Shipyards, File: Command Conference #3190
[15] New Republic Archives, Section: Military Operations, File: Imperial Communications at Kuat—Surrender Order

that Grand Admiral Sloane made contact with Chancellor Mon Mothma to discuss the possible terms of a peace treaty that would bring the conflict to a close.

The Chandrila Deception

To understand the nature and intentions of the supposed peace talks at Chandrila, it becomes necessary to address the emerging command structure of the Empire at the end of the war. As previously mentioned, there were no shortage of figures who had designs on the vacant throne, but simply desiring it was not enough to make others follow your orders. So, who was actually in charge? Rae Sloane had emerged from the Battle of Endor with what appears to have been much of the loyalty of the Imperial fleet. She was a proven battle commander and—as evidenced at places like Derra IV—had a solid reputation for being able to fight effectively against the Rebel Alliance. While Mas Amedda had been reduced to little more than a mouthpiece for the civil aspects of the Empire, Sloane appears to have had actual control over the Empire's surviving military. It is possible, however, that appearances may have been deceptive.

Following the defeat at Endor, an emergency summit was held between various representatives on Akiva to discuss and plan the Empire's overall strategy. In attendance was Rae Sloane, then still only an admiral; Grand Moff Valco Pandion, a promotion he'd apparently awarded himself; General Jylia Shale; Arsin Crassus, who was a key financial expert within the Imperial economy; and Yupe Tashu, who was apparently some sort of dark side cultist that Palpatine had humored while still alive. This meeting was largely unsuccessful given that Admiral Ackbar sent New Republic fleet assets into the system before it could conclude. Pandion and Crassus were killed while Shale and Tashu were captured by the New Republic. Only Sloane herself was able to escape. Subsequent interrogations of Tashu produced little of worth as he seemed relatively impervious to questioning.[16] But Shale was far more cooperative.[17] She reported that a significant part of the meeting had revolved around attempts to ascertain the current status and location of the Super Star Destroyer *Ravager* that Admiral Sloane claimed to be under her command. What is interesting is that Shale also reported that the *Ravager* had previously been under the command of Admiral Gallius Rax. This is a figure who does not appear in any of the surviving Imperial archives. Sloane apparently told the summit that Rax was dead, but we know now that was not the case. Numerous prisoners taken at Jakku reported that Rax had been orchestrating the fleet's presence there. So, who was he? And an additional question to be asked is: at what point did Sloane rise from the rank of admiral to grand admiral? The information available to us about Sloane does not suggest that she was the sort to summarily promote herself.[18] So who granted her that rank? Is it possible that it was Gallius Rax, and if that was the case, was Sloane perhaps just as much of a figurehead at the end of the war as Mas Amedda?

Following the Empire's defeat at Kuat, Sloane contacted the New Republic to begin a process of peace talks. She also identified herself as an asset within the Imperial hierarchy known as "the Operator" who had been feeding the New Republic information.[19] This seems highly unlikely given what we know about Sloane's other actions at this time. I do not believe that the Imperial leader who was so proactive in trying to destroy the Starhawk project and who sent additional ships to try and defend Kuat was also aiding the New Republic. Regardless, the New Republic—eager for peace—accepted Sloane's admission and arranged

[16] New Republic Archives, Section: Imperial Prisoners, File: Yupe Tashu* *File outlines Tashu as uncooperative.
[17] New Republic Archives, Section: Imperial Prisoners, File: Jylia Shale—Interrogation
[18] New Republic Archives, Section: Imperial Analysis, File: Admiral Rae Sloane—Profile
[19] New Republic Archives, Section: Intelligence Assets, File: The Operator

for a ceremony on Chandrila. Among the plans for this event was a festival broadly termed Liberation Day, designed to showcase the hopeful and tyranny-free future that the New Republic imagined. It would not last long. Among those in attendance were many representatives of the New Republic's command staff as well as a group of rebel prisoners recently freed from Imperial captivity. As is now known, those prisoners had been subject to intense chemical and ideological brainwashing activities by the Empire.[20] They had been programmed to try and eliminate the New Republic's leadership, and opened fire, causing significant casualties.[21] Mon Mothma herself only narrowly avoided death, while rumors that Crix Madine had been killed in the attack—never confirmed or denied by the New Republic—circulated for years afterward. The ceremony descended into violence and Grand Admiral Sloane vanished in the chaos.

Again, we must now wonder exactly what role Sloane had in this attempted assassination. Whether she would have desired the destruction of the New Republic's leadership seems rather a moot point. The two states were still at war after all. But would she voluntarily have appeared at the scene of the crime? It is of interest that she apparently managed to escape under her own power—there was seemingly no underlying plan to whisk her off-world. Although there were later reports of her being seen on Jakku, it is clear she was not in command of that battle and it would take years for the New Republic to properly account for her fate, though many of those files remain heavily embargoed.[22] If Sloane was no longer in command of the Imperial fleet, then who was? Many of the signs point toward Gallius Rax as the one in control behind the scenes, who now gathered the apparent remaining

[20] New Republic Archives, Section: Imperial Sleeper Agents, File: Postmortem of Chandrila Agents—chemical signatures
[21] New Republic Archives, Section: Attack on Chandrila, File: Casualty list
[22] New Republic Archives, Section: Imperial Personnel, File: Grand Admiral Rae Sloane* *Record encrypted at level 10 classification

strength of the Imperial Navy above Jakku for what appeared to be a final showdown. The New Republic now came to realize that there could be no peace without victory.

Last Stand

If Gallius Rax hoped that the presence of the massed Imperial fleet, including the long-absent Super Star Destroyer *Ravager*, would provoke an immediate reaction from the New Republic he was likely disappointed. No sooner had the New Republic Senate been established, then it appears that some within it proved to be open to exactly the sort of corruption that had marked the previous Republic, and it took time for a resolution authorizing military action at Jakku to gain approval. While he waited, Rax seems to have initiated a variety of training programs for the gathered Imperial forces that were designed to, for want of a better term, brutalize them into an almost feral state.[23] Whatever it was that Rax had planned, he appears to have wanted to burn away what little restraint or compassion that still existed within the Imperial military. This may not have been a battle that Rax intended to win.

When the New Republic eventually mobilized their forces to attack Jakku, they found the Imperial fleet in an initially haphazard deployment around the planet. However, upon the arrival of the New Republic, the Empire coalesced its forces into a running shield formation around the *Ravager*. Various Imperial Star Destroyers screened the larger ship with their own shields before opening up gaps that allowed it to shoot back. Down on the planet's surface, the New Republic landed an increasing number of troops to try and storm the Imperial facilities. The two battles raged simultaneously with the added danger to the ground forces of debris falling from orbit. While the Imperial fleet had been driven to

---

[23] Imperial Archives, Section: Jakku, File: Training regime* *Records retrieved from the *Ravager*'s computer

the breaking point by the defeats since Endor, the New Republic's forces were not in much better shape. They too were exhausted by the ongoing nature of a war they'd hoped had been won already. With nowhere seemingly left to run, the Empire and the New Republic fought out one last climactic battle on the edges of the galaxy. The victors would get the chance to rule.

In military terms the battle's turning point came when the New Republic brought their three Starhawks—*Amity*, *Unity*, and *Concord*—into the battle to try and disrupt the Star Destroyer formation. It appears that Captain Groff of the Star Destroyer *Punishment* panicked and elected to crash his vessel into the *Amity*. The impact also caused significant damage to the nearby *Concord*. It was at this point that Commodore Agate of the *Concord* sacrificed her own life in order to secure a New Republic victory. As her ship fell into Jakku's gravity well, its weaponry opened fire on the *Ravager*, and then its huge tractor beam dragged the Super Star Destroyer out of orbit behind it. The two ships crashed into the planet's surface—causing huge casualties—and the Imperial formation in orbit began to disintegrate. While the battle continued to rage for some time, Imperial morale and forces dwindled and ships and units began to surrender. Amid the chaos in orbit or on Jakku's surface the Galactic Civil War was finally coming to an end.

But had this been its intended end? New Republic pilot Norra Wexley attempted to rescue her husband—who had been one of the brainwashed assassins on Chandrila—from Jakku and located him within an installation generally referred to as "the Observatory."[24] New Republic scientists who examined this facility reported that the technology within it was capable of disrupting the planet's core and therefore destroying the entire world.[25] While it had not been fully initiated

[24] New Republic Archives, Section: Jakku Observatory, File: Norra Wexley Debriefing
[25] New Republic Archives, Section: Jakku Observatory, File: Scientific Assessment

during the battle, it appears that this facility was activated and operational. Perhaps this had been Rax's plan? To lure the New Republic fleet into a battle at Jakku and immolate both them and the forces of the Empire. But to what end? What was the planned outcome of this mutual destruction? Norra Wexley reported that she saw Grand Admiral Sloane kill someone who was, presumably, Rax in a confrontation within the Observatory, and that she vanished shortly afterward. Sloane was not the only leading Imperial officer to be missing at the conclusion of hostilities. Many more had disappeared in the war's final days and there were numerous ships—including the Emperor's flagship Super Star Destroyer *Eclipse*—that were unaccounted for.[26] Given recent events, it seems likely that many of these personnel and weapons made their way into the Unknown Regions to bide their time.

In the aftermath, confronted with an opportunity to finally achieve peace, the New Republic—understandably—took it. With the Imperial military defeated, suddenly Mas Amedda was the only recognizable figure left in the Empire's hierarchy. He agreed to sign the Galactic Concordance treaty that would end the war.[27] On Jakku the remnants of the vaunted Imperial fleet were left to decay beneath the dunes, a symbol of a regime that all hoped would be lost to the sands of time. However, this was not the end. Having won their war against the Empire, the New Republic now had to take control of what remained of the galaxy's infrastructure, while also deciding how best to heal the rifts caused by the brutal conflict.

[26] New Republic Archives, Section: Military Intelligence Assessments, File: Missing Imperial Assets—*Eclipse*

[27] I strongly recommend the account of these negotiations written by Terag Liman: *Ending the Empire: Peace Conference at Chandrila.*

Chapter 23

Truth and Reconciliation

T he end of the Galactic Civil War and the collapse of the Empire represented the ultimate victory for what had once been the Rebel Alliance. However, the New Republic found various distinct challenges amid their triumph. The vacuum left by the departed Empire required filling and, in many ways, this was easier said than done. As mentioned in previous chapters, the New Republic was largely composed of soldiers who had waged—and been exhausted by—war. There was not necessarily much administrative experience within their ranks. The return to public life of ex-senators who had been dismissed by the Empire was of some help, but not universally so. The new government had to face up to the fact that most contemporary knowledge of actually running the galaxy now resided in those who had until very recently been on the opposing side of the war. Reconciling this was not going to be easy.

This was not the only problem facing the New Republic. In the latter days of the war the Imperial military had disintegrated, even before the final crushing defeat at Jakku. As a result, the New Republic was now in possession of countless ex-Imperial prisoners. Processing them would require time, resources, and space. But how much preference could the housing of prisoners of war be given, when there was also a burgeoning refugee crisis? The collapse of the Imperial state had led to the discovery of just how many prison, labor, and concentration camps existed across the galaxy. The prisoners there also now required help. Where was the New Republic supposed to direct its attention? And what would be the fate of those who had served the Empire to the bitter end? There were many voices who clamored for vengeance and harsh punishments for those who had oppressed the galaxy. Could an enduring peace be built upon such foundations? What were the limits of justice?

But perhaps the most difficult issue was one that was not entirely within the New Republic's control. Because the Galactic Civil War had not just been played out on distant battlefields and star systems. It had split families apart. There were some who, for various reasons, had viewed those who suffered under the Empire as having brought it upon themselves and therefore deserving of it. Those for whom loyalty to Palpatine or compliance with the law was the way to live your life. Others saw the Empire's crimes and were either repelled by them or horrified by the precarious nature of existence in a totalitarian state. These two states of being could not easily survive under the same roof. How could the galaxy begin to move forward and heal when many households, lodgings, tribes, and domains were split, with each half viewing the other as traitors or monsters.

The Aftermath

As the war came to an end, many of the pillars of the Imperial state that had previously been viewed as permanently secure just faded away. In many ways this was exactly what the New Republic had wanted. The complete collapse of the Empire left the way open for them to replace it. But it is probably fair to say that they had not fully considered all the ramifications of the Empire's fall. Infrastructure on various worlds ground to a halt with nobody left to facilitate it. With nobody left to pay workers, and no guarantee that their jobs even existed, food shipments stopped, transport services froze, sanitation repairs ended. In time this uncertainty could be solved, and some workers continued to return each day with the acknowledgment that it was necessary. This was one of many problems now facing New Republic administrators, but it was by no means the most concerning.

While a significant number of Imperials in the armed forces were held captive either by the New Republic or by the security services of individual systems, by no means all were gathered up. Many who had worked for COMPNOR or the ISB erased their own identities within Imperial archives and simply walked out the door never to return. It did not take long for planetary populations to find what they had left behind. Hidden offices for Imperial Intelligence that contained a wealth of surveillance records. The covert interrogation and torture facilities. The execution chambers. The death camps. Riots nearly broke out on various worlds when populations tried to storm these offices to find details of missing loved ones, or to try and burn records of family members being Imperial informants. The New Republic recognized early on that the records within these locations would be absolutely necessary for any future trials.[1] But how could they best protect them? Were they supposed to use lethal force against those trying to break in, or against the prisoners in camps trying to torch facilities that had confined them? Some of these worlds had not yet even formally joined the New Republic. Who had jurisdiction? Did the demands of justice and history override the claims of innocent civilians to know what information the previous government held about them, and then to destroy it if they so chose?

The transition between Empire and New Republic led to a period of almost peculiar lawlessness. Surviving civilians on Ivera X looted the local Imperial headquarters but, rather than dividing the wealth between themselves, used it to hire a bounty hunter by the name of Xegan Miatt. She was tasked with locating senior Imperial officials who had ordered the destruction of their cities and drag them back for summary justice. Miatt had successfully captured two majors and a

---

[1] New Republic Archives, Section: Emergency Legislation, File: Imperial Black Sites

lieutenant governor—officials who were promptly executed by the Iverians—before the New Republic stepped in.[2] There could be no charges against Miatt or the civilians though—what laws had they broken? What laws even existed anymore? The New Republic's resources were already being stretched to the breaking point, and the worst was yet to come.

There is a record in the New Republic archives on the briefing of the governing council on the first intelligence gathered from Wobani after the world had been abandoned by the Empire. Curiously the timings of the meeting suggest an unaccounted delay early on of 27 minutes.[3] It is only when viewing the actual holovid of the meeting that this gap becomes explainable.[4] Agent Joris Vegen—who had been the first New Republic personnel to arrive on the world—was so upset by the images she presented that she broke down in tears twice, while it appears that at least three other senators in the audience were similarly stricken. I have seen many awful things both as a historian and as a soldier. All wars and suffering are tragedies. There is no hierarchy of horror. But even so, I wish I had not seen the evidence she presented. When it became clear that emergency aid was required Leia Organa immediately reached out to the only group she could be sure would answer. Within days three heavy freighters full of bacta and food were chartered and delivered to Wobani, all paid for and piloted by Alderaanian refugees, led by Commander Rutowan Cannter.[5] It was a start, but it was not enough. Not for the entirety of Wobani nor for the entirety of the galaxy. While the Empire was gone the suffering it left behind continued.

[2] New Republic Archives, Section: Bounty Hunters, File: Xegan Miatt Testimony
[3] New Republic Archives, Section: Briefings on ex-Imperial Systems, File: Wobani Notes
[4] New Republic Archives, Section: Briefings on ex-Imperial Systems, File: Wobani Holovid* *This record has a number of—well-founded—warnings regarding its distressing contents.
[5] New Republic Archives, Section: Relief Efforts, File: Alderaanian Convoy to Wobani—Leia Organa's Official Request

On the Core Worlds things were a little better. These systems had not been occupied or devastated in the way that others had and there remained enough of a bureaucratic infrastructure to govern the worlds. But many of those who had previously held power found themselves forced out, tarnished by their service to Palpatine's regime. Suspicion weighed heavily across many planets. Those who had cooperated with the Empire were viewed as being complicit with its worst crimes. Those who had long been occupied by Imperial forces did not necessarily know any other way of life and were also viewed with suspicion by those who wondered if they would always harbor some desire for the return of the Empire. Entire cultures had effectively been institutionalized.[6] Freedom and liberty were exciting concepts, but they were not solutions to every problem.

The galactic economy began to shrink into recession at just the point when the New Republic needed funds more than anything else. Aid, medical supplies, and food were not free. There was scarcely enough to go round. Soldiers and fighter pilots also needed paying before they were demobilized. Many of them had been left scarred and traumatized by their war service. Some would now return to worlds and families who had previously rejected them for turning against the Empire. Could they even go home at all? How was any of this supposed to work? Having won the war, the sudden peace threatened to rip the New Republic apart.

The Dream

I do not know how they did it, Mon Mothma and Leia Organa. They are better people than I. While I have recently been a soldier, at heart I am a historian and an educator. Or am supposed to be. I'm supposed to be

---

[6] I strongly recommend Chir Ugille's groundbreaking study *Life under the Empire, Peace under the New Republic* on this very topic.

able to look at events and analyze and understand them. I'm supposed to be better than this. And yet I feel so angry and filled with horror. I felt that way at the end of my own war, and the research for this study has only exacerbated it. And I do feel the pull toward revenge. To see the people who committed these awful acts punished. But not just them. The ones who stood by. Who facilitated. Who watched. And my war only lasted a fraction of the time of the Empire. I do not know how Mon Mothma, who had worked toward peace for decades having seen the Empire unfolding before her, and Leia Organa, who watched her whole world be destroyed, were able to stand up at the end of their war, at the point of victory, and understand that vengeance would not solve the galaxy's problems. That the only way forward was to give people something to believe in. They needed it after Jakku in the same way that I think we need it now.

As the New Republic tried to get a grip of the situation in the aftermath of the war, the newly forming Senate passed various pieces of emergency legislation designed to begin overhauling the old Imperial legal framework and give the new state license to govern. However, the implementation of new laws and rules was not the most important part of this process. The Empire had plenty of laws and rules. The problem with them was that they operated in a similar manner to a hand of sabacc cards—constantly changing at random. What the New Republic needed to provide the citizens of the galaxy was not a new set of laws but rather an understanding of what justice and the law consistently and fairly applied could look like.[7] They had to see that life under the New Republic was better than its equivalent under the Empire. That they did not have to be afraid anymore and that transgressions of the law would be treated the same in every instance. This would not take place overnight—and there were undoubtedly setbacks—but it was a crucial first step.

---

[7] New Republic Archive, Section: Legal Framework, File: Report for the Committee of Democratic Implementation

The New Republic also recognized that in order to try and direct proceedings across the galaxy they would need to make use of as much of the bureaucracy that still existed. This meant Coruscant. There appear to have been many, fairly heated, debates about whether to shift the New Republic's capital from Chandrila to Coruscant. Those in favor argued that it had been the seat of the Republic before the Empire. One of those against pointed out that "in order to avoid the appearance of becoming a new Empire, it might be best to avoid moving straight into Palpatine's old house."[8] However, the tools and levers of power were located on Coruscant. Even if it was only to be for a short while, the New Republic needed that system. The world had previously been promised to Mas Amedda, but he continued to cut a variety of highly advantageous deals with the new government that kept him out of prison and living in a style to which he was accustomed.[9] Many symbols of the Empire were quickly removed, or publicly destroyed, to try and banish the specter of the fallen regime.

This was not an easy time for Mon Mothma. There were any number of issues related to trying to build a new government, but perhaps one of the most pressing was both political and personal. While her roots were in the democratic mechanisms of the Senate, she had been a wartime leader for years. As the New Republic reverted the galaxy back toward a democracy, she was the obvious choice to lead it. And yet she had seen what Palpatine had been able to do as the last supreme chancellor of the Galactic Republic. How could she ensure that the New Republic would not head back down the same path again? How could she restrict her own powers while also allowing the future occupants of her position the freedom to administer the government? Her first decision seemed like a semantic one, but it really underlined the extent to which Mon Mothma

[8] New Republic Archives, Section: Capital, File: Coruscant Debate #13* *The speaker here was anonymized.
[9] New Republic Archives, Section: Mas Amedda, File: Additional Legal Immunity Agreements #1-73

was planning for a decentralized system of power. Where Palpatine had once been the supreme chancellor, she would just be the chancellor. "Supreme" had very unwelcome connotations that could have no place in the new galaxy.

Furthermore, having lived through the Clone Wars, Mon Mothma was aware of another significant difficulty that many of her younger comrades may not have considered. The Empire had been born at the end of that conflict and had swiftly begun the process of reabsorbing— or conquering—those worlds that had been part of the Separatist cause and seceded from the Republic. Trying to convince the populations of those planets that the solution to Imperial tyranny was a return to a form of Republic that they had once rejected was not going to be easy.

Perhaps in partial response to both these issues and the lingering shadow of Palpatine's rule, she began instituting a variety of checks and balances on both her own personal power and that held within the Senate. One of the enduring criticisms of the previous Republic was that the bureaucracy had slowed the body politic to the point of inaction. Mon Mothma must have been wary of doing the same but, at the same time, how else could she show the people that power controlled at the whims of a single individual was designed to be abused? This process was then coupled with the implementation of her planned Military Disarmament Act. This was probably the most controversial policy that Mon Mothma forced through. Her reasoning was that violence and centralized armed forces had long ruled and ruined the galaxy. That a large standing military would always produce the circumstances for further conflicts. Peace could not be achieved through the mass stockpiling of weapons of war.[10] The New Republic's military would be reduced in size by 90 percent, leaving just a peacekeeping force behind. There were many opponents to this. Some questioned whether this was at all wise

---

[10] New Republic Archives, Section: Chancellor Mon Mothma, File: Notes on the Military Disarmament Act

when remnants of the Empire could—and sadly did—still exist out in the galaxy. But Mon Mothma stood firm. The New Republic—as will be discussed in the next chapter—had various flaws and weaknesses, but to just focus on those is to misunderstand the rationale behind decisions such as these. So many had fought and died in the Rebel Alliance in service of the dream of freedom. It was left to those like Mon Mothma to find a way of making the dream a reality. As so many others were—as I myself may be—perhaps she too was scarred by her wartime experiences. So desperate to avoid the appearance of Empire that she rushed the New Republic too quickly into changes it was not ready to make. But, as I previously stated, I do not know how she managed to navigate the horrors bequeathed to her at the end of the war. In understanding the limits of implementing the new government I cannot bring myself to critique it too closely. They had to believe their war was worth it. As I must believe the same of mine.

The Vanquished

While the New Republic and Mon Mothma struggled to find ways of building their new government and helping those emerging from the shadow of Imperial tyranny, it was not the limit of their problems. They now held, in various prisoner of war camps and other facilities, significant numbers of ex-Imperial personnel from various branches of the military, COMPNOR, the ISB, and governing positions. What was to become of them all?

To begin with, the New Republic had to try and identify exactly who they now held. Most prisoners saw no reason not to give their real identities—especially as many had been captured with their command cylinders or similar—but undoubtedly among the mass were those individuals wanted for high crimes against the galaxy. A widescale process of interrogation and questioning would have to be instituted in order to identify all these people and also try and gather information as to the extent of their potential crimes. Responsibility for this was split between various New Republic Intelligence agents and specially programmed droids. A system of evaluation based upon each individual's perceived *value* and *risk* was applied in various combinations.[11] Those identified as being *high value*—meaning they were either notable Imperial officers and leaders or possessed important information—always caught the attention of interrogators first. While those deemed *high risk* were kept in secure locations to prevent either escape or suicide attempts. For those who registered further down the rankings of *value* and *risk* the wait for processing could take a very long time. It was also causing plenty of issues within the New Republic regarding what to do with these prisoners when processed. Not every Imperial who'd worn a uniform could spend the rest of their lives in prison. Where were they supposed to go? Would they be welcomed into New Republic worlds?

One of the most interesting outcomes of the interrogations of those leaders deemed as being *high value* was an insight into just how badly the Imperial military had been faring at the end of the war and, perhaps, a way of navigating the obvious post-war tensions between those who had recently fought to liberate the galaxy and those who'd fought to rule it. This is perhaps most notable in one of the final interrogations of Vice Admiral Corf Ferno who had been taken prisoner at Kuat. When asked why he had advised Moff Maksim to offer a surrender he replied: "I have fought enough wars and battles to know when one is lost. Why did I surrender? Because I'm tired and I want to go home."[12] Whether this was actually true or not is obviously hard to prove. Ferno would, after his eventual release, go on to write his memoir *Fighting with the Galactic Empire* which—having read these previously restricted

[11] New Republic Archives, Section: Imperial Prisoners, File: Assessment Criteria
[12] New Republic Archives, Section: Imperial Prisoners* *Vice Admiral Ferno's interrogation reports constitute files #139-152 within this section. The low numbers are indicative of his high level of importance to the New Republic interrogators, as one of the few senior fleet commanders captured alive.

interrogations—differs noticeably from the account of events he gave the New Republic. Having now gained access to these previously sealed interrogation reports, I believe discrepancies such as this will need further additional examination and investigation. But regardless, his apparent weariness at the end of a war he believed had long been lost was not an unusual response. There were many others who seemingly felt the same.

This was an opportunity for the New Republic to solve several problems at once. One of the most pressing issues faced by the new government was a dearth of experience. For 20 years the galaxy had been orchestrated and administered by those within Imperial service. Not all of them were cold-hearted villainous mass murderers. On many worlds it was not even possible to apply to join your own planetary civil service without also becoming an employee of the Empire. But these were the people who knew how everything worked. If they spent the rest of their lives either in detention or under suspicion, then the New Republic may take a generation to fulfill its promise. Nobody could wait that long. So, a process of de-Imperialization was instituted. Those who were seen as *low value* and *low risk* were moved through as quickly as possible to enable them to take up the jobs they'd previously held, but now for the New Republic.

Other ex-Imperials were not released quite so quickly. The New Republic held in the Hall of Imperial Records on Coruscant the details of all crimes committed by personnel under the Empire. This would take years to go through, and there were undoubtedly those now in captivity who had serious charges to answer. But for those who were adjudged to have committed lesser offenses they would, eventually, be released back into the civilian population with various restrictions—regarding ownership of weapons and voting rights—until such a time as they were judged to no longer be a potential threat.[13]

---

[13] New Republic Archives, Section: Legislation, File: Restrictions for ex-Imperial Personnel

To aid with the reintegration process, the New Republic Amnesty Program was established on Coruscant to give those who had been conditioned by the Empire the opportunity to adjust to the new shape of the galaxy.[14] Counseling was undertaken by droids and accommodation provided within the Re-Integration Institute. There were plenty around the galaxy who refused to accept that these ex-Imperials could ever be rehabilitated to any acceptable level, but the New Republic persisted. This program was not—as we will see—without its flaws, but the rationale behind it was sound.

But perhaps the most important measure taken to draw a line under the war was the wide-ranging Reconciliation Project, where ex-Imperials would be paired up with those who had suffered under the Empire— often at specific locations that tied into the ex-Imperial's service records—and would attempt to undergo some form of healing and closure together. There were, of course, numerous ex-Imperials who were tried for war crimes and genocide after the conflict, but attempts like the Reconciliation Project offered a solution to the horrors of the war and Imperial rule that did not simply increase the death toll. Mon Mothma seems to have believed that ongoing fatalities were no solution to the galaxy's need to live freely, so she attempted to institute as many ways as possible for the galaxy to learn from what had just happened, to heal, and then to move forward. It is perhaps one of the most noble undertakings in recent galactic history.

If only it had been successful.

[14] New Republic Archives, Section: Legislation, File: New Republic Amnesty Program* *Records show this was strongly supported by Leia Organa.

Chapter 24

Complacency and Appeasement

G iven the recent destruction of the New Republic and its capital on Hosnian Prime, there will undoubtedly be a great many pieces of analysis and investigation into the flaws of that fallen government. This is both understandable and inevitable. As we will discuss in this chapter, the New Republic was by no means a perfect state and laid many of the foundations of its own destruction. But, as with the Empire, it is necessary to really consider the nature of those failings. How many were inbuilt and how many only manifested themselves because of circumstance? Was the New Republic an institution doomed to failure and destruction? How much of its failure can perhaps be understood as the outcome of post-Imperial agents or activities within the new system? In such close proximity to the collapse of the New Republic, we may not yet fully understand the various strands and threads of the way the government both functioned and fell. In time it may become clearer.

However, given what I have already been able to uncover about the state that replaced the Galactic Empire and led the galaxy for 30 years, it is apparent that responsibility for its failure should not be assigned solely to either its own administrators or entirely to the—many—ex-Imperials who found a home within its bureaucracy. For every former soldier of the Empire aiming to bring down the government from within, was another who had abandoned Imperial ideology for the hope of a better life. For every Centrist politician who was secretly working with the First Order, there were devoted senators and politicians trying to lead the galaxy out of the horrors of Empire. I refuse to blame them all for the disaster of appeasement and the Hosnian Cataclysm. Similarly, I refuse to believe that the 30 years of relative peace that the New Republic provided were pointless. I would give a great deal for another 30 years of it. There were times during the recent conflict that I would have accepted 30 minutes. Or even 30 seconds.

But none of this is to say that the New Republic is above critique and criticism. To understand how Imperial ideology managed to have such a resurgence so long after Palpatine's death at Endor and the end of the Galactic Civil War at Jakku, it is necessary to stare unblinkingly at the flaws that appeared within the New Republic over its 30-year lifespan. There is already a tendency to point at the Centrist faction who appear to have secretly collaborated with the First Order while in elected office and then more overtly as war loomed. There are clearly many who will need to face justice for what they have done. But they were not the only groups dividing the New Republic and splitting its focus. What is interesting when undertaking a retrospective such as this is the fact that—in the early years after the Galactic Civil War—the greatest split was between those who had fought in the conflict and those who had not.

A Fractured Peace

As mentioned in previous chapters, the Rebel Alliance was a military organization, not a political or governing one. The combat skills many had gained during the war did not easily transfer into administering the galaxy they had just liberated. Furthermore, given the mix of different groups, factions and cells that had composed the Rebel Alliance, a return to the Republic that had died under Palpatine's chancellorship— a Republic that was hardly a shining example of representative democracy—was not necessarily the type of radical revolution some had envisioned. The situation was further complicated by the appearance—in some cases reappearance—of various political figures who had not actively taken a role with the Rebellion. Just as various ex-Imperial bureaucrats had skills and knowledge that could not easily be turned away, so too did those politicians who had remained—charitably speaking—neutral during recent hostilities.

While, as will become apparent in due course, the New Republic's political make up would eventually split into the Populist and Centrist factions that made governing a difficult balancing act, before this evolution of the Senate's affiliations, there was a more noticeable split between the combatants of the Rebel Alliance and the politicians who had not been involved. These two groups both engaged in a variety of internal contests over the wider direction of the New Republic and the best ways in which to navigate the peace.

Much of the basis for this split within the New Republic's political leadership revolved around competing concepts of moral superiority. Those senators who were either newly elected, or had previously served in the Old Republic and had sat out the war—such as Senator Hamato Xiono—seemed to believe that by remaining neutral they had not been tainted or corrupted by the manner in which the conflict had been fought. Because they had not engaged in combat they were somehow purer and more politically objective and not so minded to see threats and ex-Imperial plots everywhere they looked. By contrast, those who had been involved in the Rebel Alliance believed those who had sat on the sidelines to await the outcome were at best cynical opportunists and at worst Imperial sympathizers. While these competing viewpoints would often hamper or paralyze the New Republic, especially when it came to dealing with the Imperial remnant, I believe that at its roots the difference could best be described as differing interpretations of peace and hope.

The ex-rebels in the New Republic government believed that the best way to ensure peace was through vigilance. That while the Empire had been defeated, enough military leaders and other officials had slipped away at the end of the war to potentially pose a problem in the future. Furthermore, they also harbored ongoing concerns as to the number of ex-Imperials who still retained political offices in the aftermath of the war. While many of them may well have become loyal to the New Republic, as a collective, the group was still viewed with suspicion. While these ex-rebels hoped and believed in a future that could exist without a return to warfare, they were not willing to simply trust to hope in the face of what they perceived to be an enduring Imperial threat.

In contrast, their political opponents viewed the ex-rebel faction to effectively be warmongers and individuals who were incapable of abandoning their military past and accepting that the recent conflict was over. They believed that the constant concern over ex-Imperial sabotage was "little more than paranoia from those who did not realize that compromise was the best form of government."[1] The result of this position was the view that the possibility of peace was being constantly undermined by those endlessly looking to begin another war. Rejecting this pessimistic view of the galaxy, Xiono and others believed that in order to fulfill the hope of a better future held by the New Republic's citizens, every effort should be made to avoid conflict and to accept that with the war over, it was now the job of impartial politicians to steer the galaxy rather than soldiers.

Matters were not helped by the ongoing shadow of the Galactic Civil War that manifested itself in unexpected ways. In the years after that conflict a swathe of memoirs and "reflections" were published by those who had either participated in it or had watched it from afar. While many of the major figures of the Rebel Alliance—such as Mon Mothma, Leia Organa, or Luke Skywalker—did not participate in this movement, there were plenty of others who did. Some, like Alexsandr Kallus, who

---

[1] New Republic Archives, Section: Mon Mothma Collection, File: Memo from Senator Xiono to Chancellor Mon Mothma

had served on both sides, produced works that reflected on both the Empire and the Rebel Alliance. His memoir, *Honor Lost on Lasan: Serving the Empire, Fighting for the Alliance* is a surprisingly moving account of his own war service before his retirement to Lira San. His narration of how he had come to realize quite how evil the Empire was, became incorporated into the education system on some worlds in order to help teach the next generations about the war. However, there were many others who were nowhere near as reflective or honest in their own published works.

Haolp Joruth, who had served as a senator for Eufornis Major during the Clone Wars and the Empire before the Senate was dissolved, did not take any role in the Rebellion. However, in the aftermath of the peace treaty he returned to lead his people into the New Republic while also publishing *The Folly of War: An Analysis of the Rebel Alliance*, which critiqued the tactics and leadership of the Rebellion and, certainly to my mind, appears to have questioned whether the overthrow of the Empire was necessary at all. It cannot have been easy for those who had fought for the Alliance to build bridges with someone like Joruth who seemed quite content to slander them in text while also constructing his own reputation as an insightful genius.

Joruth was not alone in attempting to rebrand himself for a new era. While Mon Mothma herself refrained from publishing her own account of the war, she was the subject of various published works— some of them of highly dubious quality—that sought to analyze or debate the ways in which she had led the Rebel Alliance and what it might mean for the New Republic. The popular demand for insights and reflections on the war fed a growing trend where many authors tried to argue that they themselves had been a hero or the crucial difference in winning the war, or that those who had fought in it should now step away and leave the governing to those who knew best. Each new work complicated the entire picture. While the Galactic Civil War was still relatively fresh in the memory, the overall image of it was becoming muddied. It became increasingly difficult for the public to say who had done what or why events had played out as they had. Against this backdrop of voices clamoring for both attention and legitimacy how was the New Republic supposed to deal with its own inner problems, or understand the gravity of a crisis unfolding in front of it?

The Remnant

While, as we will shortly discuss, there were those across the galaxy not yet ready to fully abandon their loyalty to the ideology of the Empire, they were not the only ex-Imperials. There were certainly those who had found a role within the New Republic who still aimed to either bring down the new government or perhaps corrupt it from within. But there were also a tremendous number of individuals who had served the Empire in some format who were either traumatized by their past or deeply regretted their actions. Did the New Republic really do enough to help these people adapt to post-war life? Did it really consider the best ways of assisting them with the difficult process? When you now look at the actual approaches taken by both the Amnesty Program and the Re-Integration Institute, I believe there are serious questions to be asked and lessons to be learned about the ways in which the New Republic went about their de-Imperialization program.

To begin with we must consider the way the process was designed and where they drew their ideas and inspirations from. It must first be acknowledged that trying to create a program that would help ex-Imperials be rehabilitated back into wider galactic society was not easy. Many within what had been the Rebel Alliance had not really interacted with or lived on Core Worlds for years and were slightly out of touch with Imperial culture toward the end of the war. They needed input from those who could give advice on exactly what needed to be dealt with when assisting ex-Imperials. Unfortunately, there are suggestions that the New Republic was far too trusting and receptive to ideas from those who were not acting in good faith. When you compare material relating to the development of what would become the Re-Integration Institute with meetings and interviews by those same New Republic officials with Mas Amedda, a very concerning correlation begins to appear.[2] While there was no more senior figure for the Empire left available to the New Republic after the war that does not mean that Mas Amedda's suggestions should have been trusted. The Chagrian was a cruel and spitefully petty figure, and if Amedda did make recommendations to the New Republic then I now worry about how much damage he may have caused behind the scenes.

If you take a critical eye toward the de-Imperialization initiatives created by the New Republic then it does not take long for the problems to become visible. Most—but not all—of the ex-Imperials who entered the system were humans. As previously mentioned, this should not be a great surprise given the ideology of the Empire. But the knowledge of how the Empire promoted human interests, and the contempt in which other species were sometimes held, should have been a useful starting point in undertaking rehabilitation. However, it seems that a great deal of the work, particularly the one-on-one counseling interviews, was undertaken by specially programmed droids.[3] Most of us have been around droids all our lives and understand how helpful and, in their own ways, individual they can be. But would ex-Imperials recognize that? On many Imperial worlds droids had been considered to be little more than tools and less personable than pets. They certainly were not viewed as equals. How many Imperials, even those who wanted to, would really be able to open up about their problems to a droid? Would not a living being

---

[2] These records can be found in: New Republic Archives, Section: Imperial Rehabilitation Program, File: Planning and Development Outlines #11-59; and New Republic Archives, Section: Imperial Prisoners, File: Mas Amedda—Interrogation Notes #418-501.
[3] New Republic Archives, Amnesty Program, File: Droid Programming and Responsibilities

have been a better choice? Someone who could react from a position of empathy rather than from a more clinical programming? Records of the interviews droids were expected to undertake leave a very formulaic impression. Rehabilitation by numbers. Is this what these people needed?

Similarly, the Amnesty Housing Program that provided accommodation on Coruscant also dictated that each resident be effectively stripped of their identity and replaced by a number.[4] Again, there were some good reasons for this. It allowed the participants to leave their past lives behind to an extent and begin anew. But the Empire had removed the names of many of its soldiers and replaced them with a number as well. Even with the best intentions, was replicating the—for want of a better term—dehumanizing practices of the Empire the right approach for those who were trying to free themselves of its past control? Matters are then exacerbated when you consider that, for those who relapsed during their rehabilitation, the New Republic repurposed the infamous "mind flayers" so beloved by Imperial torturers.[5] The rationale for this was that on much lower voltages, the equipment could be used to help ease or remove painful memories and emotions. But the subjects it was likely to be used upon knew exactly what it was originally intended for and must have been greatly distressed by the treatment. Furthermore, there are also instances where the equipment appears to have malfunctioned and caused lasting damage to the patient within it.[6]

When examining the ways in which the New Republic approached the matter of rehabilitating captured Imperials I am constantly left to question where exactly the empathy could be found. The use of mind flayers and effective social isolation cannot have been what Mon

[4] New Republic Archives, Section: Imperial Rehabilitation Program, File: Numeric Identification Protocol
[5] New Republic Archives, Section: Imperial Rehabilitation Program, File: Explanation on the safe use of the Six-O-Two Mitigator
[6] New Republic Archive, Section: Imperial Rehabilitation Program, File: Amnesty Scientist L52—Emergency Medical Assessment

Mothma had in mind when she proposed her policy of truth and reconciliation. So why did the New Republic settle upon this approach?
Perhaps, understandably, it was difficult for many to have much in the
way of sympathy toward those who had stood with the Empire until the
very end. In among all of those undertaking rehabilitation were probably a great number who could count themselves very fortunate not to
have ended up in front of a tribunal. But I do not know if I can bring
myself to hate all of these people. If they required help and assistance in
leaving the Empire behind, then that is what they should have been
given. The Rebel Alliance had relied upon many ex-Imperials during the
height of the Galactic Civil War. Could circumstances not have prevented the likes of Crix Madine or Wedge Antilles the opportunity to
defect? Perhaps the Imperial associations of Jan Dodonna or Han Solo
would have meant they were excluded from the Alliance. Where would
the rebel cause have gone then, stripped of some of its most important
heroes and warriors? What would have become of the dream? We would
do very well to learn some important lessons when now dealing with
prisoners from the First Order, many of whom have been effectively
indoctrinated from birth and prevented from making their own escapes.

Disappointingly, however, and of great concern to some within the
New Republic, was the reality that although many ex-Imperials willingly entering rehabilitation, there were those working within the
government who had little interest in abandoning the Empire. It is here
that the complacency of the New Republic is further noticeable, not
helped by those like Senator Xiono and his allies who refused to accept
that there was any danger to be found from within the new system. One
of the most serious examples of Imperial-driven sabotage could be
found on the shipyards of Corellia that had previously been administered by the Imperial industrialist Morgan Elsbeth.[7] After the Galactic

---

[7] Imperial Archives, Section: Corellian Infrastructure, File: Santhe Shipyards
Facility #301G

Civil War, these shipyards were then absorbed into the New Republic and generally used to dismantle vessels that had previously served in the Imperial Navy.[8] But many of the workers, managers, and administrative staff remained the same. As mentioned in a previous chapter, this should not be too surprising. They were, after all, the ones who knew how to work the machinery. However, there does not appear to have been any real interest or consideration as to whether their loyalties may have been compromised by their time serving the Empire. As a result, when General Hera Syndulla and the former Jedi Ahsoka Tano visited the facility, they discovered that workers there had been removing the hyperdrives from Super Star Destroyers to assist Morgan Elsbeth—who had recently escaped New Republic custody—in building a gigantic hyperspace ring. Given the repercussions this plot had for the galaxy, could this not have been prevented if someone within the New Republic government had shown the slightest interest in what ex-Imperial workers might be doing with their time?

Because these neo-Imperials were not just undertaking subversion and treason for their own benefits. They were working to serve an Imperial remnant that was still lurking out among the stars. Though the war had ended, there was no shortage of loyalists who were not yet ready or willing to lay down their arms. Again, the New Republic largely turned a blind eye to the presence of Imperial troops on worlds like Morak and Nevarro that lay outside their jurisdiction. It appears that the idea of the last remnants of the beaten Empire scrabbling around in the outer reaches of the galaxy was not an immediate problem for many New Republic leaders. But those Imperials were not looking to waste their own time. Figures like Moff Gideon were able to build up power bases of their own, secure in the New Republic's disinterest. So difficult did New Republic forces on the Outer Rim find confronting the Imperial

---

[8] New Republic Archives, Section: Ex-Imperial Industry Requisitions, File: Corellian Shipyards

remnants existing just across the border, that it appears at least one officer found inventive ways of hiring bounty hunters to try and solve the problem.[9]

The New Republic was painfully slow in recognizing the real threat of the Imperial remnant until it was effectively too late. The return to this galaxy of Grand Admiral Thrawn proved to be a turning point in the balance of power between the neo-Imperial forces biding their time and the New Republic ones trying desperately to raise the alarm. Much of the military campaign waged against Thrawn's forces was still classified by the time the New Republic fell. At the time of Thrawn's return, Chalm Plesk—a historian from the University of Coruscant—was embedded with the New Republic fleet. His planned work, *The Last War Against the Galactic Empire: On Deployment with the New Republic Fleet* was highly anticipated for years, but various military figures refused to permit its publication.[10] Plesk eventually took his case to the New Republic Senate on Hosnian Prime but, tragically, was on the world when it was destroyed by the First Order. We can only hope that copies of his work exist elsewhere in the galaxy and can now be released to us.

Seeds of Destruction

While the Imperial remnant was largely defeated, Imperial ideology did not go with it. It had survived Palpatine's death, and it was more than capable of surviving this. Out in the Unknown Regions, a new form of Empire was rising. They called themselves the First Order, and from what we can now ascertain from New Republic Intelligence and recently captured prisoners, their origins—which will be discussed further in the next chapter—lay in the aftermath of Jakku. Though much of the

---

[9] New Republic Archives, Section: Adelphi Base, File: Requisition Form #1837p— Subcontract for fulfillment of refuse collection
[10] New Republic Archives, Section: Military Intelligence, File: Notice Prohibiting Publication #1310

Imperial military was defeated in the final battle of the Galactic Civil War, a sizeable number were able to flee separately into the Unknown Regions to begin their rebuilding process.

While the New Republic, slowly, became aware of this new entity that was emerging beyond their own territory it seems they largely treated them with disinterest.[11] The Galactic Concordance that had ended the previous war placed strict limitations on the military technology and production that ex-Imperial factions were permitted. The First Order continually broke these restrictions, and the New Republic did not act. The First Order slowly began to expand its own borders, and the New Republic did not engage with them. The First Order—through various Centrist faction puppets in the Senate—also worked hard to undermine the New Republic's government, and still, inaction. So concerned were many Senators at the prospect of starting a new war while still recovering from the last, that they allowed the First Order to build up its own military forces with no consequences at all. At the same time Mon Mothma's Military Disarmament Act had whittled the New Republic fleet down to a fraction of its previous size. Many vessels had been broken up entirely while more famous ships, like *Home One*, were now effectively museum pieces.[12] The intended plan for this reduction in state firepower was that, in theory, individual systems and sectors would have their own defense forces, which could then form ad-hoc coalitions should a greater threat arise. An idea vaguely in line with how the High Republic had organized military forces across the galaxy.[13] The hope was that such an arrangement would encourage a feeling of communal defense—and possibly help avoid a rise in inter-system rivalries that had

[11] New Republic Archives, Section: Military Intelligence, File: First Order Surveillance

[12] Mon Cala Archives, Section: Galactic Civil War Commemoration, File: *Home One* museum inauguration

[13] New Republic Archives, Section: Military Disarmament Act, File: Proposal for decentralized defensive operations

been suppressed by the Empire. However, there was more than a touch of naivete behind this plan and, as the recent war has shown, it left the galaxy unable to cohesively react to a burgeoning threat when the central government was destroyed. In the face of the First Order, many systems and sectors effectively locked themselves down in an attempt to defend their own borders.

Of additional concern was the extent to which the Imperial aesthetic and aspects of its ideology had endured within New Republic society. Many Centrists, even those who may not have been sleeper First Order agents, espoused the benefits of a single central figure who could rule the galaxy. Their image of a proto-Palpatine was horrifying to many within the Populist faction who hoped to disseminate governmental powers out to the people. Within the Centrists there were also individuals like Ransolm Casterfo who—and I say this even in the knowledge we recently served alongside each other in the Resistance—almost fetishized the symbols and iconography of the Galactic Empire. His collection of ex-Imperial militaria, which he kept on display in his senatorial office, was extensive. How he and others could look upon such objects and disassociate them from the regime that created them is still beyond my understanding. But Casterfo was not alone. There was a growing number of civilians within the New Republic who also looked to collect such relics, justifying their interest and obsession in the language of historians, without having any real comprehension as to what exactly they were playing with.[14]

In many ways it serves almost as a fitting epitaph for some of the failings of the New Republic. They had become so relaxed and assured that the Empire would not threaten them again, that it was now through a lens of good-humored curiosity that they viewed the materiel with

---

[14] See the records of *The Society for Imperial Re-enactment* who billed themselves as "The Galaxy's premier organization for those who appreciate the aesthetic of the Imperial military."

which the Empire had waged war. Not realizing that the ideology that had once produced stormtrooper armor was still producing stormtroopers. Chancellor Lanever Villecham resolutely refused to heed the warnings from the likes of General Leia Organa as to what was about to happen. It was only when the skies of Hosnian Prime ignited above them that many in the Senate were truly able to see their own doom.

Chapter 25

The First and Final Orders

Perhaps, given all that had gone before, the recent war between the Resistance and the First Order was inevitable. Maybe we were always destined to be here. Given, as I have attempted to argue throughout this work, that the worst crimes carried out in the name of Imperial ideology could very easily be separated from the actual activities of the Emperor himself, we should now not be surprised that it endured both within the New Republic and out in the Unknown Regions, biding its time to have a resurgence and threaten us all once again. Even before it became apparent that Palpatine's malicious influence had not been eradicated at Endor as hoped, we must understand that the First Order was founded and influenced by the mindset and ideals that had permeated the Galactic Empire.

The New Republic, having been profoundly weakened by the work of Centrist senators who really gave their allegiance to the First Order, was fatally unprepared for what was about to happen. They had placed their faith in the ongoing benefits of peace without being prepared to recognize the threats to that peace they allowed to exist through complacency, appeasement, and wishful thinking. The annihilation of Hosnian Prime cost innumerable lives and also marked the moment that the dream of a galaxy free of the Empire was immolated. The war that had long seemed inevitable to the likes of Leia Organa arrived and the Resistance was forced to fight it alone. While some, such as myself, joined their ranks, for a time it seemed that many in the galaxy were content to allow the neo-Imperial conquest to succeed and reimpose its view upon us all.

But that is not what happened. While in this chapter we will examine what we now know about the ways in which the First Order was formed and organized, how they intended to wage war, and the ideology behind their actions, it must also be understood that their eventual defeat and destruction was not entirely the result of the Resistance's military efforts. The role that the resurrection of Palpatine played both in covertly orchestrating the First Order and then also in provoking the galaxy's population into action should not be underestimated. Palpatine had previously shown the ways in which his own ego could prove an obstacle in achieving his objectives, and recent events have only solidified that judgment.

However, to begin with we must first come to understand what exactly the First Order intended to create and how they rallied around certain leaders and figures. One of the most interesting aspects of their ideology and structure is that, to certain extents, they had come to embody the very notion of separating the Empire from the Emperor. While figures like Supreme Leaders Snoke and Kylo Ren clearly wielded a great deal of power, it is also perhaps fair to say that—by the time of the war—there were plenty within the First Order's upper echelons who had little interest in Palpatine himself, even after his sudden return.

Generational Divides

At this stage it must be stated and understood that there remains a great deal we do not yet know about the time the First Order spent in the Unknown Regions recovering from the Empire's defeat in the Galactic Civil War. Of the great many prisoners recently captured from the First Order, and then from Palpatine's forces at Exegol, a good deal were not even born by the time the Empire fell. Those who were, have proven reticent to discuss the past in their interrogations, possibly because they are hoping to secure some form of clemency deal before divulging their secrets. As a result, much of what we can piece together is based on fragments of information and should be considered subject to revision as soon as we are able to gain new knowledge. But what we can ascertain is that, for a period at least, the organization and administration of what would become the First Order was based along military lines, and that it was likely the recipient of a great deal of covert financial support from the Corporate Sector Authority.[1]

Given how far these Imperial survivors would likely have been forced to travel to put a safe distance between themselves and the New Republic, we can only imagine what sorts of dangers lurked in the deeper unmapped parts of the galaxy. Surviving out there must have been challenge enough, let alone undertaking what turned out to be an extensive rebuilding process. What is interesting when looking at the forces of the Imperial remnant that existed on the edges of New Republic space in the lead up to Grand Admiral Thrawn's return, is the scarcity of larger capital ships. Moff Gideon, one of the preeminent figures on the "Shadow Council" of the Imperial remnant who served to link the various surviving Imperial factions, was reduced to a modified *Arquitens*-class command cruiser.[2] Where had all the remaining Star Destroyers and other vessels gone? We must wonder if perhaps when the founders of the First Order escaped the known galaxy, they took the bulk of their surviving military equipment with them. It would not be enough to reconquer the galaxy with, but it might assist them in staying alive long enough to one day make their return.

At the conclusion of the Galactic Civil War, the New Republic began to take stock of notable Imperials who appeared to have either avoided capture at Jakku or slipped through the tightening net that had

[1] Resistance Archives, Section: The First Order, File: Organization and Financing
[2] New Republic Archives, Section: Moff Gideon, File: Force evaluation

surrounded the Empire. During this—sadly all too brief—period, the New Republic undertook active attempts to track down a handful of these missing figures. Many of the operations were largely what you might expect, including an increase in surveillance and intelligence gathering activities on previously loyal Imperial worlds, in some cases working with bounty hunters beyond the New Republic's borders. One development—which was of dubious taste at the time—has proven to have been remarkably prescient. New Republic Intelligence created, and circulated, an adapted sabacc deck with each of the 76 cards featuring the last known image of a wanted Imperial fugitive. The idea seemed to be that these cards would be disseminated through tapcafes and cantinas, hopefully resulting in the wider population identifying some of those featured.[3] It later transpired that some of those on the cards had died without the New Republic knowing at the time, but others would later go on to have a key role in the creation of the First Order. Grand Admiral Rae Sloane was to be found on the Master of Sabers, Commandant Brendol Hux was the Seven of Coins, and Captain Enric Pryde was found on the Three of Staves. While there were other ex-Imperial figures who then would go on to appear within the Imperial remnant, it seems that Sloane, Hux, and Pryde played a significant part in the creation of what would follow.

There are numerous questions regarding the activities of some of these figures in the years following Jakku and even right up to the opening battles of the most recent war. Commandant Hux, according to his New Republic profile, appears to have been a ruthless but devout follower of Imperial ideology.[4] Recently captured First Order records suggest he was behind "Project Resurrection," involving the conscription—often by kidnapping children—and training of the next

[3] New Republic Archives, Section: Military Intelligence, File: Customized Sabacc Deck

[4] New Republic Archives, Section: Military Intelligence, File: Missing Imperial Personnel—Commandant Brendol Hux

generation of stormtroopers who would become loyal soldiers.[5] It appears that Hux would eventually die while in service to the First Order, though the circumstances of his death are not clear.[6] His son, Armitage, rose to replace him and was an almost rabidly fanatical follower of the First Order's ideology—we now know it was Armitage who gave the order to fire on Hosnian Prime. Grand Admiral Rae Sloane has already appeared numerous times within this study, and I remain optimistic about gaining access to the previously sealed records of her held by the New Republic.

Enric Pryde is a much more interesting figure.[7] Firstly, it is unclear how he escaped the destruction of the *Steadfast* at Jakku or how he spent the years immediately following the end of the Galactic Civil War. Clearly at some point he made his way to the First Order where his emerging role is highly intriguing. His rank of "allegiant general" strongly suggests he was tasked with instilling loyalty and ideology within the First Order's ranks. He'd served within the Empire for years, and can probably be classed as a "true believer" in that sense. However, testimony from First Order officers indicates he was not present at either the Battle of Starkiller Base, or the attempt to destroy the Resistance fleet preceding the Battle of Crait. So where was he? So far, during my opening examinations of captured First Order material, there appear to be various entries relating to the activities and movements of Pryde, but none were filed by him. Instead logs—which are proving difficult to decrypt—were filed by TK-111.[8] That appears to be an older Imperial

---

[5] First Order Archives, Section: Project Resurrection, File: Foundations and Principles
[6] First Order Archives, Section: Commandant Brendol Hux, File: Report of death*
*This item has been heavily redacted.
[7] New Republic Archives, Section: Military Intelligence, File: Missing Imperial Personnel—Captain Enric Pryde
[8] First Order Archives, Section: Allegiant General Enric Pryde, File: TK-111—Mission Logs and Reports* *Data retrieved from the remains of the *Steadfast* at Exegol

stormtrooper designation, and some of the holovids of Pryde arriving at First Order installations do suggest he was always accompanied by a stormtrooper, though that individual's identity and whether they survived remain a mystery.

As might be expected there were significant crossovers in ideology between the Empire and the First Order. This new organization was, broadly speaking, highly human-centric and possessed of considerable bias against non-humans and droids. We have already been able to uncover the education protocols put in place within the First Order to indoctrinate their children into neo-Imperialism and they are truly horrifying.[9] Records of the speech given by General Armitage Hux at the inauguration of Starkiller Base show the extent to which he, and the First Order by association, disdained the New Republic and its form of representative democracy, characterizing it as "a regime that acquiesces to disorder."[10] It is not hard to believe that the likes of Sloane, Brendol Hux, and Pryde had instilled much of this sentiment in the First Order by drawing upon Imperial ideals. What is curious though is that many of the younger generation within the First Order did not appear to have any particular interest or loyalty toward Palpatine himself. This is perhaps understandable given he was thought to be dead, but when he began to make his presence known once again, it was only older officers like Pryde who seemed minded to flock back to his side. Initially at least, the likes of Kylo Ren and similarly aged officers viewed him as either a rival or an irrelevance.[11] In the figures of, firstly, Snoke and then Kylo Ren, the First Order already had leaders who could seemingly wield the dark side of the Force. Why did they need to look to a man who had

[9] First Order Archives, Section: Loyalty and Indoctrination, File: Educational Edict #15
[10] First Order Archives, Section: General Armitage Hux, File: Address at Starkiller Base
[11] First Order Archives, Section: Command Council, File: Briefing regarding Palpatine's return* *Holo-recording recovered from the *Steadfast* at Exegol

failed the last time he held power? Ignoring the likely damage such a realization may have caused to Palpatine's already fragile ego, it also serves as an alarm for the rest of the galaxy that neo-Imperialism did not require the presence of Emperor Palpatine in order to flourish. Nor did the First Order require him to instruct them on how to perpetrate atrocities.

The Last War

Even in the years before overt hostilities broke out against the Resistance, the First Order had been making its presence felt in the galaxy. They seized control of worlds like Hays Minor and forced the local population into the mines. Like the Empire before it, the First Order needed considerable resources to power its emerging military. As it began developing its weapons it also tested them at Hays Minor and began rounding up the local children as part of their expanded stormtrooper program.[12] Further incursions and attacks on other outlying worlds, like Tehar, became an increasing occurrence as the First Order sought to flex its muscles and test the boundaries of the New Republic's patience.[13]

The New Republic had, for some time, believed that the First Order was nowhere near militarized enough to pose a serious threat. However, given what we now know about the expansion of their fleet based around the *Resurgent*-class Star Destroyers, the construction of enormous weapons like Snoke's flagship the *Supremacy,* and the conversion of the former Jedi world of Ilum into the terror weapon Starkiller Base, this cannot have been true. Though the First Order undoubtedly had their own hidden shipyards—the locations of which we must now establish as quickly as possible—it also seems likely that various Centrist worlds

[12] Resistance Archives, Section: First Order Military Activities, File: Hays Minor—Testimony from Paige and Rose Tico
[13] First Order Archives, Section: Military Operations, File: Attack on Tehar

such as Arkanis, Kuat, and Orinda must have been supplying either financial support or construction expertise. Each of these worlds—alongside a number of others—all wanted a return to a central dominant ruler and all of them broke with the New Republic when the First Order fully emerged. Furthermore, there appears to be a great deal of evidence to suggest some of the galaxy's wealthiest industrialists continued to fund both the Resistance and the First Order in a cynical attempt at war profiteering.[14]

If the New Republic had the chance to regret not taking a firmer stance against the First Order, then it was only a brief one. The opening shot of the wider war was targeted from Starkiller Base directly at Hosnian Prime and it succeeded in destroying the seat of government, almost the entirety of the Senate, and much of the New Republic Defense Fleet.[15] Although Starkiller Base itself was destroyed shortly afterward, the damage already done was devastating. For all intents and purposes the New Republic ceased to exist or function. While the Resistance continued to put up a fight it rapidly became apparent that the military forces available to the First Order dwarfed what we could put into the field. Though the First Order dispatched a significant fleet to pursue the Resistance from D'Qar, and then engage them in battle firstly at Oetchi and then at Crait, this was not the limit of their aggressive expansion. It seems that, aside from an ongoing desire to destroy the remnants of the Jedi, the First Order was utterly focused on securing legitimacy to rule the galaxy it was attempting to conquer. It seems that at least two sizeable battlegroups made a push for Coruscant in the apparent hope of seizing it and ruling the galaxy from the Empire's former seat of power.[16] It appears that the forces sent to achieve that were defeated, but there is still a good deal of confusion regarding recent events at the end of

[14] Resistance Archives, Section: Canto Bight Clientele, File: Testimony by Finn and Rose Tico
[15] Resistance Archives, Section: Hosnian Cataclysm, File: Casualty Estimates
[16] First Order Archives, Section: Military Operations, File: Coruscant Deployment

the war.[17] Elsewhere the First Order moved swiftly to try and seize worlds that had either been stripped of protection from the defeated New Republic or that had been "neutral" on its borders. Planets like Kijimi found themselves under an ongoing occupation as the First Order attempted to pacify the world despite the activities of its lawless inhabitants.[18]

Much as the Empire had done before it, the tactics and strategies of the First Order relied heavily on fear and force. Their use of Star Destroyers, stormtroopers, and various TIE fighter designs allowed them to make overt shows of military strength that could then be backed up by destructive power. There are some elements of interest in this aspect, however. Aside from the fact that some of the TIE fighter variants appear to have had shield generators, which was a break from Imperial norms, the replication of particular kinds of military weaponry and tactics strongly suggests—and we should now cross reference First Order records with surviving Imperial ones to check for this—that many of those who had founded the First Order and influenced its doctrines had their roots in the "firepower" lobby that had previously split the Imperial military. Regardless, if the main founders of the First Order were, in some way, selected in advance for this rebuilding task it is highly likely that the main criteria for their inclusion was their loyalty and adherence to Imperial ideology rather than any great military skills. This might explain why the Resistance was often able to successfully use tactics adapted from the Rebel Alliance, because the First Order was no better at dealing with them than the Empire had been. The determination to hold onto the ideals of the fallen Empire meant that tactical innovation in battle beyond that which Imperial forces had attempted

[17] Resistance Archives, Section: Post-War Intelligence Gathering, File: Planned Operation on Coruscant
[18] Resistance Archives, Section: First Order Military Activities, File: Kijimi—Testimony from Poe Dameron

was seen as almost heretical.[19] However, if the shadow of Imperial doctrine was cast upon the war, it was nothing compared with what was about to happen.

The Fallen Emperor

When I explained to my fellow Resistance soldiers that the likeliest explanation for the apparent return of the long-dead Emperor Palpatine lay in "secrets only the Sith knew," they did not fully grasp quite how horrifying a concept this was.[20] The history of the Sith is replete with examples of terrifying experiments, attempted necromancy, and arcane rituals. As mentioned previously in this study, Palpatine likely spent decades attempting to discover the secrets of eternal life. If the version that he enacted on Exegol was not quite what he had intended, it was successful enough. On the hidden fortress world of the Sith, Palpatine, as hobbled and deformed as he was—according to Rey's testimony—bided his time and gathered his power. And, just as he had many years before, began to tug on the galaxy's threads to sculpt events.

For years the Resistance attempted to gather information on Supreme Leader Snoke.[21] It remains unclear exactly when and where he encountered the First Order or what he did to seize control of that organization. His abilities with the Force clearly provided him with an advantage over the other First Order founders and leaders and left him effectively unchallenged at the start of the war. From what we have been able to ascertain about Snoke's appearance he was noticeably taller than humans, but he had also been left with horrifying scars and damage that

---

[19] First Order Archives, Section: Military Doctrine, File: Adaptation of Imperial Military Approaches

[20] Resistance Archives, Section: Command Meetings, File: Sinta Glacier Debriefing—Minutes taken by AD-4M

[21] Resistance Archives, Section: Supreme Leader Snoke, File: Intelligence Gathering—Speculated Origins

we had assumed were signs of some form of battle. Now that appears not to be the case. Here on Exegol we have discovered the various vats in the laboratory and have extracted the various "Snokes" from within them that appear to have been failures. Snoke did not discover the First Order and take control of them by chance. He was created by Palpatine for that express purpose. How very telling that in his arrogance the defeated Emperor could not bear to allow the offshoot of his Empire to be under the control of anyone but himself. It seems that an additional part of Snoke's—and therefore Palpatine's—plot was to try and lure Ben Solo to the dark side, therefore weakening the Jedi cause. Solo—adopting the identity of Kylo Ren—seems to have been fascinated by the legacy of his grandfather Darth Vader and embraced the sense of purpose it gave him. Kitrin Braves is continuing to explore this complicated aspect of the Skywalker legacy and I will happily leave it to her. But there certainly appear to be traces of Palpatine's scheming and his need for pliable Force wielders both in Ben Solo's fall and in the circumstances that left Rey abandoned on Jakku as a child.

While the First Order built its own forces and, over time, began to both weaken the New Republic and draw its attention away, Palpatine was also gathering his own strength. In the shipyards below Exegol he continued the construction of hundreds of new Star Destroyers, each armed with a scaled down version of the Death Star's superlaser that was more than capable of destroying a planet.[22] Surrounded by Sith acolytes and his most loyal followers, Palpatine was effectively breeding an army that was conditioned to be absolutely loyal to him and him alone. While he expected the First Order to join him, he was prepared to annihilate them if needed. The Emperor had not shared power when alive, he had no intention to do so while rising from the grave. When he saw that the time had finally come, he made his announcement. The broadcast

---

[22] Exegol Excavation Project, Section: Industrial Facilities, Files: Shipyards and Design Plans

from Exegol revealing that Palpatine had returned is interesting for various reasons. Firstly, it was not immediately apparent to anyone listening that it was actually true. For the Resistance, it was only when we discovered that the First Order was convinced as to its veracity that we were able to accept it with some confidence. For those out in the galaxy it must have been much more confusing and terrifying.

Additionally, while Emperor, Palpatine—as we have previously discussed—had seemed to undertake at least some efforts to hide his true appearance and nature. He dropped all those pretenses upon his return, declaring that, "At last the work of generations is complete. The great error is corrected. The day of victory is at hand. The day of revenge. The day of the Sith."[23] The mention of the Sith, a group that were little understood by the galaxy's population, was presumably targeted at both the First Order—by reminding Kylo Ren of something he was not—and any Jedi within the Resistance. But the most striking part is Palpatine's declaration that he would soon correct a great error and have his day of revenge. His return was, as ever, motivated by his ego and his inability to accept that the galaxy had rejected him. Palpatine's vanity and pettiness had been resurrected with him. He did not realize it yet, but it was going to cost him dearly once again.

Following Palpatine's emergence, and especially after his ordering of the destruction of Kijimi, there was a blurring of the lines between what had been the First Order and what was emerging as the "Final Order" of the Sith Eternal. Leaders like Allegiant General Pryde and Captain Edrison Peavey immediately moved to rejoin Palpatine's side however they could. Other vessels crewed by the younger generation of First Order loyalists were not as motivated. However, the apparent defeat of Kylo Ren at Kef Bir meant that there were no alternative orders coming down the chain of command aside from Pryde's. Willingly or not, they began to obey orders that were essentially coming from

[23] Resistance Archives, Section: Palpatine, File: Exegol Broadcast

Palpatine. It was against this backdrop of emerging power that the Resistance moved against Palpatine's fleet at Exegol. I will leave the retelling of the various movements and phases of that battle to my colleagues who are currently reconstructing it. For my part the experience was terrifying. Trapped upon the hull of the *Steadfast* confronted by Sith troopers, while the Resistance fleet was being overwhelmed and destroyed around us, there were many moments where I could feel the tug of despair. It continues to shame me now.

But that is not entirely how I look back upon that battle now. Because while the nightmares continue to visit me with regularity, there is something else that helps me sleep sounder when the horrors have passed. Because what I had feared during the darkest days of the Resistance was proven to be untrue at Exegol—we were not alone. Down on Exegol itself Rey and Ben Solo—returned to the light side of the Force—did battle against Palpatine. It appears that the pair of them had a form of unique bond through the Force: a dyad. By draining some of this power, Palpatine was able to return to his full strength and shed the life support equipment that had previously been keeping his ruined body together. Power is all that Palpatine had ever been interested in, and while he could channel a tremendous amount of it, he was still the same deeply flawed human underneath it all. That same arrogant weakness was once again his undoing. When he stood against Rey he believed he faced a single opponent. He was wrong. The lineage and strength of the Jedi stood behind Rey, and as she turned Palpatine's lightning barrage back upon him he was annihilated by it.[24]

However, that is not where I believe the true victory came from. What Rey achieved on Exegol is beyond my comprehension. But it was not just the Jedi that brought Palpatine to defeat. Not really. It was us. It was the great mass of people who had been forced to repeatedly stare into the depths of Palpatine's evil intentions and then chose to reject

[24] Resistance Archives, Section: Battle of Exegol, File: Rey Skywalker's Debriefing

him. Starships, fighters, freighters, and cruisers from across the galaxy had come to Exegol not just after hearing the call from General Lando Calrissian, but because Palpatine's broadcast had terrified and motivated them in equal measure. It is not yet even clear if many who came were totally convinced it even *was* Palpatine. But it didn't matter. Because regardless of what the Centrists, or the Imperial remnant, or the First Order had believed—the galaxy did not long for a return to Empire. While there have been so many mistakes and errors made over the last three decades in how we have talked about the years of Imperial rule, enough of the message had made it through. Enough people knew what the Empire stood for. What it meant. What it promised. And they came out to fight against it.

The Resistance has spent a great many hours going over the various transponder signals and communication records from Exegol and they have found something truly heartening.[25] There were ex-Imperials there among the Citizens Fleet as well. Some, like Imanuel Doza, had long left their Imperial past behind them and begun to move toward the Resistance. But he was not the only one there. We have not yet identified all of the ships or pilots present at Palpatine's final destruction but the fact that some of his own, once loyal, soldiers were present in rejecting his return and risking their lives to fight against him, should provide all of us with the most precious element in the entire galaxy: hope.

Now, together, we must decide how to spend it.

[25] Resistance Archives, Section: Battle of Exegol, File: Communications and Ship Analysis

Conclusion

As I now reflect on this study and the motivations behind it, I must accept that I have failed with one of them. When I decided to revisit the era of the Galactic Empire, to go through as much material as possible, to examine and analyze the records that had never been considered before, I had objectives that were both important for the galaxy and for myself. It is in the latter of these where I have been unsuccessful. The current era of war and horror was not supposed to have been my life. I was a historian. I focused on the history and materials of the Sith. I taught at Lerct Historical Institute and, in many ways, I was happy. And then I looked around the galaxy and saw what was coming.

My realization that the First Order was set on waging war against the New Republic terrified me. I could see how unprepared we were for what was about to happen, and after the Hosnian Cataclysm I joined the Resistance. I do not regret that choice. I could not stand by and allow such a vicious organization as the First Order to plunge the whole galaxy into darkness. But now, after the war, I do not know how to retrace my steps. I do not know how to once again be the historian who left Lerct because I do not know if that person still exists. I do not know how I am supposed to teach students the same age as the stormtroopers I have killed. I do not know how to interact with my older colleagues who stayed silent and neutral as Hosnian Prime burned and as the First Order cut a swathe across innocent worlds and systems. I do not know how to live with myself for the things I have done and seen. Necessary though they may have been, I now struggle to move beyond them.

It is here where I had hoped this study would help me. I had hoped that by coming to fully understand the roots and foundations of the Imperial system that brought us to this point, the way they had intended to structure and rule the galaxy, the reasons and methods behind their worst atrocities—that this knowledge would help me. Help me come to terms with what has more recently happened and give me a route out of it. Sadly, it has not. I now find myself assailed by the horrors I have lived through and haunted by those of the past. This galaxy has suffered and lost so much that it is hard not to look around now, as I sit amid the wreckage on Exegol, and wonder if there is any way to truly break this cycle.

But it is also here where the second rationale for this study rises in importance, and where the hope for the future might be found. Because for all of the power, and the terror, and the destruction of the Empire and the First Order one thing is also true: they always lose. If one half of the legacy of the Empire is death then the other is defeat. Given enough time and enough people dedicated to resisting them, then the Empire— and the First Order that followed it—can be defeated. The galaxy did it at Endor and Jakku and we have recently done it again here at Exegol. There is much hope that can be found in the realization that resistance and rebellion will always rise to meet totalitarianism. But how many times do we want to repeat this process? How often do we wish to relax, complacently, upon our victories and ignore the dark slivers of Imperial ideology that lurk within the shadows, just biding their time. How do we make this time the *last* time?

I mentioned in the introduction to this study that I believed it to be one born of necessity. I continue to believe that. Because while I cannot know whether the galaxy will be able to go through this process of defeating the specter of the Empire again, I know for certain that I cannot do so. I have fought my war. I do not believe I have it within me to fight another. Equally I refuse to bequeath the horrors of the present onto the generations of the future. I will not see our children and our grandchildren face the destruction that we have, simply because we were not willing to understand how we reached this point. That is neither right nor fair. Peace must begin with us.

To begin with we must learn—really learn—exactly what has happened here and why. That is the main purpose of the work I have presented to you. To try and make all across the galaxy understand that the emergence of the First Order did not happen in isolation. They did not simply manifest into existence of their own accord in the Unknown Regions. They came from the Empire. And if they could wait 30 years before trying to reestablish what had once fallen, then so can another offshoot of patient neo-Imperials. I believe it is now fair to say that, on reflection, the New Republic failed in fully explaining the Empire. Fortunately—very fortunately—enough of the ideas made it through to help motivate the participants in the Citizens' Fleet, but that was far too close a call for us to risk repeating it. To guard against the return of the Empire in yet another form, we must start the whole process of learning about it once again.

Our galaxy has been split by warfare too many times in recent memory. Peace has always been hard won and, sadly, easily dispensed with. For things to be different this time we need to take a long hard look at the Galactic Empire and see it for what it was. Not just as a series of abstract ideas that seem to come from a different time, but as a regime that, in many cases, drew our ancestors into its grasp with promises of order and stability and then kept them there, complacent or complicit, for far longer than we may wish to acknowledge. We need to look directly at the horrors perpetrated by the Empire and accept that they were not just carried out by Palpatine himself. Responsibility for them was spread wider than we have previously wanted to accept. Among some of the younger First Order personnel I have interviewed there appears to have been an intriguing level of disinterest in the Emperor's return. They didn't seem to have overly cared. It's possible that he meant nothing to them. The dangers of the Empire and its ideology are not embodied within Palpatine, a man who craved power but disdained all around him. It is the way that ideology offers something to ordinary people. The promises it makes to them and the awful things it gives them permission to do. *That* is the Empire. *That* is what has given me so many sleepless nights.

Following the defeat of the First Order, we have taken countless prisoners. Some of whom are from the generation that served Palpatine willingly and aimed to return to his side again. They perpetrated awful crimes for the Empire and again for the replacement they helped to create. It may have taken a long time but finally justice has caught up with these war criminals. But what are we to do with the others? There are stormtroopers and naval officers who were raised within the First Order. They have had Imperial ideology hammered into them by brutal indoctrination. Many of them were kidnapped from parents and families across the galaxy. We know that the New Republic attempted a de-Imperialization process, but looking back at their attempt simply fills me with a deep sadness. Regardless of their good intentions, the New Republic failed many of those who wanted to leave the Empire behind. We should not fail these conscripts and child soldiers. They did not choose this life for themselves. They need our help. They should receive it.

Similarly, there are many planets and cultures across the galaxy that have had their worlds ravaged by the return of war. Some of them were only just beginning to recover from the damage done to them by the Empire. They cannot be abandoned to their fate. We must not trade their right to recover and prosper again with our desire to leave the war behind. We can only all share in a better future if we also spend time looking back at our recent past, and bring those left on their knees with us.

To move forward we need to do something that has seemed easy in the past but has never truly been attempted. The New Republic failed firstly to explain the horrors of the Empire to a galaxy weary and divided by recent conflict, and then failed again to combat its ideology when the First Order appeared on its borders. We cannot make their mistakes again. We need to follow thought with action. Too often we think of standing against evil as an act of bravery when recent events have shown us that it should instead be considered one of necessity. So, we need to take the necessary extra steps that the New Republic could or would not. We need to say "never again" and then, crucially, we need to *mean* it. We cannot turn our eyes away nor sleepwalk into destruction as those before us did. We must see, we must learn, and we must remember.

It is this last point that can often prove most challenging. One of the difficulties of being a historian is the constant concern that things are being forgotten. We may never know about all of those who were murdered by the Empire. Neither may it be possible to discover the identities of all the heroes and the martyrs who lost their lives fighting against its evil even before there was an organized Rebellion. But some of their words have endured and can still move and inspire us today. A long time ago a riot started on the planet Ferrix. It was begun by a hologram of a deceased woman at her own funeral. She was called Maarva Andor and she has been forgotten for far too long. She described the Empire as a disease that grew stronger the longer people refused to look at it. She was right. At the end of her speech, she made a simple plea: "Fight the Empire."[1]

It can be different this time.

And it begins with you.

---

[1] Imperial Archives, Section: Censored Seditious Material, File: Ferrix Riot—Maarva Andor Transcript

Index

Index

Index

Oyec, Ilb 74
Ozzel, Admiral Kendal 116, 114, 136,
  226–27
  Hoth attack 263–64, 265

P

Pallopides, "Lady" Ederlatth
  Nataasias 310
Palpatine, Emperor Sheev xii–xiii, 3–22,
  23, 52, 53, 310–11
  and Anakin Skywalker 11, 20–21, 22, 123
  appearance 15–16
  art collection 6, 7
  assassination attempt 12, 142–43
  Battle of Endor 286, 293, 294, 295,
    296, 297
  and Cassio Tagge 249
  clone army 31
  Clone Wars 10, 12, 26–28, 30
  and COMPNOR 57
  and Count Dooku 9–10, 11, 19, 20, 32
  Crimson Dawn 275, 278, 279, 281,
    282–83
  and Darth Maul 19–20, 278
  and Darth Plagueis 7, 19
  as Darth Sidious xii, 3, 18, 26, 33,
    123, 128
  and Darth Vader 19, 20–21, 22, 123,
    124, 126, 127, 240, 246, 251–52, 255
  death x, xiv, xv, 19, 21, 22, 129, 241, 299,
    304, 307–309, 311, 357, 362, 369, 370
  Death Star 197, 198, 232, 235, 239,
    240–41, 246, 251, 255, 284, 288, 290
  Declaration of Empire 15
  early life 5–6
  First Order 358, 362–63
  the Force 285
  galactic travels 6, 7
  and General Grievous 12, 21
  and Grand Moff Tarkin 54, 95–96,
    240–41

Imperial military 114, 140
Imperial Royal Guard 119
Inquisitorius 150
and the Jedi Order 10–11, 12–13, 16,
  32, 33, 140, 194
and Luke Skywalker 18, 21–22,
  286, 299
and Mas Amedda 128–29, 130
and Mon Mothma 47, 206
Naboo blockade 26
as Naboo senator 7, 8–9
Operation: Cinder 311–16
Order 66 11–12, 31, 33, 194
return of x, 366, 367–70
and Rey 18, 22, 369
rise to power 5–11
and the Senate 37, 39–40, 41, 42, 43,
  46–48
Sentinels 311–12
servants and underlings 121–36
and the Sith 7, 17–22
superiority of 168–70
support for 76, 77–78
as supreme chancellor 3–4, 10–11,
  12–13, 55
and the wealthy elite 67, 68
and Yoda 21
Palpatine family 5, 6
Pandion, Grand Moff Valco 324
Parau VI 192
Partagaz, Major Lio 61, 169
Peavey, Captain Edrison 368
Pellaeon, Captain Gilad 226
Perlemian Trade Route 191
Persecutor 219
Pestage, Sate 13, 130, 308
Phelarion 117
Phoenix Squadron 147
Piett, Admiral Firmus 116, 136, 266,
  282, 291, 292, 294–95
Plagueis, Darth 7, 19
Plesk, Chalm 353

Index

Index

Acknowledgments

The series of events that led to me writing this book are so wildly improbable as to stretch credulity to breaking point. This is probably the most important history book I will ever write, and it certainly would not exist in any recognizable form if it were not for the *many* people who have supported both me and it along the journey. It appears to take a star system to write a book.

First among these is my editor, David Fentiman. It was he that reached out to invite me to participate in *Star Wars: Battles that Changed the Galaxy*. He also then understood the vision I had for this book and was incredibly invested in it from the start. It's entirely possible my emails inquiring about the progress of the pitch became a regular part of his work life, but he never ignored them, or me. Together I think we've produced something to be really proud of, even if—at times—we kept forgetting that the events laid out here were not "real." Matt Jones at DK was also very helpful in the last stages of compiling and editing the full draft.

From Lucasfilm I am hugely grateful to Brett Rector for reading and liaising constantly and for kindly coordinating my visit to Lucasfilm HQ in San Francisco. From Story Group: Pablo Hidalgo, Emily Shkoukani, Leland Chee, and Matt Martin provided an unbelievable amount of help, information, assistance, and direction. Furthermore, Mike Siglain also saw something in this book and the conversations I had with him about it at Celebration London helped a huge amount in the earliest stages of the project. I am aware of the tremendous amount of trust and faith that all of the Lucasfilm employees I have named (and undoubtedly many more) have placed in me with this book and I am supremely grateful for it.

Similarly, the stable house of *Star Wars* authors is one of the kindest, nicest, and most supportive groups you will ever meet. I cannot be any more certain than to say that without the support and advice of Amy Richau, Amy Ratcliffe, Clayton Sandell, Jason Fry, Cole Horton, and Phil Szostak—I would have failed. Adam Christopher also very graciously allowed me to pick his brains regarding Enric Pryde, which was extremely helpful. Special thanks must be reserved for Kristin Baver. There is a reason why she was identified in a bookstore in London as "the *Star Wars* Lady" but I do not believe you will easily find someone who so kindly, graciously, and genuinely offers her time and support in facilitating other people's projects or joy. You are, in the most *Star Wars* way imaginable, a hero.

It is not possible to play, even for a short time, in the universe made by George Lucas without also thanking him for its creation and maintenance. What a truly wonderful thing he has gifted to us all. I have spent many years now considering the historical nature and implications of *Star Wars* and much of my understanding of Lucas himself has informed my thought process.

I am also hugely grateful to my academic colleagues and co-workers. Catriona Pennell, Ann-Marie Foster, Ann-Marie Einhaus, Jessica Meyer, Angus Wallace, and Vanda Wilcox have all supported my descent into this—the one thing I've wanted to do more than anything else in the world. There are also countless historians who have allowed me to ask them very strange questions about tiny aspects of the past and very graciously did not push when told I couldn't explain why I was interested.

My dear friends Steve Newman, Tom Akehurst, Roger Johnson, Sylvie Lomer, Tash Silk, Richard Guille, Ruth Canter, James & Lola Knopp, Bethany Tranter, Jessica Pinkett, and Matt Wheeler have all—unknowingly at times—provided fun and distractions when the burden of writing got a little heavy.

Acknowledgments

Sincere thanks must go to my whole family and especially my mother who may not have realized what me buying *Star Wars: Specter of the Past* in a bookshop in Florida in 1997 would lead to. Or perhaps she did. But she supported me all the way regardless.

To my partner Jo: thank you. For all your love and support, from the moment I was first contacted by David Fentiman, to my return from Celebration Anaheim suddenly unsure how to navigate a world where I'd now discovered what I desperately wanted to do, and now as I write these acknowledgments having completed my very own "Star War." I don't know how to repay you. I'll attempt to do so with High Republic books and Chopper merchandise.

But final thanks are reserved for you. Whoever you are. Wherever you are. If you are holding this book, if you are reading it, if it's your first *Star Wars* book or just your most recent. You are why I wrote this. *Star Wars* is for everyone. And that includes you.